The Reading Group

Della Parker

Quercus

First published in Great Britain in 2016
This edition published in 2017 by

Quercus Publishing Ltd
Carmelite House
50 Victoria Embankment
London EC4Y 0DZ

An Hachette UK company

A CIP catalogue record for this book is available
from the British Library.

PB ISBN 978 1 78648 972 2
EBOOK ISBN 978 1 78747 066 8

This book is a work of fiction. Names, characters,
businesses, organisations, places and events are
either the product of the author's imagination
or used fictitiously. Any resemblance to
actual persons, living or dead, events or
locales is entirely coincidental.

10 9 8 7 6 5 4 3 2 1

Cover design © 2017 Dawn Cooper

Typeset by CC Book Production
Printed and bound in Great Britain by Clays Ltd, St Ives plc

The Reading Group

For Gran, who taught me to read

PROLOGUE

Books had saved her life when she was a child. Was that too dramatic? No, she didn't think it was. Reading had taken her away from the pain of being born into a family that didn't understand her. A family into which she had never truly fitted.

That's why she had started the Reading Group. She had wondered for a while if the other women felt the same way. Maybe not, although she did know that all of them – Jojo, Grace, Kate and even little Anne Marie – loved the monthly escape to her house on the cliffs. It was a time out of time. Somewhere they could leave the stresses of their daily lives behind and just be themselves for a couple of hours.

When she was a child reading had transported her into worlds where anything was possible. Worlds where the baddies always got their comeuppance. Worlds where there were always happy endings ... even if they did sometimes take a while.

Serena stood in her orangery and looked out at the sunset that was beginning to pink the sky. *Wouldn't it be wonderful,* she thought, *if real life were a little bit more like fiction?*

She pressed her fingers to her forehead and smiled at her foolishness.

One could always hope, she thought.

One could always dream.

JANUARY

Anne Marie

CHAPTER 1

Anne Marie was sweeping the bathroom floor of Flat 10, The Moorings when a text came through on her phone, which was in the pocket of her overalls. She didn't bother checking it because the only messages she'd had lately had been from her service provider updating her on their latest offers or telling her that she could now check her bill online (*so good of you to think of me so often, O2. Thank you very much!*).

For a moment she allowed herself to fantasize that the text was from a mysterious stranger asking her out to dinner. He wouldn't actually be asking *her* out – obviously: he wouldn't know who she was at that stage. It would be a misdial. But by the time they had chatted for a while and had realized they were actually soulmates, well, by then they really would be going out for dinner.

Where would they go? Calypso's, probably. It was the classiest restaurant that Little Sanderton had to offer.

Although occasionally she went to Ocean Views with one of the girls from the Reading Group. That might even be better. What could be more romantic than the ocean stretching out behind you while you tucked into a pint of prawns?

No, maybe not prawns: they had their tails on and could get messy. A prawn leg stuck in your teeth was not a good look either.

She blinked a few times. Where on earth had all that come from? She wasn't even interested in dating. She was way too busy. A man would mess everything up. She needed a man like . . . she frowned, hunting for a suitable analogy . . . like she needed unreliable cleaners.

Sophie Smith, her youngest and prettiest member of staff, was supposed to be cleaning this flat, but she'd phoned in sick this morning so Anne Marie had been obliged to do it herself. Not that she'd had far to come. She lived in the same building. Four floors above, to be precise. She had the penthouse, thanks to Daddy. The Moorings had been his previous project.

To be honest, she could have got someone else to clean number ten, but she'd been curious. It was interesting seeing what other people did to what was basically the same foot-print of rooms. This flat was a lot smaller, of course, than hers: only two bedrooms, and much lower spec – it had laminate for a start instead of proper wood floors, but it was still very interesting.

And it wasn't such a bad thing to keep your hand in. Even if you were the boss. Never let it be said that she wasn't prepared to pitch in and get her hands dirty – she could do humility with the best of them.

Her phone pinged with another text and Anne Marie paused. Not the phone company, then. They only ever sent one text at a time. It might actually be someone who wanted to speak to her. Hopefully not someone else phoning in sick.

It pinged again.

She hooked it out of her pocket and discovered that all three texts were from the same person: her long-time friend and confidante Manda Crippins.

The first was long and began: *You are invited to the wedding of Jack Taylor and Manda Crippins on 28 January 2017, to be held at St Augustine's Church, Stamford Green, Ashmore at 3.00 p.m.*

Then it said ****incomplete text****

Flaming phone.

The rest of the invitation came through separately with a PS at the bottom: *Sorry for text invite. Proper invite to follow. Cock-up at printer's. Please reserve date.*

Anne Marie raised her eyebrows. No wonder they'd texted: 28 January was only three weeks away. And it was the first she'd heard of any wedding – it was clearly last-minute.

The last text was a personal one to her, also from Manda: *Darling, please come, it's your fault we're getting married. I'll phone you later. Mwah, mwah.*

Anne Marie smiled. Manda was right: it was all down to her. She'd introduced them, hadn't she? So they'd met, fallen in love and were getting married inside six months. And she was responsible. She felt a little glow of pride.

Clearly she should be in the matchmaking game. Maybe she should organize a speed-dating event at Little Sanderton. That might be fun. A lot more fun than organizing a troupe

7

of cleaners anyway. Daddy was always saying what a good organizer she was.

Less charitable people might call it meddling. People like her first – and, as it turned out, only – boss, but as Manda had pointed out when Anne Marie had been sacked, the woman was probably just jealous because Anne Marie was blonder, prettier and thinner than she was.

She wished she was thinner now. Not that she was actually fat, but the festive season had landed her with an extra half-stone she could have done without. She glanced at her reflection in the mirror that took up one wall of the luxury bathroom. The sunshine-yellow overalls didn't help. They would have made anyone bigger than a size eight look enormous, especially when worn over jeans and a chunky jumper. Well, so what? It was cold today!

As for the huge logo, Clean Living, emblazoned across her breasts in shocking pink, it had probably been a bit OTT, even for her. She should have gone for a more stylish uniform when she'd set up the company, but there hadn't been a lot of choice in the Corporate Clothing catalogue. And she'd liked the colours. Yellow was cheery, friendly and outgoing, just like her.

Anne Marie stopped looking at her reflection and thought about the man who owned this flat: Dominic Peterson, his name was. She'd met him only once, when he'd first contracted her company. He was a sales rep. For Jaguar, she thought. She'd spotted a whole pile of brochures on the bureau in his lounge when he'd been fetching his bank details to pay her. It was handy to know what your clients

8

did for a living. Made it easier to strike up a conversation and, of course, check that they were solvent.

Yes, a speed-dating event in Little Sanderton would be just the thing. She could even invite Dominic! He was single. He deserved someone nice. His current – soon to be ex – girl-friend was a two-timing minx. Anne Marie knew this because just after she'd got there today she'd heard a message come through on the answerphone. It was the type of machine that plays the message aloud as it's being recorded.

She'd been in the kitchen when the phone had rung, but she'd dashed through to the lounge in case it was important. She'd been just in time to hear a woman's voice: 'Dominic, I'm sorry, it's over. I've met someone else. Bye.'

That had been it. Just like that. Anne Marie had been outraged on Dominic's behalf. Dumping someone by answer-phone message was seriously crappy. Worse than dumping them by text.

Never mind. She'd invite him to her speed-dating event where he could meet someone lovely.

She should probably finish cleaning his flat first.

Oh, it would be so nice to see Manda again. She hoped that Jack wasn't going to drag her too far away from Little Sanderton once they were married. Not everyone wanted to live in a sleepy little coastal village ... Just the floor-mopping to do now. She put some dance music on her iPod and turned up the volume. Getting fit and losing the half-stone she'd put on over the festive period were two of her New Year resolutions.

Another of her resolutions was to read some classic novels, which she hadn't bothered with before because they were so tedious (apart from *Far From the Madding Crowd*, which they'd had to do for GCSE at school). But, thanks to a decision they'd made at Reading Group a couple of months ago, that resolution was already in hand too.

It was Reading Group tonight. They met on the first Thursday of the month. Anne Marie hummed as she got ready. She hoped January's novel would be exciting. Preferably something that was on television, in case she was too busy to read it. This speed-dating event was going to take a bit of organizing, that was for sure.

It was Kate's turn to pick this month's novel. Kate was clever and sassy. Maybe she'd choose something amusing.

Anne Marie grabbed the keys to her Mazda as she dashed out of the door. Reading Group was great. Not because of the reading bit – she wasn't a big reader – but because of the friendship, the female solidarity. They were a really solid gathering of women. It was like having a whole bunch of extra sisters. She only had one older sister, whom she hardly ever saw, and no brothers. Mum had died when she was tiny and Dad had never remarried.

Bless his cotton socks. She ought to go round and see him soon. He had a house on the cliffs. A great dark Gothic monster with about nine bedrooms and four bathrooms. Well, actually they were classrooms, not bedrooms – the place had once been a primary school. He'd bought it as an investment a few years ago and was living in it until he got planning permission to knock it down and build a block of flats.

It was one of the very few projects that wasn't going well.

He was a savvy property developer-cum-landlord. He owned quite a few places in Little Sanderton. It was down to him that she'd set up Clean Living. He bought the flats and let them. Her company cleaned them. In fact, it had been his idea that she start the company. He'd helped her set it up through Companies House and register it as a limited company and all the other boring stuff like that.

Anne Marie was the last to arrive at Reading Group. Everyone else was already in the snug, enjoying the warmth of the log-burner and a glass of red. Kate, who was closest to the door, handed her a glass. 'Hello, lovely. We're on mulled wine as it's still kind of the festive season. How are you?'

Anne Marie breathed in the scents of spice and cinnamon. She felt the warmth of the room and the camaraderie of her friends, and she beamed. 'All the better for seeing you guys. And I'm definitely up for extending the festive season. Do you think we can get away with it till the end of January?'

'Well, at least until the end of tonight, angel.' That was Jojo. She held out a plate of mince pies.

Anne Marie took two. They were only tiny, after all, with little pastry stars on them, and was that edible glitter? Yum. Besides, if they were extending the festive season then technically the New Year hadn't started yet. So the diet could begin tomorrow.

There was a lot to catch up on.

Grace told them that Harry, her little boy who had been sick with cancer, was doing really well. 'No more scares. He's still in remission,' she said.

'And on a somewhat more mundane note, Anton's finally agreed we can get a new kitchen,' Kate said. 'We're going to look at units in the January sales. We might even get a breakfast bar.'

'And I'm going to start a new business,' Anne Marie announced to the group. 'I'm going into matchmaking, starting with speed-dating events in Little Sanderton.'

Her news did not bring quite the roars of approval she was hoping for. In fact, she thought she saw Serena and Grace exchange a quick look of horror. 'There are plenty of singles in Little Sanderton,' she added.

'Yes, but most of them are over eighty,' Jojo said, with a frown.

'Over-eighties deserve a love life too,' Anne Marie said, waving a hand. 'Maybe I'll do a knitting speed-dating evening for them.'

Serena seemed to be choking on her mince pie. Anne Marie paused while Grace patted Serena on the back and refilled her glass. Then she went on, 'I know I did get it wrong with that couple down the road, but you have to admit, they did seem a perfect match . . . apart from the age difference, I mean. It was a shame it ended so badly.'

'And there was the woman on the checkout at Waitrose,' Serena pointed out. She seemed to have recovered from her coughing fit. 'The one you tried to set up with a customer – remember?'

'Well, yes, but how was I to know the guy was a shop-lifter? That wasn't really my fault. I have had a major success, though,' she went on blithely, and told them about Manda and Jack's wedding.

'Well, I think it's . . . um . . . a lovely idea,' Grace said diplomatically. 'Anyway, a commercial enterprise is different from ad-hoc matchmaking, isn't it?'

'I suppose so,' Serena said, taking another sip of wine. 'Now, moving swiftly on to the main business of the evening: our classic novel. Over to you, Kate. What are we reading this month?'

Kate had gone a little pink, Anne Marie noticed. Maybe they were reading something saucy? She clapped her hands in expectation.

Kate was shuffling around in her bag. 'I can't seem to – er – find it,' she said. 'How odd.'

Jojo bent down and hooked out a book that had been accidentally kicked half under the chesterfield. 'Looks like you'd dropped it, angel. Here we are.' She handed it back to Kate with a smile.

'Ah, thank you.' Kate didn't look too happy, but she held it up to the group. 'We're going to read Jane Austen's *Emma*,' she said. 'I hope you like it. Now, I must just nip to the loo.'

'That's one of her later ones, isn't it?' Jojo said. 'What's it about?' Kate had already fled, so Jojo held up the book and read out the blurb on the back. 'Emma Woodhouse is the character Austen was sure no one would like. She delights in meddling in the romantic lives of others . . .' She tailed off.

Anne Marie frowned. Why was everyone looking so uncomfortable? She shook her head. It sounded like a really fun book to her.

CHAPTER 2

When Anne Marie rang her father's doorbell the next day there was no answer. She let herself in through the front door, and was greeted by the smell of dogs – and then by an actual dog. Digby, Dad's wet springer spaniel, had clearly been swimming.

He wagged ecstatically as she bent to stroke him, flicking water everywhere.

'Where is he, then?' Anne Marie asked Digby, though she knew exactly where he'd be – in his office at the back of the house. She was pretty sure he slept in there sometimes, workaholic that he was.

'Dad!' she called, as she walked along the corridors of parquet flooring. On either side, doors opened into class-rooms, still full of the old desks and school chairs, all gathering dust.

She'd offered to get a team in to clean the place, but her

father wouldn't hear of it. 'What's the point when most of the rooms are shut up?' he'd said, and she'd been unable to argue with that.

Knowing Dad, letting the place fall down around his ears was probably also a tactic – he was working on the assumption that the planning department would decide they'd rather have a block of nice new flats than a derelict eyesore on the outskirts of town.

She tapped on the glass upper pane of the office door. It still had the old sign in situ. *Headmaster*. She smiled. She had a feeling Dad rather liked the idea of being Headmaster, even if he did only have her to boss around.

'Hello, Princess.' He turned from where he had been hunched over a computer screen, tapping away into a spreadsheet. 'What's happening? I wasn't expecting to see you today.'

She bent and kissed his bristly cheek. 'What are you doing? Counting your money?'

'Something like that. Is it coffee time?' He got up stiffly and rubbed his arm. 'I've got tennis elbow.'

'You don't play tennis.'

'From using the mouse.'

'It's probably RSI. Shall I book you an appointment with Thomas?'

'I'm ahead of you. He's due any minute.' He peered at the clock on the wall, which had stopped. 'Well, I think he is. What time actually is it?'

'Ten to ten.' She sighed. 'I'd better leave you in peace, then.'

'Nonsense, you can make us a coffee. Thomas will be pleased to see you. He always asks after you.'

'Are you matchmaking, Daddy?' She smiled at him.

'Hardly!'

'Actually, it's matchmaking I want to talk to you about, as it happens. Have you got five minutes?'

'Darling, I've got all the time in the world to talk to you. Especially if it involves your love life.'

Anne Marie winced. Oops, she'd probably given him the wrong impression.

'I don't have a love life and I don't want one, as you very well know,' she said, as she carried a cafetiere of coffee and a plate of ginger nuts into the assembly hall, which was what currently passed for a lounge.

'So you keep saying. It's not normal, you know – a gorgeous young thing like you. I was out playing the field when I was your age.'

'You were a boy,' she pointed out.

'Your sister was too.' He slurped his coffee. 'Playing the field, I mean. Not a boy.' He winked.

'Yes, and look where it got her. Four children and she's only just turned thirty.'

'It's nice having children when you're young.' Having a conversation with her father was like playing table tennis. He batted each sentence back before she'd had a chance to formulate the next.

'Thomas Hanson is a world authority on blood-spatter, he told me, last time I saw him,' her dad remarked.

That was a bit random, even for him. 'I'm sorry? What?' Anne Marie raised her eyebrows.

'He's versatile, is what I'm saying. He's clever. Educated. Solvent. Tall too. You could do a lot worse.'

'You forgot "know-it-all",' she said, suddenly remembering she was supposed to be on a diet and feeding the remaining half ginger nut to an enthusiastic Digby. 'The trouble with Thomas Hanson is that he's got an opinion on absolutely everything. No wonder you get on so well.'

She'd said that rather too loudly in view of the fact that approximately ten seconds later Thomas appeared at the door. 'Good morning. Sorry to barge in, but the bell doesn't seem to work. I did try.'

He was smiling equably. Had he heard what she'd said?

She offered him a ginger nut.

He refused it. 'No can do. New Year resolution. Cut down on sugar.' He patted his perfectly flat stomach and added, 'How's the toilet cleaning going?'

Ouch. She decided not to rise. 'Actually, I'm branching out,' she said. 'That's what I was saying earlier, Daddy. I'm going into the matchmaking arena, running speed-dating events in the village.'

Her father nodded.

Thomas narrowed his eyes.

She ignored him. 'I shall hire the village hall, advertise in the local press, charge people to come along.' She clapped her hands together. 'What do you think? We've never had anything like that in Little Sanderton before, and I do have a track record.'

'You do?' Thomas said, with irritating scepticism.

'I do. Yes.' She popped another ginger nut into her mouth, enjoying its melting sweetness on her tongue, and told them about Manda and Jack. 'They met at my twenty-first birthday party. On the boat – do you remember, Daddy?'

'How could I forget? Manda fell overboard, didn't she, and Jack jumped in to rescue her?'

'Well, he threw her the life buoy, anyway.'

Her father shuddered. 'Good job it was summer. So now they're getting married, are they? Well, I guess that's a happy ending. Well done, Princess.'

'Anyway,' she went on, 'as you said, Daddy, all's well that ends well. I've been invited to their wedding. I can take a plus one. Maybe you could come along. It's at the end of January.'

'Thank you, Princess, but I think it'd be better if you went with someone your own age. You busy, Thomas?'

'My diary's usually pretty full,' Thomas said quickly. 'Speaking of which, we'd better have a look at that elbow of yours, hadn't we?'

Honestly, Anne Marie thought, as she caught up on her invoicing later that evening. Why did no one believe her when she said she wasn't interested in having a relationship? Manda was just as bad. When they'd chatted on the phone earlier Manda had asked her if she'd fancied being bridesmaid, then spent ages telling her about the best man.

'His name's Todd and he works with Jack on the trains,' she said. 'It's really well paid, that job. He's just in the process of buying his own house in Poundbury – you know, the estate in Dorchester that Prince Charles built.'

'Lovely,' said Anne Marie. 'But I'm not on the market for a train driver called Todd.'

There was a pause. 'Don't tell me you've met someone else!'

'No,' Anne Marie said. 'I haven't. But I'd love to be your bridesmaid. Do you mind if I bring my dad?'

'Of course I don't. Your dad's pretty cool.'

She certainly wouldn't be bringing Thomas Hanson – that was for sure. They had absolutely nothing in common. Every time she saw him he insulted her. The only reason she let him get away with it was because she'd known him for ever. He'd been a friend of the family for as long as he'd been an osteopath. He was superb, apparently. Thankfully she had never needed his services.

The thought of him touching her with those long-fingered hands was – oh ... She shivered. No, definitely not.

The door buzzer sounded as Anne Marie was packing up for the day. It was Sophie, she saw on the entry-phone screen. She must have recovered from her sore stomach. Well, that was good. She let her into the block.

'Hello, honey-bunny, you feeling better?' She ushered her through to the kitchen.

Sophie nodded. 'I'm fine now, thanks.'

'You're not coming to tell me you've had enough of cleaning for a living, are you?'

'I'm not, no.' Sophie blinked rapidly several times. 'But you might decide you've had enough of me when you hear what I've done.'

'I doubt that.' Anne Marie looked at her properly. Her eyes were glittery and her face really quite pale. 'You're my best cleaner.'

'I've broken my Henry,' Sophie said, and burst into tears.

Anne Marie hugged her. She had no idea what she was talking about, but the poor girl was clearly distraught. For a few moments she let her sob and wished she knew what to say to make her feel better. 'Who's Henry?' she ventured, when Sophie had finally stopped crying. 'Is he your boy-friend?'

'He's my vacuum,' Sophie said. 'My really expensive vacuum you told me not to break. On pain of death.'

Gosh, she hadn't really said that, had she? How tactless.

'I'm so, *so* sorry. I don't know how it happened. I think I must have sucked up something too big.'

'Oh,' Anne Marie said. 'Is that all? I thought you were upset about something serious.'

'That *is* serious, isn't it?' Sophie looked at her, wide-eyed. 'They're really expensive, you said.'

'Yes, but it's only money, isn't it?' Anne Marie felt very maternal and wise. 'It's replaceable. I can probably claim on my insurance. I thought someone had died or you'd split up with your boyfriend or something.'

'What? You mean Gary?' Sophie rolled her eyes. 'No, I haven't split up with him. He proposed the other day. He did it on my birthday. Got down on one knee and everything in McDonald's.'

'McDonald's?' Annie Marie gasped. 'That's not very romantic.'

'No, I know, but we like McDonald's. It's where we met. He was on the griddle and I was waitressing. Before I got the job with you, I mean. Gary's still there – he's Head Chef so he gets us a discount.' Sophie had brightened considerably now she knew she wasn't in trouble.

'Did you say yes?' Anne Marie had a horrible feeling she already knew what was coming.

Sophie studied her blue-and-pink fingernails. 'I said I'd let him know in a week. I don't want him to think I'm a complete pushover.'

'Good girl,' Annie Marie said. 'You're far too young to go rushing into marriage. It's a massive step.'

Sophie nodded uncertainly. 'I *was* going to say yes, though,' she said, screwing up her forehead. 'Do you think I shouldn't, then?'

Anne Marie settled her at the breakfast bar and opened a pack of extra special Belgian-chocolate cupcakes with edible glitter that she had left over from Christmas. Desperate times called for desperate measures. 'Have I ever told you about my sister Julia?'

Sophie shook her head.

'Julia got married when she was just a few months older than you are now. She was supposed to be going to Cambridge. She was offered a place and she turned it down. Can you believe that?'

Sophie's eyes popped. 'She turned it down because she wanted to get married?'

'She turned it down because she was pregnant. How

21

someone that brainy doesn't have the sense to take proper precautions, I'll never know.'

'I'm on the pill,' Sophie said promptly.

'You're clearly more intelligent than my sister.' Anne Marie drummed her fingers on the breakfast bar. 'Guess what happened next.'

'She lost the baby?' Sophie ventured.

'No. She did not. She got married to this oik,' that was a bit harsh – her brother-in-law was a doctor and quite a laugh – but she wanted to make her point, 'and now they have four children and Julia's only just turned thirty.'

'I see.' Sophie started on her second cupcake. 'Is that bad?'

'It's not bad, exactly.' She was going to have her work cut out here. 'The point I'm trying to make is that you're a bright girl. You're doing a college course, aren't you? The last thing you want is to throw it all away on a burger-tosser – I mean fryer.'

'I see.'

'Unless you really love him. Do you love him?'

'I like him a lot.' Sophie batted her eyelashes thoughtfully. 'And we do get on well. He makes me laugh.'

'Yes, but does he make your heart go into overdrive?' Anne Marie asked. She couldn't remember ever feeling that way about a man – but that was a standard indicator of love, wasn't it? 'Look, Sophie, if you're not sure I think you should say no.'

'Really?' Sophie looked alarmed. She was a pretty little thing, blonde with brilliant-blue eyes – that were, at this moment, sparkly with tears. She was petite too, with a delicacy about her that put Anne Marie in mind of an elf. Sophie didn't look at all chunky in the yellow Clean Living overalls. And now she was on her third cupcake. How did she do it?

'You should definitely say no.' She took hold of Sophie's shoulders and gave her a gentle little shake. She'd just had a brainwave. Dominic Peterson – who lived in this very block! – was a *far* better proposition than some griddle chef, whose main asset was being able to get a discount on burgers! Dominic had a very nice home. And a well-paid job. Also, Anne Marie was sure she'd seen a Jag in the car park this morning – it was probably his. Although it might have been a company car, of course. Still, a temporary Jaguar was better than no Jaguar.

'What sort of car has he got – this Gary?'

'He hasn't got one at all yet. He's learning to drive in his dad's Fiesta.'

That clinched it. 'Tell him to sling his hook,' Anne Marie said firmly. 'There's someone I want you to meet.'

CHAPTER 3

Matchmaking was harder than it sounded, Anne Marie thought the next day. It had seemed easy. All she had to do was arrange for Sophie to bump into Dominic Peterson and let Fate take its natural course.

There were two fatal flaws to this plan.

Number one was that Dominic was never in when he had his cleaning done. That was the whole point – he liked to be out of the way when it was taking place. Most of her clients were like that, although she did have the odd controlling one who liked to oversee every move the cleaner made and – as one woman had pointed out – make sure they didn't go nosing about in her 'privates'.

Number two was that – pretty as Sophie looked in her Clean Living uniform – Anne Marie wasn't sure that Dominic would think it appropriate to chat up his cleaner, even if he did bump into her. He was happy enough to chat to

Anne Marie on the odd occasion they bumped into each other in the car park, but that was slightly different. After all, Anne Marie wasn't just a cleaner, she owned the business. She had a feeling that Dominic was an upwardly mobile kind of guy. He might be looking for an upwardly mobile girlfriend.

She sat in her kitchen making notes. What exactly did she know about him?

He was twenty-two.

He was single.

He was five foot nine at a push. (Sophie was only five foot five so that was fine. She could still wear heels when they went out.)

He had dark hair and was reasonably attractive. He had a nice flat and he paid his rent on time. (She'd checked with her father.)

He worked out. (She'd spotted his joggers in the laundry basket.)

He had a Jag (which might or might not be a company car, but at least he had one).

He was nice.

The last point was the most important in Anne Marie's book. She could have forgiven him a lot as long as he had that one attribute. She began a list about Sophie:

She was seventeen. (Good age ratio, girls of that age liked older men.)

She was single (or would be once she'd kicked griddle-
   chef Gary into touch).
She was blonde and very pretty.
She lived with her parents. (Who didn't at that age?)
The cleaning job was temporary. (She was studying
   for . . . what was she studying for?)
She was reliable and honest. (She'd owned up about
   breaking the Henry.)
She was nice.

Anne Marie paused. They had loads in common, didn't they?
They both liked eating out, too. Sophie liked McDonald's
and Dominic was bound to like eating out. Everyone liked
eating out and they probably both went to gigs. Dominic
liked Maroon 5. She'd seen one of their CDs on his coffee
table.

A perfect match.

They just needed to meet.

She could, of course, invite them along to her speed-
dating event. She'd already phoned up to ask the price of
the village hall. Unfortunately it was fully booked for January. The WI had it twice and some obscure am-dram
company had it the rest of the time.

The answer came in a flash of inspiration. She could
arrange a meeting at hers. She could hold a supper club.
She couldn't just invite Dominic and Sophie – that would
be weird. There would have to be more people. Who else
could she ask? Who was the right age? And who was single?
While she had her pen in her hand she made a list . . .

There was Matt, Manda's elder brother – they had always got on well, in a friends kind of way, and he was good company. She added him to the list. Her thoughts turned to Reading Group. She could invite anyone who was single. Which counted out Grace and Kate but left Serena and Jojo. She'd need a couple of guys for them – maybe Thomas Hanson could be one of them. He was nice when he wasn't being sarcastic and, at twenty-nine, was in the right age group. Maybe train-driver Todd – Jack and Manda's best man – could be the other. He was probably too young for Jojo, who was thirty-seven, or even Serena, who was thirty-three. Unless either of them wanted a toyboy ... Probably not. Although you never could tell.

She pictured the scene.

Her dining table – which got precious little use in the normal course of events – set for twelve with a topless butler (where had that thought come from? Bad girl!) serving hors d'oeuvres. No, he definitely couldn't be topless. He'd have to be wearing a bow tie at least. A bow tie and a six pack. Mmm.

Anne Marie sighed.

She was probably only fantasizing because her own social life had been so quiet lately. A lot of her uni friends were now one half of a couple, which made it a little more awkward because she hadn't had a boyfriend for ages. It wasn't so much fun having people round for dinner when you had to do absolutely everything yourself. Shop for the food, cook, stress about whether it was all going to be ready at the same time, then clear up afterwards with no one to help.

Actually, she didn't really mind having no one to help clear up. She had a dishwasher so it was no big deal. But it would have been nice to have someone to dissect the evening with afterwards. That had been one of the best bits about parties at uni – the drunken recap held in the kitchen at the halls of residence afterwards. That had always been such a laugh. More fun in some ways than the evening itself.

University had been such fun. The social side – not so much the qualification she had ended up with. And what had she done with that? Set up a cleaning business. She could probably have managed that without a degree in business studies.

Oh, for goodness' sake, stop feeling sorry for yourself, girl! Having a matchmaking supper club would be fun. A sit-down meal, even for six or eight guests, would be hard work. A buffet would be just as good. That way it wouldn't cost too much – she could cook loads in advance. She would be free to circulate, making sure the right people met the right people, so to speak.

She designed some invitations on her MacBook Air, then printed them out and decided they would be best hand-delivered. There would be no texting people at the last minute for *her*. She wasn't going to leave anything to chance. Although she did have to invite train-driver Todd via Manda, as she didn't have his contact details.

She had asked them to RSVP (phone or email) by Wednesday, which wasn't very far away. She'd better get her act together.

*

By Wednesday everyone had RSVP'd.

Jojo and Serena both said yes. Thomas Hanson said yes. Dominic Peterson said yes. Matt said yes. Train-driver Todd said no, via Manda. Not surprising, really, as he didn't know her from Adam. And Sophie also said no.

Crap. Sophie was the reason she was having the supper party! The whole thing was pointless if she didn't come. Anne Marie decided desperate measures were called for and went round to see her.

Sophie didn't answer the door until the third ring. When she appeared, it was obvious she'd been crying.

'Oh, sweetie, what's wrong?' Anne Marie crooned.

'I've split up with Gary.'

That was a good thing, surely. Aware that such an observation wouldn't be entirely tactful, Anne Marie gave her a hug. 'He's not worth your tears.' After his proposal in McDonald's – that was an understatement. 'There, there. Dry your eyes and tell me why you're not coming to my supper club.'

'I'm not really in the mood,' Sophie said.

'Oh, but you'll soon cheer up when you see Dominic. He's dying to meet you.'

'Is he?' Sophie blinked a couple of times.

'Absolutely.'

Dominic wasn't actually aware of Sophie's existence but if he had been she was sure he'd be dying to meet her. She'd have to redress that before Saturday. Maybe she should phone him in advance and mention Sophie.

First, there was the more pressing matter of getting her to come.

'I think Dominic has a Jaguar sports car,' she said. 'I think it's a soft-top – now *that's* what I call class. I wouldn't mind a go in it myself.'

'Nor would I,' Sophie replied. 'I've never been in a Jag.'

'Imagine it,' Anne Marie told her. 'Driving round the country lanes with the wind in your hair . . . I'm sure he'd take you for a spin if you asked him.'

Sophie was nodding. 'My dad's got a mate with a Jag – it's dead posh.'

'So you'll come to my party?' Annie Marie said.

'Go on, then.'

'Excellent.' Anne Marie breathed a sigh of relief. And hoped she was right about the Jag.

CHAPTER 4

Anne Marie stood back and surveyed her efforts. Not bad, if she did say so herself. The long dining table was set with plates, silver cutlery, crystal glasses, napkins and several bottles of wine – two reds already opened to breathe. Through the floor-to-ceiling windows of the dining room there was a panoramic view of the bay. It was a beautiful evening. A silver moon path angled across the sea, which was black glass. Stars were beginning to pinprick the dusk.

On the horizon she could see the flickering lights of distant ships. Anne Marie clasped her hands as she stood on her balcony, looking out, and breathed in the aromas of scented candles dotted around (rose musk and vanilla), just in case anyone should step outside. It was a perfect night for romance.

Dominic was the first to arrive. He was ten minutes early – perhaps that wasn't entirely surprising since he lived downstairs. He held out a carrier containing two bottles of wine. Nice touch. Except that when she glanced into the bag they were screwtops. Not so good. She took his coat and he leaned in for a kiss. Both cheeks.

Mmm, nice aftershave. He was freshly shaved. A whiff of smoke. She hadn't known he smoked. That could be a deal-breaker. She was sure Sophie didn't smoke. Well, never mind, he could always give it up. Perhaps she should mention it now. No. Too soon.

She frowned, trying to see him through Sophie's eyes, then realized, with a start of embarrassment, that she was staring at him a bit too openly.

'Thanks for asking me.' He was smiling. 'I was blown away to get your invite. I'll be interested to see your pad too – I'm imagining it's kind of similar to mine, yah?'

'Yah.' She echoed his rather posh accent unconsciously. 'I mean, yes. It's similar.' *Pad*? Who said *pad*, these days? Now was the time to tell him about Sophie. 'I'm pleased you could make it,' she began. 'At such short notice.'

There was an awkward little silence. She leaped in to fill it. 'Um, do you by any chance own a Jaguar sports car? Only I thought I saw one in the car park—'

'Not mine.' He gave a rueful sigh. 'I've got a Skoda.'

'Blimey.' She covered her shock with a cough. That was going to take some getting out of when Sophie was expecting a ride around the neighbourhood in an open-top Jag.

'They get a bad press,' he was saying. 'But they're very good cars. Economical, reliable, easy to park.' He ticked off each attribute on his fingers. 'Great cars. Very underrated. Yah?'

'Soft-top by any chance?' She knew she was clutching at straws.

'Er, no.' He looked puzzled. 'What do you drive?'

'A Mazda.' Maybe she could lend it to him. Sophie would probably be quite impressed with that. 'But you didn't come here to talk about cars.'

'No.' He gave her a great big cheesy grin. 'I came here to see you.'

'And Sophie,' she said, taking a step back. He was getting a bit too much into her personal space. She hadn't had a chance yet to close the front door. Perhaps that was just as well.

'Who's Sophie?'

'Someone I think you should meet. Ah, Sophie!' To Anne Marie's horror Sophie, clearly eager to meet her prospective soulmate, had also turned up early. She'd just appeared at the open front door. Anne Marie hadn't heard the lift doors ping. She hoped Sophie hadn't heard what he'd just said.

'Sophie – we were just talking about you. This is Dominic. I think you two have an awful lot in common.' Actually, she wasn't so sure about that any more.

Fortunately at that moment Thomas Hanson arrived too. He'd taken the stairs, judging by the way he was puffing. He was closely followed by Serena and then Manda's brother, Matt.

Gosh, everyone was very prompt.

33

Anne Marie got them all into the lounge, poured drinks and introduced people.

'What a beautiful room,' Serena said, looking admiringly at the minimalist décor, acres of real wood flooring rolling away to the cream blinds at the windows, currently rolled back to display the lights on the balcony beyond.

'Thanks.' She smiled, surprised because Serena's home was the opposite of hers: all rustic and *Country Living*. Although they both overlooked the Devon coastline, the two couldn't have been further away from each other in style. Compared to Serena's, her home was a bit cold, she thought, but that was partly because there wasn't much of her in it. She liked the minimalist look. The pale walls, the blank, bland surfaces, the fact that everything, even the television, was out of sight . . .

Anne Marie bit her lip. Did she *really* like bland? Or was the truth that she didn't know what she liked? Well, this was no time to be reflective. She should be entertaining her guests. She was beginning to wish she'd hired the topless butler. Or asked more people. Or gone for a sit-down meal. Or taken everyone into the lounge where the comfy chairs were. There were only a couple of dining chairs in here, pushed back against the walls – not exactly inviting – and people were standing around in stiff little groups.

After the initial 'What a lovely place you have here' comments the conversation didn't seem to flow. It was too quiet. Ah – she'd forgotten to put on the music! She darted across the room and prodded her iPod. It went straight into the Maroon 5 album she'd bought to make Dominic feel at home.

She stole a glance at him. He was chatting to Sophie, who was looking bored. Still, at least they were standing together. Serena and Matt had struck up a conversation too. Matt was pretty sociable and Serena was good at this sort of gathering. They were talking about the education system and student grants.

Thomas was sipping his drink – a lime and soda – and gazing out of the window. He certainly scrubbed up well. He actually looked as if he'd made an effort. Was that a Jasper Conran shirt? She felt a bit guilty. She'd only really invited him to make up numbers. He must have felt the weight of her gaze because suddenly he turned and winked at her.

Oh, hurry up, Jojo! Everything would liven up when Jojo got here – she was so warm and outspoken. She wasn't usually late . . . Maybe she'd got held up somewhere delivering a baby.

Anne Marie grabbed a couple of plates of canapés and went around offering them to people. The entry-phone buzzer rang while she was in the middle of it. She escaped gratefully to answer it. 'Jojo! It's so lovely to see you.'

Jojo smiled at her. 'You too. So sorry I'm late. I had a call – you know what it's like.' She shrugged off her coat, jingling bangles. Anne Marie wondered if she took them off when she was delivering babies.

'Now, lead me to the food and the men in that order.'

By the time they returned to her guests, Serena and Matt

were laughing at something. Maybe this was going to work, after all. Thomas was helpfully unwrapping food – he smiled as she came in with Jojo, so she took her to meet him.

'Thomas is the world authority on blood-spatter,' Anne Marie introduced them.

'Really?' Jojo helped herself to a Dorito and crunched loudly. 'Well, I've just had a labour from hell. In fact, you could say I'm something of an expert on blood-spatter myself.'

It was a conversation-stopper, that was for sure. And as Jojo had quite a loud voice everyone in the room had heard her. There was a slightly stunned silence. On the other side of the room Dominic curled his lip in distaste. Sophie screwed up her face. Thomas nodded politely and looked at Jojo with interest. Anne Marie didn't know what to do, so she poured everyone more wine.

After that you'd have thought things couldn't get any worse. But they did. Dominic kept abandoning Sophie and starting up conversations with Anne Marie.

'You've got great taste in music,' he said. 'I really love Maroon 5.'

'Thanks.' She beamed at him. 'You seem to be getting on well with Sophie.'

'Yah, she's cute.' He frowned. 'Is she your little sister? Only there is a definite resemblance. Both beautiful blondes.' He put out a hand to touch her hair and she leaned back-wards to avoid him. At the exact same moment she caught Sophie's eye across the room. This was not working out as she'd hoped.

Jojo was now chatting to Serena and Matt. At least they all seemed to be getting on well, which was a blessing. Thomas was on his own again – now looking at his phone. Ah, he'd just noticed that Sophie was twiddling her thumbs. He slipped his phone back into his jacket pocket and headed across to her.

When he got there he said something that made Sophie smile. Anne Marie breathed a sigh of relief. He had his uses, bless him. She excused herself from Dominic, saying she had to see to something in the kitchen.

Things got marginally better when she invited everyone to help themselves to food. It was delicious and sparked off a few conversations between the women over which was the best diet for losing your post-Christmas belly. Which brought them on to a conversation about Sophie's Fitbit, which was on her wrist busily monitoring every movement she made.

'Where did you get it?' Serena asked. 'I think one of those would be perfect for me.'

'It was a Christmas present from my boyfriend.' Sophie glanced at Anne Marie. 'My ex-b-b-boyfriend.' Her lip wobbled, and in the next moment she was in floods of tears, with Serena patting her shoulder comfortingly and Jojo offering a mini-pack of tissues.

All the men in the room suddenly got very interested in a picture of a cornfield on the opposite wall. Anne Marie went to put the kettle on.

The party broke up not long after that. It seemed that everyone except Dominic had somewhere else they'd remembered they needed to be. He hung about in the kitchen, ostensibly stacking the dishwasher but clearly just eager to chat.

Anne Marie gave up dropping hints that she was tired. 'So how did you get on with Sophie?' she asked him. 'Did you two swap numbers?'

'No. We didn't.' He gave her a sharp look. 'Once she'd established that I drove a Skoda and not a Jag she wasn't very interested. Hang on . . . You thought that too! Did you tell her I owned a sports car?'

'Yes,' Anne Marie said, deciding it was best to come clean. 'Well, you *do* work for Jaguar, don't you?'

'No.' He frowned. 'I work for Clearly the Best Windows. I sell conservatories.' He straightened his collar (definitely not Jasper Conran, that shirt) and huffed a little.

It just went to show that you shouldn't make assumptions. You definitely shouldn't read too much into leaflets you see lying about in people's flats. 'Right,' she said. 'I see.'

'I thought you'd invited me to your party because you liked me,' he mused.

'I *do* like you.' She could feel heat starting on her neck.

'But not like that.' He gave her a direct look. 'I only talked to your little friend to humour you. She's a bit young for me. It's you I'm interested in, Anne Marie, not Sophie.' He took a step forward. 'You know that, right?'

'Um, no. No. That's not how I feel at all. I'm happily single. More than happy.'

It was as though he hadn't heard. He gripped her arms and zoomed in clumsily for a kiss. She turned her face just in time.

38

The kitchen door swung open. 'Sorry to interrupt.' Thomas appeared.

Anne Marie had never been so relieved to see anyone in her life. 'I thought you'd gone!' she squeaked.

'One of your friends got as far as the car park, then realized she'd forgotten her umbrella. I said I'd get it for her. Luckily the door was on the latch.' He smiled charmingly at Dominic. 'All right, mate?'

'I'm just going,' Dominic said, and charged past him, head down. When they'd heard the front door slam, Anne Marie turned to Thomas. 'I'll help you look for that umbrella.' She paused. 'There was no umbrella, was there?'

'No,' he said softly. 'But we were all chatting in the car park, and Serena was a bit worried that Dominic might be outstaying his welcome so I said I'd pop back up.'

'I'm glad you did. He'd got the wrong end of the stick. Not that I couldn't handle him.'

'I'm sure you could handle him fine.' His eyes softened. 'You're a very capable lady.'

She sighed. 'Tell me honestly, Thomas. Tonight was a complete disaster, wasn't it?'

'That depends on what you were trying to achieve. If it was lovely food and good conversation with a few friends, then you did great.'

She bit her lip. 'That's very generous of you. I hope you weren't too bored.'

'I've been to worse parties.' He looked around the chaos of her kitchen. 'Need a hand clearing up?'

'No, it's OK. I'm a professional – remember?' She had no

idea how she managed to sound so bright when part of her just wanted to burst into tears.

Thomas hesitated. 'Well . . . if you're sure?'

The kindness in his voice was nearly her undoing. She blinked. 'I am.'

He still didn't go.

'Really, Thomas.' She made 'go away' motions with her hands. *Go now, because you're the last person I want to see me crying,* she thought. *The very last person.*

'Well, I'd best get back down and let your friends know that all's well then.' His eyes were grave.

'Thanks again.'

'Any time, lovely.' And he was gone, leaving the echo of his rather nice aftershave in her hall.

CHAPTER 5

By Tuesday morning everyone except Dominic and Sophie had either phoned or texted her to say thanks for the party and that they'd had a great time. There had been varying levels of enthusiasm. Matt had sent her a one-line text:

Cheers, great to see you. Mwah.

This had been swiftly followed by another text saying,

This is Matt using Manda's phone. Mine's bust.

Tee-hee. Actually she'd worked that out from the *Mwah*. He probably hadn't realized the phone had done it.

Serena and Jojo had both phoned and said they'd had a lovely time. Thomas had sent a little card in the post. It had a picture of a bluebell wood on the front and inside it said:

Thank you for Saturday. Hope it's the first of many successful supper parties.

She held it in her hand and smiled. How politely old-fashioned he was. He'd always been thoughtful. Her earliest memory of Thomas Hanson was of him coming to the house to sort out Dad's back problem. In his youth, although it seemed hard to believe now, Dad had been a bit of an action man. He'd had to stop after he'd broken several bones in his back following a nasty fall from a tor on Dartmoor when he was in his twenties. All before she was born, of course.

He was pretty much an adrenalin junkie at work too. He'd earned his money from stocks and shares, which he seemed to have a sixth sense for, and had invested the profits in property. He'd left city life behind when he'd met her mother and seemed to get most of his kicks, these days, from battling with planning departments. He always won.

Luckily he had Thomas, who as well as being the world blood-spatter expert – why on earth had she mentioned that last night? – was a very fine osteopath. Every time Dad had a problem he consulted Thomas. He could be staggering around, barely able to walk, when Thomas arrived, and a mere two hours later he'd be skipping about like a spring lamb.

Anne Marie decided to head over to Dad's now and see how he was getting on. On her way out of the door she spotted that month's novel, *Emma*, on the hall table. Which was where she'd left it when she'd come in from Serena's. She really should read it some time. They were halfway through the month and she hadn't so much as glanced at the blurb.

Not that it mattered too much if she didn't read it. She could look up the plot on Wikipedia and blag it. It wouldn't be the first time. Reading Group wasn't so much about the actual reading as the friendship, she told herself. It had been really nice of Serena to send Thomas back to check on her on Saturday night. It was good to know her friends were looking out for her.

What was *Emma* about again? She picked it up. Ah, yes, matchmaking. Hey, perhaps it might give her some tips. She hadn't done very well on Saturday, had she? Despite what Thomas had said.

She owed Sophie an apology, too, she thought with a prickle of remorse. This matchmaking business wasn't as easy as she'd imagined. Goodness knows how the poor girl was feeling after Saturday. She'd call in and see her on the way to Dad's.

Sophie was in surprisingly good spirits when Anne Marie turned up on her doorstep just after lunch.

'Oh, hi. Come in. Mum and Dad are away.'

She was still in her Clean Living overalls. Anne Marie had been right – she looked great in them – and she hummed as she made them a drink.

'Thanks for inviting me to your party. It was – er – different.'

'Um, yes. I'm sorry things didn't work out with Dominic. I—'

'Who?' Sophie asked. 'Oh. You mean Skoda Man.'

Anne Marie winced. 'My mistake. I really did think he had a Jag.'

'To be honest, he could have had a Rolls-Royce and I wouldn't have been interested. "So what do you do for a living, then, Sophie? Oh, you're a cleaner. I guess someone has to be. Yah!"' Her imitation of Dominic's rather pompous voice was so good that Anne Marie snorted with laughter.

'I'm sorry about him. I got it wrong. I misinterpreted the – um – situation.'

'It's cool, don't worry. It happens. Thomas is nice, isn't he?'

'Yes. Yes, he is.' Surely Sophie wasn't interested in Thomas?! He was twice her age.

'I like older men,' she went on dreamily.

'Thomas is way too old for you.'

Sophie stopped what she was doing. 'Er . . . I didn't say I *fancied* him. I'm actually thinking about Matt. Did you know he's in the RAF? He's just signed up. But he's not doing the training till March. Until then he's only up the road. He lives with his sister.'

'No, I didn't. Well, not the RAF bit.'

'I've always gone for a man in uniform,' Sophie said. 'I think that's why I fell for Gary. He looked really hot in red.'

'He did?' Anne Marie was starting to relax again, although she could foresee one or two problems on the horizon. Still, at least she'd perked up a bit. It could have been a lot worse.

Her father was on fine form too.

'Thomas had a lovely time at your party,' he told her, when she saw him that afternoon. 'Well done, Princess. It sounds like it was a great success.'

'How do you know about that? Has Thomas been here?'

'This morning. Yes. My arm needed another session.' He circled his elbow. 'That's much freer.'

'Clever old Thomas,' she said, hoping he didn't hear the edge in her voice.

'It's a shame you don't like him. He has a soft spot for you.'

'No, he doesn't. He humours me because you two are friends.'

'I'm sure that's not true. He wouldn't have gone to your supper club unless he wanted to see you. He's a busy man.'

She supposed that could be true. *And* he had rescued her from Dominic, which had been sweet. Not that she'd needed rescuing, but even so . . .

Her father looked at her keenly. 'Mind if I ask you something?'

'As long as it's got nothing to do with Thomas Hanson.'

'Are you happy?'

'What a strange question. Of course I'm happy . . . I have a wonderful home, a business I love – some really great friends.' She went across to him and put her arms around his shoulders. 'I have you.'

He smiled. There was a weird mixture of pain and pride in his eyes.

'I don't need a boyfriend to be happy,' she added.

'I know you don't, Princess.' He looked reflective. It wasn't a mood she saw him in often. 'When your mother died . . . well, you two were very young. Especially you. You were only three. I didn't have the inclination or the time to go out and look for anyone else.' His face went very solemn and his voice a bit gruff. 'You were my life, you two girls.

And I had my work, of course. That was enough. But, well, latterly I've sometimes wondered if I did the right thing.'

'It's not too late,' she said. 'You're only fifty-three. Hardly over the hill. You could start dating again now.'

'Yeah. I guess I could. But I'm too busy.'

'No, you're not.'

He huffed and puffed. 'I am, actually. I just got planning permission – *finally* – to redevelop this place. The Old School House will very shortly be the Old School House flats, one to ten.' He waved a piece of paper at her. 'Ta-dah!'

'Ten flats? That's awesome, Dad. Well done.'

He smirked. 'Knowing the right people helps. Those afternoons on the golf course finally paid off.' He winked at her. 'But enough about me. When's your next matchmaking event?'

'I'm not sure,' she said. 'Maybe I ought to give that up. Saturday night wasn't terribly successful, if I'm honest.'

'You can't give up yet. Perhaps you need a different venue. Somewhere further afield?'

'Perhaps I do,' she mused.

All thoughts of matchmaking venues were pushed out of Anne Marie's head when on her way home she had a phone call from Manda.

Manda's voice sounded tight with tears. 'Jack and I've just split up.'

'What?'

'Can you come over?' Manda went on tearfully. 'I don't know what to do.'

'I'm on my way,' Anne Marie told her. Blimey O'Reilly. Manda and Jack were her main success story – her *only* success story. They couldn't split up! She'd have no credibility at all.

She found Manda in a right old state. She was puffing away on her e-cig and gulping a glass of wine. It was barely four o'clock.

'Want one?' Manda asked, waving the bottle.

'Why not?' Anne Marie said. Not that she could have more than half a glass if she was driving, but it would show solidarity.

'Thanks so much for coming,' Manda sobbed, once they were ensconced on the settee with a man-size box of tissues between them and plenty of Dairy Milk to accompany the wine. Anne Marie was never going to achieve her New Year resolution to slim down at this rate.

'What happened?' she asked.

'I don't know what to do!' Manda wailed, ignoring the question. 'I've decided. I'm going to give him his ring back.'

She held out her hand, glanced at the huge sparkly stone with a small sigh of regret and began to wiggle it off.

'No, wait,' Anne Marie said. 'You don't have to do anything straight away. Did you have a row?'

'Not really.' Manda stopped tugging at her ring. 'I don't think I can get it off. How am I going to throw it in his face if I can't get it off?'

'You're not,' Anne Marie said firmly. 'No ring throwing. I want you to tell me exactly what happened.'

47

Manda took a deep breath. 'We had a disagreement over the place settings. He wants black-edged and I want silver.'

'Is that it?' Anne Marie was aghast.

'No, of course that's not it. That turned into a row about the invites. They still haven't come, by the way, so arguing about the place settings was probably immaterial, seeing as we don't even know who's coming because we haven't even been able to send out any flaming invites!'

'I'm coming.'

'I know you are, bless you. Train-driver Todd's really looking forward to meeting you.'

'Mmm.' Anne Marie was beginning to think that train-driver Todd was as aware of her existence as Dominic Peterson had been of Sophie's before Saturday. 'So what happened next?' she prompted.

'Well, then we argued about the timing – Jack said everyone would think it's a shotgun wedding because we haven't known each other that long.'

'It's not, is it?'

'No, we just thought it would be romantic to have our wedding day on the same day as my parents had theirs because they're not around anymore.'

Anne Marie nodded and her heart went out to her friend. Manda's parents had died in a car accident two years earlier.

'I suppose we could have put it off for a year,' Manda went on quietly, 'but it seems an awfully long time to wait. And I haven't got any patience.' She gave a watery smile.

'I haven't any patience either,' Anne Marie said. '"Please, God, give me patience, but I want it now."'

Manda giggled, but whether this was at the weak joke, or because she was well on the way to being drunk, Anne Marie wasn't sure.

'Manda, do you love him?' Anne Marie asked, realizing with a little shock that it was the second time in a week she'd asked someone that question. Love – it was what her father had been talking about earlier too. In a roundabout way. Everyone needed it, didn't they? The world revolved around it.

'I love the way he opens doors for me and walks on the traffic side of the pavement,' Manda said. 'And he's a really good foot-rubber.' She hiccupped. 'Is that love?'

'I guess so,' Anne Marie said, wondering if it was. *What made up love?* Was it tiny little bits or was it one big thing? And why the hell was she getting so hung up about it? She never had before Sophie had had her romantic crisis.

Sophie hadn't been having a romantic crisis, she remembered. Sophie had been jogging along perfectly happily until Anne Marie had got involved.

No – she'd been right to do it. OK, so she might have made a slight misjudgement as far as Dominic Peterson was concerned, but Matt was nice enough. And being in the RAF didn't preclude him and Sophie from being happy. Lots of people were in the armed forces and had perfectly nice lives.

'Hey,' she said, remembering that Manda probably didn't know about that. 'Your brother enjoyed my singles supper. Did he tell you?'

'Yes.' Manda looked cheered. 'He said he met a hot chick.

I didn't know you had any hot friends. Apart from me, of course.'

'Cheeky!' Anne Marie made a slapping motion with her hands. 'He's talking about Sophie. She's lovely. She's one of my cleaners.'

'No it wasn't a cleaner, I'm sure it wasn't.' Manda bit her lip. 'Though I think her name did begin with S. Have you got a friend who's a teacher or something? No, not a teacher. Headmistress. That's it.'

'Serena? But she's way older than Matt. She's thirty-three.'

'There's not that much difference. Six years. He's always liked older women.'

Oh, no, this could be a disaster. 'Poor Sophie. She's got the hots for him. And she thinks he likes her too.'

'Oh dear,' said Manda. 'Anyway, enough of him. We're supposed to be talking about my love life, not Matt's. I think I'm going to phone Jack. You're right. I'd be mad to let him go.'

When had she said that?

'And it doesn't matter when the wedding is – you were right about that too,' Manda went on. 'It's been great talking to you. You've put everything in perspective. Thank you.'

'You're welcome.' Anne Marie smiled at her. She was pretty sure she hadn't done anything, but it was nice to be appreciated. She might have mucked up Sophie's love life, but she'd sorted out Manda's. All was not lost.

CHAPTER 6

Now that all her friends had their love lives in order perhaps she should turn her attention to her own, Anne Marie mused the next day. She wouldn't have given it a thought had not a very fit guy just turned up on her doorstep – or, to be more precise, Dad's doorstep. She'd gone over to help out.

'I'm here to see Mr Hambledon,' the man said, giving her a direct look. Wow, those eyes were blue. 'We've got a meeting for a quote about house clearance. I'm Jamie Wright.'

'Hi, I'm his daughter,' Anne Marie said. His name was 'Mr Right'! It couldn't be a coincidence. No sooner had she decided to sort out her love life than Mr Right had appeared. Literally. 'Do come in,' she said. 'Daddy's had to go out, but he asked me to show you what needs to go so you can get an idea. There's rather a lot of stuff. This used to be a school.' She glanced back over her shoulder and caught him looking at her butt. Naughty. She pretended not to notice. 'I hope you've got a big van,' she said, as she showed him the first classroom. 'There are another eight like this.'

He didn't seem fazed. 'It's not just me,' he said. 'It's a family business – my three brothers are involved. We're a team.'

Family was good. Everyone liked family.

'Your wives too?' she asked. Was that too obvious?

It seemed not. He shook his head. 'Simon's the only one who's married. The rest of us are still looking for the *right woman*, if you'll excuse the pun!' There was a twinkle of flirtation in his eyes. She betted it wasn't the first time he'd used that joke, but she wouldn't hold it against him.

As they filled in the paperwork she nibbled the end of her pen and touched her hair. 'Are you local boys – you and your brothers?'

'We are, ma'am, yes.'

Why hadn't she bumped into them before?

'Oh, please don't call me "ma'am" – it's Anne Marie.' She smiled.

'Nice name.'

'Thank you,' she said. 'I'll give you my mobile number – just in case.' She hooked out one of her Clean Living cards and handed it to him. 'This is my company – just in case you should ever need a cleaner.'

'Cheers. Cool.' He turned the business card over in his hands. 'Another family of entrepreneurs.'

They were back at the front door when he finally got his act together. 'I don't suppose you, er, fancy a coffee or any- thing one night, do you?'

Alleluia! She liked his shyness, the way he dipped his head a little as he spoke. 'That could be fun.' She gave him an encouraging smile.

'I'll ring you.' He put her card in the top pocket of his denim jacket. 'In the meantime I'll sort out a final price then get this stuff out of your way.'

'Thank you, Jamie.'

She watched him walk back to his van, his step jauntier now that he'd got the job – and the girl. She frowned.

Retrospectively, had the whole thing seemed a little forced? Would he have even asked her if she hadn't dropped so many hints? She wished she had a bit more experience, but although she was twenty-two in August she hadn't had what you could call a serious relationship. OK, make that a relationship full stop. She'd been on plenty of dates at uni but hadn't got involved with anyone. She hadn't met the right guy, she'd told herself, but the truth was she'd been a little afraid and had backed off if anyone got too close.

She hadn't wanted to do what Julia had done. She hadn't wanted to get pregnant and have to drop out. It didn't seem fair on Dad. And even though he'd never once complained, after Julia had turned down her place at Cambridge . . . well, it played on her mind.

When she got home she phoned Manda. 'How'd it go? Is the wedding back on? Am I still a bridesmaid?'

'You are.' Manda sounded happy. 'Jack loves me and I love Jack, and that's all that's really important, isn't it?'

'It is,' Anne Marie said, feeling warmed because Manda sounded so happy. 'Manda, guess what.'

'OMG, what? Tell me now. Tell me immediately.'

'I would if I could get a word in edgeways.'

'Sorry. Go!'

'I've just met Mr Wright.'

'You've what? OMG, how? What's his name?'

Anne Marie loved it when Manda was like this. 'His name's Jamie Wright,' she said. 'Wright with a W. We're going on a date.'

'Somewhere nice?'

'I'm not sure yet – he's confirming the details later. In the meantime I was just, er, wondering, if you're not too busy with wedding stuff . . . have you got time to go shopping later? I'm going to need something to wear.'

'I am *never* too busy to go shopping. I'm there.'

They went to Exeter on Wednesday afternoon. Manda did shifts – she was a nurse at the Royal Devon and Exeter Hospital – so Anne Marie met her in town.

'So . . .' Manda said, running across the car park to meet her. 'What kind of outfit are we looking for? Have you got a picture of the man on your phone you can show me?'

'No, I haven't.' They air-kissed. 'Although you can check out his website – he's got a house-clearance company with his brothers. Hang on a sec.' Anne Marie rummaged for her phone. 'Here they are. The Wright Brothers House Clearance. "Let us do right by you."'

Manda clapped her hands. 'Which one is he?'

'The good-looking one in the middle.'

'Mmm – nice eyes.' They stood on the tarmac in the middle of the car park and Anne Marie felt light and happy. As if she'd just joined a club at which membership had hitherto been withheld. 'Ocean Views,' she said happily. 'Tomorrow night. He's picking me up at six thirty.'

'How exciting.' Manda stood back and looked at her appraisingly. 'Shall we start in Monsoon?'

They bought two outfits: a lovely little carmine wool dress with a bomber jacket – it looked amazing on and would go with the shoes she'd bought a couple of weeks ago; and a more casual ensemble of light-pink skinny jeans and cream silk shirt with little diamonds on it. 'You're lucky – you're so tall and slim,' Manda gushed.

'I'm not that slim.'

'Yes, you are. Don't argue with your Auntie Manda.'

Anne Marie stroked her arm. 'It's so lovely to see you looking happy.'

'Ah, bless. You know what I'm like. I'm not happy unless there's something exciting going on.'

'But splitting up with Jack! You're not going to do that again, are you?'

'No, I'm not.' Manda paused. 'Hey, you can bring Jamie as your plus one to the wedding.'

'I know. Isn't it brilliant?'

'Maybe we'll be going to your wedding in a few months' time?'

'Steady – we haven't been on our first date yet.'

'Every epic voyage starts with a single step.'

'Indeed.' Anne Marie's phone buzzed in her bag. She

ignored it, not wanting anything to distract her from shopping with Manda in this little bubble of happiness.

She didn't look at her phone till she got home. It was a missed call from Dad. He'd left a voicemail. She played it.

'Hi, Princess. Just got the quote in from the Wright brothers about the house clearance. Seems a bit steep. Can you phone me, please? Want to clarify what you asked them to do.'

It wasn't like her father to quibble over price. It really must have been steep. She phoned him back. The quote made her eyes water. 'What are you going to do?'

'Tell them to stick it where the sun doesn't shine,' he said. 'I'll find another house-clearance firm.'

'Oh,' she said, trying not to let her disappointment sneak into her voice. 'Course.'

She set the phone down. She felt as though the bubble of hope and excitement she'd been living in for the past few days had been pricked.

Perhaps it would be fine and she was just being paranoid. As if in answer to her thoughts another text came through. It was from Jamie: *Hi, just to confirm I'll pick you up at 6.30 tomorrow. Hope that's cool? J x*

Oh, blimey. A kiss. Only one, but that was good. She jumped off her stool, grabbed her shopping bags and went and tried everything on again in the bedroom. Decisions, decisions.

Even though she'd already chosen the dress – it was really slimming and the jacket was cute – she still found herself standing in front of the mirror the following day, agonizing.

Was this outfit too posh for Ocean Views? It would have been perfect for Calypso's, but they weren't going there. Maybe she should change into the pink jeans. She tried them on. They were really nice, but they were quite tight. She wouldn't be able to eat very much (if anything) if she wore these.

She changed back again. Maybe the blouse and a different pair of skinny jeans? She had about sixteen pairs. But none was quite the right colour. Why hadn't she bought a size fourteen instead of twelve? It was only a number.

She put the pink jeans back on. They were perfect. Never mind eating. But what about sitting down? She tried perching on the edge of her bed. Muffin tummy. No, she couldn't wear these.

Why was she so vain? Why was she so rubbish at making decisions? How come she could sort everyone's love life except her own?

She glanced at her phone. It was a quarter past six. He'd be here soon. What if he was early and she was half dressed? Her heart started to pound. She had to calm down.

She put the dress back on, retouched her make-up. Redid her hair. Read a text that had just come through from Manda: *Have a great time. Don't do anything I wouldn't do, so pretty much anything goes!! Mwah mwah.*

It was 6.32.

She ran out on to her balcony from which she could see the far edge, including the entrance, of the car park. Not that that was really going to help as she didn't know what car he drove. Anyway, she might not hear the entry-phone buzzer from out here. She ran back in. She went and checked her teeth for lipstick in the bathroom. All good.

It was 6.37.

Better check her phone in case he'd texted. Perhaps he couldn't find the place. She frowned. That was unlikely. Finding addresses was his job – or, at least, a big part of it. He hadn't texted.

At 6.54 she picked up the copy of *Emma* from the hall table by the door and looked at page one. She'd read the first chapter while she was waiting. Then at least she could say, hand on heart, that she'd started it, but had run out of time.

At 6.55 she decided to go down to the car park and make sure he wasn't sitting there waiting. What if he'd lost her number and couldn't remember her address?

The car park was quiet. There were no lone men sitting nervously in cars, all togged up ready for a date.

At a minute past seven, standing in the middle of the tarmac, looking out towards the sea, Anne Marie dialled his number. There was no answer. When she tried it again a minute or so later it went straight to voicemail without ringing at all and she knew he'd pressed a button to reject her call or turned off his phone so he didn't have to speak to her.

She could no longer deny that she'd been stood up. She'd run out of excuses for him. He just wasn't coming.

CHAPTER 7

When she got up the next day, Anne Marie's overriding emotion was of humiliation.

Was she ugly?

Was she too fat?

Had she been totally naïve?

She called Manda, who'd just finished a night shift.

'You're not ugly. You're not fat. I don't think you're naïve. Remind me again what that means?'

'Stupid,' Anne Marie said.

'You are the most unstupid person I know.'

'"Unstupid" isn't a word.'

'You know what I mean. The man's a bad-mannered tosser. He's definitely not good enough for you.'

'Thanks,' Anne Marie said, smiling despite herself. 'I was so disappointed, Manda. I know it was only a date, but . . .' She tailed off. 'Well, I guess I expected too much, didn't I? In my head I was already bringing him to your wedding.'

'Sweetie, I get it.' Manda's voice softened. 'It's human. There are nice guys out there. Don't waste another second of your life on that one. And speaking of weddings, the bridesmaids' dresses are here. You're going to love them. When can you come over and try yours on?'

'As soon as I've done the wages and emailed the rotas,' Anne Marie said.

She put the phone down. She felt a thousand times better already.

The bridesmaids' dresses were *gorgeous*. They were hanging in a row from the dado rail in Manda's bedroom: hers and two smaller ones for Manda's eight-year-old twin cousins. They were pale-blue silk (almost aquamarine), with detail on the bodices. They went beautifully with the ivory dress Manda had chosen.

'Where did you get them?' Anne Marie said, brushing her fingers across the delicate material. 'They're stunning.'

'Aren't they?' Manda said smugly. 'A shop in Exeter. They're straight off the rack. They fit the girls and you're a size twelve, right?'

'Maybe not at the moment. I've been comfort eating.'

'Well, I reserved the fourteen too, just in case. But try it – they're quite generously cut.'

To Anne Marie's delight, the dress fitted her perfectly. 'That colour really suits you,' Manda said, as they stood in front of the full-length mirror. 'It matches your eyes. You should wear it more often.'

'Do you think?'

'Yes. I used to envy you so much when we were younger,' Manda said. 'You're a real English rose, aren't you? I hated having olive skin and dark hair.'

Anne Marie could feel herself going pink. 'That's mad! You're stunning,' she said, as they stood side by side. 'All sultry and exotic. Lovely long hair and it's so gorgeously thick. What are you going to do with your hair anyway? Are you putting it up?'

'Up, but not too formal,' Manda said. She twirled a dark strand around her finger. 'I know it was a bit mad to pick a date so soon, but in some ways it's a lot easier. I think people go really OTT with weddings, these days. It can cost an absolute fortune – twenty or thirty thousand pounds just for one day. That's insane, isn't it? It's house-deposit money.'

'You're going to buy a house, then?'

'Yes. That's why I've been sharing this tiny little shoebox with my brother. I'm saving like mad. So's Jack. We haven't got that much now, but we will have eventually.'

Anne Marie was struck, as she often was, by the disparity between Manda and her. She'd never had to think about house deposits or mortgages or how she was going to pay them – she'd never had to worry about money at all. She felt fleetingly guilty. 'Where will you live when you're married?' she asked. 'I mean, I assume you'll move in together. Will you go to Jack's?'

'We thought we would, but his landlord wants the flat back because he's selling, so we'll probably both stay here.'

'With Matt? Isn't that going to be a bit of a squeeze?' Understatement of the year.

Manda waved a hand. 'Jack doesn't take up much room. And Matt's joining the RAF soon. When he's on active service he won't be here much.'

Anne Marie nodded. But for the rest of the evening she was imagining Manda and Jack cooking in the tiny kitchen, which smelt of curry, or watching the television in the boxy lounge. There wasn't even a proper garden, just a paved terrace about ten foot square with a boxed-off bit to put your bins in.

It seemed wrong that her best friend would be starting married life with so little when Anne Marie had so much.

'Have you got a wedding list set up anywhere?' Anne Marie asked.

'Um, no. There's not enough people coming for us to bother, really,' Manda said. 'Just buy us some nice bedding or something.' She smiled. 'I'm so excited, Anne Marie. I never thought I'd be marrying my soulmate before I was twenty-two.'

'And he's definitely the *one*?'

'He's absolutely the one. I've never been with anyone who's made me laugh so much. I guess we're just on the same wavelength. Do you know what I mean?'

Anne Marie nodded, although she wasn't sure that she did. You had to be relaxed to laugh out loud in someone's company, and she wasn't sure she'd ever been that relaxed around a man.

The front door slammed and ten seconds later Matt appeared in the doorway.

'Oh, hiya, Anne Marie. How's things?' He smiled. *He looks like his sister*, she thought, the same dark hair, the same black eyes. He lounged in the doorway, one hand on the jamb. 'You seen much of the lovely Serena lately? Only she's not answering my texts.'

Oh, crap, she'd forgotten about his crush on Serena. 'Isn't she? No, I haven't. I mainly see her at Reading Group, and that's not for a couple of weeks.'

'Reading Group . . . Hmm, what do you do there?'

'Er – the clue's in the name,' Manda said, raising her eyebrows. 'They read literary *classics*. Don't you, Anne Marie?'

'Absolutely,' Anne Marie said, trying to remember if she'd read more than the first paragraph of *Emma*. She'd certainly intended to, but when Jamie had stood her up she'd got side-tracked and watched five episodes of *Loose Women*, accompanied by a giant-bag of Doritos and a couple of packets of Haribo instead.

'Can anyone join Reading Group?' Matt asked. 'I love a good book, me.'

'Since when?' Manda asked. 'The closest you get to reading is going on Buzzfeed!'

Matt glared. 'You have no idea what I do on my phone. I've got the Kindle app downloaded on here.'

'No way.'

'Yes way.' He showed it to them. 'Ha,' he said. 'I'm not

just a pretty face. See? . . . OK, I downloaded it to impress Serena. She said she was into books.'

'Are you sure you don't fancy Sophie?' Anne Marie asked.

He shot her a look. 'Too young. I'll tell you what, though. I do have a mate who likes blondes . . . Shall I pass her number on to him?'

'No,' Manda said. 'She's not a raffle prize that you can pass around your mates.'

He looked affronted. He held up his hands, palms facing them. 'Only trying to help, ladies. Only trying to help. So how do I get to join this Reading Group then, Anne Marie? Can you put in a word for me?'

'It's at Serena's house, so it's up to her who comes,' she told him. 'And if she's not answering your texts I'm not, um, sure . . .'

'Maybe you should just take the hint,' Manda suggested. 'The woman doesn't want a toyboy.'

Matt didn't look in the least bit fazed. 'She's probably worried she wouldn't be able to handle me.' He did a mock strut up and down the lounge.

Anne Marie fled before she got any more involved.

When she got home there were three messages on her answer machine, which was unusual as most people phoned her mobile.

The first was from her father. 'Call me when you've got a minute, could you?' He sounded stern.

The second was from Sophie. 'I'm still on the rota to clean Dominic Peterson's flat and I'd rather not, if that's OK.'

How had that happened? Anne Marie could see that might be embarrassing.

The third was from Serena. 'Give me a tinkle, darling, when you get a second, can you?' Her voice was over-bright.

Anne Marie phoned her first.

'Sorry to bother you,' Serena said. 'This is a bit sensitive. It's about your young friend Matt.'

'Ah.' Anne Marie sighed. 'I think I know what you're going to say. He's been texting you, hasn't he?'

'Seventeen times to date,' Serena said. 'I've had to turn my phone off. Which is a nuisance because it's mostly for work, you see. I only gave him my number because he said he was going to send me the details of this book about applied maths.' She hesitated. 'I thought it might go down well in the school library.'

'Applied maths?' It was hard to keep the incredulity out of her voice. Matt knew as much about applied maths as he did about women's handbags, as far as Anne Marie was aware.

'I mean, it's very flattering,' Serena said. 'But—'

'You're not feeling it,' Anne Marie said. 'I'm so sorry.'

'It's not your fault,' Serena said. 'But maybe if you could have a quiet word?'

'Of course.'

There was an awkward little pause. 'How are you getting on with *Emma*?'

'Who?'

'Our novel of the month, darling.'

'Ah. Yes. I've read quite a bit.' Anne Marie crossed her

65

fingers behind her back. 'She's a fabulous matchmaker, isn't she?'

'Er ... well, I have to say that is an interesting view of it ...' She could hear the frown in Serena's voice.

The door buzzer went. Never had Anne Marie been so relieved. 'That's the door. Lovely to talk to you. Sorry again.'

Saved by the bell. But as she moved out into the hall to press the door-release Serena's words echoed in her ears: *It's not your fault ...*

But it was really. Her supper evening had been a match-making attempt, but things hadn't gone at all to plan.

Dominic was cross. She was surprised he hadn't sacked her. Maybe he still would – he hadn't paid last month's invoice yet. Sophie fancied Matt, and Serena was being besieged by texts she didn't want. It hadn't even been that much fun.

She was totally responsible for it all. If it hadn't been for her, none of this would have happened.

The door buzzer went again. 'Hello?' she said breathlessly.

'It's Thomas,' said a deep voice. 'Any chance of a quick word?'

Oh, no, she thought, as she waited for him to arrive. *Not more trouble. Please don't let anything have happened to Thomas.*

CHAPTER 8

Thomas didn't look upset. In fact, he seemed pretty laid back. He was dressed casually, Calvin Klein jeans and a pastel shirt, not pink or anything, but certainly not stiff white, like he normally wore. Anne Marie realized that she usually saw him in his work clothes. Oh, and at her party. What had he been wearing then? Oh yes, that nice Jasper Conran shirt.

'Everything OK?' She suddenly remembered her father's message. 'Dad's OK, isn't he?'

'Yep. As far as I know.' He shot her a glance. 'Why?'

She rubbed her forehead. 'No. It's just me being paranoid. He phoned earlier and I haven't called him back yet. I haven't had a very good day.'

'Ah.' He hovered in the hall. He was wearing that lovely aftershave again: a hint of citrus with the tiniest underlay of spice. 'Say if it's a bad time. I was just passing so I thought

I'd pop by and check you'd had no more unwanted visits from the guy downstairs.'

'No, I haven't.' She smiled at him. 'It's not a bad time. It's never a bad time for you to call, Thomas. You're practically family. I see you as my honorary big brother.'

'Ah.' There was something in his eyes that was gone before she could fathom out what it was – or even be sure it had ever been there.

'Actually,' she added, 'I could really do with a friendly ear.'

He gave her a quick smile. 'Honorary Big Brother Thomas is at your service.'

They sat in the lounge. She perched on the corner sofa and he sat on the matching coffee-coloured armchair opposite.

'This really is a beautiful room,' he said, looking towards the plate-glass windows, beyond which you could see a ribbon of crystal sea.

'Thank you. I'm really lucky. You can see the sea from practically every room in this flat. People assume the sea is blue, but it isn't. It ranges from aquamarine to black – it goes through every shade of green and grey on the way and when the sun sets across it, it turns pink—' She broke off. 'Sorry, I'm ranting. I really love it here. That's what I'm trying to say.'

He nodded. There was something very calm about him – very easy and relaxing. She guessed that was because she knew him so well – or, at least, had known him so long because, actually, in some ways she didn't know him at all.

She had never even been to his house, she realized, because he always came to Dad's – or sometimes Dad went to his practice, which was near Exeter.

'Where do you live, Thomas?'

'Ashmore,' he said. 'It's about halfway between Little Sanderton and Exeter. I've got a cottage. It's not as big as this flat, but it suits me perfectly.' He smiled peaceably, and she thought, *That's why he's so relaxing. He's at ease with himself. He's totally comfortable in his own skin.* She couldn't think of anyone else like that – not even Dad. In fact, especially not Dad. He was always itching to move on to a new project, a new challenge.

She hesitated. 'I know I'm a spoiled little rich girl. I know that's what people think. That Daddy – well, that he gave me all this . . .' She spread her hands to encompass the flat. 'He helped me set up in business – I didn't have to work very hard for any of it.'

She looked at him. He had grey eyes. There wasn't a scrap of judgement in them. But he didn't speak so she rushed on: 'I don't take it for granted, you know.'

'I'm sure you don't.'

'Do you think I'm naïve, Thomas? Tell me the truth.'

'How are you defining naïve?'

'I don't know . . . stupid, I guess . . . silly, not understanding the consequences of things I do.' She was trying to find the words to explain. 'It's easier if I give you an example.' She told him about her failed date with Jamie Wright. 'I can't even call it a failed date,' she finished miserably, 'because actually it was just a date that never was. I mean,

I thought he wanted to go out with me, but did he actually just want to rip Daddy off and taking me out was part of the deal?'

Thomas leaned forward, his face serious. 'Truthfully, Anne Marie, he's the only one who knows the answer to that. But I can tell you something I do know.'

She smoothed her palm across the cool leather of the sofa arm. 'What?'

'You're worth a great deal more than a man who behaves like that. If I were you, I wouldn't give him another thought.'

'That's what my friend Manda said.'

'Sensible.'

She sighed. 'There's something else.'

'OK?'

'You know my supper-club evening? That wasn't exactly a resounding success either.' She told him about Sophie and Matt and Serena.

'It doesn't sound as if there's any real harm done,' Thomas said, when she'd finished. 'And just because you introduced everyone, it doesn't mean you're responsible for their inter-actions with anyone else. We all make our own choices.'

'But there's something else. This is a really, really silly thing. You'll laugh.'

'Try me.'

'I'm supposed to have read this novel for Reading Group – we're doing the classics at the moment and they're really boring. It's a Jane Austen – and she's supposed to be the greatest novelist ever born – but I can't get past the first page.'

'Which one is it?'

'*Emma.*' She leaped up and went to fetch it. 'I don't suppose you've read it, have you?'

'I'm afraid not. But I do know the plot. Emma's the main character. She's young, she lives in a big old Gothic house with her father, who's extremely well-off and a bit of a hypochondriac and she decides to do a bit of matchmaking among her friends. Which doesn't . . . um . . . go that well . . .'

'You're making it up,' she said. He handed the book back to her and she stared at it.

'Oh.' Cogs were whirring in her brain. 'No wonder there was such a strange atmosphere in Reading Group. I'd just been telling them about my plans to set up speed-dating events in Little Sanderton and . . . Oh! What I was telling you earlier about me being a spoiled little rich girl? Well, this book could have been written about me, couldn't it?'

'No, it couldn't,' he said. 'You're not spoiled.'

'But the rest is true. Anyway, I *am* spoiled.' She fixed him with a steely glare. 'I don't do anything for anyone else. My best friend Manda lives in a tiny little flat with her brother where you can barely swing a cat and I live in this huge penthouse that I don't even need. And it's never occurred to me to try to help her.'

'Anne Marie, listen to me. You are not responsible for other people.'

She felt suddenly deflated. 'But I do want to do something, Thomas. I want to help. How can I help without Manda thinking I see her as a charity case?' She raked a hand through her hair.

Thomas got up and stood in her path so she was obliged to stop pacing. She looked up at him. He was taller than her by a good four inches.

He rested his hands gently on her arms and she thought, *He's got nice hands.* Osteopath's hands. Firm and professional. Confident. Neatly cut nails. She looked up into his eyes. There were little flecks of dark in the grey.

'You'll figure it out,' he said.

She bit her lip.

'If it's any consolation, that novel, *Emma*? Well, it does have a very happy ending.'

'Are you going to tell me what it is?'

'Google it,' he said.

'Thomas?'

He raised his eyebrows.

'You've really inspired me. I'm now on a mission. I'm going to start helping other people – properly, I mean. But I won't just go diving in – I'll find out what they want first.'

He didn't look as impressed as she'd thought he might. But it didn't matter. Her mind was made up.

'Mission Unselfish,' she said, 'has begun.'

When he had gone she phoned her father. 'Are you OK? You sounded grumpy on the phone.'

'I'm not grumpy. I'm stressed. I'm still trying to find a house-clearance firm and my shoulder hurts like hell.' He huffed.

'Can I help at all?'

'That's what I was hoping you'd say. Yes, you can. Is there

any chance you could stay here for a few days? I need someone I trust. Don't worry if you're too busy.'

'I'm never too busy to help you,' she said.

'Thank you,' he said. 'You're a good girl, Anne Marie. I don't tell you that enough.' She could hear the smile in his voice.

She put the phone down. Mission Unselfish would just have to wait a while.

CHAPTER 9

The next few days did not pan out quite as she'd expected. She'd forgotten how chaotic living with her father was. But it was surprising what you could get done if you were totally focused. By Monday afternoon she'd arranged to have the Old School House cleared by a very professional company she'd found in Ashmore. Funny how that name kept cropping up.

Everything was back on schedule, and before long this building would be no more. The classrooms where children had once learned and laughed, the corridors where they had run and the pegs where they had hung their school bags and coats would be razed to the ground. A block of smart modern flats would take their place.

Not that Anne Marie was nostalgic about such things. OK, so the Old School House had a few nice old fireplaces and some lovely wooden staircases, but it was a relic of the past.

Who'd want a mouldering, dusty old building when they could have a nice new modern flat? Certainly not her.

But her most pressing question at the moment was where Dad was going to live when this building was gone.

She hoped he didn't want to come and live with her. Much as she adored her father, they had completely different lifestyles. Dad was an owl: he got up around nine, but worked well into the night. And she was a lark. She was usually up at dawn, which was when she did most of her paperwork. She was meticulous, while Dad was far more creative and random. He also never put anything away and he got cross if she did because then he couldn't find it.

Maybe he'd want me to rent him somewhere, she thought, nibbling the end of her pen – or maybe one of his own flats was empty, although she suspected not: they were usually all tenanted.

In the meantime, the architect, Chris Clarke, was supposed to be coming round to drop off a set of drawings. On cue there was a knock at the back door and Digby started barking. She went to let him in.

'Your father about?' The architect dipped his head to come into the kitchen. He was a man of few words.

'No, he's out having a row with the builder,' she said. 'But do come in, if you've time.'

He checked his chunky gold wristwatch. 'I've a ten-minute slot. I'm in Blandford at five.'

'I'll put the kettle on,' she said, and he nodded in agreement. He put an A4 envelope on the kitchen table, then sat on a wooden chair, drawing his long legs up underneath him and looking around at the mess with distaste.

'So you're working late in Blandford, then?' she asked, in an attempt to start a conversation.

'Not work,' he said.

'Right,' Anne Marie said, putting his tea in front of him and waiting a beat for him to elaborate. He didn't. 'I see. Well, I hope it's nice, whatever you're doing.'

'Homeless centre,' he said, and raised his white eyebrows. 'I help out. In my spare time.'

'Really? What do you do there? I mean, not that it's any of my business.'

'I cook.' He took a sip of his tea and studied her over the rim of his cup. 'Nothing elaborate, although it's not soup, usually – contrary to popular belief. I imagine it will be egg and chips today because it's Wednesday.'

'Wow,' she said, and then, because she was so surprised and because he had lapsed back into silence, she said it again. 'Wow! How on earth did you get involved?'

'I've been doing it for years,' he murmured, glancing fleetingly at the pile of newspapers on the table, then meeting her eyes again. 'In 1983 I experienced a brief period of homelessness myself.'

She stared at him in amazement.

'I don't usually tell people that,' he said.

'Gosh, no.' She felt suddenly very privileged. 'I won't tell anyone.'

'Yes,' he said. 'I believe you.' He put his cup on the saucer and gestured to the envelope. 'Please pass those on to your father.'

'I will. Thanks.' He was standing up to go and she knew it was one of those now-or-never moments. Her chance, maybe, to do some good – it was as if the universe had just handed it to her on a plate. She cleared her throat.

'Chris, I – er – well, I . . . um . . . Do you ever need any help there? At the homeless centre. I'm good at washing up. And cleaning. As a volunteer I mean.'

It was his turn to look surprised. His eyes widened a fraction. Then he drew out a neat wallet from the pocket of his suit, opened it and retrieved a gilt-edged card.

She half expected it to say, *Chris Clarke – Ambassador for the Homeless*. But it didn't. It said, *Chris Clarke – Architect*.

'If you're serious about that,' he said, 'ring me.'

She rang him the next day. She couldn't believe quite how nervous she was. He sounded a little surprised to hear from her – did everyone think she was a spoiled little rich girl? Then again, what had she ever done to prove that she wasn't?

'If you really want to help,' Chris said, 'come down tomorrow evening. We're based at St John's Community Hall. It's behind the church. You can have a trial session, so to speak.'

She'd thought he meant a trial so she could see if she liked it. But it quickly became apparent that she was the one on trial. The kitchen staff, Jules and Ben, were both older than she was. Thirty-something, she guessed. Jules had a hard, sharp voice, but a nice smile, and Ben was stocky and kindly.

Jules handed her an apron. 'Save mucking up yer nice clothes,' she said, and Anne Marie nodded, even though she was only actually wearing her really old Vivienne Westwoods and an ancient T-shirt.

'Ben usually washes up,' Jules added, 'but as you're here, I'm promoting him to server. You wanna drink before you start? It'll be busy by six.'

She drank tea from a green cup and saucer. Not the chipped mug she'd half expected. In fact, over the next couple of hours all of her preconceptions about what a soup kitchen might be like – right down to the lack of soup (Chris was cooking egg and chips as he'd predicted) – were blown out of the water. The plates they used mostly matched. The homeless people were mostly polite. They didn't come shuffling in looking bedraggled, clothes tied up with pieces of string and hay in their hair. She wasn't quite sure where she was getting the hay-in-their-hair bit, possibly because this was a rural community and they might be sleeping under haystacks.

They joked with Chris, Ben and Jules as if they'd known them for years. *Perhaps they have*, Anne Marie thought, feeling humbled. To think she had never even known this place was here.

There was only one guy who matched the homeless stereotype she hadn't even been aware she had. He was clearly angry and also drunk, judging by the way he was swaying around, but Chris, pausing briefly from cooking duties, handled him with tact and sensitivity. His calmness worked perfectly there. She couldn't imagine him ever getting ruffled or cross, or being a high-drama chef, who hurled spatulas at people. He just fried egg after egg and continually filled up the chip fryer with the mound of chipped potatoes he must have peeled earlier.

It was hard work washing up. Very, very hard work. There was no dishwasher, just a big old sink and a stainless-steel drainer, which she had to empty periodically so she could fill it again. The kitchen grew incredibly hot and steamy. It had been pointless putting on make-up – even her waterproof mascara didn't fare well. And her back ached from stooping over the sink. *Perk of being tall*, she thought, wondering if she would do permanent damage to herself if she did this on a regular basis. She'd have to employ Thomas to sort her out. That might be fun ... *Where had that thought come from?*

She wondered how Thomas was. She hadn't spoken to him since he'd called at her flat last week. She should have phoned and thanked him, she realized belatedly, for sitting and listening to all that nonsense she'd been spewing out. Poor Thomas. It was all very well her telling him that he was her honorary big brother, but it had hardly been fair, had it? She'd spent the best part of two hours pouring out all her problems and he'd not said a single thing about himself. And she hadn't even thanked him!

She would text him later. No, she would phone him. He wouldn't know, of course, that she was at Dad's. So that was a good excuse to phone him. Also, she was pretty sure Dad needed to see him on a professional basis. That was another good excuse to phone him. She'd never needed one to phone him before.

'Anne Marie, you're doing a great job.'

Chris was speaking to her. She'd been on autopilot for a while. Wash, dry, stack. Wash, dry, stack. But the flow actually seemed to have slowed, and when she turned round, she saw that Ben was eating an egg sandwich, perched on a stool in the corner, and Jules was drinking tea.

'Um, thanks,' she said. 'Have we finished?'

'Yes,' Jules said, coming across the small kitchen and taking the damp tea-towel from her hands. 'We have, love. And I bet you're thinking, Thank the Lord for that, aren't you? You've worked like a Trojan.'

'She has.' Chris smiled.

Ben, who clearly had his mouth full of egg sandwich, gave her a thumbs-up.

'I've enjoyed it,' Anne Marie said, realizing with surprise that it was true. She had liked the camaraderie – it was ages since she'd been part of a team. But, most of all, she'd liked that she was actually doing something useful.

'When can I come again?' she asked Jules.

'You can come whenever you like, my lovely,' Jules said. 'You've been a little star tonight. You really have.'

The two men nodded. Anne Marie felt a glow of pleasure warming her entire body.

Much later, when she lay in her room at Dad's, she thought about the evening. She wasn't given to long periods of reflection. She didn't look back and think, *If only I'd done this or that*. She mostly just reacted to what came up in her life and got on with it, and she tended – she realized with surprise – to do a fair bit on impulse.

Tonight had been an impulse, but it had been a good one. The little glow of warmth she'd got from seeing the appreciation in other people's eyes, well, that was what she'd hoped to get from her supper-club evening.

She'd wanted Sophie and Dominic to look at her with smiles in their eyes and say, 'If it wasn't for you we'd never have met and now look at us. Thanks so much, Anne Marie!'

Instead she'd made a huge mess of it. She really should check on Sophie again. She hadn't heard from her lately.

She'd do that tomorrow. She would call Thomas too. She'd thought of a brilliant plan – she'd invite him to Manda's wedding as her plus one. That was a good way of saying sorry. Dad had seemed to think Thomas would like to go when she'd mentioned it. It was worth a try.

Last, but not least, she would go again to the St John's soup kitchen. Not every day, but maybe on Wednesdays, which Jules and Ben had said was their regular shift.

It had opened her eyes to a whole new world.

CHAPTER 10

Before Anne Marie had a chance to phone Thomas with her carefully prepared apology he turned up at the Old School House. He took her completely by surprise. He rapped on the kitchen door the following morning. She'd overslept, which was almost unheard of for her, and she hadn't put any make-up on and she'd only just finished washing the breakfast things.

'Oh, hi, Thomas,' she said, letting him in. 'I didn't know you were coming. Dad's just nipped out to get some milk.'

'Don't worry, I'm early,' he said. 'How are you? Better than the last time we met, I hope?'

'Much better, thank you,' she said, feeling irritated because now anything she said about how much she'd appreciated their chat would look as though she was just being polite because he was there. 'I wanted to apologize to you, actually,' she said, because at least she could get that in.

'Oh? What for?' He looked intrigued.

'Ranting on about my problems. None of them were that important . . . but thank you for listening.'

'Comes with the territory,' he said. 'Of being an honorary big brother, I mean.' He smiled at her and she felt warmed.

'So how are you, Thomas?'

'Quite excited, as it happens. Tonight I'm going on a blind date.'

Why on earth did she feel as though she'd just been punched in the stomach?

His eyes were a little sparkly. 'It's my sister's fault. She's been trying to set me up with a friend of hers for ages and I've been resisting, but yesterday I thought, Why not?'

'Absolutely why not?' Anne Marie said, as brightly as she could.

There went her plan for asking him to be her plus one on Saturday. She couldn't do that now. He might think it weird.

'Her name's Lucy and she's an anthropologist.'

Anne Marie hated her already. Before they could say anything else, the door opened and her father breezed in.

'Thomas, my man. Am I glad to see you! I can barely move.'

'He's been overdoing it,' Anne Marie said, relieved that she didn't have to hear any more about the gorgeous, clever Lucy. Who had said she was gorgeous? She was bound to be, though. Anyway, she should be pleased for him. So why was a red-hot poker twisting and turning in her belly?

Jealousy, said a little voice in her head, and then a little louder, JEALOUSY. Bloody hell. She was jealous. But why?

83

Thomas was nothing to her. He was a friend, that was all. He'd just said it himself: he was an honorary big brother. Actually, she'd said that first, hadn't she? Not Thomas. She had told him that the last time they'd met.

Oh, my God. It hit her like a bolt of summer lightning. She was jealous of Thomas because she had feelings for him. She wanted Thomas for herself!

He must never know. It would be hideously embarrassing and humiliating if he realized the truth. A rerun of when Jamie Wright hadn't turned up.

There could be nothing worse than realizing you had the hots for someone and them telling you that they were 'very flattered an' all' but they weren't actually interested in you. *Thanks, but no thanks.* She'd have to avoid Thomas now – preferably for ever. But also there could be no more honorary-big-brother jokes. Her feelings towards him definitely weren't sisterly.

Unfortunately, Fate wasn't on her side. She could hear her father hollering for her from the other room. She knew it was pointless ignoring him – he'd just shout louder till he got what he wanted.

'Yes?' she said, popping her head around the classroom door where the treatment couch was.

'Have you seen my towel?'

'I think I washed it. I can get you another.'

'Would you, Princess? It's a bit slippery without. An old bath towel would be best.'

She fetched it for him and retreated rapidly. Half an hour later, just as she was beginning to think it would be safe to stop hiding in her bedroom, she heard her father's voice again. 'Anne Marie, have you got a minute?'

She came out into the corridor with a smile fixed on her face. 'How can I help?'

'I thought you were asking young Thomas here to be your plus one for the wedding?'

Thomas was behind him. He looked as embarrassed as she felt. 'Maybe Anne Marie has someone else she'd rather go with,' he began tentatively.

'Of course she hasn't,' her father said. 'You haven't, have you, love?'

She shook her head. 'No, but maybe Thomas has somewhere he'd rather—'

Her father cut her off. 'He's just said he's free on Saturday.' He beamed at them both, completely oblivious of any tension. 'That's settled, then. I'll leave you two to sort the details.'

And then they were alone again.

There was a pause. Thomas smiled at her. 'Your father's quite a force of nature, isn't he?'

'Yes. And I'm sorry if he bullied you into Saturday.' She sighed. She might as well be honest with him. 'I was going to ask you, but when you mentioned Lucy I thought maybe you wouldn't want to go – you know, maybe she wouldn't like it if you went out with me.' That hadn't come out quite as she'd planned.

He was looking slightly puzzled. 'If a woman I haven't yet met took offence at plans I'd made before I met her then I'm not sure we'd have much of a future, would we?'

'True,' she said miserably.

'So, Anne Marie, I'd be delighted to be your plus one for Saturday. If you'd like that?' There was amusement in his eyes.

'Thanks,' she said. 'Did Dad mention that I'm a bridesmaid, so you'll have to get to the church under your own steam?'

Thomas nodded. 'I'm sure I can manage that.'

When Thomas had gone Anne Marie sat in the kitchen. Suddenly all of her lists, the soup kitchen and the possibilities that had seemed so shiny and bright last night now felt tarnished. Her world had a grey edge to it. Nothing, absolutely nothing, had changed ... But that wasn't true. Everything had changed.

A couple of weeks ago it wouldn't have bothered her one bit that Thomas Hanson, her father's osteopath, had a blind date – or any other kind! She'd have been pleased for him. When had her feelings changed and why hadn't she seen it coming? What a mess.

The one thing she was sure about was that she couldn't sit there feeling sorry for herself. She forced herself to concentrate on her work. She answered some emails and arranged an appointment with the caretaker of a block of flats in Exeter. It would be good if they could get that contract. New work was the lifeblood of a company. Her father had taught her never to get complacent.

What a pity he hadn't taught her to apply the same rules to her love life. Well, his track record wasn't good on that score, was it? He didn't even *have* a track record. Dad had been so much in love with her mother that he'd never wanted another woman. Whereas she had never been in love at all. Not with anyone. Well, until now.

In a bid to stop the endless circling of her thoughts, she went to call on Sophie. She had half expected to find her out – she'd only just have finished cleaning – or miserable, having discovered that Matt wasn't interested in her. But she was neither.

'Hi, Anne Marie.' She smiled happily. 'No one's complained about me, have they?'

'No, of course not.' Anne Marie did a double-take as they entered the kitchen. A lad was sitting there, looking very relaxed and comfortable, and he wasn't Matt.

'I don't think you've met Gary, have you?' Sophie said cheerfully. 'Gary, this is my boss, Anne Marie.'

So griddle-chef Gary was back on the scene. Anne Marie wasn't sure whether to be relieved or disappointed.

Gary leaped to his feet and gave her a lopsided grin. 'Aw right, boss?' he said, with a wink.

Just as eloquent as she'd thought. Ah, well. As long as Sophie was happy . . . . 'Nice to meet you,' Anne Marie said, hoping he didn't know she was the reason Sophie had turned down his proposal.

'Yeah. Likewise.' He winked again. She had no idea whether that meant he did or he didn't. Maybe he just had a nervous tic.

'We're going to Scotland for a short break,' Sophie said.

'The third week in March. That's if it's OK for me to have the time off?' She fluttered her eyelashes hopefully.

'Of course,' Anne Marie said, and got out her diary to make a note. She should really have said no. The third week in March was already busy with holiday-goers. But it wasn't as if she couldn't cover Sophie's work herself. She was good at cleaning. Judging by her evening at the soup kitchen, she was good at washing up too. At least she was good at something. *You're in danger of feeling sorry for yourself again, Anne Marie.*

She turned down Sophie's offer of tea, dropped off the amended rota, which was her excuse for calling, decided it would be wise not to mention that Sophie no longer had to clean Dominic Peterson's flat, and then she fled.

She decided to spend what was left of the week focusing on work. She was not going to think about other people's love lives any more. She was not going to be drawn into any of her father's dramas. And she was definitely not going to think about Thomas Hanson and his date with Lucy. Definitely not.

CHAPTER 11

Not thinking about Thomas was the most difficult thing of all. What if he'd changed his mind about coming to the wedding with her? She decided to leave it until the last minute before confirming all the details, but in the end he beat her to it by phoning on Friday afternoon.

She knew she should ask him how his date with Lucy had gone. But she couldn't. Because she genuinely thought she might be sick if he told her.

'The actual wedding is at eleven o'clock,' she told him. 'Then afterwards we're all going for the sit-down reception at Ocean Views bistro.'

'Ah, yes, I know it,' he said.

A horrible thought struck her. What if he'd been there with Luscious Lucy the previous night? What if he spent the whole time he was at the wedding lunch having fond reminiscences about how wonderful their evening had been?

She forced herself to concentrate. He was saying something about presents.

'Don't worry, I've got them one,' she said. 'And I'll sign the card from us both.'

'OK – if you're sure? I'll see you at the church, then. I'm looking forward to it.'

'Me too,' she said, and she was. She was looking forward to watching her best friend get married anyway. She wasn't so sure if she was looking forward to sitting next to Thomas and making polite conversation throughout the meal. There wasn't going to be an evening reception. Jack and Manda were on a budget. They were going to be staying for one night at a B & B in Exeter, then going straight back to Matt's. Ha – that was what *they* thought, anyway. Anne Marie had other plans.

Her father interrupted her musings over supper together, which was takeaway pizza. They were eating it from trays on their knees in front of the TV, which was muted, as her father liked to have what he called Intelligent Conversation over supper. This rather defeated the object of sitting in front of the TV, but at least there were pictures. In fact, Anne Marie had got used to it and was thinking of making it a habit, even when she didn't have anyone to make Intelligent Conversation with.

'I've been thinking about where I'm going to live when this place is knocked down,' her father said.

Uh-oh. Here it comes. 'What are your options?' she asked, picking a piece of pepperoni off her pizza and hoping she sounded casual.

'There aren't many. I wanted to ask though – are you serious about moving out of The Moorings?'

'Yes,' she said. 'Only temporarily. I'm loaning it to Jack and Manda for a fortnight as a wedding present. But if they like it . . . Well, I was thinking of offering it to them for a bit longer, at a peppercorn rent while they save up for their own place.' She sighed. 'They could have it for nothing, as far as I'm concerned, but Manda would never go for that – she's too proud.' She looked at him. 'Would that be a good thing to do? Or might it be construed as meddling in other people's lives?'

He looked at her seriously from his end of the sofa. Only the sofa and the TV were left in the assembly-hall lounge. Everything else had been cleared.

'It *is* meddling, isn't it?' she said, with a sigh, when he still hadn't responded.

He moved the pizza box from his lap to the floor, then leaned across and hugged her. She looked at him in surprise.

'Darling,' he began, and his voice was ever so slightly husky. 'I think that it's a very, very good thing that you're doing.' He cleared his throat. 'You put me in mind of your mother. You're just like her – sensitive, thoughtful, kind.'

'I'm not.' She thought about all the dire fates she'd been wishing would befall Luscious Lucy and blushed.

'Yes, you are,' he said. 'I was speaking to Chris Clarke this morning. He was singing your praises. I was so impressed when he told me what you'd done.'

'Ah,' she said. 'I enjoyed it, actually. I might make it a regular thing.'

'I'm very proud of you, you know.' He paused. 'Now, where were we? Ah, yes, accommodation. Don't worry, I'm not going to suggest we share a house.'

Phew!

'However, I do have an idea. Number ten The Moorings is about to come vacant. The tenant's given notice. He wants out as soon as possible.'

'Dominic Peterson,' she said in surprise.

'Yes.' Her father clearly didn't know what had gone on there and she wasn't about to enlighten him. 'Seems his company's transferring him to Manchester. I was thinking of using it myself, but you could have it, if you like. Alternatively you could stay where you are and Jack and Manda could have that one. For a peppercorn rent,' he added.

'But then you'd be down on the deal if you weren't getting a proper rent,' she said, aghast.

'Pay me whatever Manda and Jack pay you,' he said. 'That'll be fine.'

She began to protest and he added, 'Look, Anne Marie. You might think you're getting the better half of the deal here, but, believe me, I'm pretty sure I am. If it wasn't for you helping out this past week I'd have punched the builder and sacked the architect, which would have held everything up and cost me a fortune.'

She didn't say anything, just chewed her lip.

'Having you around is like having a very efficient PA,' he said. 'Have you any idea how much they cost?'

Anne Marie shook her head.

'Well, a lot more than I ever give you.' He smiled at her.

'Let me know what you'd like to do when you've spoken to Manda.'

She nodded. 'They can have my flat for their honeymoon. I'd like to do that anyway and then maybe once Dominic moves out we can think again.' She hesitated. 'But what about you?'

He tapped his nose. 'Well, once this building's under way I'm going to need another project, aren't I? So watch this space.'

And that was as much as she could get out of him.

It was the morning of the wedding. They'd arranged that Manda would come over to Anne Marie's place to get ready, ostensibly because there was more space, but really because Anne Marie wanted to tell her closest friend about her plan.

She had come back last night to sort it out. It had been odd stepping back into the clean, uncluttered space of her flat. Such a contrast from the Old School House, which felt messy and disorganized even though it was echoey and half empty.

She had walked around the high-ceilinged rooms, pausing to look at pictures she'd chosen to enhance the space but actually reflected very little of her personality. She wondered sometimes if she really knew what that was.

When she went to Manda's there were touches of her everywhere, from the selection of colourful tops hanging on the back of the bedroom door to the antique candlestick in the shape of a seahorse, which she'd found in some junk shop somewhere. Manda had a passion for junk shops. Manda's bedroom was a reflection of Manda. Loud and warm.

When Anne Marie went to her sister Julia's there were the children's toys everywhere, and bowls of water for the dogs that someone had always just kicked over, and bits of her husband's motorbike. Julia's house screamed 'Family!'

Even Dominic Peterson's bachelor pad had reflected its owner's personality. *What does my flat say about me?* Anne Marie wondered, looking around with a critical eye.

Does it say that I don't know who I am?

The one good thing about not having much stuff was that there wasn't a lot to move. All she'd have to do to accommodate Manda and Jack would be to remove her clothes from the fitted wardrobes and her personal stuff from the bathroom. It would take an hour, tops, to clear the space for them.

She glanced at her watch. Manda would be arriving any minute. She was going to text when she got here so that Anne Marie could give her a hand to lug everything upstairs. Wedding paraphernalia wasn't light.

On cue her phone beeped. Anne Marie hurried to the front door. How exciting this was: her best friend getting married and herself a bridesmaid. Maybe she would meet her soulmate at their wedding. Manda was still banging on about Todd, the best man, who was 'dying to meet her', apparently.

What did it matter if Thomas and Lucy had fallen in love? Good luck to them. She skipped out to the lift and wondered whether to tell Manda about the flat before or after they got ready.

An hour later they were standing in Anne Marie's bedroom in front of the mirrored wardrobes and she still hadn't mentioned it. Not that they were actually ready yet, although they did have their dresses on. A lot more chat than action had been taking place, which was what tended to happen when Manda was around. Even, it seemed, on her wedding day.

So far Manda had changed her mind three times about what to do with her hair. It had been up, then down, and now it was back up again.

'I think it looks best up,' Anne Marie said. 'It shows off your eyes better.'

'Do you think?' Manda tilted her head this way and that in front of the mirror.

'I do,' Anne Marie said firmly, knowing that Manda could easily change her mind half a dozen more times if she let her. 'Let's do make-up and you'll see what I mean.' She handed Manda an old folded bed sheet.

'What's that for?'

'To protect your dress while we do your make-up.'

'You think of everything.'

Anne Marie smiled. 'Maybe I should go into wedding planning,' she said. 'Any news on the house front? Are you still planning to stay on with Matt?'

Manda looked thoughtful. 'Yes, although we did have a slight hitch with that – he's not actually leaving till April now. So at first it'll be a bit of a squeeze. But we'll manage.'

'OK,' Anne Marie said, but her heart was beating very fast. This was the moment. She reached for Manda's hand. 'Manda, I want to show you something.'

Ten seconds later they were outside the spare room. Anne Marie glanced at her friend. She pushed open the door to reveal the inside, which was the size of most people's master bedrooms and was currently made up with her poshest White Company bed linen. On the dressing table there was a vase of red roses, echoed by a soap in the shape of a red rose, which lay on a pair of fluffy towels on the right-hand corner of the bed. There was also a little box of Belgian chocolates and a bottle of champagne, and alongside them a gift-wrapped package (it was a gorgeous wooden clock from Next, which she knew Manda would love).

'This is my wedding present to you,' Anne Marie said. 'I thought you and Jack might like to stay here for a few days – as you said you weren't going on an actual honeymoon. I won't be here obviously. I'm not actually living here at the moment – I'm staying at Dad's.' She trailed off. Manda's face was frozen, and Anne Marie thought, *I've made a terrible mistake. She doesn't want to stay here – but she doesn't know how to say no.*

Manda turned towards her. Her eyes were glittery. 'Gosh,' she said. 'I don't know what to say! I think that's the nicest thing anyone has ever done for me.' She bit her lip. 'I mean, are you sure?'

'Yes, of course I'm sure.' Anne Marie felt a huge wash of relief. She went over to the dressing-table and picked up a white sealed envelope. 'You don't have to come back here tonight. I know you've got the B & B booked but this is the spare key so you can come back the day after – you're welcome to stay here as long as you like.'

'But what about you?'

'Like I said, I'm at Dad's at the moment. Long-term, there's another flat in this block and Dad needs a reliable tenant. You might want to consider that?' She held out the envelope.

'We'd want to pay a proper rent.' Manda was blinking rapidly. 'That's only right.'

'We can sort that out later,' Anne Marie said. 'You'd be doing me a favour, staying here for a bit,' she added, seeing that Manda was about to argue. 'At least I'd know someone I trusted was taking care of the place. And it would be nice if we were neighbours in the future, wouldn't it?'

Manda nodded. She still looked faintly shell-shocked.

Anne Marie smiled at her. 'Haven't we got a wedding to go to?' she said softly. 'We'd better get ready.'

CHAPTER 12

At just after eleven the taxi disgorged the six of them outside the old church. Manda, Anne Marie, Matt, who in the absence of their parents was giving her away, and the eight-year-old twin cousins, who looked stunning in their blue silk dresses and kept glancing at each other, then giggling behind cupped hands. They were clearly both very excited to be bridesmaids.

Matt scrubbed up well, Anne Marie thought. The dark suit was really smart. He didn't look anything like his usual laidback self.

Except for Matt, they all carried posies of carnations (he had a cream one in his buttonhole). Anne Marie was standing so close to her friend that she could feel her trembling. Although that might have been the temperature – it was a frost-tipped morning. The grass in the sheltered half of the churchyard still had a sprinkling of silver.

'Oh, my God, Anne Marie, it's really happening, isn't it?'

'Yes,' she said. 'It really is.'

'Yeah, it really is,' Matt echoed from her other side. 'Well, we'll go in, shall we? Before your intended starts thinking we're not coming.'

'We're not even fashionably late yet,' Anne Marie pointed out.

'No, but it's too cold to stand around out here,' Manda said. 'Let's get going.'

The service went by in a blur. Afterwards, Anne Marie could recall only impressions. The way the light flooded in through the high stained-glass windows and lit up the old wooden pews, the sonorous voice of the ageing vicar, the rustling of Manda's dress on the old stone floor, and the mixed perfumes of the guests, citrus and musk mingling with the scents of the wedding flowers. But mostly she was aware of Thomas.

He was wearing a dress shirt and little gold cufflinks, and a tie with little smiley faces on it – a fun tie, which still managed to look serious. He had a statement jacket on – definitely not high street. There was something else about him today too. Were his teeth whiter? (He was smiling a lot.) His grey eyes sparklier? Had he had a haircut? She couldn't work it out, but the overall effect was gorgeous. There was no other word for it. Maybe it was because he was out of her reach now. The one who'd got away.

She wondered if he was smiling a lot because he was thinking of Lucy. She was torn between wishing she hadn't invited him and being relieved that she had.

Jack's best man had done little to take her mind off Thomas. He was cute, she'd give him that – he had spiky hair and a cheeky smile – but he was a boy next to Thomas. It was like comparing candyfloss to wedding cake. A sweet taste in your mouth that's gone in seconds or a substantial slab of fruitcake with yummy marzipan and crunchy icing. Why did she keep thinking of food? Probably because she was starving, she realized.

It was gone two o'clock and they'd only just arrived at Ocean Views. They weren't in the main restaurant but in a small private dining room that she hadn't even known the bistro had. There was a table plan on the door.

Not that there were many guests. Sixteen or seventeen, max, most of whom were currently hanging out at the bar or sneaking a quick cigarette on the terrace that overlooked the slate-grey sea. Anne Marie looked around for Thomas and found him talking to one of Manda's uncles. They were swapping anecdotes about boats, from what she could gather. Thomas was the kind of man who fitted in anywhere, she thought. He was also the kind who didn't need to be looked after. Even though he didn't know anyone, except her, he wasn't holed up in a corner. Rather, he was quite happy circulating and chatting to people.

She went over to him now. 'Apologies,' she said, 'for abandoning you so much.'

'No apologies necessary,' he said. 'You had bridesmaid duties. And I'm enjoying myself.'

'Are you really?'

He smiled at her. 'Absolutely.' He nodded at Manda's uncle. 'It was a lovely wedding, wasn't it?'

The uncle nodded happily. 'Beautiful bridesmaids too,' he quipped.

Anne Marie blushed.

'I think we're about to sit down,' she said. 'We're on table three.'

They were with the uncle, as it happened, and his wife Carrie. It turned out they were the parents of the eight-year-old twins, so lunchtime was pretty lively. The girls had got over their shyness now and were chatting to each other animatedly.

'So,' Mike began, glancing at Thomas then back to her. 'How long have you two been together?'

'Oh, we're, um, just friends,' she said.

'Very good friends, I think,' Thomas said, giving her a sideways look that made her insides melt.

She nodded. She felt hot and miserable and happy all in the same moment.

Carrie caught her eye across the table and she saw her glance at Thomas and frown. But she said nothing. While they ate their main course and dessert they chatted about Manda and Jack, boats and a little about osteopathy when Mike and Carrie found out what Thomas did.

Then between dessert and coffee, Carrie and Anne Marie ended up in the Ladies together, waiting for a cubicle.

'You look very comfortable together, you two,' Carrie said. 'Have you ever considered being more than just friends?'

'Oh, you know – maybe . . .' Anne Marie was about to

brush off her question with a casual wave of her hand, but suddenly she didn't feel very casual. 'I don't think he's interested in me,' she said sadly.

'That's not how it looks to me,' Carrie said. 'I think he likes you very much.'

Liking her very much as a brother wasn't much use, though, Anne Marie thought disconsolately, as she went back to their table.

Thomas glanced at her as she sat down. 'You OK?'

'I'm fine,' she said, putting on her brightest smile.

'Anne Marie, it's me you're talking to, honorary big brother – remember?' He touched her hand and suddenly she was blinking back tears.

'Hey,' he said. 'Why don't we take our coffee somewhere and have a quiet chat? I'm sure Carrie and Mike wouldn't mind.'

'OK,' she said, although there was a part of her that definitely did not want to sit in a quiet corner with him. In company at least she could hide. Alone, she wasn't sure that would be possible.

She was right. As soon as they'd sat at a table in the corner of the bar he zoomed in. 'What's wrong, sweetie? You haven't been yourself today. Would it help to get it off your chest?'

Unconsciously she glanced down. She wasn't used to wearing dresses and she had a cleavage in this one. Now he'd mentioned the word 'chest' she was very aware of it. Not that he was looking. She hadn't caught him sneaking a peek once. He was the perfect gentleman. Or not interested. That was worse.

102

'Did you have a nice time with Lucy?' Where had that come from? It had just slipped out somehow. 'You came here, didn't you?'

'Er, no.' He looked puzzled. 'As in, no, we didn't come here. What gave you that idea?'

She remembered belatedly that she'd made it up, but she could hardly say that. 'Not sure.' She felt herself blush. 'Maybe it was something Dad said.'

'And, yes, we did have a nice time.' He smiled. 'But I don't think we'll be seeing each other again.'

'Why not?' She found herself looking at his lips.

'There was no chemistry,' he said.

'Ah,' she said. She dragged her gaze away from his lips. 'And you need that, don't you?'

'You do.' A little pause.

Why was her heart going so fast? She looked at his eyes. Were they grey – or were they very light blue? It was hard to tell now. 'Maybe you'd have chemistry if you went out again,' she ventured, unable to take her gaze away from his.

'I don't think so.' He seemed to have edged his chair a little closer to hers – or had she done that? Either way their knees were almost touching. 'I think with chemistry it's either there or it's not. What do you think, Anne Marie?'

Oh, this was torture. She couldn't bear being so close to him.

'I think you're right,' she said, and it was then that he touched her hand with the side of his index finger, very lightly, but quite deliberately. She felt the voltage run up her arm and travel onwards in an arrow-straight path to her heart.

'I may be way out of line here,' he said, 'but there does seem to be a certain amount between us.' Another little pause. 'Although I accept that it could be just wishful thinking on my part.'

She was aware only of him. There was no one else in the room, no one else on the planet. This feeling of utter connection, and peace – he had always given her peace. She looked back into his chameleon eyes. 'It's not wishful thinking, Thomas.'

'I'm so glad,' he said.

Soon afterwards they said their goodbyes to Manda and Jack, Carrie, Mike and the twins, and they slipped away from the wedding celebrations, which still seemed to be going quite strong, considering Manda had said the whole thing would be over by four that afternoon.

It was then that she told him she'd donated her flat to the happy couple for a honeymoon.

He smiled. 'That's so good-hearted. I doubt you've got a bad bone in your body, have you?'

'I hope not,' she said, deciding not to tell him what horrid fates she'd been hoping would befall Luscious Lucy. Because actually she didn't feel like that any more. She hoped Lucy would find love, happiness and the man for her. In fact, maybe she could invite Lucy to her next speed-dating supper. No, maybe not. Hadn't she decided her talents were better spent washing up at the homeless centre?

They went back to Thomas's house for coffee. Not that either of them wanted any more coffee, but it beat going back to the chaos of Dad's.

'How do you suppose he'll react to us, um, seeing each other?' she said, as she sat in Thomas's lounge.

'I don't think he'll be too surprised,' Thomas said. 'He's known how I feel about you for a while. He's not stupid, your dad.'

She digested this. 'For how much of a while have you actually – you know . . . ?' Why was she blushing?

'Thought you were someone I'd like to know better?' he offered. 'A year or two.'

'Gosh.' Her cheeks were on fire now. 'Why didn't you say?'

'I planned to – the last time I came to yours. I'd finally plucked up the courage, but then you hit me with the big-brother line and I thought, Well, that's that, then. It was why I agreed to go out with Lucy.'

'I see.' She shook her head. 'Sometimes I think I'm quite dim.'

'You're not in the slightest bit dim,' he said. 'To be honest, Anne Marie, I was worried I'd scare you away. I'm older than you, aren't I? And I was happy to wait.'

'Eight years. That's hardly anything. I bet Dad was pleased you liked me. He's always liked you a lot.'

'I get the impression he wouldn't be averse to the idea,' he said.

'Mmm,' she said, thinking that it was odd how many times Dad had put his shoulder out lately – especially considering he hadn't been doing much. Was it possibly he'd been dragging Thomas to the house under false pretences? Perhaps she wasn't the only one who'd been doing a spot of matchmaking.

They were sitting close on the sofa now, and their hands seemed to have naturally linked together and the chemistry was all around them – enclosing them in a little bubble that she wanted to stay in for ever. It was the best feeling.

His eyes were tender as he dipped his head towards her. And she thought, *This is it – our first kiss. I'm going to remember this moment always.*

It was so much better than in chick-lit novels. It was tender and exciting and beautiful, and everything else in the world was put on hold.

The fact that she was temporarily homeless didn't matter. The fact that she hadn't read *Emma* – that she didn't even know where the book was any more ... Well, that didn't matter either.

Hadn't Thomas said that *Emma* had a happy ending?

Two years – he'd been waiting for her for two years. Heaven above, two days had been torture enough.

There's a right time for everything, she thought. As they kissed again, and then again, she knew that this – *finally* – was theirs.

FEBRUARY

Kate

CHAPTER 13

'Do you have to go tonight, darling?' Anton put on his little-boy voice, the one that Kate had found so endearing when they'd met, but that right at this moment sounded more petulant than cute.

'I do, sweetie, yes.' She glanced back over her shoulder. He was on the sofa, his long legs sprawled in front of him, his shoes unlaced but not off, mussing up her cushions. She kept her voice light, but inside a thread of panic was rising. Reading Group was her escape, especially lately. Since things had – well – changed.

She'd never thought she would need an escape from her marriage. She wasn't one of those women who didn't take it seriously, like her sister when Ben had proposed: *Oh, go on, then, I'll give it a go. Try it for a couple of years. Why not?*

When Anton had proposed Kate had been thrilled, excited and in love. When she'd stood at the entrance of the sixteenth-century church beside her father, pausing to smooth down the pale silk coolness of her dress, and seen him waiting there, it had been the best moment of her life. She had meant every word of her vows.

Till death us do part. In sickness and in health. Through good times and through bad. That line wasn't in there, but it should have been.

'Kate, sweetheart. Stay.' Anton shifted his feet on to the floor and patted the space on the sofa next to him. He was still in his work shirt, although he'd taken off his tie and undone the top button. 'We can look at those brochures you got for the kitchen. Make some decisions. The builder's coming tomorrow at nine thirty. You are in, aren't you?' He paused. 'Then I thought maybe ... after ...' He raised his eyebrows. 'We could get an early night.'

An early night was the last thing she wanted.

She tapped her watch. 'I don't want to let the girls down. I made a commitment, darling. Reading Group, first Thursday of the month. No matter what.' She smiled to soften the blow.

His beautiful mouth twisted a little. He was too used to getting his own way.

'OK. You won't be too late, though, will you?'

'I won't be too late.'

Outside she breathed in the sharp February air with relief. Freedom. Three hours a month. It wasn't too much to ask, was it? She was a good wife, wasn't she? *A good wife.* Such an old-fashioned phrase.

She wasn't the first to arrive tonight, she saw. There were four cars in the turning circle at the front of the house. As her feet crunched across the drive and her breath rose like smoke into the air she could see light pooling out of the front door, picking out the glints of frost on the leaves of a holly bush beside the porch. She heard voices in the hall. Jojo's raucous laughter. Anne Marie's lighter tones.

It was one of those universally held beliefs that where there was a group of women there would be bitchiness. An element of conflict. But it wasn't like that with them. Well, she supposed there was plenty of conflict, but not between themselves. The conflict came from outside. From the husbands and children and ageing parents. And they all rallied round and reassured each other and they fought each other's corners and sometimes it was enough that they were just there for each other. To listen.

Kate felt a little glow of warmth as she stepped over the threshold. She joined in with the niceties, the chit-chat, the fragments of a dozen conversations they'd started last month and would pick up again seamlessly, as good friends could, and the evening – well, at least, the bit before the books – began.

At around eight o'clock Serena clapped her hands. 'Right, you lot. Pay attention.' She cleared her throat. 'Is anyone listening to me? How about if I say sex? Yep, that's right. Sex. Sex, sex and more sex! Sex, glorious SEX!' Her voice rose an octave and on the last throaty rendition of the word 'sex' the room fell quiet.

Serena smiled around at them, her eyes alight with laughter. 'Now I have your attention. And it's not entirely irrelevant – sex, I mean.'

'Sex is never irrelevant,' Jojo said.

There were a few titters.

Serena raised a hand. The room hushed again. Serena was a headmistress. Kate imagined an assembly hall of kids all looking up to her wide-eyed.

'It's my turn to choose a book,' Serena continued. 'And so to continue in our current vein, I have chosen a classic.'

There was a groan.

'Ah-ah,' Serena said, wagging a finger. 'No groaning. At least, not that kind. You're going to love it, I promise.' She delved into a bag beside her on the floor and produced a book with a flourish.

'Ta-dah!'

It had a fairly plain cover, Kate saw. She couldn't see the title.

'Looks innocuous enough,' Serena said. 'But it caused quite a stir in its day. *Lady Chatterley's Lover.*'

Her words hung in the air. There was a little ripple of interest.

'I bet it's pretty tame by today's standards, though,' Jojo said, faking a yawn. 'Not many handcuffs and red rooms in that baby, are there?'

'Which version is it?' asked Anne Marie. 'I mean, which ending does it have? Didn't Lawrence write an alternative ending?'

'More than one, I believe,' Serena said. 'You are very well

112

informed. Am I wasting my time here? Have you all read it already?'

There was a general shaking of heads and more murmurings.

'I've seen the television drama,' said Grace. 'I have one word for Richard Madden: *Phwoar*.'

'Right. Naturally, we'll be discussing the book's *themes* too,' Serena continued, eyes sparkling. 'The class issues – working class versus the aristocracy, wealth and poverty, the role of love in a marriage.'

'Infidelity,' Grace added, and ran the tip of her tongue over her top lip in a way that implied she didn't entirely disapprove.

'And because it's a classic you can of course get it free for your e-reader. Which is another advantage, don't we think?'

'Result!' Jojo said.

'Although I know some of you prefer a paperback. A proper book that you can read in the bath.'

'In the nuddy,' said Anne Marie. 'Is that wise – reading *Lady Chatterley* in the nuddy?'

'I think it should be encouraged,' said Grace with a wicked grin.

The conversation drifted away from the book after that. Kate found herself telling them about their planned house renovation.

'Our kitchen makeover is imminent.' She paused. 'I should be more excited about it, shouldn't I?'

'All that mess and disruption,' Jojo pursed her lips. 'And

you'll be the one living with it, won't you, angel? He's never there, is he?'

Anne Marie was nodding sympathetically. 'Definitely best not to be there mid-renovation. Could you move out?'

Kate shook her head. 'He's home a bit more since, you know ...' She broke off. They had talked about Anton's demotion in depth when it had happened back in November, but she still didn't like saying the word.

Demoted. Dropped down a rung. So that one of his old staff – a woman – had become his new line manager. It had affected Anton in ways Kate hadn't dreamed it would. Ways that were too personal, too intimate to share – even with these, some of her closest friends.

At least he hadn't been made redundant. They'd all said that. And she knew it was true. She should feel lucky. She *did* feel lucky. He hadn't had a salary drop either. They could afford a new kitchen. Anton had even talked about getting a hot tub in the garden. None of this stopped her wishing that things were back to how they'd been before.

'It'll be lovely when it's finished,' Serena said, her eyes kind.

Jojo leaned forward, her bangles clashing musically on her plump wrists. Everything about Jojo was plump: her voice, her laughter, her beautiful face. 'Hey, Kate – you might get a hunky builder! A Richard Madden.'

'He's called "Oliver Mellors" in the book,' added Grace.

'I bet I don't,' Kate said. 'I bet I get a balding, tubby little man with dirty fingernails.'

'And BO,' Anne Marie added wickedly.

'Brash and insensitive.'

'Someone who burps loudly in public.'

They all laughed and laughed.

Kate didn't get any of these things, though. She got Bob.

'Yeah, I know. Bob the builder,' he said, when she answered the door to him the next day. 'You couldn't make it up, could you?'

Kate shook her head, temporarily lost for words. And not because his name was Bob, but because he was stunning. There was no other word for it. He was tall, taller even than Anton, who was six-two in his socks. He had very blue eyes and very dark hair. Classic Irish colouring. But he didn't have an Irish accent. He had a voice that was at the lower end of gravelly. A voice with a smile in it.

'You are expecting me, right? I'm here to quote for the kitchen. Am I at the right house?'

'Of course. Yes. You're at the right house.' She recovered her composure. 'Sorry. Come in.'

'It's the name,' he said, stepping into the hall. 'It throws people.'

It wasn't that. It was . . . a connection? An attraction? The huge regret that she hadn't made up her face? That she was wearing her third-best jeans? She clocked the wedding ring on his left hand. Down, girl. You've got one too. They both belonged to someone else. And for no good reason that she could put her finger on she heard Grace's voice saying, *Infidelity*. And in her mind's eye she saw Grace running her tongue over her top lip once more, and she felt a little heat come to her cheeks.

'Through here,' she said, clearing her throat. 'I'll show you what we need doing.'

CHAPTER 14

It was all arranged. Bob the builder's quote was very reasonable, Anton agreed, and he could start straight away. 'That can't be his real name,' Anton said. 'It's probably a PR thing. I bet he gets loads of work just because people google *Bob the Builder* and they find his website.'

'You're probably right,' Kate agreed. She would ask him, if she remembered. *Is Bob your real name?* She imagined him nodding seriously, ultra-seriously, and then caving in and laughing and saying, *What do you think?*

Why was she having an imaginary conversation with a builder she'd met only once? A stranger who was going to be coming into her house and dismantling her kitchen, probing around in her dark nooks and crannies and exposing them all to the light? That sounded way too intimate.

Kate gave herself a little shake. It was that novel. It was not a good thing to be reading right now because it put sex so firmly in the limelight and sex was the last thing she wanted to be thinking about. She wished Serena had chosen something else. Maybe she should stop reading it. But having started it, she couldn't. She was involved. She already empathized with Connie, could feel her yearning, her frustration with her impotent husband.

But then it had been different in those days. Women had been much more defined by their husbands. Connie would have had very little to focus on outside of her marriage to Clifford and her home.

Kate had her work, which was home-based. She was self-employed. She built websites for corporate clients. It was the type of work she knew she could one day fit around children. They had decided to put off starting a family until they'd been married a few years to give them time to establish their careers. There was plenty of time. They were both young. She was now twenty-seven and Anton twenty-nine.

Still, she had come off the pill a month before Anton had been demoted. She hadn't told him she was no longer taking it. She decided she would eventually – but not straight away; maybe after the first couple of months she would mention it.

She didn't want to pressure him, make him feel he had to perform – that it was somehow more important than usual. She had heard nightmare stories from friends about how 'trying for a baby' could put men off. About how it could sometimes even ruin a couple's love life completely.

It had given her an extra little frisson, though, knowing that each time they made love, she might conceive. Sometimes, in the afterglow with her head nestled against Anton's smooth chest, she lay and dreamed that she had conceived. That there was a unique little person already starting inside her. A boy or a girl who would end up with Anton's dark eyes and her brown hair. Hopefully it would only get their good bits and wouldn't end up with her pointy nose or Anton's knobbly knees.

Then, before she had the chance to say anything to Anton, something had happened which had swept all thoughts of starting a family out of her mind.

He had come in from work one Friday night at the beginning of November. A little earlier than usual, but he hadn't said anything straight away, just nodded from the kitchen doorway and put his briefcase on the floor with a small thump. An irritable thump, Kate noted.

'I'm doing a stir-fry,' she had said, turning from chopping up peppers and onion. 'I'd hug you but my fingers are garlicky.'

He nodded. Did he look stressed?

Before she had time to ponder this further he told her, 'I'm getting a shower.'

'We're seeing Louisa and Geoff for drinks later, remember?' she called after his retreating back.

She hoped he wouldn't try to back out of it. They were her friends really, not his, but the date had been booked for ages. She and Louisa had been at uni together at Exeter. Louisa was now in PR and Geoff did something clever in banking. They lived in Budleigh Salterton, which was about fifteen miles away from Little Sanderton, closer to Exeter where they both worked. They only saw them once in a blue moon, usually around Christmas so they could exchange presents and gossip. Well, so that she and Louisa could exchange presents and gossip.

The first time they'd met the two men had danced around each other like wary Dobermans and things had never really got much better. They didn't have dinner these days, just drinks. Kate suspected that one day they wouldn't meet as a foursome at all. Maybe that would be better. Maybe she shouldn't keep trying to forge a friendship between two people who had so little in common.

No wonder Anton looked stressed, Kate decided, and got on with cooking the stir-fry. When he'd come back into the kitchen she hadn't immediately heard him. She'd been absorbed in the hiss and spit of the bean shoots and pak choi and the scents of garlic and ginger and anise rising up from the wok.

Then she'd turned and seen his face.

It wasn't just stress. It was something much worse. He looked ashen. And her first thought had been, *someone's died*. His father? *My* father? Both of them were much older than their wives.

She turned off the gas. Abandoned the wok. 'Darling, what is it?'

He shook his head. His eyes were terribly dark.

'Can we sit down a sec?'

'Anton, you're worrying me.'

He'd pulled out a kitchen chair, the scrape of its wooden legs loud on the old flagstones.

'Has someone died?'

He gave a mirthless snort. 'No. It's work.'

'Have you been made redundant?' She had felt a little chill in her heart.

'No.' He swallowed and his Adam's apple bobbed. 'I've been . . . I've been . . . demoted.'

'What? Why?' He was blinking crazily. He looked as though he might burst into tears. Anton wasn't a man who cried. He'd told her once that he wished he could. That he envied men who could sob and wail and let it all out. He wasn't used to letting it all out. His father and his mother were both so stiff-upper-lipped. Old-style English – his father from a long line of dictatorial men, his mother still believed there were pink jobs and blue jobs and a strict dividing line between the two.

For a few seconds Anton put his head in his hands and said nothing at all, and Kate could feel his pain. It was coming off him in waves.

She shuffled her chair alongside his. 'It's not your fault,' she said, hearing her own voice come out fierce and protective. He was shaking his head and she waited for him to compose himself.

The kitchen smelled of aniseed and steam. There was a part of her mind that thought, *If we don't hurry we're not going to make it to the pub to meet Louisa and Geoff.* Why was it the minutiae of life that came up and smacked you bang in the face in times of crisis?

'We had to reapply for our own jobs,' he said. 'About a week ago.'

She nodded and wondered why he hadn't told her this before.

'I didn't get mine,' he said quietly. 'They gave it to Suzanna.'

'Suzanna! Your deputy?'

'Yep.'

For the first time she was as shocked as he was. 'But they can't do that.'

'They did it,' he said. 'They said they want new blood. New perspectives.' His eyes were bleak.

'What do you think's behind it?'

'Office politics. When Suzanna joined us she didn't come through the usual channels. She was headhunted by someone on the board. I was more or less told I should employ her. I was happy to – she had a great CV. A little overqualified.' He sighed. 'Now I know why.' There was another little pause. 'I suppose I should be grateful I still have the same salary.' He didn't sound grateful. He sounded bitter.

She put her arm around his shoulders. 'Tossers,' she said. 'When you get another position you can tell them where to stick it.'

He gave her the glimmer of a smile. 'It won't be that easy to get another job, not at this level. Especially when they find out that I didn't make the grade at Chalmers. But I will look.' There was a tiny pause. 'I love you, Kate.'

'I love you too,' she said. 'And Anton?'

'What?'

'We'll get through this. It's not the end of the world. We've got each other.' They were all platitudes, but she meant them with every beat of her heart and Anton must have heard the passion in her voice because he said, 'Yes. Yes, I know we will.'

They never did eat the stir-fry. It had gone limp in the wok. And that night in bed, for the first time in their marriage, the same thing happened to Anton.

'I'm sorry,' he said. 'It's been a bit of a day.'

'It doesn't matter,' she said. 'Let's just cuddle.' She spooned around him and just before they fell asleep they swapped round so that he was cuddling her. Some time around dawn she woke up and she could feel his hardness pressing against her. He was snoring softly. He had an erection in his sleep. She smiled to herself. It had been one hell of a day.

But his body clearly hadn't forgotten what it wanted to do. And the last thought she had before she fell back into dreamland was that the previous night's let-down was unlikely to happen again.

CHAPTER 15

But that's where she had been wrong. Since that day in November their love life, which had always been brilliant, had slowly disintegrated. They had never been big on quantity – more than twice a week, unless they were on holiday, was rare. But they had always been hot on quality. Anton wasn't a wham-bam-thank-you-ma'am kind of guy. He liked foreplay as much as she did. He liked to do a lot of the work and when they both wanted each other too much to hold back a second longer he liked to spend a good long time on the actual act itself; stopping, starting, titillating, teasing, swapping the power back and forth between them, sharing the pleasure and the control.

Suddenly it was as if he had changed into another person. A lightness had gone out of him, somehow. He seemed tense and anxious and keen to get on with things as soon as possible. She wondered if he was worried that if he didn't then he might miss his opportunity, so to speak. She had no idea what it must be like to be a man, but the one thing she did know was that their penises weren't always under their control. Up or down did not depend on whether the timing was appropriate or not.

She wanted to talk about the problem with Anton. But finding the right time was difficult; finding the right place even more so. Not in the bedroom. All the agony aunt pages she had ever read said that you should never mention sexual problems in the bedroom. You should wait until you were somewhere else, in a nice relaxed environment, and then introduce the subject with sensitivity and tact.

Yeah, right! How did you do that exactly? She didn't remember a single agony aunt giving guidance on appropriate wording. She practised in her head.

You know how you can't seem to . . . um . . . maintain . . . um . . . an erection anymore?

No. She shouldn't say *you*. If she said *you* it would sound accusatory.

OK then, how about: *I've noticed lately that when we make love it's not how it used to be.*

Too much pressure.

Maybe light-hearted: *Hey bud – what happened to the fore-play? Oh, and while we're on the subject, didn't you use to have working apparatus?*

Definitely not.

Why did everything she could think of sound like an accusation?

Maybe simply: *Do you think it might help to see a doctor?*

No chance. Anton hated seeing doctors. She'd have more chance of persuading him to go skydiving. They'd had the 'scared of heights' conversation early in their marriage when they'd gone to New York and she'd wanted to go up the Empire State Building.

'I'll wave to you from down here,' he'd said with a wink.

So the closest they got to discussing the problem at all was in the bedroom where Anton said a couple of times a week, 'Sorry, maybe we should just cuddle,' and she said, 'OK.'

But it wasn't OK.

It was the elephant, the great, grey elephant, sadly swinging its massive trunk – oh, the irony – in the corner of the room.

One of the worst things was, she couldn't talk about it to anyone else. It would have felt disloyal. Louisa was one of her closest friends but she couldn't tell Louisa, not even in an oblique way. If the slightest hint of his problem got back to Geoff, she thought that Anton would probably divorce her.

Neither could she tell anyone in the Reading Group. Lovely as they were. And she definitely couldn't tell her mother. They'd never had a 'discuss anything you like' kind of relationship. Kate thought sometimes that, in their way, her own parents were as stiff-upper-lipped as Anton's were.

She might have confided in her sister who lived in Manchester, but Emma had recently got pregnant with their second child, so clearly Ben didn't have any problems in that department.

Kate's thoughts were driving her mad. Maybe *she* should see a therapist?

She sure as hell knew she wouldn't get Anton anywhere near one. 'Therapists,' he'd told her once, 'are fine for people who can't sort their own lives out, but definitely not an option I'd ever consider.'

She had never thought of herself as being particularly sexual. But then it had always been there for the asking. She missed it. She missed him. She missed the warmth and the connection it gave them.

It was a dilemma, and the longer it went on the harder it got to know what to do about it.

Also, Anton hadn't lost his mojo entirely. There was the occasional time when everything worked perfectly. It wouldn't be *quite* like the olden days, but they'd be able to make love and afterwards he would smile down at her and say, 'I love you so much.' And she would say, 'I love you so much too.'

And her heart would hold on tightly to the fact that it would be OK now. That they were on their way to being back to normal, that the last few weeks had been an un-repeatable blip. Then a few days later it would happen again and Anton would get edgy and irritable and she would put on her forced smile and say, 'It doesn't matter, darling. There is absolutely no rush.' Because the one thing she did know about all this was that she must stay endlessly patient and reassuring. She must not ever, ever get irritable herself because that would make Anton ten times more insecure and then they would spiral downwards ever faster and they might never make love again.

In truth, Kate didn't know how much more of it she could take. She'd begun to hope that Fate might intervene.

But Fate – bless her little cotton socks – clearly had a warped sense of humour.

Being given *Lady Chatterley's Lover* as their February novel was evidence of that. There was nothing worse than reading about how wonderful other people's sex lives were, when your own was below par.

She hadn't told Anton what novel they were reading this month, and she hadn't left it lying around anywhere, either. She didn't want him to come across it and think she'd resorted to reading about sex as a replacement for actually doing it. Perhaps she was being oversensitive. He didn't usually take much notice of what she was reading anyway. He wasn't a big reader himself, at least not of fiction.

The Thursday after Reading Group, Kate and Anton went for dinner at Ocean Views. It had amazing views across the sea and they had a table by the window. Not that you could see much of the sea right now, because beyond the lit terrace it was dark.

They were halfway through their main course when Anton said, 'I've got to go to Brussels next Monday.' He put his steak knife down, and looked at her.

Kate's first instinct was to say, 'Can't Suzanna go?' The meetings in Brussels were something that hadn't happened since his demotion. But that would have been terribly tactless, so she just took a sip of wine and waited for him to elaborate.

'Suzanna has to be somewhere else,' he continued, as if reading her thoughts. 'It'll mean I'll be away about five days. Is that OK with you?'

'Of course it's OK.' She wondered why he was asking. He'd been away often enough in the past.

He wiped his mouth on his napkin and blinked. 'I feel like I'm abandoning you. It's the same week that the builder's coming in to rip the kitchen out. Had you forgotten?'

Yes, she had. She frowned. 'I'm sure I can survive on takeaways for a few days,' she said, because he really did look very guilty.

'I don't like to leave you with all the dust and the mess. And we'll miss Valentine's Day as well.' Ah, so that's what it was about. Anton was hot on special occasions. It was one of the things she loved about him.

'We can do Valentine's Day when you get back,' she said. 'It'll be cheaper and we'll probably get better service.'

He nodded. He was looking happier. 'Maybe I should put the builder off – although it could be tricky to get him back. You know what these people are like to pin down.'

'It'll be fine,' Kate said, thanking the waiter who had just arrived to clear their plates. 'I'll keep the office door closed.' She thought about Bob working in their house while Anton was away and somewhere in her stomach – or was it lower down? – there was a little involuntary ping of lust. *She should probably keep the office door closed anyway*, she thought. The less contact she had with the attractive builder the better.

'Can I offer you dessert?' the waiter was saying, handing them menus. He was new. He had dark eyes and a faint

Italian accent. He was what Louisa would have called 'hot', or maybe that was just the way Kate's mind was working lately. Since her sex life had become so diminished, every man she saw who was in the right age group seemed hot. Bob the builder probably wasn't even remotely attractive. It was just her frustration.

'What do you recommend?' she asked the waiter.

He smiled. He had very white teeth.

'I can offer you the crème brûlée – this is our house special. Or we have a dessert of chocolate mousse. It is for Valentine's Day, but Chef – he is practising to be perfect. It is an aphrodisiac . . .'

'Bread-and-butter pudding will do me.' Anton shut his menu with a snap.

'Me too,' Kate said swiftly, catching her husband's expression.

The waiter retreated.

There was an awkward little pause. Kate jumped in to fill it by saying the first thing that came into her head. 'It'll give me the chance to finish my novel. If you're not around for a few days.'

'What are you reading?'

Oops – she'd set herself up for that one.

'Are you still on those tedious classics?'

'We are.' She smiled at him. 'They're not *all* tedious.'

'So which one is it this month?'

'*The Wind in the Willows.*'

'Isn't that a children's book?'

'Um, yes. Yes, it is. Well, young adult, really – you know,

with Mole and Badger and the river.' Hell, she didn't even know what *The Wind in the Willows* was about. It did have a badger in it, didn't it?

'Well, you can't say the books aren't diverse,' Anton said, raising his eyebrows.

'No.' She could feel heat in her cheeks. Why on earth hadn't she just told him the truth?

CHAPTER 16

Anton was gone by 6 a.m. on Monday. Once he'd woken her, Kate couldn't get back to sleep, so she got up and started work too. When the doorbell rang at just before 8.30 she thought it must be the postman.

It wasn't. It was Bob.

'I'm not too early, am I?' he said. 'I like to crack on.'

'I've been up for hours,' she said truthfully. 'In fact I'm about due for a break. I'll make you a coffee.'

'I'd prefer tea if you've got it. Builder's.' There was irony in his voice.

'Coming up,' she said. He accepted it gratefully.

'Is your real name Bob?' She tilted her head curiously. She had put make-up on today. And she was wearing her favourite top. Not because it mattered what Bob thought, obviously, but just because she worked better if she felt better. *Really, Kate?* said a voice that sounded suspiciously like her mother's. *Who are you trying to kid?*

'My name is Bob, yes. Well, Robert, if we're being strictly accurate, after my father.' He left it a beat. 'In truth, I mostly get called Big Bob.'

'I see,' she said, looking for laughter in his eyes but not seeing any. Was he flirting with her? It was hard to tell. His face was deadpan.

'Most women ask why,' he said idly, leaning one hand against the fridge, slightly away from her, but with the faintest hint of challenge in his voice.

Her mobile beeped in her pocket.

'Saved by the bell,' he said.

It was Anton, letting her know he'd arrived safely and was just about to board. She took the opportunity to escape.

It was odd, she mused, as she got her breath back in the bathroom and contemplated her handsome builder. He was one of those guys who knew he was attractive. She could see it in his eyes. She bet flirting came as naturally to him as breathing. But there was something very likeable about him too. Something a bit vulnerable.

She showed him where she was working, in the downstairs office – just off the lounge. 'I'm going to keep the door closed,' she said. 'But if you need me, just knock.'

'I'll try not to disturb you too much,' he said, his gaze taking in the boxes of plates and saucepans that were piled up in one corner. At least Anton had helped pack up the kitchen yesterday. 'What is it you do, Mrs Collins?'

'Kate, please,' she said, and told him.

'Maybe I could employ you some time. I could do with a new website.'

'Do you get a lot of work via the internet, then?'

'Not so much building work, no – I mostly get that from recommendations. Word of mouth, you know. But I have another job too. If I had my way it would be my main job. But it's a bit harder to make a living from being a voice actor than from refitting kitchens.'

She hadn't been expecting that. She looked at him. His demeanour had changed somehow. He was no longer flirty builder but someone altogether softer and a great deal more unsure of himself. Was he actually blushing or was it the light in her office? The sun had just come out and it was a south-facing room.

'Wow. That sounds really interesting. What kind of stuff do you do?'

He cleared his throat. 'Radio advertising, mostly. The odd voiceover for a website, nothing you'd have heard of. Unless . . .' He hesitated and she saw that flash of vulnerability in him again. 'What radio channel do you listen to?'

'The local one, when I can get a signal.'

'Have you heard the ad for Topps' Recruitment Agency? It's a dialogue between a posh bloke and a Scotsman.'

She frowned. 'I have. Aren't they having a row? Which one do you do? No, let me guess. The posh guy.'

'I do both.'

'No!'

'"How da ya mean you got nae work for a Scotsman? Call

yerself an agency?' I don't write the scripts,' he added, returning to his normal voice.

Kate clapped her hands. 'That's fantastic,' she said. He cleared his throat again and looked a bit abashed. 'I don't usually tell people about the voice acting. I'm not sure why I told you.'

'Because you may want me to build you a website,' she reminded him. 'Let me know what you want some time and I'll give you a quote. Once you've finished my kitchen,' she added.

'Apologies.' He blinked. 'I'll get on.'

He disappeared and she thought he was one of those people who fill up a room. When they go you can feel the space they've left behind.

She gave herself a metaphorical slapped wrist. Yeah, so he was attractive. Yeah, so he had hidden depths too. But that didn't make her any less married. Or him, she thought, although he wasn't wearing his ring today. Maybe he took it off when he was working in case it got damaged.

Her mobile rang. She jumped guiltily. She usually switched it to silent when she was working. But she hadn't in case Anton rang. It was a relief to see it wasn't Anton, but Jojo from the Reading Group.

'Hi, angel.' Jojo's throaty voice brought blessed normality back into the room. 'Are we still on for lunch today? I'm assuming you're knee-deep in brick dust. How's it going? Was the builder hunky? No, don't tell me. We can gossip later.'

Blimey, it wasn't like her to forget a diary date. She must

135

be even more distracted than she'd thought. 'Er, yes, I'm definitely up for lunch. Where are we going?'

'Ocean Views – my shout. You paid last time.'

'I look forward to it,' Kate said with feeling.

They sat at the same table where she and Anton had sat the Friday before. It was one of those clear, bright days with just enough sunshine to take the edge off the chill – a couple of people had braved the terrace and were eating outside. One of them had a dog tucked under their table. Kate caught a flash of its brown head and lolling pink tongue. The Ocean Views was a popular spot for anyone walking the South-West Coast Path, which ran in an unforgiving roller coaster of almost vertical ups and downs along the Jurassic Coast.

There was no sign of the handsome waiter today; their order was taken by a smiley teenager with an eastern European accent. When she'd gone, Jojo leaned forward, bangles jangling musically, and said, 'So, how are you, my lovely? I have to say you've been looking a tad stressed lately. Is everything OK?' Jojo was one of the kindest people Kate had ever met. She was one of the oldest, if not the oldest, in the Reading Group. Thirty-seven or thirty-eight, Kate thought. She was a midwife. Kate bet she was amazing at it. Exactly the kind of person you'd want by your side when you were in labour.

'I'm fine. I'm really—' She'd been about to say 'good', but something in Jojo's eyes stopped her.

'Someone once told me that FINE is an acronym for Fed Up, Insecure, Neurotic and Emotional,' Jojo said. 'Actually they didn't say fed up. There's a ruder version. You are not fine, my angel. Any fool can see that.'

'And you're not a fool,' Kate said softly. 'Far from it.'

'You don't have to go into any detail,' Jojo said. 'I'm not trying to pry.'

'It's OK.' Kate swallowed. 'If I don't tell someone soon I'm going to explode. It goes back to when Anton got demoted,' she said. 'Well, since then things have changed between us,' Kate said. 'In the bedroom department, you know . . .'

'Ah,' said Jojo. 'I see.' And Kate knew that she did. She was nodding slowly, her eyes sympathetic.

All these months, Kate thought, *I've been worrying myself sick – and it was as easy as that.*

Their food arrived. When they were both full of clam chowder and had decided they would have a break before they chose dessert, Kate told Jojo what had been going on.

'Poor you,' she said. 'And poor Anton. What's she like, the woman who got his job?'

Kate shrugged. 'I don't know. I've never met her and Anton doesn't say much about her. At least, not since they've been working together.'

'Well, the important thing is – what do you do about your love life?' Jojo paused. 'It would be good if you two could go on holiday somewhere hot and lovely. Somewhere you can lie on a beach and totally relax.'

'We've kind of spent our holiday budget for this year on the kitchen,' Kate said. 'That was probably a mistake. But Anton was keen.'

'Mmmm.' Jojo frowned. 'Tell me if I'm teaching my grandmother to suck eggs here, but are you aware that there are several, er ... options on the market? It's a much more common problem than people think.'

'Like Viagra, you mean? I'm not sure Anton would be *up* for that.' She turned pink and clapped a hand over her mouth. 'I can't believe I said that.'

They both smiled at each other.

'I feel much better just having talked to you – in confidence,' Kate said, suddenly panicking.

'Of course, in confidence,' Jojo said softly. 'Also, angel,' she added thoughtfully, 'the issue might just resolve itself – given time. These things usually do.'

CHAPTER 17

When Kate got back Bob had gone. He'd left her a note. *Not much more I can do today. See you first thing in the morning.*

The cupboards had all been removed. The kitchen was back to the bare walls and it sounded echoey when Kate walked across the flagstone floor.

She took a deep breath. It had been good talking to Jojo. OK, so it hadn't resolved anything but she felt lighter than she had for ages. It was true what they said about a problem shared.

When Anton rang her that night she felt really affectionate towards him. She lay on her side of their double bed, her mobile pressed to her ear, feeling sleepy and full of love for him.

'Did the meeting go well?'

'Yes,' he said. He was obviously in the hotel bar. She could hear the buzz of chatter in the background behind him. 'And I'm getting a few things sorted out with Suzanna.'

'I didn't realize she was there.'

'There was a last-minute change of plan. She is here.' There was a burst of laughter behind him. 'We've been having a bit of a chat.'

'Is that good?' Kate asked.

'It's very good.' There was a softness in his voice that she hadn't heard for a long time. 'I'll tell you more tomorrow.'

'Cool,' she said, feeling a little flutter of hope. If things had been sorted with Suzanna then perhaps everything else would be on the way to being sorted too. Maybe Anton would come back from Brussels refreshed and uplifted – in more ways than one! She smiled at her own joke. *That* was something to look forward to.

It didn't stop her dressing up again for work the next day. *This has nothing to do with impressing Bob,* she told herself, as she applied a second coat of mascara. Is it wrong for a girl to want to look her best when there's an attractive man around? Anton wasn't the only one who had a fragile ego. Her self-esteem had taken a battering lately too. Even though Anton had reassured her a couple of times that it wasn't because he didn't fancy her any more, it was impossible to still feel completely desirable.

Bob arrived at 8.30. He wasn't interested in flirting today. He gave her a quick, polite nod and got straight to work. She felt slightly rebuffed. Had she imagined the friendliness between them yesterday? He was plastering today, which at least meant there wasn't so much banging about.

When she made herself a coffee – she had moved the kettle into her office – she did him a tea and took it into the kitchen. Not that he needed her to, she saw, spotting a flask on the sink. He was clearly self-sufficient.

'Thanks,' he said, looking up in surprise.

'You're very welcome.' He looked strained.

'Are you OK?' she asked, concerned. 'Do you need anything?' She spread her hands apart. 'For the job?'

'No, I'm fine. I'm good.' He made a visible effort to smile at her. 'I'll probably be building the breakfast bar tomorrow. That could be noisy for a while. You OK with that? If there's a time you have to be out I could aim to do it then?'

'I wouldn't worry too much,' she said. 'You're not bothering me.' There was a pause. 'Are you doing anything special tonight?'

He frowned.

'I mean for Valentine's Day? With your wife,' she added hastily, glancing at his ringless finger.

'No,' he said, draining his tea in a couple of large swallows and banging his cup down on the windowsill. 'I'm not.'

'Right,' she said, a bit taken aback. Where had yesterday's easiness gone? Maybe she'd just imagined him flirting. Or maybe she hadn't and he was just a moody bugger. One of those men who went up and down for no reason. Her sister's husband was a bit like that.

She left him to it. He could make his own flaming tea in future.

*

At lunchtime there was a knock on her office door. Then it opened a crack and his head appeared round it. His eyes were cautious. 'May I come in?'

'Sure.' She raised her eyebrows – stern headmistress style. 'Did you need something?'

'I owe you an apology,' he said, looking directly at her. 'I was rude earlier. I was angry. But you were not – *are* not,' he amended hastily, 'the reason.'

There was a tense moment, then he stepped right into the room. 'Am I interrupting?'

'I was about to stop for lunch,' she said and waited for him to say something else. He looked as if he wanted to.

'My wife and I are separated,' he said eventually.

She was tempted to say, 'What's that to me?', but she didn't because for a moment just then he had looked quite lost and she wasn't a cruel person.

'I'm sorry to hear that,' she said at last. 'Have a seat.' There was a love seat in the room – old, purple and very comfy – that had once been in their bedroom and had been re-located here in case she spoke to clients at home.

Bob sat on it, stiff-backed. There was a rip in the knee of his jeans; not a fashionable bought-to-look-old rip – but one that looked as though he'd caught it on something sharp.

'Did you separate recently?' Kate asked. 'I mean, please don't talk about it if you'd rather not.'

'Eighteen months ago.' He bit his lip. Clearly he hadn't got over it. No wonder he'd been irritated by her mention of Valentine's Day. After a couple of seconds he went on, 'We have a little girl – her name's Daisy. She lives with her mother but I have her a lot too. We've had a few fall-outs about it lately. Lia, my ex, is being . . . difficult. She keeps changing the arrangements. I was supposed to be having Daisy later today, but she texted me late last night to say there's been a change of plan.'

'That must be hard,' Kate said softly. All her irritation with him flittered away.

'Not least on Daisy.' Bob glanced at her. 'I'm guessing you don't have kids?'

'Not yet,' she said. 'We're working on it.'

'It was the happiest day of my life when my daughter was born.'

The warmth was back in his eyes again. After a while their conversation drifted on to other things. He was easy company when he wasn't upset, she thought.

They talked a bit more about voice acting. He'd always been good at accents, he told her. He was a born mimic.

'Where are you actually from?' she asked.

'I would have thought it would be obvious by my colouring, so I would.'

Perfect Belfast.

'It is now,' she said, smiling. 'But why don't you always sound like that?'

'My dad's Irish. Mum's English. We've lived in England longer than Ireland.'

'Ah.' She watched dust motes swirl in a shaft of sunlight that angled from window to carpet. Even though she had kept the door closed you couldn't avoid the dust completely.

'So are you and Mr Collins doing anything special for Valentine's Day?' he asked.

She shook her head. 'Not tonight. Anton's away. We'll celebrate when he gets back.' With a little jolt she realized that Anton hadn't responded to the *Happy Valentine's Day* text she'd sent first thing. She hadn't thought too much about it at the time, thinking that maybe he'd sent a card in the post – or had ordered flowers. That would be typical of him.

But it was gone lunchtime and neither had arrived. She shrugged away these uneasy thoughts. There was plenty of time yet.

Aware of Bob's eyes on her, she moved a pile of papers from one side of her desk to the other. 'So, what other nationalities can you do? Can you do Australian?'

'Not so well.' He tipped his hand from side to side in an unsure gesture. 'Maybe a little.'

'Say something,' she demanded.

He smiled. 'I need a situation – a script.'

'Say something about surfing.'

'Not that we're stereotyping or anything.'

She laughed.

'You'll have to give me some time to think about it,' he said. 'I'd better get back to work or I'll have the boss on my back.' He winked.

When he'd gone, pulling the door tight behind him, Kate felt a blush creep up her neck. What was wrong with her? Since she'd fallen for Anton she had never even looked at another man.

'I'm just not interested in other men any more,' she'd confided once to her sister Emma.

Emma had rolled her eyes and poked her none too gently in the ribs. 'You're such a romantic, Kate. It's called the honeymoon period. That's all.'

'Not for us,' Kate had said. 'It's the real thing.'

'See if you still think he's wonderful after picking his smelly socks up off the floor for a couple of years. See if you still love him when you've shouted yourself hoarse about him putting the flaming toilet seat down and washing his shaving mess off the sink. Sometimes when I look at Ben, I just go, like, *what was I thinking?*'

'You wouldn't ever cheat on him, though, would you?'

'I might.' Emma winked. 'If the right man came along.'

Kate hadn't known whether to believe her or not.

Had she been smug back then or just naive? She certainly hadn't seen this coming. She hadn't realized how bad it would make her feel – Anton turning away from her, time after time. Anton not seeming interested in her body any more. He'd even taken to keeping his pants on in bed. As if he wanted an extra barrier between them, as if the unspoken one wasn't enough. That hurt.

But none of that gave her any excuse to be fantasizing about Bob.

She decided she would keep out of his way, particularly while Anton wasn't here.

When Bob finished for the day and came to tell her he was off, she didn't engage him in conversation, just said simply, 'Have a good evening.'

'Sure,' he said. 'Don't work too hard. I'll see you tomorrow.

I'm heading down to the timber merchants on my way home to get the wood for the breakfast bar.'

About half an hour after he'd gone, she had a text from Anton: *Happy Valentine's Day, darling. Miss you. Love you. I'll phone on the landline later. Bad signal here.*

So he hadn't forgotten her, then. Warmth crept up through her.

Hope the trade fair's going well, she texted back.

The landline on her desk rang almost immediately. Ah, bless him. He obviously couldn't wait to talk to her.

A man said in a strong Scottish accent, 'Em I speakin' tae the hoose ooner please?'

'I'm busy,' Kate said, irritated. 'Whatever you're selling, I'm not interested.'

'Please. Dae nae hang up! Ah promise you it's nae PPI I'm bothering you with and it's nae dibble glazin', bu' ah do have an amazin' dill you dae nae wanna miss.'

Kate sighed. 'No,' she said, and was about to disconnect when another voice said, 'Mrs Collins, I do apologize. Hamish is training. He can come across as a little overenthusiastic. This is not a hard-sell call. We are not that type of company. Please let me assure you that this is a genuine offer.'

She hesitated. 'A genuine offer of what, though? He hasn't actually said.'

'Mrs Collins, I am so sorry.'

There was something oddly familiar about the man's voice. And how on earth did he know her name? Then it hit her. 'Bob? Is that you?'

146

There was a silence and in it she felt her face colour up. Maybe it really was just a sales call.

'Impressive,' Bob said. 'I thought I'd be able to keep you going for a lot longer than that.' There was laughter in his voice – his real voice now.

She laughed too.

'You're good.'

'Thank you.' A beat. 'Actually I didn't just phone to offer you an "amazin' dill". I've – rather stupidly – left the measurements I need there. Would it be inconvenient to pop back? I don't want to disturb you if you're working.'

'It's fine,' she said. 'You won't disturb me.'

No more than you already have, she thought, as her heart, irritatingly, treacherously, quickened its beat.

CHAPTER 18

He rang the bell about fifteen minutes later. He had a half-smile on his face. 'I'm not usually so forgetful,' he said.

'You've clearly got too much on your mind. You should stop moonlighting.'

He raised his eyebrows.

'Cold-calling poor unsuspecting clients.'

'Ah. You didn't mind, did you? It was spur-of-the-moment. I really did phone up to ask if I could come back for the measurements, and then after what we'd been talking about earlier—'

'It's fine,' she said. 'You made me laugh.' She gestured him ahead of her into the echoey kitchen. He still had dust in his hair from the day spent working there.

He picked up a piece of paper from the side, folded it and put it in his pocket. 'Here it is. Thanks.'

'Now if you'd phoned up trying to sell me a surfboard I'd have sussed you out straight away,' she said.

'You think?'

'Definitely.'

He smiled. 'Well, maybe we'll put that to the test one day.'

'Are you dashing straight off or can I offer you a drink?' He hesitated and in the gap she thought, *Why am I offering him a drink? He's not here on a social call.*

'Go on, then. If you're sure I'm not holding you up?'

Well, she could hardly backtrack now, so she carried their wine through to the lounge.

'What's your husband doing in Brussels?' he asked her and she felt like saying, *Your guess is as good as mine.* What was Anton doing there when Suzanna had gone as well? And why were they in a bar? There was something not quite right about that. A little nugget of unease had been jiggling about in her subconscious since last night.

'He's in pharmaceuticals,' she said. 'Their head office is in Brussels and he had to go for a meeting.'

Bob sipped his wine. 'He sounds like a clever bloke.'

'He is.'

There was a little silence. Not uncomfortable. In fact he looked quite at home on their pale leather sofa, in the place where Anton usually sat. Kate tried to imagine the room as he might see it. The neutral colours, the beige woollen rug on the stripped oak floorboards, the brass uplighters, the flat-screen television, the glass coffee table, and – uh-oh – her novel, carelessly flung beside an *Ideal Home* magazine.

She didn't think Bob had spotted it … did it matter if he had? She could explain that it wasn't the kind of thing she usually read. She hadn't chosen it. The Reading Group had. She gave herself a shake. She didn't need to explain anything.

For a while they chatted about inconsequentials: a celebrity customer he'd been to quote for lately who had a mansion up on the cliffs and steps down to her own private beach.

'Wow, that must be amazing,' she said. 'How the other half live.'

'When I was there she and her husband were just buying a 1.6 million pound Sunseeker,' he said. 'They had the brochures on the table.'

'Hard to believe that a boat can cost that much,' she said. 'And that's a relatively cheap one, isn't it?'

He nodded.

'Do you sail?'

He nodded again. 'I've got a third share in a boat – myself and two mates. It's nothing fancy, and it's not just a sailboat – which upsets the purists – it's got an outboard motor as well. That's handy around here. But not much beats heading out on a nice day with the wind in your sails and the sun on your face. Daisy loves it.' He lit up when he talked about his daughter.

Kate smiled. 'I bet.'

After he'd finished his glass of wine he said, 'I'd better get back to the timber merchants. They close at eight.'

'Of course,' she said, feeling oddly disappointed.

He put his empty glass on the coffee table beside *Lady Chatterley's Lover*. The title blared out loud and proud. Kate struggled to remember what bit she was on. She was still amazed at how explicit the love scenes were. She remembered thinking that Lawrence did the female viewpoint very well. That the writing was strangely beautiful.

Their eyes met across the table and he said, 'That book caused a right old furore in its time, didn't it? What do you think?'

Suddenly it was hard to breathe. She said, 'I'm not surprised,' feeling a little frisson of something in her groin, 'It's much more shocking than I expected it to be.' A beat. 'I'm in a reading group. It's their choice. Not mine.'

She held his eyes, trying to read his expression and failing.

'Of course,' he said. 'Well, enjoy it. I'll see you in the morning. Thanks for the wine.'

At the front door he passed by her so close she could feel the heat of his body – or imagined she could.

'Night, Mrs Collins.'

'Kate, please.'

'Night, Kate.' There was amusement in his eyes. A kind of knowing. Or was that her imagination too? Yes, it must be. They'd been having a perfectly innocent conversation about boats over a glass of wine. She doubted very much that he'd ever read *Lady Chatterley's Lover* anyway. Most blokes didn't read fiction, in her experience. Anton didn't.

The most Bob was likely to know about the plot was that Lady Chatterley had fallen for her husband's gamekeeper, her bit of rough. That they'd had a steamy affair. That was all she'd known about it herself before this month. Mind you, that was probably enough.

It was impossible to get back into work after he'd gone. She was too hot and distracted. She picked up the book instead and carried on reading. It didn't help. She kept replacing Oliver's face with Bob's.

As she read on she realized that the book wasn't just sexually explicit and shocking. It was very intimate. It was a love story between two people who didn't just connect physically but emotionally too, and the fact that they were from such different classes – which was highlighted frequently – only added to the sense of poignancy.

Suddenly she realized that she was missing Anton terribly. He hadn't phoned back on the landline as he'd promised and it was nearly 9 p.m. She wondered what he was doing. She pressed his number on her mobile and got the international ringtone, which almost immediately went into a number-unobtainable flatline. When she tried again she got only an anonymous recorded message.

This number is not available. What did that mean? Kate drew her knees up on to the settee and hugged them. It wasn't like him to ignore her completely on Valentine's Day. He made a big thing about special occasions. He was extravagant at birthdays and Christmas. *But you did agree that you'd celebrate when he got back,* her sensible voice reminded her.

It was difficult when he was working away – he'd told her that before: you weren't just on duty in normal office hours, you were on duty the whole time. You couldn't just say to a client, 'Hang on, I've got to call my wife, she gets a bit needy in the evenings.'

But she wasn't being needy. It was bloody Valentine's Day. And he was with Suzanna, not her. Suzanna must have a husband or a boyfriend. She would surely need to head off and chat to him for a bit. Or maybe she was single. On impulse, Kate fetched her iPad. It would be easy enough to check that out. Well, she could check whether or not Suzanna was married, anyway. She typed Suzanna's name into a search engine and found her on Facebook.

It would have been handy if Suzanna had had a face like the back of a bus. She didn't have a face like the back of a bus. She was stunning. Ms Suzanna Jones had the kind of cheekbones that ensured she would never lose her looks, glossy dark hair, come-to-bed eyes and a kind of sultry little smirk. Kate hated her on sight.

The only saving grace was that she was older than Kate, a couple of years older than Anton, too – around thirty-one, according to her profile. That wouldn't put him off. He'd confessed to her once that he had a bit of a thing for older women.

For heaven's sake. Kate's sensible voice snapped back into action. This is the woman who stole his job. She's the reason he can't perform in bed any more with you. He is hardly going to get off with her. He would be too worried that he might fail. He would be far from home, it would all be super stressful.

. . . Or would it actually be an escape? A time out of time? Away from his own bedroom where he'd had so many frustrating failures. Holed up in a little fantasy capsule with a beautiful woman.

She was letting her imagination run away with her.

So why hadn't he phoned, then?

She would try him one more time when she was in bed. She fetched a glass of water and went upstairs slowly, brushed her teeth, took off her make-up and creamed on moisturizer.

Then she sat up on her side of their bed and tried him again. This time his phone was switched off altogether.

CHAPTER 19

In the morning he rang her, full of apologies. She was driving, but she answered him on hands-free.

'I had a problem with my phone,' he said. 'I'm so sorry, darling.'

'It's fine,' she said, feeling slightly mollified. 'How's Suzanna?'

'Suzanna?' he said, as if he'd never heard the name. 'Oh, I've hardly seen her.'

'I didn't realize she was so attractive,' Kate couldn't resist saying.

'Do you think so?' His voice was dismissive. 'I hadn't really noticed.'

Kate didn't know if she believed him. He sounded just a bit too casual. She was about to change the subject before he asked how she knew what Suzanna looked like, but he beat her to it.

'How's the builder getting on?'

'Very well,' she said. 'He's doing the breakfast bar today. I'm just on my way to see a client in Exeter.'

'You've left him in the house alone? Is that wise?' Anton sounded worried.

'He's hardly going to steal anything, is he? We don't exactly have a heap of family silver.'

'Well, all right, darling, if you're OK with it.'

'I'm OK with it,' she said. 'How's the trade fair going?'

'Oh, you know . . .' His voice faded a little.

'Anton, are you still there?'

'I think I'm losing the signal again, darling. I'd better go.'

'Can we talk later?'

'Yeah, hopefully.' And then he was gone.

What did he mean, 'Yeah, hopefully'? She felt that niggle of unease again. The sensation that something wasn't quite right. Not that she had time to worry about it now. She was in the centre of Exeter, not far from her client. It was a big company; she'd been recommended by a mutual contact. She needed to focus. It would be excellent if she could pick up this contract.

The client turned out to be short and balding and clearly had a chip on his shoulder about it.

'It's a pleasure to meet you, Mr – er – Short,' she said. Gosh, she hoped she'd got that right.

It seemed she had. 'Duncan Short at your service. Short by name and short by nature,' he said, puffing out his chest before leading her into a glass office on the ground floor of the glass building.

He had an enormous desk. There was room behind it for at least five people. Kate had read a feature recently in *Business Plus* called 'Big Desk Syndrome'. The more insecure the manager the bigger the desk they needed and the more controlling they tended to be. It certainly seemed to be true in Duncan's case.

Duncan Short was pedantic in the extreme. She'd met his type before. A control freak who couldn't bear to hand anything over. No matter that he knew absolutely nothing about building websites and would be paying a large chunk of his company's money for her to do it!

By the time she came out of his office – having refused his offer of luncheon in the roof-terrace canteen (just in case she gave in to the urge to push him off the edge of the building) – Kate was feeling thoroughly frazzled.

Her phone rang as she emerged onto the street.

'G'day, ma'am,' said a deep voice with an Australian accent.

Well, Bob hadn't left that long. Clearly he was buoyed by his last success and thought he would catch her out again. Well, he had another think coming.

'Am I speaking to Kate Collins?' the voice continued pleasantly. Hell, he was good.

'Yes, you are, and I can tell you now I'm not remotely interested in buying a surfboard.'

'Well, that sure is a relief, 'cause I'm not trying to sell you one.'

'And I'm also incredibly busy. I've just spent a very trying morning with a jumped-up little idiot who thinks he knows

157

how to build a website.' She paused for breath. 'How's the breakfast bar going?'

There was a brief silence.

'Bob?' she went on, feeling the first little prickle of foreboding. 'That is you, isn't it?'

'No, ma'am. This is Matt Williams, Mr Short's PA – he asked me to call you and give you his direct line so you don't need to go through the switchboard.'

Kate went cold. What had she called Duncan Short? A 'jumped-up little idiot'. Oh God. She took a deep breath. 'I'm so sorry,' she began. 'I – er – thought you were someone else.' She'd accused him of trying to sell her a surfboard! She could feel her face heating up. In fact, she wouldn't have been at all surprised if she wasn't heating up the entire street, she was so red. Well, there went that job, then.

'I'd figured that one out, ma'am.' He didn't sound particularly perturbed. 'So shall I give you that number?' he said.

'Um, I don't suppose you could possibly email it to me? I don't have a pen to hand.'

'Sure.'

'That's very kind of you.'

He was never going to send that number. Why would they want to use her services after that little performance? She just hoped that word wouldn't get back to the client who'd recommended her. He wouldn't be too amused either.

She had planned to ring her friend Louisa to see if she fancied doing lunch, but she wasn't really in the mood now. Louisa would probably laugh at her faux pas, but if she told Louisa about the surfboard conversation then she'd have to explain all the backstory too. Which meant Louisa would know she'd been flirting with her builder. And Louisa was terribly traditional when it came to marriage.

And if Kate mentioned that Anton was currently away with his stunning boss doing goodness-knows-what, Louisa would very likely suggest that Kate drop everything and fly out to Brussels to confront him. Louisa could be a bit dramatic at times.

Kate decided to drive straight back home.

Bob's van wasn't outside and her house was empty. The keys were back through the letter box, which presumably meant the job was finished.

How odd, Kate thought, as she walked through to the kitchen. It didn't look as though he'd completed the breakfast bar. Everything was in a bit of a mess, which was unusual for him. It looked as if he'd been called off somewhere in a hurry. Maybe she should phone him? She decided she wasn't that bothered. She trusted him, she realized, as she grabbed a supermarket chicken tikka salad from the fridge and took it through to her office. That was interesting: she trusted Bob and she'd only known him a few days, yet there was a part of her that still didn't trust Anton. What did that say about her marriage?

When she opened up her laptop there was an email from Matt Williams. Her chest tightened as she opened it.

Dear Mrs Collins,
Here is Mr Short's direct line as requested. If you will resend your agreement with the amended terms and conditions he will get that back to you by return.

159

I will be your main contact for the project.

I'll look forward to hearing from you.

Kind regards,

Matt Williams

PA to Duncan Short

PS. You are not the first person to voice such an opinion of my esteemed boss.

PPS. FYI not all Australians sell surfboards!

He had a sense of humour; thank goodness for that. She could feel the smile starting in her chest. It bubbled up inside her and spilled out until she was laughing hysterically. Maybe it was a good job Bob wasn't around to see her. It was certainly a good job Anton wasn't around to see her.

She sent Anton a text: *Got the contract at Maynards. Yay. How's it going your end? Can't wait to see you. Are we going to talk tonight? What time are you back Friday?* About two hours later she got a brief reply. *Well done, darling. I didn't doubt you would get it. Will ring tonight.*

Her landline rang just after six and she picked it up with a sense of expectation. But it wasn't Anton, it was Bob.

'I just wanted to let you know that I had to leave early today,' he said. 'Apologies that I didn't clear up properly, but I was rushing. Daisy was taken ill at school and Lia couldn't get her, so I went.'

'I'd guessed something had happened. No problem. Is she all right?'

'She's fine. Slight tummy upset. You know how kids are.

Lia has her back now. I'm having her this weekend, fingers crossed, if she's better. So I'll be with you tomorrow as planned.' A beat. 'How did the meeting go?'

She told him. Then she told him about the surfboard conversation and he laughed.

'It's not funny,' she said. 'I thought I'd blown it.'

'You didn't, though, did you?' His voice sobered instantly.

'No. Fortunately the guy had a sense of humour.'

'You're fairly safe from Australian sales calls on your mobile,' Bob added. 'At least from me. I don't have the number.'

'Of course you don't!' Kate groaned. 'I wish I'd remembered that. It would have saved a lot of embarrassment. Look, if you like, I'll give it to you. You never know when you might need it.'

'Sure. Thanks.' He waited while she gave it to him.

'I'll see you tomorrow as planned, then.'

'Look forward to it,' he said.

CHAPTER 20

The phone rang again as soon as she put it down.

'Who have you been talking to?' Anton asked.

'Bob,' she said. There was a pause. 'Our builder,' Kate explained. 'He had to leave early today to go and get his little girl.'

'I hope he's not going to do that on a regular basis. His childcare arrangements aren't our problem.'

'I'm sure he's not,' she said. 'Are you OK? You sound snappy.'

'I'm tired, that's all. It's been a long day. It's not all fun and games being over here, you know. I'd rather be at home.' For a moment he sounded like a petulant small boy.

Kate bit her lip. 'How's Suzanna?'

'Inconsistent and contrary. Like most women. One minute she wants us to do this – the next minute she wants us to do that—'

'What kind of things?' Kate asked, registering that he'd

162

said 'us' and feeling slightly unnerved. In normal circumstances she'd have pulled him up on the sexist comment, too, but she didn't want to antagonize him further. A part of her was pleased that things weren't rosy with Suzanna.

'Dinner arrangements,' Anton said. 'First we're having dinner at six, then we're having dinner at half seven. First we're staying in the hotel – then she's booked us a table in town.'

'Dinner arrangements?' Kate felt that quiver of unease again. 'Well, surely it's not compulsory to have dinner with her every night, is it? Just tell her you're eating alone.'

'I can't.' Anton's voice was flat.

'I'm sure you can—'

He broke across her. 'I just can't, OK? I've got to stay on the right side of her. It's imperative.'

'Because of your job?'

'No.' An awkward pause. 'Well, yes, I suppose so. Look, I've got to go, Kate.'

'But I thought you weren't having dinner until 7.30?' Now she felt hurt. 'Anton, what's wrong? Please tell me what's going on.'

'Nothing's going on.' She heard him take a deep breath, in the way he did sometimes to compose himself when he was talking to an awkward client on the phone. When he spoke again his voice was softer. 'I'm feeling a little stressed, that's all. It'll be fine when I'm back. Look, why don't you book us somewhere nice for Saturday? How about Calypso's? We can celebrate Valentine's Day with a slap-up meal like we said.'

'All right,' she said, only slightly reassured. 'I love you,' she ventured.

'Yeah, you too.' And he was gone.

Kate felt empty and a little raw. *They needed to talk*, she thought. Anton being away had given her some perspective on things. The problems they'd been having in the bedroom. Maybe it had done the same for him. Maybe that's why he'd sounded so uptight on the phone. Maybe he'd come to the same conclusion she had: that they couldn't put off talking about it any longer.

The demotion and its consequences were the first big thing that had happened to them, she realized with a little start. The first time that their marriage had ever been truly tested. It was quite sobering.

Kate allowed herself a little fantasy in which Anton would come back and the problem would be sorted. That him spending time away would have resolved everything. If Suzanna had been the cause of the problems, maybe she would somehow be their resolution too.

In her fantasy he would have returned completely to his old self. They would have a fabulous meal at Calypso's – which was an uber-posh but really friendly bistro on the edge of Little Sanderton – followed by amazing lovemaking with gorgeous foreplay that went on for hours. It would be just like it had been in the old days.

She thought about a line she'd read in *Lady Chatterley's Lover*: 'She was always waiting. It seemed to be her forte.'

But Connie hadn't been waiting for her husband. She had been waiting for her lover. Suddenly Kate was awash with grief and nostalgia because it hadn't been so long ago that Anton had been both. Where had the old Anton gone? Would they ever get back to the way they had been before?

She thought about what Jojo had said when they'd had lunch – the suggestion that they should go away somewhere hot and lovely. OK, so they might not be able to afford to do that, but it didn't mean that she had to meekly hang around waiting for the end of their marriage, did it?

She could take the initiative. She got up and went into their bedroom and had a good long look at herself in the mirror. She'd put on a few pounds lately – too much sitting at her desk; she hadn't been to the gym in ages. She slopped around in jeans, mostly – there didn't seem to be much point in dressing up when you worked from home. Also, when was the last time she'd done anything with her hair other than its six-week trim? No wonder she and Anton were stuck in a rut.

Maybe it wasn't even his fault. Maybe the fault lay with her and she was just in denial.

On Thursday morning, after a bit of cajoling, she managed to get an afternoon appointment at her salon for some balayage. Ellie, her stylist, had been trying to persuade her to try balayage for ages: 'It'll look wow in your hair, it will really lift the colour.'

'Brighten the brown, you mean,' Kate had quipped.

'Yes, if that's how you want to put it. But honestly, hun, I know you don't like hassle but it's the opposite of that. It looks so natural.'

Faked natural, Kate thought. Now there was an irony if ever there was one.

She booked an appointment at the nail bar, too, while she was at it. A new outfit would be good as well – something slinky and sexy – she could wear it when they went to Calypso's.

Anton wouldn't know what had hit him. He'd think he had a new wife.

By the time she'd had her mini-makeover she felt a hundred times more confident. On impulse she nipped into a lingerie shop on her way back to the car park. She wasn't completely sure about this part of the plan. Would Anton feel pressured if she were wearing new undies? Actually, he probably wouldn't even notice. He had no idea what was in her underwear drawer.

Bob's van was still outside when she got back to the house, close to six. As she let herself in she could hear the sound of drilling. He stopped when he heard her and turned. He was covered in wood dust.

'Hi, don't worry, last bit of noise. I've been taking full advantage of you being out. In the best possible way, I mean.' His lips quirked. He had nice lips. That was a random thought. She blinked.

'It's fine. I appreciate you staying on.'

'I said I would. After yesterday, I mean.'

'Are we still on target for it to be done by the end of next week?' she asked, thinking of Anton's call.

'I should think so. I'll be quicker if I can. I know what a

pain it is not to have a kitchen.' He raised his eyebrows quizzically. 'You done something different with your hair?'

'Just been to the salon.'

'It looks good.' He turned back to his drill, but she felt absurdly pleased that he'd noticed.

Anton would notice too. Anton would fall in love with her all over again. He wasn't due back until the following day. His plane landed at four and by the time he'd driven back Bob would be gone. She'd have plenty of time to have a shower, dress up a bit, and they'd have the house to themselves.

She would get a pizza delivered. They could watch a box set. He would come into the lounge where she'd be curled up on the sofa, put down his bag, come across to give her a big hug and say, 'I've really missed you.'

He was back just after 5.30.

She hadn't put on the Calypso's dress – that was for tomorrow – but she'd ditched her jeans and put on some dark-green leggings and a cream top which made her look slim. Her hair didn't look quite as good as it had fresh out of the salon the previous day, but the colour was perfect: touches of blonde through her shoulder-length brown. Ellie had been right, it was very sexy. Anton *had* to notice. She did her make-up, too, that old trick of 'get it on but make it look like you haven't'. Anton much preferred *au naturel*.

Anton came straight into the lounge when he got back. She was curled on the sofa reading *Lady Chatterley's Lover* inside an *Ideal Home* magazine (she didn't want to put any kind of pressure on him).

He plonked his bag on an armchair and frowned.

'The kitchen's a mess.'

'We're having it refurbished. What did you expect?' She looked at him. He looked rumpled, as he did sometimes when he'd had a few late nights on the trot. There were faint bluish shadows beneath his eyes.

'What have you been doing for meals, then?'

'M&S salads, mostly. But I thought we could have a pizza tonight – if you fancy it? Treat ourselves.'

'Don't think I could manage a pizza. I think I'll skip tea. You carry on with your salad.'

She frowned. 'I didn't get a salad for tonight.'

He nodded and she knew he hadn't heard her.

'I think I might run a bath,' he said.

'I might come and join you.'

He didn't smile. When she went upstairs a few minutes later the bathroom door was shut.

They had a code. When the door was shut you didn't go in. However much you loved each other, there were certain things you wanted to do on your own.

She hesitated outside the closed bathroom door for a few seconds. Maybe she should knock. This was mad. He actually felt further away from her now than he'd done when he'd been in Brussels twelve hours ago.

She didn't knock. Instead she went into their bedroom and lay on the bed, her hands behind her head, staring up at the ceiling. She felt like Connie again. As though she was waiting, but this time for a moment that would never come.

When Anton pushed the door open about ten minutes later he was fully dressed and had his phone in his hand. He looked startled when he saw her, and Kate felt curiously guilty, as if she'd barged in on him doing something private.

'Just got a couple of work calls to make,' he said.

'But you've been working all week, Anton. Can't they wait?'

'I suppose they could.' He slipped his phone back into his pocket and fixed a smile on his face. She could see it was a huge effort – that smile.

She patted the duvet beside her. 'Come and talk to me.'

'What about?' His gaze flicked around the room. He had the look of a trapped animal.

'I don't know. Anything. Tell me what you've been up to.'

'All right. But could we go downstairs? It's a bit early for bed.' That forced smile again.

It was downstairs, with him on one end of the sofa and her at the other, that he told her he had slept with Suzanna.

CHAPTER 21

At first she didn't think she'd heard him right. Typically, Anton didn't try and sweeten the pill or even build up to it; he just looked at her and said quietly, 'I've done something stupid. I went to bed with Suzanna.'

'You did what?' She frowned at him. One part of her jumped straight into denial mode. 'That isn't funny, Anton.'

Another part of her, a deeper part of her intuition, wasn't surprised. She had been waiting for this, had known it was coming.

'I'm really sorry,' he said, plucking at a thread on one of the cushions, his movements jerky and distracted. 'It's unforgivable, I know.'

He sounded as though he were rehearsing a line that he'd practised. He didn't sound real. Or maybe it was the situation that didn't feel real. He stopped plucking the cushion and chewed the edge of his thumb in that way he always did when he was stressed.

Kate could feel her heart pounding and adrenalin whooshing in her ears and yet there was also a stillness in her so that she noticed every little detail in the room: a tiny chip out of the skirting board by the door; the scent of wood from the newly carved breakfast bar in the room next door; and a smear mark on the television screen, highlighted by the floor lamp beside it. A smear mark in the shape of an 'S'.

'S' for Suzanna.

So, this was shock, she thought. This was one of those moments she would always remember. For years to come she would remember that smear mark in the shape of an 'S'.

'Say something.' Anton's gaze was on her.

'When?' she said, in a voice that sounded throaty and low and nothing like hers.

'Tuesday night. I'd had too many drinks.' He blinked several times and began to say something else.

She cut across him. 'Valentine's Day! But we spoke. We spoke on the phone. Was that before you did it or after?' She'd gone from having nothing to say to having too much.

'Does it matter?'

'Yes, it matters. Yes, it bloody matters! I want to know.'

He bit his lip. 'I can't remember.'

'No, hang on a minute … you know what? We didn't speak on Valentine's Day. You just sent me a text in the morning. And when I tried to phone you, your phone was switched off. Because you were with her, weren't you? You were fucking her.'

The ice-cold stillness had worn off and in its wake came a trembling hot anger. 'You got your mojo back, I take it. You didn't have any problems with Suzanna. You got it up for her. So how does that work, then? Did she manage to entice you into action? Or was it just not a problem?' She couldn't stop the vitriol spilling out of her mouth. She hated it, but she couldn't stop.

'Don't,' Anton said. He was on his feet now, holding his hands out in front of him to ward her off, even though she wasn't anywhere near him. 'Just don't.'

He backed out of the door and shut it. Kate ran across the room. 'What did you expect?' she said, pulling at the handle and realizing he was holding it shut from the other side. 'What did you expect me to say, Anton? *Oh, well done – you're cured.*' She pounded on the wood. 'Open this door, you coward!' The last few words trailed into a sob. They'd never had a proper emotional row, she realized suddenly. They'd never needed to. They'd never been in a place where she hated him like she hated him now. She hated him so totally and utterly.

She stopped trying to open the door. The first rush of powerful anger had disintegrated into pain. She sank down on to the floor and hugged her knees to her heart and sobbed. There couldn't be any coming back from this. There was nothing he could have done that would have hurt her more.

Some time later, she heard him move from the other side of the door. She heard him go into the kitchen and the sound of his footsteps echoing across it and then on into the hall, and then the bang of the front door. After a while she got up and went and checked to see if his car had gone. It had.

Had he gone to her?

You go and tell her and we'll meet up later.

Bastard.

Did Suzanna have someone to tell? Was Suzanna even married? She realized she had never actually found out. She didn't know where Suzanna lived. So she couldn't have followed Anton even if she'd wanted to. She knew nothing about Suzanna, his deputy-cum-manager . . . and lover. The thought of them together brought fresh pain.

She didn't want him back. She didn't want him in the house. She wanted it purged of him. She suddenly understood why the women in old films threw their unfaithful partner's possessions out of the window. There was some mad part of her that wanted to race upstairs and rip all his clothes out of the wardrobe, tear them off the hangers and bundle them up and throw them into the street.

She went into the bathroom and checked the towels he'd used. They were barely damp. Had he even had a bath? She put them in the washing basket in the corner. Then she went into their bedroom – but it was too painful, seeing the ghost of his image by the door and the ghost of hers on the bed, waiting to seduce him. Earlier she'd put a Jo Malone candle on her bedside table. Dark amber and ginger lily. It had sounded sensual and erotic and had smelled gorgeous.

She picked it up, the glass cool beneath her fingertips, and put it away in a drawer.

There was bergamot massage oil, too. They hadn't massaged each other for ages. Anton had a little dark mole high up on his right shoulder. Her touch had snagged on it a thousand times.

She shut the drawer before she could think about Suzanna's fingers on him, or worse, his fingers on her. Him unwrapping her on Valentine's Day, uncovering her breasts, kissing each one, because he could never take off Kate's bra without doing that, spending equal time on each breast in case the other should feel left out. The pain spiked again and Kate moaned softly.

She couldn't bear to sleep in their bed. She went into the spare room and got into the double bed there, which she kept made up for visitors. At some point during the night, though, she must have got out and moved back into their bed – although she had no recollection of doing it.

In the morning when she awoke she was on Anton's side, curled up like a child. She must have been crying in her sleep, because his pillow was damp with her tears. She felt headachy and tired, as though she had a hangover, and for a few seconds she had no memory of the previous night's events. Then they came crashing back.

In the bathroom she splashed water on to her face. Her eyes looked puffy. Her hair still looked good, though. So did the foils on her nails. They were a bronze colour with little flecks of gold. *Understated*, the nail-bar girl had said, *under-*

stated and classy. She hadn't been very understated and classy last night. She'd been raucous with anger and very loud. It was a good job they lived in a detached house. Jean Barnes and her cat on the right and the nice older couple on their left would be none the wiser.

It was lucky that she didn't have any work scheduled. She'd left today free for her and Anton. She had planned that after their night of lovemaking they would have a lie-in, followed by a leisurely breakfast of toast with Nutella. Totally decadent: toast crumbs and chocolate in the bed. And if their lovemaking hadn't gone according to plan, well then, Plan B had been that they would have talked – they would have talked with honesty and tenderness about Anton's – no, *their* – issue. And they would have slept spooned in each other's arms because they'd cleared the air and had such a frank discussion. They would still have had Nutella on toast when they got up. Because in either Plan A or Plan B everything had been resolved and today had been a new start for them both.

Kate didn't have a Plan C.

Kate went downstairs. She wasn't hungry. That was one thing she was clear about. The second was that she wasn't going to stay here. She needed to talk to someone she could trust and she needed to get out of this house.

Jojo's. She would go to Jojo's, she decided. She was single. There was no husband to judge her. Jojo lived in a cottage at the other end of the village. She was even closer to the sea than Serena; her garden trailed down on to the sand and when the tide was in it lapped a few metres away from her stone front wall.

Although she wasn't in the habit of calling on Jojo unannounced, Kate had a feeling she wouldn't mind, and so it proved to be when she turned up half an hour later. Jojo took one look at her face, tutted quietly – so much for her brilliant cover-up job, then – and said, 'I'll put the kettle on, shall I, angel?'

CHAPTER 22

Kate stood in Jojo's galley kitchen while she brewed tea in a large brown teapot. The room smelled of fruitcake. There was one cooling on a rack.

'Have I interrupted you?' Kate said, feeling suddenly needy as hell.

'Only baking,' Jojo said. 'I was going to do cupcakes next, but I'd only eat them, so you've saved me from myself.'

'Sorry.'

'Don't apologize, angel.' She turned and smiled at Kate. 'Shall we take this through to the conservatory? Grab the cake.'

Kate did as she was told, dipping her head to avoid banging it on copper kettles and bunches of herbs strung from the central beam, and followed her friend into the conservatory, which was so bright she found herself blinking. Her eyes still stung from crying. She felt light-headed and empty and she remembered she hadn't eaten anything.

'Sit yourself down,' Jojo said, moving a pile of newspapers and a black cat from a cane armchair and settling herself in it. 'Is it Anton?'

Kate nodded and swallowed. She could feel more tears rising in her throat. *Where did they all come from?*

'Have some cake,' Jojo offered. 'Cake is good for stress. Well, this one is – it's a new recipe. I got it from a vegan website.'

'Vegan?'

'Yes, I'm trying to lose weight so I'm experimenting with vegan recipes.'

'Wouldn't you be better off cutting back on cake?' Kate asked, slicing them both a piece. The cake smelled gorgeous.

'Where's the fun in that?'

Half an hour later Kate had told Jojo everything and somehow in the telling she felt better. She had even smiled. She couldn't believe that was possible.

'I didn't think I would ever smile again,' Kate said. 'I thought smiles had gone forever.'

'It's the cake,' Jojo said. 'It's Step One of my Three-Step Feeling Better Plan.'

'What's Step Two?'

'A walk on the beach. Did you bring a coat? It's pretty nippy out there today. Don't worry if you didn't. You can borrow one of mine.'

Jojo's coat swamped Kate, but it was comforting to have it on. She felt as though she were a pale and fragile thing and the coat was a protective layer between her and the world. They didn't speak much as they walked. Jojo was surprisingly fit for her size and she set a brisk pace. Kate was glad – it was hard to think much when you were striding along. Also, Jojo had been right about it being nippy and it felt good to get her muscles moving. The salt wind buffeted their faces. It would have been difficult to talk even if they'd wanted to.

To their left the waves broke on the sand in a rhythmic pattern that was endlessly soothing. At some point Kate felt rather than heard her mobile phone vibrating in the pocket of her jeans, but she didn't get it out to see who it was. She didn't much care. All that existed in the world was the motion of their footsteps on the hard sand by the shoreline, the shushing of the waves, the cries of the gulls and the cool touch of the wind.

After a while her calves began to ache and Jojo turned to her and said, 'You ready to head back?'

It was easier walking back, the wind behind them now. The world was quieter. Her head seemed quieter, too, as though the walking had soothed away some of the anguish. The sea stretched out in a glassy dark expanse to the horizon, chopped up by white horses.

Jojo didn't say very much. She occasionally glanced at Kate and smiled, and Kate found herself smiling back. When they got back to the cottage her face felt hot and tingly from the change in temperature, and she was amazed to discover they'd been out for two hours.

'You ready for a spot of lunch?' Jojo asked. 'I've got some

leftover chilli which should be even tastier today. I made it yesterday.'

'Is this Step Three of your Feeling Better Plan?' Kate asked as they ate it. 'It's delicious. I didn't even think I was hungry.'

'Irresistible, isn't it?' Jojo agreed without a trace of smugness. 'But no, it's not Step Three. Although perhaps it should be. You can't make plans on an empty stomach.'

'So Step Three is making plans?' They were sitting at the small round table in the conservatory. Jojo's tastes were a mixture of vintage and vibrant, Kate thought. The floors were sand-coloured tiles and there was a wind chime of blue and orange seagulls strung up beside the door. There were a lot of ceramic pots trailing green foliage and a couple which held cream orchids, beautiful and fragile. Something sweet that she hadn't yet identified scented the air.

'Step Three is thinking about what you want to do next,' Jojo said. 'Not necessarily making plans. It might be a bit early for that. Has he been in touch?'

'No.' Kate remembered her phone and pulled it out.

'Yes,' she said, seeing his name flash up on the missed call. 'I wonder what he wants.'

'Do you know what *you* want?' Jojo asked. 'Sometimes it's best to get that clear in your head first.'

'Not really. I mean, I don't really have a choice. He's made the choice. He chose Suzanna.'

'Is that what he said?'

Kate shook her head.

'Don't you think it's odd that he asked you to book Calypso's for tonight?' Jojo asked thoughtfully. 'When did he do that again?'

'I'm not sure . . . a couple of days ago—'

'I mean, was it before or after he'd . . . done the deed?'

Kate winced. 'After,' she said, realizing that it did seem odd. 'So he was still planning that we go out to celebrate Valentine's Day. That's mad! Why would he do that?'

'Maybe it was a crazy one-off mistake. Maybe he isn't with her at all.'

'But where did he go?' she said, as much to herself as to Jojo.

'Who knows? But he obviously felt guilty as hell. Maybe he just couldn't face you last night.'

Kate nodded slowly. That made sense. In fact, it made much more sense than her assumption that Anton and Suzanna were holed up somewhere planning their future together.

'So what do *you* want to do?' Jojo repeated. 'Do you still love him?'

'Of course I still love him.' Kate sighed. 'You can't just turn that off.'

'That's true. I still love my first husband. My second one, too, on a good day.'

'You've been married twice?'

'Yes,' Jojo said, clicking her fingers sharply at the black cat, which had just strolled in and looked as if it were contemplating leaping up on to the table. 'I'm still married to the second one – Alan, his name is – I used to call him Big Al. Six-foot-four of strapping muscle.'

'What happened to him?' Kate asked, fascinated despite herself.

'He went to a retreat in Marrakesh to find himself. Only he never came back. That was four and a half years ago.'

'Blimey. You must have been worried sick.'

'I was at first. But he always had a habit of going off on his own. I was used to it. And he kept in touch by text. He still does text me from time to time.'

Kate leaned forward, resting her chin on her hands and realizing how little she knew about Jojo. It was because Jojo was the listener of the Reading Group, she realized. The nurturer. She was the one who took care of the others. Not bossy like Serena, not full of madcap plans like Anne Marie and not the entertainer like Grace. Jojo could be a bit tactless – she had a habit of putting her foot in it sometimes – but she was also very kind, very solid and direct and dependable. They all knew that about her.

'Don't you mind?' she asked.

'I do mind on some levels. I'd prefer it if he was here. It gets quite lonely sometimes. And I don't really know where I stand.'

'No,' Kate said in awe. 'Do you want to divorce him?'

'Sometimes I do. Then I could just move on.' Jojo rested her chin on her hands. 'Then again, I've never met anyone I wanted to move on with. If I did, I would probably date them anyway.'

'Will Big Al be dating other people?'

'I expect so.'

Kate felt a bit shocked, and clearly Jojo picked up on this

because she said, 'It's OK, angel, I've kind of got used to the idea that we don't have a normal marriage. It's not the same as what Anton's done. You two had different rules and he broke them. If you agree to be monogamous then you should stick to it.'

Kate nodded. 'I think I'm too shocked to know what I want at the moment. One thing I do feel is that the trust has gone.' She paused. 'The thing that hurt the most – that still hurts the most – is that he could sleep with Suzanna when he couldn't sleep with me. He could sleep with some woman he didn't even like.'

'He might actually have found that easier,' Jojo said quietly. 'No strings attached. No emotional fallout.' Her candid gaze met Kate's. 'Men are weird creatures.'

Kate's mobile began to ring. It was Anton again, she saw as she glanced at it. 'I may as well speak to him,' she said. 'I'm going to have to do it sooner or later.'

She pressed connect and Anton said, 'Where are you?' And she realized he must be at the house.

'I'm at a friend's.'

'Please come home.' His voice was low. 'We really need to talk.'

CHAPTER 23

Kate had no idea what she was going to say, even as she unlocked the front door. There was no script for this. Anton met her in the hall. She shot him a warning look: *Don't try to touch me.*

'I deserve your scorn,' he said. 'I'm so sorry, Kate. But I want you to know there's nothing between me and Suzanna.'

'Where did you go last night?' she asked.

'To Liam's.' Liam was Anton's oldest friend. He had been their best man. 'I told him we'd had a row.'

His eyes were dark and she thought Jojo was right. He didn't want this to be the end of their marriage. And he hadn't been planning to tell her about Suzanna – but he'd never been very good at keeping secrets.

'What did you want to talk to me about?' She couldn't believe she felt so calm.

'I want to know if you can forgive me,' he said. 'Shall we

go and sit down?' She followed him through the bare kitchen and into the lounge. They sat at either end of the sofa, remote as bookends.

She could still feel the echoes of last night's pain. It was in the air like dust. It felt like a long time ago and yet no time at all since they'd been here.

'I don't know if I can forgive you,' she said truthfully, 'until I know a bit more. I think you're going to have to tell me what happened.'

'In detail?' He looked shocked.

'Yes. I want to know why. Was it just the once? And I need the truth.'

He sighed. 'It wasn't just the once. It was four – maybe five times.'

'Which?'

'Five.'

She felt a fresh wave of shock. So it hadn't just been because he was drunk. He had lied about that.

'All when you were away?' she whispered, feeling something die inside her. 'Whose room were you in?'

'Hers,' he said. 'She invited me in for a nightcap. It was difficult to refuse.'

'Really.' She could feel the anger rising in her voice.

Anton got up. 'This isn't helping,' he said. He paced across to the window and stood facing her with his arms folded across his chest. 'I've told you all you need to know already. It was a dreadful mistake. I couldn't be more sorry. I've come to my senses and I think we should move on.'

He sounded as though he was repeating lines rehearsed for a film. There was no genuine remorse in his voice. There was no genuine anything in his voice. Suddenly Kate was angrier than she'd ever been.

'I don't know if I can move on,' she said. 'You've been making love to another woman. In case you've forgotten, we haven't been able to do that. We haven't been able to do that for months.'

'No, I know.' He took a step towards her. 'Having sex isn't the same as making love, Kate. What we do – *did* – I didn't do that with her.'

There was something in his eyes she couldn't fathom. It looked like a mixture of relief and contempt. But it was gone so quickly she wasn't sure if she'd imagined it. Anyway, she didn't want to look at him anymore. 'You're right, this isn't helping,' she said. 'I think you should go.'

'Go where?'

'I don't care. Back to Liam's if you like.'

'I don't want to go back to Liam's.'

'I'll go, then. I'll stay with Mum for a bit. You can oversee the kitchen renovations.'

'No,' he said with a deep sigh. 'You're right. I'm sure Liam won't mind. It'll give us both some breathing space.' He hesitated in the doorway. 'How long for?'

'What did you say?' Jojo asked when Kate relayed this conversation to her over the phone on Sunday evening.

'That I didn't know,' Kate said. 'Because I don't. I can't believe that he wants us to just carry on like nothing has happened.' She paused. 'It was almost as if he thought it wasn't that big a deal. Thank you for yesterday, Jojo.'

'Any time,' Jojo said. 'Have you got a busy week?'

'Very. How about you? I don't suppose you know exactly with babies, do you?'

'Spot on. They just put in an appearance when they're ready. Bless them. I've got one definite this week. Mum's being induced on Wednesday.'

'Good luck with that.' They said their goodbyes and Kate hung up. She was glad she was busy. She could forget everything when she was inside the code of a website.

She didn't realize quite how well this worked until Monday morning when the doorbell rang for the third time. She'd ignored the previous two rings but the caller was clearly determined. Irritated, she swung the door open, an angry retort on her lips.

'G'day, ma'am.' Bob doffed an imaginary cap. 'Thought for a moment you'd forgotten I was coming and gone out.'

'Sorry.' How on earth had she forgotten Bob? 'I didn't hear the bell.'

'Figured it might be something like that.' He strolled into her kitchen and ran his hand over the breakfast bar. 'This is looking good. Was your husband pleased?'

'Er – yes,' she said, caught off guard.

He gave a satisfied nod.

'Did you have a good weekend?' she asked, relying on pleasantries to get them back into normality.

'Great. I took Daisy fossil hunting down at Lyme Regis.

She loves being beside the water. You?' He turned to smile at her and she had a sudden urge to say, *Wonderful. I split up with my husband on Friday and cried for the rest of the weekend.* But she didn't say this, of course; she said, 'Not bad. I was by the sea too. I went walking with a friend.'

'Lovely weather for it.'

'Yes.' She excused herself and went into her office, but it wasn't as easy now to get back into work. She couldn't concentrate. All she could think about was the pride in Bob's voice as he ran his hand over the breakfast bar. Would she and Anton ever sit at that? Have croissants and coffee on a Sunday morning? Or would they end up selling the house? Would their fabulous new kitchen end up belonging to another couple who were starting off on their journey – with all that optimism, all that hope?

She pushed those thoughts away: dangerous territory. Their marriage didn't have to be over. It was up to her. She just had to tell Anton she forgave him. Except she couldn't because she hadn't.

On Thursday afternoon Bob knocked on the door of her office, which she'd taken to keeping closed. She was in hideaway mode. She didn't feel like being sociable. He hadn't been as relaxed with her this week. But then, to be fair, she hadn't seen much of him. She'd barely come out of her office.

He looked hesitant now.

'Everything OK?' she asked.

'I'm hoping you'll think so. I'm done. Would you like to come and see?'

'You mean done as in "finished"?' She blinked. 'But you're ahead of schedule.'

'Yes,' he said proudly. 'Although you haven't signed the job off yet. I like to leave a bit of time for a snag list.'

'Of course.' She followed him into the kitchen. She'd noticed it was coming together. The units had been in for a while. They were ivory – the colour of her wedding dress. The bespoke breakfast bar, in matching ivory, dominated the centre of the room. It looked superb.

'It looks . . . brilliant,' she said with a slight catch in her throat. 'Just what we planned.' She burst into tears.

'Hey.' He stared at her in alarm. 'That's not quite the reaction I was hoping for.' He started patting his pockets, clearly looking for a hanky and failing to find one. 'Are you OK?'

'I'm fine.'

'Well, I'm no expert, but you don't look fine. Not that it's any of my business.' He coughed and looked embarrassed.

Kate found a tissue in her pocket and blew her nose. 'Sorry.' And then, because she felt she owed him some sort of explanation, she added, 'Anton and I have had a row. Quite a big row. Well, actually, he's moved out.'

'Ah,' he said and there was an awkward little silence.

'I'm, um—' she began.

'If you—' he said at the same time.

She gestured for him to go first.

'I was just going to say if you're worried about paying my bill – I can wait a few weeks.'

His eyes were kind. And it was that kindness that was her

189

undoing. She felt herself unravelling. The nice comfortable numbness that she had been feeling all week, aided by a few glasses of wine every night, was suddenly gone and beneath it she felt raw and terribly, terribly vulnerable.

'I really am fine,' she said, aware that the tears were pouring down her face and dripping onto the worktop. 'The bill's fine too. Give me the invoice.' More tears. 'I'll pay it . . .' She couldn't seem to stop them. Bob nodded with each gulped out little phrase.

When she'd finished he said, 'I'll make you a cup of tea.' There was a no-nonsense tone to his voice. She sat at the new breakfast bar with her head in her hands and listened to him filling up the kettle.

CHAPTER 24

Anton came back on the Saturday. 'I can't stay at Liam's any more. He's got his family coming for the weekend. Also, I've run out of clothes.'

He eyed her warily from the centre of the kitchen. 'You must have had time to think things through.'

'Yes, I have,' she said. 'I'm going to Mum's.'

'What are you going to tell her?' She knew he was more worried about that than anything else. It was so strange – she'd been married to him for nearly a decade and she'd never noticed how often he worried more about how it would look to people outside.

Maybe she was guilty of that too, because after she had thought it through she decided not to go to her mother's after all. She would go to Jojo's. Jojo had offered and Kate knew she had meant it.

She would only go for the night – after that she would book into a B & B and stay there for as long as it took to decide what to do. Which she didn't think would be long, because she almost knew already.

On the way there she called round to drop off Bob's payment. She could have put it in the post, but he'd been so kind the last time she'd seen him. She hadn't gone into any detail and he hadn't asked any questions. He'd simply said, 'Relationships are tough. I know that one.'

He lived in a semi on the new estate on the outskirts of Little Sanderton. They'd been edging back onto the conservation area for a while, but the houses were nice: pretty sandstone buildings with integral garages and pocket-sized front gardens. Quite expensive, probably, because they were in sniffing distance of the sea and this was Devon, darling!

She rang the bell, but no one came. Pity, she'd have liked to see him one more time. She was about to let herself out of his front garden when she heard her name.

'Kate – hi – sorry, I didn't hear the bell.'

She turned. He was standing in the open front doorway, holding his phone. She retraced her steps. 'I just wanted to drop off your payment. And to say thanks.'

'You don't need to say it. I assume this is my thanks.' He took the envelope.

'I didn't mean for the kitchen.'

'Ah. So how are you doing?' There was that kindness in his voice again. She blinked. She wouldn't cry. She was four days stronger. Four days wiser.

'Have you got time to come in?' he said, looking at her face.

She hesitated. There was something very peaceful about Bob.

'If you're sure,' she said. 'Thanks.'

His house was not what she expected – first off, he led her straight through to the garage, a corner of which had been converted into a recording studio.

It had egg-box soundproofing on the walls, two large speakers on stands, a Mac computer with an enormous screen and a selection of mics set at different heights.

'I was in here when you rang the bell,' he told her. 'I'd just finished an audition for an ad for Dorset cookies, would you believe.'

'When will you know if you've got it?'

'A couple of weeks. Fingers crossed.' He gestured to a plate of them balanced on one of the speakers. 'Help yourself.'

'Thanks. Do you do a lot of auditions?'

'Hundreds. Well, OK, slight exaggeration. Dozens. My hit rate isn't very high.'

'I'm sure that's not true.'

'I'm afraid it is,' he said. 'It's an incredibly competitive industry. Hence I do kitchens while I wait for fame to come knocking.'

His voice was light, but his eyes told her he cared a great deal more than he was letting on. 'Enough of me,' he said softly. 'Are you OK? I don't want to pry. Tell me to mind my own business if you like.'

'You're not prying.' She looked into his very blue eyes. 'Anton wants to carry on. But . . .' She looked away. 'I'm not so sure I can.'

'I'm guessing he hurt you,' Bob said simply. 'And now you don't know if you can trust him again?'

'Is it that obvious?'

'Yes, if you've been there yourself.' He paused.

'And you have?' she asked, wanting very much to know.

He nodded. 'My ex-wife, Lia. Very soon after we got married she told me that she was in love with someone else.' He frowned. 'I was completely oblivious. The man concerned – he was a friend of Lia's family. They more or less planned to get married, but then I came along and Lia had her head turned. She's quite impetuous,' he added softly. 'She's Italian. And this man was also Italian.'

'Oh, no.' Kate looked at him. 'That must have been very tough.'

'It was. I had no idea that he and Lia had been so close. I just saw this beautiful, passionate woman and I fell head over heels in love with her.'

'But she must have loved you too. She married you.'

'We'd only known each other a few weeks when she got pregnant,' Bob said softly. 'After that she didn't really have a choice.'

'Oh my gosh,' Kate said, looking at Bob's serious face. 'So what happened?'

'I found her crying one night. Daisy was only a few weeks old at the time. Lia had been very low. I thought that she was just tired out. But then I realized there was much more to it than that.

'She told me she thought she had made a terrible mistake marrying me, but that she would honour our agreement, even though she loved someone else.' He gave a wry little smile.

'What did you do?' Kate said.

'I let her go. What else could I do? We waited a few months and then we invented a lover. A lover for me,' he said. 'Not for Lia. It meant that she could leave the marriage with her head held high. It meant she could go back to this man with impunity.'

'That was incredibly generous of you,' Kate said, touched beyond belief.

'It wasn't entirely altruistic. I wanted the best for our daughter – for Daisy,' he said quietly. 'And that meant a mother who was happy – not a mother who was living a life she didn't want to be living. It was the only sane thing to do.'

She touched his arm and he smiled at her. 'Yet Lia still messes you around,' she said. 'With the arrangements for Daisy.'

'Often,' he said with a little shrug. 'That's people, though, isn't it? They have incredibly short memories. And Lia has always been a little irrational. It was what I liked about her,' he said.

'Thank you for trusting me with it,' she said softly.

They were sitting very close, by virtue of the fact that there wasn't much room in his studio, just a director's chair and a visitor's chair, side by side. There was a moment when she thought, *I could lean over and kiss him.* Kiss away that pain. Not even in a romantic sense, but in a meeting-of-souls sense. *I know you. I know who you are. I know you.*

And she thought of Connie Chatterley in the woods that first time. When she had gone to Oliver in the little hut and he had very gently laid out the rug and unwrapped her and she had lain there so passively and so quietly while the sun had slanted in on them and he had taught her with such tenderness about connections and about intimacy and about love.

She sat there very still, thinking about Anton and wondering how much about intimacy they really knew. Because it wasn't just about foreplay, was it? It wasn't just about teasing and titillating in the bedroom, and cooking meals and watching films and buying a kitchen and having a code for the bathroom. It was about honesty and caring and doing what was best for each other. It was about putting the other person first no matter how hard that was. It was about doing what was right.

Bob's phone beeped with a text and the moment was broken. He picked it up and she saw his face change.

'I'm sorry,' he said, 'but I need to go out. It's urgent.'

'Of course.' She put down her half-finished coffee and picked up her bag. 'Is it Daisy?' she asked as they went back through the house.

'Yeah.' He gave her another apologetic look. 'I've been trying to get hold of Lia for the past couple of days. It's a long story . . .'

'Sure. Don't worry.' She touched his arm. 'If there's ever anything I can do to help, just call.'

'Cheers.' He flashed her a smile.

As she drove away she saw in her rear-view mirror that he was getting into his van.

She hoped that whatever the problem was he would sort it out. It was strange: she barely knew the man, but she liked him very much.

CHAPTER 25

Kate was just pulling up outside Jojo's when her mobile began to ring. Half expecting it to be Anton, she was tempted to ignore it. But as she pulled it out of her bag Bob's number flashed up on the screen.

Curious, she answered it.

'Kate, are you still nearby?' The urgency in his voice straightened her spine.

'Yes.'

'I need a lift to the airport. My van won't start. Can you help?'

'Sure,' she said. 'I'm about ten minutes away.'

'Heathrow, not Exeter,' he said. 'It's quite a trek.'

'Heathrow's fine,' she said, even as her sane voice kicked in, *Are you crazy? That's a three-hour drive.*

He was waiting outside his house. She had barely pulled up when he opened the passenger door and was climbing in.

'I appreciate this. How are you fixed for fuel? Do we need to stop?'

'No.' She glanced at him.

'I'll reimburse you.' He paused. 'Don't take this the wrong way, but are you a fast driver? I'm not expecting you to break any speed limits, but the timing's critical.'

'I'll put my foot down,' she promised, and did so as soon as they got on to the dual carriageway.

She glanced over at him. He looked white. 'I'm aware it's none of my business,' she said. 'But what are we trying to achieve? Do you have to catch a flight?'

'No, I'm not trying to catch one. I'm trying to stop one,' he said. 'I'm trying to stop someone getting on one.' He sighed. 'I think Lia is taking Daisy to Italy.'

A beat.

'This has been brewing for a while. She wants to go back to her family in Verona. I'm not keen. I'll never see Daisy if they're there.' His voice went a little gruff. 'The last thing Lia said to me was that I couldn't stop her.'

'Can she do that?' Kate felt herself gripping the steering wheel a little tighter.

'She can get on a flight any time she chooses,' he said. 'That text I had earlier was from Lia's sister. She lives in Exeter. We've always got on well.' He paused. 'She texted to warn me about Lia's plans. She thought I should know.'

'Oh my goodness.' Kate felt herself go cold. 'What time is their flight?'

'It's nine twenty-five. We should make it before that. I'll just have to pray that they haven't gone through departures.'

199

'Can the authorities stop her going?'

'I think it might be a bit late for that.' He hesitated. 'Lia has family all over Italy. If they wanted to they could pass Daisy from place to place for years. I might never see her again.'

'Would she do that, though – after all that you did for her?' Kate could hear the shock in her own voice.

'She might,' Bob said. 'If she's desperate enough.'

Kate broke the speed limit. Not enough to get pulled over, but enough to make sure they got there as fast as humanly possible. 'I'll drop you off,' she said, as she pulled into the airport at just gone 8.15. 'And I'll wait in the short-stay car park.'

'You don't need to do that. I can find my own way back. I can get a train.'

'I'm very happy to wait,' she said. 'Now go. Phone or text when you know what's happening.'

'I owe you big time.' He was out of the car before she could answer. She watched him running towards the doors. His tall frame was highlighted briefly in the lights from the other side. Then he disappeared into the mouth of the terminal. She went to the short-stay car park and found a space. It was cold once the engine had been off for a while. She was glad she'd had the foresight to put a fleece in the back, in case Jojo had decided to take them for another bracing walk on the beach. She grabbed it and put it over her knees. Then she put the radio on for company and texted Jojo.

So sorry. Change of plan. Could I come later instead?

Jojo's reply came back a few minutes later.

Open invitation, angel. You're welcome any time. You know where key is.

Then another text, a few seconds after that. *PS. Good luck!*

Jojo clearly thought she was talking things through with Anton. What would she say, Kate wondered, if she knew she had just driven three hours into the night to help out a man she barely knew? Knowing Jojo, she'd probably just smile.

This was the difference between novels and real life, Kate decided. In *Lady Chatterley's Lover* Connie had gone on a trip to Venice. She had hired her own gondola. She had already been pregnant with her lover's child. She had already decided she was never going back to her husband.

They had that one thing in common, Kate thought. She was never going back to her husband, either. She had been almost sure when she'd packed up her rucksack this afternoon. Somehow during the mad drive up here, with her head full of someone else's problems, she had become totally sure. She couldn't trust Anton again. She was no longer certain whether she still loved him. She looked at the time on her mobile. He'd been gone half an hour. It was 9 p.m. She really hoped Bob had found them.

She must have dozed off because the next thing she was aware of was waking up in the car, fuzzy-headed and unsure of where she was. Her mobile was ringing, she realized.

She swiped the answer icon. 'Hello?'

'Kate – it's Bob. I'm so sorry I haven't phoned you before.

I didn't realize the time. I'm hoping you had the sense to head on back to Devon.'

'No, I'm still in the car park. I'm not very sensible,' she added, half in sleep mode. 'What time is it, anyway? Did you stop them?'

'It's just gone ten. And no, I'm afraid not.' He sounded exhausted.

'I'll come and pick you up.'

'Don't worry, I'll come to you. Tell me which car park.'

A few minutes later he was there, a dark shape outside the window. She took the central locking off to let him in.

'It's far too late to drive back to Devon,' he said. 'There's a Premier Inn up the road.'

She yawned. 'They might be full.'

'I took the precaution of phoning them. I couldn't face going back tonight. They only had one room, but it is a twin. Would that be OK?'

'It's fine with me.'

Twenty minutes later they were standing in reception: she with her holdall, and he clutching his phone and wallet. The receptionist handed them a key. 'Our last twin,' she said, glancing at Kate. 'It's on the thirteenth floor. If you're superstitious I could do you a double on floor 10. I didn't realise we had any doubles left.'

'A twin on the thirteenth floor is fine,' Kate said.

But as they went up in the lift she thought that she wouldn't have minded a double on floor 10. She wouldn't have minded a double anywhere with him. That was probably because she was still sleep-addled, she told herself.

By the time they got into the room, she felt wide awake again. She perched on the twin furthest from the door. 'Do you want to talk about what happened?'

He yawned. 'I think I owe you that at least. I'm really grateful to you, Kate.'

'You don't owe me anything.'

'Nevertheless.' He sat on the other single bed and rubbed his eyes. 'I didn't stop them but I did get a chance to talk to them. Their plane was delayed, which helped.'

She nodded. Something told her that he was only just holding it together. That if she tried to comfort him he might break.

'Paolo was with them,' Bob said quietly. 'He thought the story about my affair was true. Lia had never told him we'd made it up.' His voice hardened a little. 'Which meant that his conscience wasn't pricking him overly much about taking my daughter away.' He bit his lip. 'It seems that by trying to do the right thing I shot myself in the foot.'

Kate nodded. She was beginning to dislike Lia more and more.

'Anyway, he knows now.'

'But they still went?' she said quietly.

'Yes, but Lia has promised me – they have both promised me – that they will bring Daisy back.'

'Did you believe them?'

He nodded. 'I have to. Or I'll drive myself insane.' He gestured towards the window. The curtains were undrawn and beyond the glass the sky was an inky blackness. 'I *have* to believe them,' he repeated and his voice cracked a little. And this time Kate couldn't help herself. She went across to him and she put her arms around him and she held him tightly. For a minute or so they stayed like that, side by side on the edge of the single bed. She held him until he had calmed, like a mother would, with his head against her breasts.

Eventually he shifted so he was looking at her. 'Isn't Anton going to be worried about you? Where does he think you are?'

'With a friend.' She paused. 'It's over between us. I think maybe it has been over for a while.' She told him about Suzanna. 'The truth is, things haven't been right for ages.' She wouldn't tell him about the impotence. 'Anton having a fling just put it into perspective.'

He nodded slowly. The air was suddenly charged with something different. Something new. They still hadn't touched each other, but she knew that it wasn't far away. There was chemistry between them. It had been there from the moment they'd met and it had been building, even though neither of them had acknowledged it along the way.

For some reason she found herself thinking of the hut in the woods: the hiding place where Connie and Oliver met secretly. A place that only they knew. A hut in the woods versus a room on the thirteenth floor of a Premier Inn. She and Bob sitting on a single bed, both of them fully dressed. And she had an urge to laugh. But that would have been so entirely inappropriate that she managed to restrain herself.

'What are you thinking?' His voice was soft.

'That maybe we should have got the double.'

It was out there now. She knew she hadn't shocked him. His eyes were dark for a different reason now.

'We could probably push these two together,' he said. 'If we were both sure that we wouldn't regret it come the cold light of day?'

'I wouldn't regret it,' Kate said.

He touched her face with fingers that were feather-light. 'I wouldn't regret it either.'

CHAPTER 26

It was very tender, their lovemaking.

They kissed for a very long time. First when they were dressed and then a lot more when they weren't. She had forgotten what it was like to kiss someone new. Actually, she had forgotten what it was like to kiss.

Because that was one of the first things to go when you grew apart. She could remember the last time she and Anton had made love but not the last time they had kissed. And she had forgotten what it was like to know without a shadow of a doubt that you were desirable, that you were wanted.

She was aware of the smile in Bob's eyes, of the slight stubble of his chin, of his breath, the scent of his skin and his hair, the hardness of him. The wonderful, life-affirming, confident hardness of him. The rhythm of his body. The totality of him. And then, finally, the totality of them.

*

In the morning the first thing that made it into her conscious awareness was the warmth of him behind her. They were spooned together in the narrow confines of the bed, covered with just the sheet. The room smelled of sex. She couldn't remember when she'd last felt so safe.

'Are you awake?' he said.

'Yes.'

'I've been waiting for you to wake up so I could move my left arm. It's gone to sleep.'

'Sorry.' She shifted her body to release him.

She rolled over, propped her head up on her elbow and looked at him. His eyes were laughing and his face was crumpled with sleep. 'I'll make the tea.' He gave her a quick sideways glance as he pulled on his pants. 'What? I'm shy.'

'You weren't shy last night.'

'It was dark last night.' A beat. 'Seriously, though, it's been a long time since I was ... with a woman. Like this.' His ears were actually going pink. It made her like him even more.

'It's been a long time for me too. Except for Anton,' she said. 'But we haven't – hadn't – for a while.'

He nodded. She watched him fill up the kettle. Although he was tall he wasn't skinny. He was lean and well-muscled with a smattering of dark hair on his chest, running downwards in a thin line. She drank him in.

Aware of her gaze, he came back to the bed. 'You're staring.'

'I know. Do you mind?'

He shook his head. 'No regrets?' he asked.

'None.' She held out her hand. 'You?'

'No regrets. I thought you were beautiful the first time I saw you. But I also thought you were as far out of my reach as the moon. You were married, for one thing.'

'You flirted shamelessly with me,' she reminded him. 'You told me your nickname was Big Bob.'

'Did I?' His face went pink to match his ears. 'That was probably just nerves. I get nervous around beautiful women.'

'And now I know why that was your nickname,' she said, giggling at his embarrassment.

They sat in the stillness of the morning sipping tea with UHT milk. 'What time's checkout?' she asked. 'I think I might take a shower.'

'Not till midday. You've got plenty of time.'

She stood in the shower letting the hot jets of water stream over her and feeling a faint regret because there was a part of her that didn't want to wash him away. She wanted to keep the scent of him on her, in her. She didn't want this to be just a lovely interlude. Because she knew that whatever happened from now on, it wasn't going to be easy. As he'd said not five minutes ago, she was still married. Anton might have been the first to stray, but he didn't want the marriage to end. He'd said as much, *Can you forgive me? I want to know if you can forgive me.*

She had to go back and tell him that, yes, it was possible she could have forgiven him in time. She might have been able to forgive him for sleeping with another woman in the heat of the moment – but not for doing it so many times, and not for doing it with Suzanna.

Divorce wasn't going to be easy. But forgiving him was impossible.

Then of course there was Bob.

She had thought him beautiful too on their first meeting. Not that it would ever have gone any further, she was sure. He'd have stayed in her head, a gorgeous fantasy, but circumstances had conspired against her . . . or was it *with* her?

Until they'd made love there had been a chance that she could still have stepped back. But Bob had made her feel things that Anton never had. She kept getting flashbacks to last night. The memory of his fingertips on her face, the expression in his eyes, his breath in her hair, the taste of his mouth.

A shiver of lust melted her legs and she shut her eyes. The sound of the bathroom door opening hooked her back into the present and there he was standing on the other side of the glass, his eyes on her face.

'Is it OK if I join you?'

They made love again in the shower with the water running down their backs, the newness of it all overwhelming, and Kate thought, *I want to remember this moment forever. Just in case I lose him. I want to get it out on the darkest days and let it warm me.*

'What are you thinking?' he said, cupping her face very gently with his hands and looking down at her.

'That if I died now I'd die happy.'

He smiled at her. 'I hope that neither of us is going to die for a very long time. But we should talk about the future.'

*

They talked about it in the car. It was a long drive back, made longer by an accident on the motorway. For an hour they crawled in a stop–start fashion at less than 10 mph.

'I'm going to ask Anton for a divorce,' she told him.

'It sounds like he still loves you,' Bob said. 'Maybe Suzanna was a mistake.' He hesitated. 'Just as I was a mistake for Lia.'

'It's possible,' Kate said, and she could feel her fingers gripping the steering wheel a little tighter. 'But I don't think so.' She paused. 'And we both know that love has to be a two-way thing. It doesn't work otherwise.'

'You're right.' She heard the sigh in his voice. 'Are you sure a divorce is what you want? It's so final. Wouldn't you like to try a separation first?'

'I'm guessing we'll do that anyway,' she said. 'We'll have to sell the house. One of us will have to move out. I think that'll be me. At least we have a new kitchen.' She paused for a moment, and added with a flippancy she didn't really feel. 'That's a good selling point.'

'Aye, darlin', you've a grand wee kitchen, so you have.' He was straight into Belfast. Which made her smile and took the sting out of the thought of selling the house. Of the practicalities, of the dividing things in half – *this is yours, this is mine*.

'What about you?' she asked him. 'Do you think Lia will honour her promise?'

'I guess I'll soon find out.' Kate glanced at him and saw his face twist a little in pain. 'I live in hope.'

'Yes,' Kate said, thinking about hope. She and Jojo had talked a little about *Lady Chatterley's Lover* when she'd been there last. 'The ending's terribly sad, don't you think?' Kate had said. 'They're totally in love with each other – Connie and Oliver – but they can't be together. Because neither of their respective spouses will give them a divorce.'

'At least that's improved since 1928,' Jojo had said. 'These days you can get a divorce even if your spouse doesn't want one.' Her eyes had gone a little reflective and Kate had known she was thinking about Big Al. 'Besides,' Jojo had gone on thoughtfully, '*Lady Chatterley* finishes – as all good love stories should finish – on a note of hope.'

It was true, Kate thought now. She had actually gone back and read it. It had finished with Oliver writing to Connie and telling her that whatever lay ahead of them, however long they had to wait for each other, he still had a hopeful heart.

The traffic was still crawling along. Kate flexed and unflexed her fingers on the steering wheel.

'What about us?' Bob said quietly. 'I mean, I don't want to put you under any kind of pressure – I would like – I would if you – well, I'd . . .' He stuttered to a halt. 'Oh, bugger.'

A beat. 'I would really like to see you again, Kate.' His voice was quiet. 'I would like to have dinner with you. I would like to take you out on my boat. I would like to walk by the sea with you, holding hands. I would like very much to watch a sunset with you and maybe a sunrise.'

She felt her heart fill with warmth. 'I would like to do those things with you very much, too.'

They smiled at each other and for a while they drove in silence but for the drone of the engines – theirs and the rest of the cars' on the M25. All travelling together, stop start, stop start, stop start, in a little loop of eternity. There was a part of her that wanted to stay forever in the logjam of traffic so that she could be close to him, instead of going home to confront all that awaited her there.

Kate wished she could fast-forward into the future to a time when she and Anton were separated. To a time when she and Bob were free to start something of their own. She imagined taking him to meet everyone in the Reading Group, introducing him as her friend, her lover, this man who had become so important in her life in such a short time. This man she hoped would become even more important as time went on.

She hoped that she and Bob – like Connie Chatterley and Oliver Mellors – could have the kind of love that until now she hadn't known was possible.

The sound of a text coming through on one of their phones interrupted her thoughts. She hoped it would be his – she hoped it would be Lia keeping her promise to stay in touch. She hoped for him all the very best that there was of life.

Unconditional love, she thought. Pure and brave. She hoped that they would have that for each other, too – she and Bob. One day soon.

MARCH

Jojo

CHAPTER 27

Jojo was the first of the reading group to arrive on that rain-speckled March evening. She usually was, she thought, as she kissed Serena's cheek.

'Mmm, you smell nice. Go through to the snug,' Serena told her. 'I've just got to send an email for school before I forget. I don't suppose you could open the bottle of red, could you? I don't think I did it.'

'Certainly, angel.' Jojo did as she was bid. Serena's snug was one of the most relaxing rooms on the planet. The wood-burner was aglow, picking out the muted reds and golds of the two chesterfields, which sat at right angles to it. There was a plate of little pastries on the side. Oh, my – they looked homemade and she hadn't eaten. She wouldn't be able to resist. She'd have to start the diet tomorrow.

She sat in her usual place in the seat furthest from the fire and gave a deep sigh of contentment.

'That was a big sigh.' Serena appeared in the doorway. 'How are you, dear?'

Serena called everyone 'dear'. A habit from school, which, she'd once confessed, saved her having to remember everyone's name.

'I'm good,' Jojo told her. 'In fact, I'm very good. That was a happy sigh, not a sad one.'

'Oh, yes?' Serena was on it immediately. 'Tell me more – is there a man involved?'

Is it that obvious? Jojo felt her cheeks flame scarlet. 'What on earth makes you say that?'

'You've got a glint in your eye,' Serena said thoughtfully. 'An I've-just-met-a-man-I-like glint. Although it could also be an I've-just-finished-work-and-I've-got-a-nice-glass-of-wine glint.' She frowned. 'And now you're blushing. I'm right, aren't I?'

To Jojo's immense relief the doorbell rang and Serena didn't wait for her reply.

Moments later the hall was full of chattering voices. It seemed that everyone had arrived at the same time.

She poured wine for them all. They would worm it out of her by the end of the evening.

The level of noise rose and then there they all were.

Anne Marie, pink-cheeked English rose, looking very pleased with herself. Her romance with her father's osteopath was clearly going well then.

Beautiful Kate – she had a glow about her as well. Jojo smiled. There was some news there too, if she wasn't mistaken . . .

She was right. It didn't take Kate long to confess that she had become close to the handsome builder who'd installed her kitchen. 'He's lovely,' she gushed. 'But I've only just split up with Anton, so it's very early days . . .'

'Very *Lady Chatterley's Lover*,' said Serena, with a smile, and Kate's eyes sparkled.

But the conversation led on to them chatting about how reality could echo fiction.

'And in January we were reading *Emma* and young Anne Marie here went into the matchmaking business,' Grace pointed out.

'Although the project didn't really get off the ground,' Anne Marie replied, with a giggle.

'Yes, but you did end up with a romance yourself, my dear,' Serena told her. 'Just like Jane Austen's Emma.'

Anne Marie looked surprised. 'I suppose I did.'

'And how about you, Jojo?' Serena continued.

Jojo caught her breath. *This is it. It's now or never.* And she said, 'Yes, actually. I've got a date on Saturday night. He's a paediatrician at the Royal.' She paused beneath the clamour of their reactions.

'Jojo, you dark horse. You kept that quiet!'

'What's his name?'

'How old is he?'

'His name's Daniel Mannings,' she said, 'and he's thirty-one. I've known him for years but just as a friend and colleague . . .'

'A toyboy!' Anne Marie clapped her hands.

'Only a *bit* of a toyboy,' Jojo said. 'Only six years.' It was

217

bothering her a little – the age difference. And here in the comfort of the snug she felt safe enough to let the fear out of its box. 'Do you think that's too much?'

'Absolutely not.'

'It's just a number.'

The warmth of their responses washed over her. Jojo felt a little better. 'I do like him,' she said.

'Go for it,' Grace said.

It was Serena who broke up the relationship chat. 'Right, then, ladies. Time is pressing. We should get on to our book of the month. Over to you, Anne Marie. So, what are we reading?'

Anne Marie cleared her throat. 'I hope you don't mind but I've chosen one that's not quite so ancient.'

She must have spotted that Serena was frowning, because she went on quickly, 'Don't worry, it's still a classic! But I thought it might be a bit easier to – well – you know . . . actually read!' She rummaged in her bag and produced a paperback that she held up to show the group. They all leaned forward expectantly. 'It's Daphne du Maurier's *Rebecca*,' she said. 'Haven't they made a film?'

She didn't need to elaborate. Everyone knew what *Rebecca* was about: the age-gap romance; the shadow of the dead wife hanging over the new young bride; and, of course, Manderley – the ancestral home that overlooked the sea.

Jojo blinked a couple of times. There were some disturbing parallels already. Jojo and her toyboy. And she lived by the sea. No, that was crazy. Utter nonsense.

Into the little silence that followed Anne Marie's announcement, Jojo said, in an over-bright voice, 'Don't worry, angels. My toyboy has never been married. There are no dead wives to come back and haunt us. And I'm pretty sure he doesn't live in a stately home that's been in his family for generations.'

Her friends looked back at her. Nodding. Smiling. Agreeing that it was completely different. Ridiculous to think that reality could echo fiction.

OK, so it was a bit spooky that the last two novels had echoed the lives of two members of the Reading Group. But that had just been a coincidence. It definitely wasn't going to happen again this month.

Definitely not.

CHAPTER 28

Jojo stood in front of her bedroom mirror at just after 6.30 on Saturday evening and wished she was more pleased with what she saw. She really should do something about losing the extra couple of stone she was carrying. Okay, so she would never be sylph-like: she had always been curvy, but curvy was in danger of becoming overflowing.

No wonder you're single, whispered a nasty little voice in her head.

Shut up, Mum. Jojo gave the mirror a steely glare.

A couple of years ago she'd taken a course in boosting one's self-esteem, an evening class at Exeter College. One of the things the tutor had advised students to do was to stand in front of the mirror every day and list all their successes out loud, starting with 'I am a success story,' then going on to list everything they loved about their lives. The idea being that if you reinforced all the positive things in your life while looking yourself in the eye you would begin to believe it and your self-esteem would flourish.

For a few weeks Jojo had done it religiously. But then she'd got out of the habit. She decided to try it again now. She glanced at her reflection and cleared her throat. 'I am a success story,' she began. 'I have a successful career, which I love. I love my home.'

Sinbad, who was curled up on the bed, opened sleepy green eyes and yawned at her in the mirror. He probably thought she was talking to him.

'I love you,' she told him, and he blinked, unimpressed.

'I love myself.'

When she said the last sentence she felt a twinge of discomfort in her stomach and couldn't quite meet her own eyes. Was that because it wasn't true? She certainly didn't love her body. Right now, it was covered up. She was wearing leggings and an oversized top, which had a flattering neckline that showed off her best asset, which was what Big Al, her second husband, had called her 'magnificent cleavage'.

That had been a long time ago, though. Was it still magnificent? Was *any* part of her still magnificent?

Right now, it didn't feel like it. 'Get a grip, Jojo,' she told the mirror. 'Of course you're magnificent . . .' She tailed off. Well, Daniel must have seen something in her that was attractive. He was very keen.

She hadn't told the girls that – some kind of false modesty, maybe. But he'd asked her out three times before she'd said yes and they had found a date they could both do. Tonight.

He wouldn't have done that if he wasn't keen.

She picked up her bangles from the dresser, a selection of gold, silver and copper, and slid them on to her arms with a *ting-ting-ting*. She spent ages doing her face. Then she looked at the bottles of scent lined up on her dressing-table and frowned. Was this a Jimmy Choo night? Jimmy Choo was reserved for special occasions and it was only a date. On the other hand it might lead on to something more important. It might be the date that broke the four-and-a-half-year sabbatical she'd had since she'd realized Big Al wasn't coming back. It was definitely a Jimmy Choo occasion. She sprayed it on liberally. Then she glanced at her watch and panicked because she was going to be late.

They were meeting in a fusion restaurant in Exeter. 'It does Thai and Italian,' he'd told her, 'so we should find something we like.'

As it turned out, the traffic was lighter than Jojo had anticipated, so she wasn't late. She arrived at the restaurant just before seven. He was there already – she spotted him through the window, sitting at a table in the corner. They had that in common at least. They liked tables in corners. He was an 'observer', not a 'performer'. Completely different, she suspected, from Big Al.

The place was quite full – he must have booked. She took a deep breath, opened the door and was hit by the delicious scent of garlic and cinnamon. Date number one. She knew she shouldn't have any expectations. She definitely shouldn't be looking into the future – imagining them going to the theatre, having Sunday morning lie-ins, eating Danish pastries in her little patio garden by the sea – but it was hard not to.

Jojo's hands felt clammy on her bag. This was supposed to be fun. And it wasn't as if they didn't know each other – they'd often bumped into each other at hospital dos and occasionally on the ward. She had always liked him.

Threading her way through the other diners, she headed for the corner table and Daniel stood up to greet her. He kissed her on both cheeks, then pulled out her chair and she felt a frisson of pleasure. *A gentleman*, she thought. You didn't get that often, these days. As much as Jojo loved people, she was appalled by how rude some of them were . . . although being a midwife definitely put you in the line of fire. You could forgive people a lot when they were scared and in pain, Jojo reasoned.

Daniel smelt of aftershave – something faintly musky – and he was wearing a pink shirt, with very fine stripes, which most men couldn't have carried off but which accentuated his olive skin and dark hair perfectly.

'How's your day been?' he asked. 'Mother Nature been on your side?'

It was a standing joke between them that the biggest problem they ever had in their jobs was with Mother Nature – where babies were concerned, she was a capricious ally.

'Mother Nature has been behaving herself perfectly,' she told him, glad to be on familiar ground. 'Although I did only have one delivery, it has to be said. Home birth this afternoon. Very peaceful.'

She passed him a breadstick. 'How's your day been?'

'Not so good.' His face sobered. 'I had to give a parent some very bad news.'

'Ah,' she said. 'I'm sorry to hear that.'

'It never gets any easier, that part of my job.' Daniel gave a little sigh. 'The ups and downs of working in medicine. But there's always hope, I guess. Sometimes we see miracles.' He smiled at her. 'We shouldn't talk shop.' He steepled his hands and rested his chin on them. 'Tell me about you. Why has it taken me so long to get you to come out with me? Do you have a queue of suitors? That's it, isn't it?'

There was a spark of humour in his eyes as he spoke, but she sensed the question was not entirely flippant. 'I should be so lucky,' she said.

'Let me guess – a bad past relationship that's left you wary?'

It was quite a direct question but his directness was one of the things she liked about him.

She nodded slowly. 'Something, like that,' she said. To her relief, he didn't push it. 'Tell me about you,' she continued. 'Why aren't you spoken for, an eligible bachelor such as yourself?'

'Would you believe I've never met the right woman?' His voice was soft, almost shy. It might have been a well-practised line, but instinct told her it wasn't.

And she wasn't all that surprised. Like a lot of doctors, he probably didn't have time to meet many women outside the hospital. He had a reputation for being compassionate and conscientious – a doctor for whom it was still a vocation.

They were interrupted by a waitress coming to take their order. Jojo had forgotten briefly that they were even in a restaurant, they'd been so immersed in each other.

Her head told her to order salad, but her heart yearned for pasta and her heart won. Daniel followed suit, and asked if she'd like garlic bread – *was the pope Catholic?* Stretchy leggings were much better for you than tight jeans anyway. She regularly told her new mums that.

Yes, but your extra weight is not the result of a baby, Jojo. It's the result of gluttony and no self-control . . .

Bugger off, Mother. Leave me alone!

After the waitress had gone again the conversation continued seamlessly. He leaned forward, his hands crossed in front of him on the table, and said, 'I was close to my mother. For a long time it was just the two of us. Dad left when I was small, you see. I think maybe I had her on a bit of a pedestal. It's hard to find a woman who matches up.'

'Gosh.' She hadn't been expecting that. She touched the back of his hand lightly. 'Is she not still alive?'

'She had a brain haemorrhage when I was sixteen.'

He hesitated and she nodded sympathetically. After a couple of seconds he seemed to make a decision and he went on, 'She'd just made our tea one night – shepherd's pie – and she was carrying the plates through from the kitchen. There was this huge crash and when I looked round she'd dropped the plates and was on the floor. At first I thought she'd slipped, you know?' He blinked a couple of times. 'I was about to laugh. There was mess everywhere – a little shepherd's pie goes a long way.' His voice was quietly wry. 'But then I realized she wasn't moving. She was just lying there with her face against the wooden floor. She was trying to speak, but she couldn't get the words out.'

'Oh, my goodness.' Jojo felt a chill of shock as the memory clouded his eyes.

There was a little pause and he went on slowly: 'I sat on the floor with her until the ambulance came – but it was too late. She was already gone.'

'I can't imagine how hard that must have been,' she said.

He frowned. 'It was such a shock. For weeks I woke up thinking it hadn't happened. I kept replaying it and sometimes I'd give it a different outcome. You know, where I'd saved her.' He swallowed.

'You couldn't have saved her, sweetie,' Jojo said, aching for the sixteen-year-old boy he had once been. 'No one could have saved her.'

'I know that now. But it was one of the reasons I decided to become a doctor. Paediatrics came later.' He took a sip of his drink. 'Sorry. I didn't mean to dump all that on you. It's not exactly a first-date conversation.'

'It's fine,' she said, liking him more and more. 'Thank you for trusting me with it.'

'You're an easy person to trust, Jojo.' His face was more composed now. 'So, why did you specialize in midwifery?'

'I wanted to help people – women . . . to have their babies in a really supported environment . . .' She tailed off. It was her stock answer, but after what he had just told her she wanted to tell him the truth.

226

For a moment she became aware of the tables around them. A couple to their left. A family to their right. Then she looked back at Daniel.

'I'm adopted,' she said, meeting his eyes. 'That was part of my motivation – I wanted to know what made a mother decide to give up her baby after she'd carried it inside her for nine months. I wanted to try to understand. I know that's not a very good reason to go into the profession but—'

'Maybe it is,' he said, and his voice was very gentle. 'Do you get on with your adoptive mum?'

She shook her head. 'Not really, no. But I don't see her often. She's lived in Cyprus for the past five years.'

He stroked the back of her hand. He had beautiful finger-nails and little dark hairs around the knuckles. But there was no spark at his touch. A little part of her was disappointed. Did that mean there was no chemistry? Big Al had set her on fire from the very first moment he'd taken her hand.

Their starters arrived. The moment was lost.

As the meal progressed she discovered that he was clever and funny. He didn't have Big Al's quick-fire banter or his sarcastic wit. Instead he was much more considered, more measured. But he was kinder too. He listened to what she said, then thought about what he was going to say back. Why was she thinking of Big Al anyway? Big Al had left her – walked out without a backward glance. Big Al had let her down very, very badly.

They were on desserts – homemade tiramisu – when Daniel asked her the question she'd been dreading.

'Haven't you ever wanted to get married?'

227

She blinked and tried to gather herself. Why hadn't she told him before? But it was hard when you first met someone to get your skeletons out of the cupboard: you wanted them to see the best bits of you, not the worst.

'I have been married,' she confessed. 'Twice.'

He nodded. 'So I wasn't far off the mark earlier. Twice bitten, eh? Did they both end badly?'

'Yes,' she said, 'but—'

'Divorce is tough,' Daniel interrupted, his eyes sympathetic. 'My elder brother had a bad one a couple of years ago.' He slapped his head. 'A bad one! I don't suppose there are really any good ones, are there?'

She had to stop him before this got out of hand. 'I'm not divorced,' she said. 'Alan, my second husband, and I are still married.' She watched his face. Watched the sympathy flitter to shock and then to wary curiosity where it seemed to settle.

He took another sip of his wine, rubbed his nose, then looked back into her eyes. 'I see,' he said. 'Um, can I ask why? Not that it's any of my business.' She saw him glance at her ring finger, which was bare, and had been for quite some time. 'I thought . . .' he said. 'I guess lots of midwives don't wear their rings.'

'Daniel, I'm sorry. I should have told you before, but it's not what you think. We are separated. Well, it's a bit more than separated. We've actually been apart for longer than we were married. You see, Alan went to Marrakesh to find himself more than four years ago. He never came back. I haven't seen him since.'

The curiosity in his eyes was turning into puzzlement and she pre-empted his next question. 'I do hear from him periodically, so I know he's not dead. We might still be married in name, but we are no longer a couple.'

He still didn't speak, so she rushed on, 'I do understand if that changes things for you, I mean . . .' She felt suddenly flustered, disappointed that her fantasies of Sunday morning lie-ins and eating Danish pastries in her garden were dissolving faster than a morning mist across the sea.

She picked up her bag and rummaged for her purse. 'I'll pay my half of the bill, of course.'

'There's no need.' His face was deadpan.

'I insist.'

'You can pay next time,' he told her, stopping her in her tracks. 'If you want there to be a next time, that is? I hope you do.'

She looked at him. His eyes were thoughtful. 'We all have baggage,' he said quietly. 'I'm sure there will be things about me that will surprise you also.'

Jojo stayed in her seat, caught in his gaze. 'It's a deal,' she said, feeling her heart give a little thump of nervous anticipation. 'I'll look forward to it.'

CHAPTER 29

Next time, they went to Ocean Views. At the end of the evening she insisted on paying and he finally conceded.

'There is a condition,' he said, as he helped her on with her coat – another gentlemanly touch.

'What's that?' she asked.

'That you'll let me cook you a meal – at my house.'

'You can cook too?' She raised her eyebrows in mock horror. 'I'm impressed!'

'Don't get too excited,' he warned. 'It'll be something simple, like spaghetti – it was my mother's signature dish.'

'Spaghetti's my favourite,' she said, and his eyes warmed.

She would need to buy some more Jimmy Choo at this rate, Jojo decided, as she got ready for date number three. She sprayed the scent liberally on to her wrists and collarbone and behind both ears for good measure.

Daniel's house was a surprise. It was a lot bigger than she'd expected. On the outskirts of Exeter, it stood alone, a great double-fronted place with ivy trailing across the walls. Jojo hadn't had time to read *Rebecca* so she'd bought the DVD instead – the Laurence Olivier version – and the last iconic image of Manderley was fresh in her mind. Daniel's house was hardly Manderley, yet she felt a little shiver as she parked on the gravel frontage and walked up to the high porch, which had stained-glass windows that reflected the evening sun.

Daniel let her in with his shirt sleeves rolled up, dressed incongruously in a green-and-white striped apron. She saw that the floors of the big old hall were of bare wood, and the ceilings high. Through a doorway off to the left she glimpsed architraves and a beautiful open fireplace, although no fire was lit there.

'Come in.' He kissed her on both cheeks, then ushered her across the hall into a dining room, where the table was laid, then on into a big kitchen where he was obviously in the throes of cooking dinner. Chopping boards were littered with red and green peppers, and the room was filled with the pungent scent of onion mixed with that of freshly torn basil. There were pots of herbs on the windowsill: coriander, basil and chives jostled for space with a stalk of feathery fennel, almost toppling over. On the worktop to her left sat a basket of beef tomatoes, plump and shiny, and an over-sized wooden pepper-grinder. Phallic, Jojo thought, feeling a little tingle in her groin – the first awakening of chemistry, maybe. No, not *quite* the first. There hadn't been the imme-diate fizz of attraction she'd felt for Big Al, but since she and

Daniel had been chatting – since they'd been opening up to each other – the chemistry had been building.

'Wow, so you really do cook,' she said, as she looked around her. She could tell he was good, just by the way he chopped garlic, handling the big knife with a speed and skill that told her he was a chef – the real deal, not just a man who could cobble together dinner.

When he opened the fridge, letting the door bang back against the worktop, she saw that inside a couple of tall glass dishes were filled with something coffee-coloured.

'Tiramisu,' he explained, when he caught her look. 'I noticed you liked it. It was one of my mother's favourites. She taught me how to make that too.'

'Your mother sounds like a very special lady,' she said, and he smiled and nodded, clearly pleased. He had been close to her – he'd told her that on their first date. Why then did she feel the tiniest hint of unease?

There was nothing abnormal in having a good relationship with your mother – it was healthy for a guy to have that. It was certainly better than a man who'd disconnected from his roots. Big Al had told her early on that he hadn't seen his mother for decades. Aside from a couple of distant cousins, none of them had even turned up to Al and Jojo's wedding. That should have been a warning sign. At the time, though, she'd understood. She'd 'got it'. She'd 'got him'.

After all, Jojo didn't see her mother much either. They had never been close. She had often wondered why the spiky, frosty woman who had adopted her had wanted a baby. Jojo had never gone without material things, but there hadn't been much warmth.

Their difficult relationships with their mothers had bonded them, not separated them, which had made it all the more devastating when Al had abandoned her.

'Penny for your thoughts,' Daniel said, and she jumped.

'I was just thinking what a beautiful house this is,' she said, opening her hands to indicate the kitchen.

'Thank you. I love it. I grew up here.'

Of course – suddenly it all made sense. 'So this was your parents' house?'

'My mum's,' he corrected. 'Dad left when I was small.'

'Yes,' she said, remembering. 'But you were so young when she died. Did you just stay on here, then, alone?'

He shook his head. 'No. I went to live with my brother. He's twelve years older than me. Mum left us the house jointly. Simon didn't want it – he was already pretty wealthy. The house is beautiful, but it's also old – it needs a lot of maintenance, a right old money pit. I think Simon was glad to get rid of it, to be honest.'

He went across to the stove – an Aga, which looked original. 'I'll just get this sauce on the go and then I'll show you round.'

'I love old houses,' she said.

There were four bedrooms, all doubles. She stood in the doorway of his bedroom, looking at the expanse of cream duvet, ever so slightly rumpled, and the old brass bedstead. It was a king-size, yet it didn't dwarf the room.

But there was a chaise-longue there – a vintage one, in pale cream with gilt edging. It was adorned with heart-

233

shaped cushions. Two plump, blood-red velvet hearts. It was a strange thing to see in a bachelor's bedroom, she found herself thinking, until she realized they had probably always been there. Another little touch from the past.

As they went around the rest of the house she saw more and more evidence of his mother's hand: the pretty little Dresden-style shepherdess with her crook on the dresser in the drawing room; the set of china dogs playing musical instruments on the fireplace; the silk flower arrangement on a dark wood bookcase. There weren't many photographs, although she thought she'd seen a frame on the chest of drawers in his bedroom. They hadn't lingered there.

Then, over dinner – the best ragu sauce she had tasted outside Italy – they used linen napkins, with silver cutlery, and had cut crystal glasses for their wine.

'Very posh,' she said, feeling easy enough with him to take the mickey just a tiny bit. 'At my house you'd get mismatched china.'

'I'm still at the trying-to-impress-you stage,' he said, his eyes dancing with amusement.

'It's working,' she said, and then, after a little pause, 'Are these family heirlooms?'

He nodded, and then he went on hesitantly, 'Do you think it's weird, keeping around so much of her stuff?' He didn't wait for her to reply, but rushed on: 'After she died I think . . . well, I was too young to make that decision so everything stayed here. I know this house reflects her personality, not mine, but I wouldn't know where to start. I don't know what to keep and what to let go.'

Compassion flooded through her. She was suddenly aware that she could really hurt him if she wasn't careful. Jojo reached across the table and touched his hand. 'What I think, sweetie,' she said slowly, 'is that you did what was best then. You can have a clear-out any time. Now, or in the future. You don't need to keep everything – you won't be betraying her memory if you let some of it go. When all's said and done, it's just stuff.'

He was nodding, his eyes uncertain.

Jojo warmed to her theme. 'Maybe you could keep a few things that especially remind you of your mum. You could get someone to help you? Simon, maybe?'

'We're not close, Simon and I.' He stared at the tablecloth, then back into her eyes. 'Would you help me?'

'Er . . .'

He heard her doubts and retracted the question almost immediately. 'No, it's too much. I shouldn't—'

'I'm happy to help,' Jojo heard herself saying. Even as she thought, *This could be a minefield. One wrong step and I'll be trampling all over his grief.*

'We can talk about it another time. But thank you.' He struggled to gather himself, she had the feeling that he did not often appear so vulnerable. He stood up to clear the empty pasta bowls. 'Tiramisu,' he said, in a voice that was close to his normal one. 'That is, if you're not too full?'

'I'm never too full for tiramisu,' Jojo said, looking up at him and feeling her emotions shift and change. Humans were such complex creatures. Sometimes when people were at their most vulnerable they were also at their strongest.

When he came back to the table he had composed himself once more. 'I was hoping you might tell me about Alan,' he said. 'If that's not too personal.'

She knew she should. He wasn't the only one who was clinging tightly to the past. If this was going anywhere she needed to be honest with him.

'I met Alan when I was thirty-two,' she told him, between spoonfuls of the dark, velvety tiramisu. 'Wow! How do you get it so smooth?'

'Secret recipe.' He winked.

She smiled, grateful to him for lightening the atmosphere. She had never found it easy to talk about her disastrous marriages.

'I hadn't been out with anyone seriously for years,' she went on slowly. 'I'd had my fingers burned the first time round. We were both too young to get married. Barely nineteen. I think I married the first time round because I wanted to get away from home. It only lasted eighteen months. He worked on the oil rigs and fell for someone else – it was as simple as that. I think that in all our marriage we probably only spent six weeks together.' She bit her lip.

Daniel nodded, his expression soft.

'Alan came along at just the right time.' This was more painful to talk about. It had been much more real. 'Mum had just moved to Cyprus. I was feeling abandoned, I guess, even though we weren't close. Alan swept me off my feet. He told me I was beautiful. Not just told me – he made me feel it ... I've never been very confident about my body. I mean, look at me. I'm not exactly petite.'

Daniel didn't comment: he just listened. He was one of those people who listened with the whole of himself, leaning forward, attentive. Jojo couldn't tell what he was thinking.

She went on, 'I thought we were soulmates. We liked the same music, the same films, the same food. Well, actually, he was vegan, but I was going through a vegetarian phase at the time. We both liked travel – although Alan had been to a lot more places in the world than I had.'

She took a deep breath. 'We met at a Christmas party and we were married by the spring. We had an amazing few weeks. Then one evening, out of the blue, he told me he wanted to "find himself". He wanted to go on a pilgrimage to Morocco. Alone.'

'And you were happy with that?' Daniel asked, his eyes dark in the glow of candlelight.

'Well, yes. I trusted him.' She bit her lip. 'I had no idea he wasn't going to come back.' She put her hands into her lap and studied them. 'Actually, I don't think he knew that either. And, like I said, he does keep in touch. He sends me pictures of out-of-the-way places. And sometimes of people he's met.' Her voice hushed.

'And that's OK with you?' Daniel's voice was neutral now.

'Not really,' Jojo said.

'Doesn't it stop you moving on?' He made a little gesture with his hands. 'Are you waiting for him to come back, Jojo?'

'I don't think so,' she said, not wanting to tell him that part of her was doing exactly that. Or had been, until now.

He reached across and picked up her hand. 'He was right about one thing,' he said, lifting her hand to his mouth and kissing the back. 'You are very beautiful.'

CHAPTER 30

Self-esteem came from inside yourself, not from what others said. Jojo knew this, but it certainly helped when Daniel had told her she was beautiful.

He had told her this on the first night she stayed over at his house, too. In the last ten days they had become very close. She wasn't sure whether this was because they knew each other from before or because it just felt right.

She'd stayed a few times now, although on this particular night – a Tuesday – she'd planned to go home. But they'd been watching a film and it had got quite late, so she'd decided to stay.

'My neighbour will feed Sinbad,' she told Daniel, having texted to check. 'Are you sure it's okay with you?'

'Of course it is. I've got a meeting in Basingstoke tomorrow so I have to be up at the crack of dawn, but that doesn't mean you do. What time's your shift?'

'I don't need to be anywhere till ten,' she said lazily, lulled by the warmth of his company.

'Just let yourself out when you're ready,' he told her.

Even so it was a shock to wake up and find that he was no longer beside her. Directly in her line of vision was the chaise-longue with its two heart-shaped, blood-red velvet cushions. Of all the little feminine touches in the house it was those cushions that reminded Jojo most of what he'd told her about his mother. She wondered if he'd object if she moved them. He probably wouldn't notice ... still, that was a bit controlling when they'd only just started seeing each other. She yawned and glanced at her mobile phone on the bedside table. Just after 7.30. She'd have ten more minutes in bed.

The next time she woke up someone else was in the room. A young, dark-haired woman standing in the doorway with her arms folded across her chest.

Jojo jolted upright, then remembered she wasn't wearing anything and grabbing the duvet for cover. 'Who are you?' she gasped.

'I am Anoushka,' the woman said, with a fierce frown and a foreign accent. '*Who* are you?'

'I'm Jojo,' Jojo said, with all the dignity she could muster. 'I'm a friend of Daniel's.'

'A leetle more than a friend, I theenk,' said Anoushka, her eastern European accent growing stronger as her voice got crosser and louder. 'Vot are you doing in his bed?'

Jojo hesitated.

'Ha,' Anoushka said, tossing her head contemptuously. 'I think you are one of his floozies – yes? I am his cleaner.'

One of his floozies. That news hit her like a bucket of ice. And she could tell by the triumphant look on Anoushka's face that it had been intended to wound. The woman gave her a contemptuous smile, then turned on her heel and flounced out of the room as quickly as she'd appeared.

Jojo waited until the sound of Anoushka's footsteps had faded downstairs before she leaped out of bed and closed the door. Then she hotfooted it into the en-suite bathroom, just in case Anoushka came back. Why hadn't Daniel mentioned he had a cleaner coming? A cleaner who had her own key!

She got dressed, put on her make-up, which made her feel slightly more confident, and went downstairs. Last night, Daniel had said she was to help herself to breakfast as usual, and before they'd gone up to bed he'd left out a loaf of uncut bread, some jam and marmalade, the butter dish, a side plate and a knife on the dining table. These had all been cleared away, presumably by Anoushka. Jojo could hear her vacuum roaring in another part of the house.

With a streak of rebellion running through her veins, Jojo got everything out again. She carved two slices of bread and slotted them into the toaster. Then she put a pod into the automatic coffee machine, made herself coffee and carried her breakfast into the dining room.

The smell of the toast brought Anoushka hurrying back. 'Vot are you doing? You make mess!' She raised her hands in a snappy gesture of irritation. 'Huh!'

'I'm having my breakfast.' Jojo gave her a placatory smile. It would probably be wise to make friends with

Anoushka. After all, in her defence, it had probably been as much a shock for her to discover a strange woman in Daniel's bed as it had for Jojo to see one standing in the doorway.

'Don't worry,' she added, spreading marmalade on a slice of toast and cutting it in half. 'I'll clear it up again.'

Anoushka glared at her.

'Daniel didn't mention you were coming this morning or I'd have got up earlier.'

Anoushka's glare didn't waver. She would have been very pretty if she hadn't looked so cross. Jojo guessed she was twenty-six or twenty-seven. She had dark eyes, beautiful cheekbones and the kind of petite slenderness Jojo could only aspire to. Not to be deterred, she went on softly, 'How long have you been doing Daniel's cleaning?'

'Longer dan you will be sharing his bed,' Anoushka said, with a narrow look. 'Like other floozies!'

Jojo felt herself colour. She was pretty sure the references to other floozies weren't true. Daniel had already told her he hadn't been in a relationship for several months. Of course, he might have been lying, but that seemed unlikely. He wasn't the type – she knew him well enough to be confident of that.

She took a bite of her toast, unsure how to respond in a way that wouldn't be rude or inflammatory – but Anoushka didn't give her the chance to say anything else: she disappeared, and a few minutes later, she began to vacuum on the other side of the dining-room door, occasionally banging into it with the machine for good measure. So much for a peaceful breakfast!

When Daniel called her at home later that evening, she said, 'I met your cleaner this morning.'

'Anoushka?' He sounded surprised. 'That's odd – she doesn't usually do Wednesdays. She didn't tell me she was changing her day.' There was a little pause. 'I hope everything was okay with her?'

'She wasn't in a very good mood.' Jojo told him what had happened. 'How long has she worked for you?'

'About eighteen months. Why?'

'She seemed to think I was one of many ... er ... girl-friends,' Jojo told him.

'Did she now? I'll have words. You're not!' he added hastily. 'She can be a bit on the sharp side, but she's a good cleaner. And her heart's in the right place.'

Anoushka's heart, Jojo thought, very likely belonged to her employer. It had to be the reason she'd been so antagonistic towards Jojo – although Daniel probably didn't have a clue.

'Remind me to tell you about her history,' he added. 'It's quite interesting.'

'I can't wait,' Jojo said, imagining him sitting at his dining table, his phone pressed to his ear, his head tipped to one side as it did when he was a little uncertain.

'What are you up to?' he asked her.

She was sitting at her own little table in the conservatory with her laptop open in front of her. When he'd phoned she'd been googling 'grounds for divorce'. She told him that now. 'I want to move on,' she said. 'I've left it way too long. I've actually just discovered we have grounds already because we've been separated for more than two years. If I wait another six months I won't even need to ask for his consent.'

'What do you want to do?' His voice was neutral and she wished she hadn't started this conversation on the phone.

'I think I'd like closure,' she said. 'I don't think I'm very good at letting go sometimes.'

'Well, I can certainly relate to that.' Daniel's voice was gentle now and she could hear the wry humour in it. And she thought again about his mother's things everywhere in his house. There was a pause and he went on, 'If you need any help with any of it, let me know.'

'Thanks.'

They said their goodbyes and she put the phone down, feeling curiously choked up. He was so nice. She swallowed and looked out of the conservatory window. Dusk was beginning to shadow the darkening sea. A silver moon path tracked across the water, angling out to the horizon. Al was out there somewhere – across the ocean in a land far away. She'd been assuming these last few weeks that he would want the same as her – want them both to be free to move on. But what if he wanted to stay married?

That could be awkward.

CHAPTER 31

Jojo didn't have time to mull over anything for very long: it was the busiest week she'd had in ages. March was always a good month for babies. The results of summer romances – or romantic holidays abroad, she'd often thought. Lucky beggars.

Daniel was busy at the moment too. They were both finishing work late so couldn't see each other, although they did talk on the phone every day. He was good at texting, too. Without fail he sent her a goodnight text last thing and another in the morning, with some little comment like *Have a good day*, or *Sweet dreams, lovely*.

They were very reassuring, those texts. She liked knowing that he was thinking about her, even when they weren't together. That their romance was growing legs that would carry them into the future, becoming something solid and real and good.

She started reading *Rebecca*. Having seen the film she was intrigued. Anne Marie was right: it was more accessible than some of the others they'd read lately. Daphne du Maurier was a superb writer, in Jojo's (far from expert) opinion. She wished she could warm to the unnamed heroine a little more, though. She seemed so paranoid and worried that her new husband might not love her – not to mention her total obsession with the dead wife. 'For goodness' sake, just ask him!' Jojo muttered to the book, one night in bed. 'Is he still in love with his ex? How can I ever match up? Blah blah blah . . .'

A thought struck her. Wasn't she being just a tiny bit that way herself? But in her case it wasn't about her new love, but her old. Wasn't she as fearful about asking Big Al what he thought about them getting a divorce as du Maurier's heroine was about asking her new husband if he truly loved her?

There was a definite parallel, and Jojo frowned as she considered this. In every other aspect of her life she was a success story. She was financially independent. She had a great career. She was well-respected among her colleagues. She had some good friends.

Yet she hadn't been able to let go of the memory of Big Al.

Jojo put the book down firmly on the bedside table, flung back the heavy patchwork quilt that covered her duvet and went to retrieve her mobile phone on the other side of the bedroom.

She clicked on her messages and read Big Al's most recent text: *Kolkata is hot. But the temples are cool. Will be offline for a bit. Hope you doing OK x*

When had he gone to India? She hadn't kept up lately. At least he had asked after her, which showed a snippet of concern – she'd lived on those for a while. After the big phone call. The phone call that had come after he'd been away for just four and a half weeks. The phone call when he had said, 'I'm sorry. I needed to get away for a while. I felt too hemmed in. It's not you, it's me.' All those crass, crass platitudes from a man she'd thought would never do platitudes.

'Are you ever coming back?' She was holding tightly to the mobile phone with her fingers all sweaty. She couldn't even up sticks and go to him. He'd never asked her to.

'One day.' She had heard the smile in his voice.

'When's one day?' And the phone had crackled and cracked, and then they'd lost the connection.

After the first six months, she'd stopped asking him when he was coming back. If anyone had ever told her she'd do that she wouldn't have believed it. But, of course, she hadn't known at first how long it was going to last. Jojo loved him so much that she'd decided to give him the benefit of the doubt – go along with the idea that this was just something he needed to get out of his system. And, after a while, Big Al being away travelling had become a new normality. One of the other midwives at the hospital had a husband who was in the forces. It was a little like that. Except, of course, Kenny came home between postings and Big Al never did.

Jojo flicked through the texts. She had kept every one. It was no way to sustain a marriage, both of them hanging on to the end of a line. No, it was Jojo that was hanging on, not Big Al. He was doing what he wanted to do. She had never been consulted. How had this become normal?

With her fingers trembling slightly, she began to type out a reply to his latest text. *I want a divorce.* No, that was too harsh. It wasn't the kind of thing you could put in a text . . . Maybe she should phone him. She had no idea what time zone he might be in. He had told her once not to phone. In case it was inconvenient.

Inconvenient! She was his wife. Jojo felt a hot anger rolling up through her. How had she ever let this go on for so long? It was insane.

She dialled his number. No answer.

She went back to the text: *Al, we need to talk. I think it's time we ended our marriage. I assume that's what you want too. Get in touch, please.*

Even as she pressed 'send' she wished she hadn't added the last word. What kind of weak, people-pleasing behaviour was that? She was so weak.

Jojo half expected to hear the answering ping of his reply that evening, but her phone stayed silent. There was no reply the next day either. By lunchtime she was beginning to relax a bit. All the night-time paranoia had flittered away beneath the weight of the midday sun, and tonight Daniel was coming to dinner. It wouldn't be the first time he'd been to hers, but it would be the first time she'd cooked for him.

The first time he'd stayed over. The first time they would have the opportunity to sit in her garden and eat pastries and drink coffee, overlooking the sea because it was Saturday morning and there was no need to rush off. So many firsts. And no chance of Anoushka gate-crashing their peace! Bliss.

Daniel arrived at 6.30, bearing flowers.

'Thank you,' she said, snipping an inch off the stems and breathing in their mixed scents as she transferred them to a chunky glass vase. 'They're beautiful.'

'I'm still trying to impress you,' he told her.

'It's still working.' She kissed him, inhaling his scent too, which was becoming familiar, synonymous with warmth and laughter and love – *could it be love*? She felt a little rush of happiness. She should have done this months ago. Years, even! Gone out on dates, asked Al for a divorce, taken charge of the situation – she should have done it all.

She led Daniel out through the conservatory and on to the patio. He stood among the mishmash of pots and looked out, past her short, sloping garden, past the little wall at the foot, past the mustard-coloured sand that ran on down to the shoreline. And beyond that to the mirror-calm expanse of sea that stretched out to infinity. Then he turned towards her and smiled. 'Wow,' he said. 'Do you ever get tired of this view?'

'No,' Jojo said, taking a deep breath of the sea-scented air. 'And I don't think I ever will.'

*

That night they made love in her enormously comfy double bed. And in the morning they ate pastries on the patio: cinnamon-scented swirls, *pains au chocolat* and chocolate and raisin twists. And the sun, surprisingly bright for an early March morning, shone down on them. Seagulls dipped and soared against the pale sky, and Jojo thought she had never felt so happy.

Daniel was just helping her take the breakfast things back into the kitchen when there was a knock at the front door. No, not a knock ... a noise. The sound of the front door banging, and a scuffling in the hall, like the sound the postman made when he was trying to put a parcel through the letterbox. Jojo went out in alarm to see what was going on. And there he was in her hall. Not the postman, but Big Al. Filling it with his presence, the sunburned scent of him. She had forgotten how large he was. How tall: six foot four of muscle – a wall of solidness in her hall.

'What are you doing here?' The words were shocked out of her. She had been anticipating a reaction – a text, maybe a phone call – not for him to turn up in person. How was that even possible? Kolkata was more than a twelve-hour flight away. 'How ... ?' She tailed off as he turned towards her, having dumped a backpack on the floor. His eyes were just as she remembered. Sharp, blue and perceptive. And that little scar on his upper right cheekbone, made whiter by his tan.

'How did I get here so fast?' He gave her a long, slow smile. 'I wasn't that far away, Jojo. How else?' His gaze raked over her. Assessing, considering. 'I was in France.'

'I thought you were in Kolkata.'

'I flew to Paris last week. The most romantic of cities. I must take you there.' A beat. 'You're looking very well, my beautiful wife. You have a positive glow about you. I wonder why . . .'

And now he grew dangerously quiet. His eyes like a cat's, narrowing on its prey.

Jojo was aware that Daniel had come up behind her in the doorway that led from the kitchen to the hall.

'Why don't you introduce me to your friend?'

She did not have to feel guilty. There was absolutely no reason she should. He had walked out on their marriage four and a half years ago. By anyone's standards it was outrageous, yet she could feel the hot shame creeping up her neck.

'Daniel Mannings,' Daniel said, stepping forward, and Jojo couldn't decide whether this was very brave or extremely foolhardy. Daniel wasn't a small man, but he was no match for Al. Jojo could smell the testosterone.

'You have no right to be here,' she said quietly to Big Al. 'You walked out of our marriage, remember?'

'Fair comment,' he said, lifting his hands in a little gesture of acceptance. 'But I thought we had an arrangement, Jojo. The odd date, the odd little dalliance.' He looked down his nose at Daniel. 'You are a woman of needs. I accept that. Just as I am a man of big appetites.'

'That's not—' Jojo broke off, as she felt Daniel's shock, heard his sharp intake of breath in the silence. When she looked at him, there was a kind of frozen stillness to his face.

'I'll go,' he said, meeting her eyes for a second before dropping his gaze. He stepped past them both and opened the front door.

Jojo's mouth was dry. She started to go after him. 'Daniel, please wait!'

He paused briefly at her gate. 'You have things to sort out, Jojo. Obviously.' The hurt she had seen fleetingly in his eyes was gone. His face was blank, closing her out, as he turned to unlock his car. But in that moment she felt something break inside her. A little precious thing shattered by that look on his face.

All the warmth had fled from the day.

When she looked back, Big Al was filling the doorway of her cottage.

CHAPTER 32

He was in her kitchen when she went back inside, busying himself with the kettle at the sink. 'Do you have any green tea?'

'No.' She walked towards him slowly. 'And I want you to leave.'

'But I've only just got back.' He had a faint twang she didn't remember, as though he'd picked up an accent on his travels, his voice sounded foreign and faintly exotic. 'I thought you wanted to talk,' he said. 'That's why you got hold of me? Well, apart from to bin me, that is.' There was something else in his voice too: an edge of hardness.

He had found the ordinary tea and had put two bags into a mug, mashing the liquid into a dark syrup the way he had always preferred it. 'Do you want one?' he added, as an afterthought.

'No.' She picked up a teaspoon and rinsed it, found a cloth

and wiped away tea stains from the work surface. She couldn't get past him in the galley kitchen. There wasn't room. They could only stand alongside each other. It brought back a long-ago memory of them cooking here – in the early days of their marriage.

She felt a bittersweet ache. 'I didn't know if you were ever coming back.'

A little silence as he sipped his tea and looked at her over the rim of the mug. 'Yeah, but you know *me*, Jojo.' He reached out a hand, and before she could stop him, he touched her very lightly on the cheek. 'You knew I wouldn't abandon you.'

'No, I didn't.' She jumped back to get out of his range. She needed to feel angry with him, but she just wanted to burst into tears.

'You can't stay here,' she said, summoning all the self-control she could muster. 'I need you to leave now.'

He rose to leave, picking up his backpack from the hall. 'Call me when you're ready to talk,' he said, over his shoulder. 'When you've calmed down.'

She drove straight over to Daniel's. Every traffic light was red, as if they were conspiring against her. Impatience thrummed in every pore of her body.

When she got there Daniel's car was outside. There was another car too. A little yellow Citroën, which turned out to be Anoushka's.

The cleaner opened the door on her first ring. Almost as if she had been waiting behind it.

'Mr Mannings eez out,' she said.

'No, he's not. His car's there.' Jojo gestured to it. 'Let me in, Anoushka, please. I really need to talk to him.'

'Is not possible.' Anoushka waved her hand in a shooing motion. 'Go away.'

Jojo shook her head. This was ridiculous. She tried an experimental push of the front door and realized, to her shock, that it was on the chain.

'Go away,' Anoushka repeated.

Jojo considered shouting for him. He would come, surely he would – after all they had shared.

But what if he didn't? She remembered that look on his face and she was suddenly doubtful. She bit her lip. 'Then would you at least give him a message?'

'Vot message?' The cleaner raised her eyebrows.

She took a deep breath. 'Could you please tell him that I'm very sorry about the misunderstanding with my husband?'

'You *very* sorry you 'ave husband,' Anoushka repeated, her voice dripping with sarcasm.

'No. I'm sorry about the misunderstanding, not the husband.'

'*Do* have husband? Do *not* have husband?' Behind the narrow gap in the door Anoushka folded her arms.

Jojo suppressed the urge to scream. 'Please tell Daniel that I will call him,' she said. 'Please tell him I came round.'

Anoushka nodded. There was a triumphant gleam in her eyes. Jojo suspected she had no intention of passing on a message to Daniel. At least not the kind of message that would help Jojo's case.

Jojo's heart was beating very fast as she walked back to her car, her footsteps crunching on the gravel. She imagined that Daniel was watching her from his bedroom window, where they'd so often made love.

He must know she was here. He would have heard the bell. The house wasn't so big that he couldn't have heard Anoushka telling her to go.

If he was here then he didn't want to see her. And who could blame him?

It was just starting to rain, the spring promise of the day dissolving into drizzle. Jojo couldn't bear the thought of going home. She didn't want to bump into Al, who might have decided to return to the house. She had forgotten to ask him for his key, which meant that her husband could drop by at any time he chose. That had been stupid.

She would have to lay down some ground rules. He couldn't just walk into her house any time he wanted to. She would have to tell him that she'd meant it about getting a divorce. In truth, she hadn't quite thought beyond that to the *implications* . . . would she have to give him half the house? Would she have to support him?

Big Al had never had a steady job that she knew of. When she'd met him he'd been a roadie for a band. He'd also done stints of long-distance driving, the odd bit of private security work. She was pretty sure he'd never voted. Had he ever even paid tax?

She needed to talk to someone. She drove around the corner from Daniel's, parked up and scrolled through her phone. Her finger hovered over Kate's number. Kate had enough problems of her own – she and Anton had officially separated now and Kate had begun divorce proceedings. But that at least meant Kate would understand. And they'd seen quite a bit of each other lately.

Kate answered her phone on the third ring. 'Jojo, how are you, lovely?'

'I'm not so good actually,' Jojo said. 'I've just had a situation with my new man. Now I'm sitting in my car wondering what on earth to do next.'

'I'm in Exeter shopping for a Mother's Day present,' Kate said. 'Why don't you come here? We can meet at the Costa in the centre. Do you know it?'

'I do,' Jojo said, thinking, Mother's Day – gosh, she'd almost left it too late to send a card. And she did send one usually, even though it was rarely acknowledged.

Twenty minutes later she and Kate were in the coffee-scented Saturday bustle of Costa. Kate kissed both her cheeks and put her bags down by the chair. 'Are you OK, Jojo?'

'I don't think I am really, no.' Jojo put her elbows on the table. The warmth of her friend's voice was sparking tears. Blinking, she told Kate what had happened. 'So now Daniel thinks I have some sort of weird polyamory set-up with my husband that he got caught up in,' she finished. 'It's not true, Kate.'

'You just need to talk to Daniel,' Kate said. 'It would help if you could get past his cleaner, wouldn't it? She sounds like a right little madam.'

Jojo managed a smile. 'Daniel says she has an "interesting" background.'

'Well, she won't be guarding his door for ever. Why don't you phone him?' She leaned across the table. 'I'll go and get us some carrot cake if you want to give it a try.' She smiled as she got up. 'There aren't many traumas that cake can't improve. A very wise woman told me that.'

Jojo felt a little choked up again. It was a weird old thing that – how kindness in the bleakest moments choked one up.

Daniel's mobile went straight to answerphone. He must have switched it off, she thought, shocked. Doctors rarely did that, even when they weren't on call. At least, Daniel didn't. Like her, he always had one ear open for his job, for the people who depended on him.

She didn't leave him a message. The last thing she wanted was to complicate the situation further. Goodness knows what Anoushka had told him, but it certainly wouldn't put Jojo in a good light.

'Any joy?' Kate came back with the cake.

Jojo shook her head. 'It's probably best if I phone him from somewhere quiet anyway. I hope we'll be able to sort things out.'

'So how about your ex?' Kate asked softly. 'Is he back for good?'

'I don't know. I barely spoke to him,' Jojo said. 'He seemed to think it would be okay for him to stay in the house, obviously I threw him out.'

Kate looked outraged on her behalf. 'The cheeky beggar.'

Jojo took a sip of her coffee. 'I'm worried,' she began, 'that he'll have some kind of legal claim on the house.'

'But didn't you buy it before you were married?'

'Yes,' Jojo said. 'Well, when I say bought, the mortgage company owns most of it!'

'And has Alan ever contributed?' Kate smiled. 'Sorry, I'm beginning to sound like a textbook. But I'm seeing a solicitor at the moment myself, as you know.' She paused. 'He didn't even live there very long, did he?'

'Barely three months.'

'Don't worry then,' Kate said. 'No court in the land is going to award him half your house. Not in the circumstances.' She rummaged in her bag and drew out a business card. 'This is the solicitor I'm seeing,' she said. 'She's really nice. And, more importantly, scarily efficient.'

'Is she expensive?' Jojo asked.

'None of them are cheap, are they? But I think you can get a half-hour's free advice. Tell her I recommended her to you.'

'I will,' Jojo said, putting the card in her purse. She leaned forward. 'Thank you, Kate. I really, really appreciate this.'

'Sweetie, you don't have to thank me.' Kate's eyes went a little sparkly. 'It wasn't very long ago that I turned up on your doorstep in absolute bits. You were amazing. You saved my life. Or, at least, my sanity.' Her voice husked over the words. 'You told me about your Three-Step Feeling Better Plan. Don't you remember?'

'Yes, of course I do,' Jojo said softly, not wanting to confess that it was much harder to follow one's own advice when it came to these things.

'Don't you remember Step Three? It was to think about what you want,' Kate added.

'Well,' said Jojo, 'I wish I'd got Alan's key back from him. I know that!'

'Would you like some help there? It would certainly be a good idea to make it impossible for him to swan in and out of your house any time he pleases.'

'How?' Jojo said, frowning. 'Are you offering to help me track him down and forcibly get his key off him? He's not going to want to give it back. And he's a big bloke.'

Kate's beautiful dark eyes held a glint of amused determination. 'No, my darling. As tempting as that idea is, I think you should change the locks.'

'Finding a locksmith on a Saturday afternoon is going to be pretty tricky,' Jojo said.

'You're forgetting that I'm currently going out with a builder.' Kate smiled. 'I'm sure Bob won't mind changing the locks for you. It won't take him any time at all.' She whisked out her phone and Jojo watched as she dialled and spoke rapidly.

'No problem,' she said, disconnecting again. 'Bob's going to meet us over there in an hour. Does that suit you?'

Jojo nodded.

'Girl power,' Kate said, with a smile. 'Well, and a little help from Bob the builder.'

CHAPTER 33

By early evening Jojo had a new front-door key in her hand and two spares in the cupboard.

Bob had refused to let her pay for anything, except the cost of the materials.

'Well, that's sorted then.' Kate sighed. 'You don't really know someone until you start divorce proceedings against them. You'd be amazed at some of the stunts Anton's tried to pull so far.'

Jojo nodded, sobered by the expression on Kate's face. 'I didn't think he'd *want* to stay married to me,' she said. 'I certainly didn't think he'd come back like this.'

'Well I wouldn't waste too much time feeling sorry for him, Jojo. He didn't have a problem swanning off round the world while he thought you were sitting at home waiting for him, did he?'

'No.' Jojo felt a deep sense of shame rising in her again.

She was very aware of Bob pretending not to listen a few feet away. 'Thanks again for today,' she said. 'I'm certainly going to sort it out now.'

'Good. And if you need any help, or if you're worried about anything at all, just call me, OK? I'm only up the road.'

It was odd when they'd gone and she was alone in the house again. She felt suddenly very vulnerable.

How long would it be before Al came back? He wouldn't be very happy when he discovered she'd changed the locks on him.

She decided to take the initiative and phone him.

There was no answer.

Frustrated, she tried Daniel again. This time he picked up. 'Hello, Jojo,' he said, in a voice so distant she could have wept.

'I need to explain,' she said.

'You don't,' he said. 'I get it.'

She had one chance, she thought. One chance to get him to listen.

'Alan wasn't telling the truth,' she said. 'About us having an arrangement, I mean. We've barely spoken for the last few years. There has never been any kind of arrangement between us. Not the kind he was talking about.'

'I see,' Daniel said, noncommittal, but at least he hadn't hung up on her.

'Please can we meet? I can come to you. Or you can come here.' She sighed. 'I've just had the locks changed so Alan can't walk in. Like he did before.'

There was a small silence. She held her breath.

'All right,' he said at last. 'But I think it would be better if you came here.'

'I'll come now,' she said, before he could change his mind.

There were no red traffic lights to hold her up this time. Neither was Anoushka's car in the drive, thank goodness, though the hall smelt of beeswax polish and citrus air freshener.

He invited her into the dining room and she sat stiffly while he made coffee. It felt so different from the times they'd been there before. She tried to imagine how she'd have reacted if their positions had been reversed: if he'd had an ex-wife who'd turned up and announced a claim on him.

She bit her lip. Yes, she'd probably have behaved exactly like Daniel. In fact, she'd most likely have run a mile and never come back. She was lucky he was listening to her at all.

He sat opposite her on one of the high-backed dining chairs. He'd been avoiding her eyes, but for the first time he looked at her and then away, as if it pained him.

'I'm so sorry,' she began. 'I was as shocked as you were when Alan turned up like that.'

He nodded, his expression wary.

'It was probably my fault,' she said, 'because I sent him a text telling him I wanted to start divorce proceedings. I was expecting him to respond, but I didn't think he'd just come back.'

He frowned. 'I see.'

Her mobile rang in her bag. She pulled it out and switched it off.

'Was that him?' Daniel asked, and Jojo so wanted to lie, but she couldn't. She nodded.

'Can I ask you a question?' Daniel said.

'Of course.'

'Do you still love him?'

'I still care about him.' She met his eyes. 'But I don't want to be with him. Our marriage has been finished for a very long time. I would never have started seeing you if it hadn't.'

For a moment he didn't say anything, but some of the tension had gone out of the air.

She sipped her coffee. 'I'm sorry,' she said again.

'No, don't apologize.' His eyes warmed a fraction. 'Maybe I overreacted. It was a shock.' He hesitated. 'I think I owe you an apology, too. Anoushka told me you came round and that she hadn't let you in.'

'You were here, then?'

'No. I'd walked up to the corner shop to get some milk. And a paper.' A copy of the *Guardian* was neatly folded on the table in front of them. She was so glad he hadn't been in the house, hiding from her.

'She's very protective.' Jojo gave a wry smile, and as it seemed a day for honesty, she went on, 'She doesn't like me. She made that clear the first time we met. She was very antagonistic, to be honest.'

'I don't think it's personal,' Daniel said. 'She may be jealous.'

'Because she wants you for herself?' Jojo asked cautiously, and he looked startled.

'No, nothing like that. Because of your profession. She saw your uniform, I think, and your bag downstairs. Anyway, she clearly knows you're a midwife and that probably didn't help.'

'You've lost me,' Jojo said, and Daniel frowned.

'Sorry. I'll start from the beginning. Anoushka is a friend of a friend. Ben introduced us because he thought I might be able to help her with a job at the Royal. In medicine, I mean.'

'She wants to be a doctor?' Jojo said, surprised.

'She *is* a doctor. In Romania she's fully qualified. She came here to work. But it's not quite as simple as it used to be. So many forms – and it all costs money . . . She doesn't have much.'

'Oh, my goodness.' Jojo remembered the young woman's anger. 'So she's ended up cleaning. Poor Anoushka – not being allowed to do what she loves.'

'It's incredibly frustrating for her. I've put her in touch with some people who will be useful to her, but it's all taking longer than she'd hoped.' He leaned across and touched Jojo's hand. 'Suffice to say, it's made me see how very lucky I am, how very privileged to have come from a background where there was enough money.'

'Yes, me too,' she said, suddenly seeing Anoushka with different eyes. 'I take it for granted.'

'When I first met Anoushka we had some pretty heated discussions about it. But then she realized I was on her side.

Since then we've settled into a kind of mutual respect. But seeing you has stirred it all up again for her. I don't think she's angry with you personally. You're just a convenient target!'

Daniel asked Jojo if she'd like to stay the night but she said, no, she would go home and return the call she'd missed from Al. She'd much have preferred to stay, she thought, as she drove back through the darkness towards home.

She'd always loved the location of her house. It was far enough away from others so she didn't feel hemmed in, but close enough to its one neighbour that she didn't feel isolated. Except that the adjoining semi was a holiday cottage and at the moment it was empty.

As Jojo parked in her space outside she felt suddenly terribly alone. There were no neighbours within running distance. If Al were to step out of the shadows she'd be at his mercy. Even in her fear she knew she was being over-dramatic. Al wasn't going to hurt her ... but the memory of his anger stayed with her, and her fingers shook as she got out her front-door key. Why was it your fingers never worked properly when you were in a hurry?

She got the door open, stepped inside and shut it behind her. All was quiet and normal. Putting on lights as she moved through the house, she checked the downstairs windows, the conservatory door and finally the two bedrooms upstairs, her own and the spare. Even though it was irrational because he couldn't be hiding in here.

Something banged in the conservatory downstairs and she jumped out of her skin, then realized it was just Sinbad, strolling in to say hello.

She made some hot chocolate and sent Daniel a text, as promised, to tell him she was safely home. A few moments later she heard the answering ping of his reply. Looking at his name on her mobile warmed her, made her feel safer.

For a while she sat in the conservatory in the dark, aware that if she put the lights on she could be seen from outside. Then she took a deep breath and returned Alan's call. She was not entirely surprised when he didn't answer. She was beginning to grasp that all the conversations they had were on his terms. Probably every conversation they'd ever had had been on his terms. Not just since he'd been away, but maybe before that, even. She'd been thinking about the past a lot lately.

Except for those first few heady weeks of their marriage, she didn't remember having much of a say. Al had moved into her house, had come and gone as he'd pleased – she'd been so bowled over with new love she hadn't minded that he didn't contribute much.

He *had* cooked, though. She remembered how cool she'd thought that was. Proper recipes that took hours to prepare, dishes that had involved soaking dried beans for days and using a wooden pestle and mortar. Recipes that had needed spices and herbs that guys hadn't usually heard of, let alone knew how to use.

It had all been so amazingly bohemian and free. She'd truly thought him to be her soulmate in those early days, even when he'd gone off to find himself without her. And she'd believed herself to be so liberal and generous. 'It's something he needs to do,' she'd told her friends. 'Why would I mind? We trust each other.'

It was funny when you were part of a couple how that happened. You became a kind of mirror to each other. You grew more aware of all the good bits about yourself from how the other person reacted to you. You grew more aware of all the bad bits too. She had tried not to feel jealous in those first few months. Of the places he was seeing, the people he was meeting. *If you love something you let it go.* She'd had that quote on a fridge magnet with a picture of a dove being released from someone's hands.

She'd stand in front of the fridge and look at it when she felt sad. Trying to will herself back into the place of peaceful acceptance where it was okay for him to go off and leave her alone. Telling herself that it was all fine and normal. Even though she knew deep down that it wasn't.

What had happened to that dove magnet? It had been years since she'd thought about it.

She felt very weary when she finally went upstairs to bed, and as she slid beneath the coolness of her duvet she wished she'd stayed at Daniel's, instead of coming home to make a call that she should have known Al wouldn't answer. She was still waiting for Al, she realized, even now. She was still letting him dictate the terms.

She switched off the bedside light and lay for a while in the darkness, listening to the cries of the gulls, the ticking of the clock on the mantelpiece, the familiar night sounds of home.

She slept fitfully, waking several times in the night to imagined noises outside and the whirring white noise of her mind. At one point she put on the bedside light and decided to read a chapter of *Rebecca* in the hope that it would distract her. But *Rebecca* was not a peaceful book. The heroine's head was still full of the shadows of the past, full of the fear that her new husband might not love her as he'd loved his late wife. She seemed to spend most of her time worrying that she might lose him.

Rebecca was not exactly a cosy bedtime read, Jojo decided, putting it down and switching off the light. She was better off with her own thoughts. And they weren't exactly peaceful either. There was a great deal to sort out, she decided, before she could feel truly peaceful again.

CHAPTER 34

Jojo was woken by her phone ringing. Suddenly she was wide awake, jolted from her tangle of dreams, convinced it was going to be Al. But it wasn't. It was Daniel.

'Hi, I didn't wake you, did I?'

'No. Well, yes. But I'm glad you did. What time is it?'

'Eight thirty. I just wanted to check you were all right. No more unexpected visits from Alan.'

'No. Thank you. It's good to hear your voice.'

'Likewise,' he said softly. 'What are you up to today? Can I take you to lunch?'

'That sounds lovely,' she said.

'I'll pick you up about half noon.'

They went to Ocean Views. It was warm enough to sit outside, and as they chatted in the soft spring sun, with the backdrop of the ocean sparkling like a mirror of blue diamonds behind them, it was almost possible to believe that everything was back to normal.

'I started clearing out my mum's stuff this morning,' Daniel told her. 'I spoke to Simon about it yesterday. He's coming over on Tuesday night to look at some bits and pieces – see if there's anything he wants to keep.'

'That sounds like progress,' Jojo said, then frowned. 'Didn't you tell me you two didn't get on?'

'We're not close,' Daniel said, 'but she was his mum too. I thought it was the right thing to do.' He hesitated. 'I won't chuck everything out. I just plan to make the house look less like a mausoleum. That isn't the right word . . . but you know what I mean?' His eyes were hopeful that she would understand, and she did.

'You want to put your own stamp on the place,' she said. 'Yes, that makes total sense. It's been a long time since she died, hasn't it?'

'It's seventeen years on Friday,' he said ruefully. 'Sometimes it feels like five minutes and sometimes it feels like for ever.' A beat. 'I was afraid at first that I would forget her. I think that's why I didn't change anything. But you said something the other day that made me realize I wouldn't.'

'Really?' She couldn't remember what it was. She took his hand across the table.

'You said I didn't need every single possession she'd owned to remember her. You said that one or two mementos were enough. That the rest was just stuff and I shouldn't feel guilty about clearing things out. That really resonated with me.' He touched his chest with the hand Jojo wasn't holding. 'In here.'

Jojo smiled. 'I'm glad,' she said. 'Would you like some help with your clear-out? Or would you rather do it by yourself?'

'I'd love you to help. Thank you. Not today, though. Maybe one evening.'

'Of course,' Jojo said, feeling warmth spreading through her. It would be a pleasure to help Daniel, despite everything that was going on with Al.

He paid the bill and they drove back. There was peace in the car now. Jojo felt as if they'd weathered the first small storm in their relationship and come out even closer than before. *What doesn't kill you makes you stronger.* Another fridge magnet she'd had. She was pretty sure that had disappeared too. What happened to all the fridge magnets? Did they end up in the same place as all the odd socks?

She was still pondering this when they drew up outside her house and discovered that Alan was waiting by the front door.

'I'm coming with you,' Daniel said. 'I don't want you seeing him on your own. Not after the locks.'

'There's no need,' she murmured, but she was glad that he ignored her. The slams of their car doors seemed overloud in the Sunday afternoon quiet.

Alan waited, unsmiling, as they approached.

Jojo was slightly ahead of Daniel. Before she had unlatched the front gate, Alan called, 'So I'm locked out of my own house now, am I? I'd like to see what a lawyer has to say about that.'

'It's not your house,' she said. 'It's mine.' She hoped he couldn't hear the wobble in her voice.

'I think you'll find that that changed when we got married. I'm not the one who committed adultery, either,' he said, glancing at Daniel. His voice was mild but she could feel his anger.

'I'm glad you're here,' she said, 'because we do have a lot to talk about.' She unlocked the front door, acutely aware of the two men on the path behind her, the tension in the air.

When they were all in her conservatory, Al said, 'Call me strange, but I actually don't fancy discussing private matters that should be between my wife and myself in front of her lover.'

Jojo turned in time to see Daniel flush. She met his eyes. 'It's all right,' she told him. 'We'll be fine. I'll phone you if I need you.'

'Yeah, mate.' Al raised his hands in a gesture of surrender. 'Don't worry. It's not about to get physical. Unless the lady wants it to get physical ... do you, Jojo?' There was a glimmer of a smile on his face.

'What I want is for you to be out of my life. Officially and for good,' she said, and now she knew her voice was strong. Because he had angered her just now with his accusation of adultery and his assumption that he had a claim on her home. The home he'd never contributed so much as a penny towards.

She saw Daniel out. At the front door he said quietly, 'I'm going to wait up the road. Text me in an hour to let me

272

know you're OK. If I don't hear from you, I'll assume you're not and I'll come back.'

'I'll text you,' she said. 'And thank you.'

When she went back into the conservatory Alan was lounging in the larger of her cane chairs. Even so, he looked too big for it, his long, jeans-clad legs at odds with the flower-patterned prettiness of the cushions.

'Finally,' he said. 'We get the chance for a proper chat.'

'I phoned you yesterday,' Jojo snapped. 'You didn't answer.'

'I must have been in a bad area.' He rubbed his chin and looked at her thoughtfully. 'I owe you an apology, Jojo. I shouldn't have stayed away so long.'

'No,' she said, disarmed by the sincerity in his voice, and by his complete turnaround. That was the last thing she'd been expecting.

'I was a fool. I should have known you wouldn't wait.'

'I did wait.' The words were stung out of her. 'I waited and waited and you never came back. You didn't even phone.'

'That was very wrong of me.' His eyes held hers. His eyes were summer-blue and guileless and his voice was softer than she had ever heard it. 'Can you forgive me?'

She had been ready to fight with him. She had been armed with anger, but she couldn't hold on to it in the face of such a humble apology.

A part of her was responding to him, and he knew it. He didn't say anything else. He didn't make a single move towards her. He just stayed perfectly still in the chair and waited, and all the while she could feel her resolve crumbling.

She could feel the well of pain that she had pushed down deep for so long trying to burst out of her. She wasn't angry any more. She wanted to sob and sob for the man she had once loved so much. She wanted to weep for all they had lost. The grief that she had kept a tight lid on these past four years was rising in her chest.

'Can you forgive me, Jojo?' he said again.

She had planned to say, 'No, it's too late, I've moved on,' but what actually came out was a muffled sob. She sank into a chair by the table and rested her elbows on the blue chequered cloth. Tears were pouring down her face. She hadn't cried for so long that it was a blessed relief to feel them soaking her cheekbones, her throat, the neck of her blouse, the top of the scarf she wore. Carrying the pain out of her, even as they rendered her defenceless.

And then he was up and he was putting his arms around her and holding her and kissing the top of her head. 'It's okay, baby. Let it all out. Better out than in, my beautiful girl. Let it go.'

His arms felt enormously comforting. As if they were the safest place in the world. He stroked her head, everything about him so familiar that she was back in the past once more, when there had only ever been him. When she had thought there only ever *would* be him. When being with any other man was unimaginable.

When she'd finished crying, when she was surrounded by bits of soggy kitchen roll – he must have fetched it at some point and handed it to her – he made her a mug of chamomile tea.

'Calming,' he said, as he put it into her hands. 'Take these too.' He got out a little bottle of pills from his rucksack and she saw they were one of the homeopathic remedies he relied on so heavily. He never touched Western medicines. 'Ignatia,' he said, tipping three of the tiny white pills into the cap of the bottle and handing it to her. 'They're good for grief.'

Jojo took them obediently. She wasn't sure whether it was the ignatia or the catharsis of so much crying, but she was beginning to feel better.

Al sat back in his chair and smiled at her. 'You're so beautiful. Even when you cry.'

'I'm not,' she said. 'But thank you.'

'And you've lost weight,' he said, his gaze leaving her face momentarily. 'It suits you. But don't lose too much more.'

He was right: she *had* lost weight. Probably a stone since he'd gone away. For various reasons.

'You look more muscular,' she observed. Not that he'd ever been a flabby guy. He prided himself on his physique. A strapping, muscle-bound vegan – he liked the apparent contradiction of it.

'Do you think so?' He sounded pleased. His vanity was one of the things she'd always teased him about – but in an affectionate way. 'I've tried gyms all around the world,' he said. 'It's important to take care of yourself.'

'Yes,' she said, remembering the weights he'd had, which were still in a corner of the spare bedroom.

'But there's no place like home,' he said, and he smiled at her. A slow cat's smile, self-satisfied and smug, and at the same moment as her brain caught up with what he'd just said, and its implications, her mobile rang.

She fumbled for it in her bag. Saw Daniel's name on the screen. She'd forgotten all about texting him. She'd forgotten all about everything, caught as she'd been in Al's cat-and-mouse game.

She pressed answer. His voice, low and urgent, brought the crash of reality back into the room.

'Are you all right, Jojo? I know it's only just gone an hour but I was worried.'

'I'm fine,' she said. She got up, opened the patio door and took the phone out into the back garden, where she could see the choppy white horses on the sea. Where the gulls wheeled against the sky and the wind blew cool on her face and she could get a sense of perspective once more.

'He's still here,' she told him, 'but he won't be for much longer. It's going quite well.'

When she finished speaking to Daniel and went back into the house she discovered Al had gone. A few minutes later a text from him came through on her phone: *Sorry, beautiful. Something urgent cropped up. I'll call you. A xx*

Jojo wasn't sure whether she was relieved or bereft. There was a kind of hollowed-out feeling in her gut, as if she were empty inside. She had planned to tell him she was starting divorce proceedings. But she hadn't. She had achieved nothing. Absolutely nothing at all.

CHAPTER 35

'He's messing with your head,' Kate said, when Jojo phoned her on Monday evening. 'And I think it's about time you beat him at his own game.'

'What do you mean?'

She sighed. 'Look, I don't know the guy, but he abandoned you, Jojo. An apology doesn't make it all right.'

'I know,' Jojo said.

The conversation she'd had with Al still felt surreal, but a long chat with Daniel yesterday had helped her put things into perspective.

'How did you get on with the solicitor?' Kate asked.

'I've got an appointment for nine thirty on Wednesday.' Jojo hesitated. 'Alan said I've committed adultery – and I suppose I have, haven't I?'

'The cheeky bugger,' Kate's voice was fierce with indignation. 'Anyway, how do you know he hasn't done the same thing? Is he likely to have been celibate all this time?'

'Probably not,' Jojo said, with a sigh.

'Well, I think we should do a bit of digging – we don't have to sit here and wait for him to dictate what's going to happen. Is Alan on social media at all? It's amazing what you can find out on the internet.'

Jojo frowned. 'I don't think so. Well, apart from a very old Facebook account he had once. That was before we were properly together. He used to put photos on it from time to time of his travels. He told me he'd closed it down when we got married.'

'I'll start there, then,' Kate said, 'if that's all right with you?'

'Of course. I wouldn't know where to start when it comes to social media.'

'How is the lovely Daniel? What does he make of all this?'

'He's being very supportive. I'm going over there tomorrow night for dinner and to help him clear out some of his mother's stuff.'

'Bless him,' Kate said. 'That's never easy, is it? I'm glad he's supportive, Jojo. He sounds like a good man.'

Daniel *was* a good man, Jojo thought, as she drove over to his house after her final call on Tuesday. Not to mention a patient one. She was well aware that most men would have run a mile if an estranged husband had suddenly turned up on the scene, however extenuating the circumstances.

He looked stressed when he opened the door, though, and it didn't take her long to work out why. A man with the same dark hair and olive colouring as Daniel was sitting on a chair in the dining room.

He stood up when Daniel introduced them. 'This is my brother. Simon – this is Jojo.'

She shook his outstretched hand. His fingers felt warm, but his eyes, a couple of shades lighter than Daniel's deep-brown, were cool. Apart from their looks, the two men weren't alike at all. Simon was dressed casually, but there was a pressed crease in his trousers and his pristine white shirt looked as though it had never been worn before. Everything about him screamed control, from his economical movements to the bland 'How do you do,' when he'd shaken her hand.

There was an odd atmosphere in the room. Had the brothers been arguing? She felt as though a lot had gone on before she'd arrived.

It looked as though they'd made a start. Several plastic storage boxes full of knick-knacks were already piled on one side of the room.

Daniel went to make coffee and Jojo glanced at Simon. 'How are you getting on?' she asked conversationally.

'Most of it should have gone to the tip years ago,' Simon said, with an edge of bitterness in his voice. Or maybe she'd imagined that. She was struggling to think of something neutral to say when Daniel came back in.

'Everything OK?' he said, to no one in particular.

'Everything's fine,' Simon said, still with that strange edge to his voice.

Jojo wondered if perhaps she shouldn't have come. She sipped coffee. 'Were you thinking of taking things to a particular charity shop? Or were you thinking of selling?'

'We should have burned the whole lot years ago,' Simon interjected. He shot Daniel a look of contempt.

Daniel held his brother's gaze for a few moments before he replied. 'I appreciate you coming over but I think you'd better go now.'

'Gladly,' Simon said, standing up. He nodded in Jojo's direction, then strode across the room. Daniel followed him into the hall and Jojo could hear their muttered voices but not what they were saying.

When Daniel came back he was frowning. 'I'm sorry. You didn't need to hear that.'

'It's all right.' She looked at his troubled face. 'Why is he so cross?'

'We don't get on,' Daniel said slowly. 'Simon didn't get on with Mum either. That's why he said what he did.'

He looked so sad and lost that she got up and hugged him. 'Families, eh?' she said. 'Well, at least you did the right thing in inviting him here. Did he not want anything?'

'No.' There was a pause and she thought for a moment he was going to say something else, but he didn't.

'What would you like me to do?' she asked. 'Are there any clothes? Anything I can just pack into boxes that doesn't need to be sorted?'

He shook his head and gave her a rueful smile. 'No clothes. I'm not quite *that* bad. Although now you come to mention it there may be a few old coats. ' He picked up a couple of the storage boxes. 'They could go in here.'

She followed him upstairs. 'I'm going through her bureau,' he said, as they got to the landing. 'I've got things like her very first driving licence and her and Dad's marriage certificate.'

His voice was wistful, and Jojo said, 'Well, maybe they're some things you might like to keep.'

'Yes.' He touched her shoulder. 'You're very lovely, did you know that?'

'I have my moments,' she said. She was still smiling as she went into the spare room.

'A few coats' was an understatement, she saw, as she opened the double wardrobe door. There must have been at least ten in there. All of them good quality, and some had barely been worn. She put everything by the chest of drawers in the corner. Then, on impulse, she pulled out the top drawer to see if there was anything else that needed sorting. It was empty, save for a crumpled leaflet. Jojo picked it up, curious. The heading was in plain black capitals and read: *AA – WHERE TO FIND.*

Jojo's heart gave a little thump of shock. She'd seen leaflets like this before. They kept a stack at the hospital and occasionally handed them out to patients they thought might benefit. It was a list of Alcoholics Anonymous meetings in the local area.

Why on earth would Daniel's mother have one? Jojo supposed that was obvious – did Daniel know his mother had possibly had a drink problem?

Should she say anything to Daniel? Her gut reaction was, no, she shouldn't. It could only upset him. He'd adored his mother, and besides it was ancient family history now.

Jojo folded the leaflet and stuffed it into the side pocket of her bag at exactly the same moment that she heard a light cough from behind her. When she turned Daniel was standing in the doorway.

How long had he been there? She smiled brightly at him, but he didn't smile back.

'What did you just put in your bag?' he asked.

She would have given anything to rewind the last five minutes. With a little sigh, she took it out again and handed it to him. 'I'm sure it doesn't mean anything,' she ventured.

'If you were sure of that you wouldn't have been hiding it from me,' he said quietly.

She could feel her cheeks flushing hot.

'That was a very sweet thing to do,' he went on, 'but there's no need. I knew she was an alcoholic.'

'You did?' It seemed an inane thing to say, but it was all she could manage.

He sat down on the bed amid the coats and drew her down next to him. 'Mum was a recovering alcoholic,' he said. 'I don't remember seeing her drunk. She gave up when I was about two years old. She went to three AA meetings a week. And she died sober.'

'Wow,' Jojo said. 'That's so brilliant.'

'It wasn't for Simon,' he said, and his eyes darkened. 'She drank all through his childhood. He was fourteen when she gave up and he was already very damaged by it. He never forgave her.'

'I see,' Jojo said softly. Everything was starting to make sense. Simon's bitterness, his comments about taking their mother's stuff to the tip.

Daniel touched her face and she was reminded fleetingly of Al. Except Daniel's eyes were tender and Al's had been speculative.

'The truth is that Simon and I had completely different childhoods. Completely different mothers. I don't blame him for resenting me. I guess it was a mistake to invite him over, but I really did think he might have softened a bit by now – it's been such a long time.'

'Yes,' she said, looking at the coats spread out on the bed. 'I'm sorry, I haven't got very far with helping you.'

'Oh, I don't know. You've unearthed a skeleton from my cupboard now too. And you haven't run for the hills yet, have you?'

She smiled at him. 'I've no intention of running for the hills.'

'Good. For what it's worth, one of Mum's favourite sayings was "What doesn't kill you makes you stronger." She used to have it pinned up over her desk.'

'Funnily enough,' Jojo told him, 'it's one of my favourites too.'

CHAPTER 36

They'd just finished dinner when Al called. 'I'm tempted to ignore it,' she told Daniel, 'but if I do I won't get hold of him for days.'

She answered the phone.

'Hi, you,' Al said, in a voice that was way too familiar.

'What can I do for you?' she said, aware that Daniel was clearing plates and tactfully getting up to go out of earshot.

'I've been thinking, Jojo.' A beat. 'The truth is, I hated seeing you so upset on Sunday.'

'I see,' she said, wondering if that was true. Despite what Kate had said about him playing games, Jojo didn't think he'd have enjoyed deliberately hurting her.

'I'm happy to agree to a quickie no-fault divorce. I won't bring up your adultery. I can see why you did it and I'm certainly not blameless.' Another little pause. 'The new guy seems like a decent bloke. I hope he takes good care of you.'

Jojo wasn't sure whether to be outraged by this statement or relieved. Some instinct told her to keep quiet. If Al really was feeling repentant enough to let her go with good grace, she should probably make the most of it.

He went on in the same soft voice. 'How do you feel about that?'

'Pleased,' she said. 'Thank you.'

'I do think I'm entitled to some financial settlement,' he went on smoothly. 'Not half the house or anything. I'd never want you to lose your home. You love that place, don't you?'

'What did you have in mind?' she said, echoing his softness, even though she could feel the anger rising. How dare he think he could manipulate her?

'Twenty-five thou seems reasonable. You could borrow it against the house. And it's probably similar to what the lawyer's costs would be if we went to court. I'd get legal aid, of course.' When she didn't speak, he went on blithely, 'This way we don't need to go to court. There'd be no costs at all involved then.'

'Apart from my twenty-five thousand.' She didn't know how she managed to stop her voice shaking. She was so angry.

'Yeah,' he said, confident now. 'What do you say?'

Jojo could feel the anger solidifying into a cold burning fire in her gut. 'Screw you,' she told him, and disconnected.

Daniel had just come back into the room. He gave her a rueful smile. 'That went well, then!'

She took a couple of deep, steadying breaths and told him what had happened. 'I shouldn't be shocked,' she said. 'But I am.'

He sat down next to her again at the dining table and stroked her arm. 'At least you know what the score is now. He's put his cards on the table.'

'Yes.' She looked at him. 'He certainly has. He's right about one thing, though. I've heard of people who've run up thirty-thousand-pound court bills because they've failed to come to an agreement. I can't afford that.'

'It hasn't come to that yet,' he said. 'See what the solicitor says tomorrow first.' He reached for her fingers. 'I know it's very early days since—'

'Since we became *intimate*. Yes.' She watched the smile warm his eyes at the phrase.

'Well, what I'm trying to say is that I hope we know each other a lot longer. In that way.'

'Me too,' she said. 'Speaking of which, shall we go up?'

They smiled at each other.

Her mobile began to ring again as they stood up. A vibrating, irritating buzz. Neither of them bothered to look at it.

'I don't care who it is,' Jojo said, grabbing Daniel's hand. 'They can wait.'

In the morning, the first thing she noticed was that the blood-red cushions were still *in situ* on the chaise longue. But, oddly, she didn't mind them anymore. Before they'd fallen asleep last night they'd had a long chat about Daniel's mum. Jojo felt as though she knew her a lot better. A troubled woman who'd had a drink problem since the day she was legally old enough to imbibe.

'People don't understand that alcoholism is an illness,' Daniel had said, 'It's genetic. It got really bad after Simon was born. She had postnatal depression, too, which didn't help.'

'How do you know all this?' she'd asked him gently.

'She told me some. My maternal grandmother told me the rest. This was my grandmother's house originally,' he'd said. 'There was a great deal of money in our family at one time. Mum did her best to drink it away – but she got sober before she bankrupted us. Gran was proud of her for that. It wasn't easy. Especially when she had me to bring up and no husband to help.

'In her later years Mum helped an awful lot of people. She kind of devoted her life to it – that and looking after me. I didn't fully grasp the extent of it until she died. There were two hundred people at her funeral. People I'd never even met.'

Jojo was beginning to see why he'd had her on a pedestal. A woman who had been so flawed but who'd finally come good.

'The only regret I have now is that Simon and I aren't closer,' he continued. 'But I don't think there's anything else I can do about that.'

'Maybe your relationship with Simon will change over time,' Jojo said.

'Maybe. You've never told me why you don't get on with your mum,' he'd said, just before they fell asleep.

'I don't think she ever really liked me that much,' Jojo said. 'She disapproved of everything I did when I was younger. My looks, my clothes, my choice of men. Although she may have had a point there.'

Daniel had stroked her hair without commenting and they had fallen asleep, spooned together. Totally peaceful. He'd got up before she had. She could hear him moving around downstairs. At least, she hoped it was Daniel clattering plates down there, not Anoushka.

Suddenly anxious not to bump into his cleaner again – especially not when she was undressed – she grabbed his robe from the back of the door and met him coming back upstairs with a tray on which there was a plate of toast and a pot of coffee.

'Breakfast in bed,' he announced. 'Only you seem to be up.'

'I was worried you might be Anoushka,' she confessed. 'I can get back in.' She tossed him a flirtatious glance over her shoulder. 'Are you joining me?'

'Yep, for five minutes.' He waited until she was tucked in and put the tray on her lap. She noticed her mobile was next to the plate.

'It rang again just now,' he said. 'And don't worry, I've had a word with Anoushka. I've told her she's to play nicely.'

'Hmm. I can't see her taking much notice of that. She thinks I'm a floozy.'

'She actually said that?' He looked startled.

'Don't worry, I've been called a lot worse.' *Although mostly by women in the throes of labour*, Jojo thought.

'We need to introduce you two properly,' Daniel said. 'Maybe I should invite her round for dinner.'

'I can't wait!' Jojo said, scrolling through the missed calls. They were both from Kate.

'She's probably calling to wish me luck with the solicitor,' she said. 'Ooh, Nutella, my favourite. You angel.'

'Is there any chance of me having any of that toast?' His voice was plaintive. 'And don't get any Nutella near mine. I'm a Marmite man.'

Jojo looked at him in horror. 'Yuck. Does this mean we're not compatible after all?'

He blinked. 'I'm not even going to dignify that with a reply,' he said. 'Are you going to phone your friend back?'

'I'll call her after I've seen the solicitor,' Jojo said. 'No doubt we'll have a lot more to talk about then.'

'OK. And, Jojo, be careful. When you get home, keep an eye out for your ex. He's not likely to be very happy about the way things are going.'

'No,' she said. 'But I don't think he'll get violent. I can handle Alan. I just need to get it absolutely straight in my head what I'm dealing with first. And Kate was right. The solicitor will be able to tell me that.'

A couple of hours later when she walked out of the solicitor's office, Jojo wasn't feeling quite as confident. It seemed that Alan could, if he wanted to, make life very difficult for her.

'We can probably prove that he was out of the country,' the solicitor had said, 'but there are also phone records that will prove you were actually in touch. So your ex could argue that you were perfectly happy with the arrangement.

A judge might wonder why you let it go on for so long. I'm not trying to worry you,' she added, her eyes kind, 'just playing devil's advocate. From what you've told me so far it does rather sound as though Mr Wainwright is likely to play dirty.'

It had felt odd hearing Alan's full name. She had loved that name, back in the early days of their marriage. Mrs Jojo Wainwright. When she'd first realized he wasn't coming back she had thought his name was the only thing he had ever given her that he hadn't taken away again.

But now it seemed it was going to cost her dearly to get rid of it.

She sat in her car outside the solicitor's and phoned Kate.

'Finally!' Kate exclaimed.

'Sorry. I've just been to the solicitor's.'

'Was she helpful?'

'Yes, thank you, she was.'

'I sense a "but",' Kate said, acutely perceptive, as always.

'I don't think things are going to be quite as straight-forward as I thought,' Jojo said, and told her about Alan's demands.

'Well, I'm not entirely surprised he's pulled a stunt like that.'

'Me neither,' Jojo said. 'I should have seen it coming.'

'Well, I may have some good news for you.' Kate had a smile in her voice. 'At least, I hope you'll think it's good news. It'd be easier to tell you face to face. What are you doing now? Can I come over?'

'Be my guest,' Jojo said.

CHAPTER 37

Jojo had barely been in five minutes when Kate rang her bell. Even so, she checked through the glass window of the front door before she let her in. She didn't feel up to confronting a furious Alan. Not just yet.

Kate had her laptop with her. 'I think you're going to find this very interesting viewing,' she said, with a wink.

'Are we going to need cake? I made a fruit one the other day. It's virtually fat-free.'

'Cake, and lots and lots of coffee.' Kate set up the laptop on the conservatory table and switched it on. 'You get that sorted and I'll log in.'

As she made the coffee and cut slabs of fruitcake, Jojo's stomach was churning. She was pretty sure that Kate was going to show her photographs of Al and various indiscretions. And while she knew that wouldn't upset her as much as it would once have done, she still wasn't sure she wanted to see them.

'Don't look so worried, sweetie,' Kate said, as Jojo set the tray on the table beside the laptop. 'Your ex isn't quite as smart as he thinks he is.' She stirred sugar into her coffee. 'Well, he isn't as smart as your clever mates, anyway. Brace yourself.'

Jojo smiled. 'I'm braced,' she said. 'I don't think anything he could do now would shock me more than he already has.'

'Right.' Kate began clicking on the screen and opening various windows. 'Let me introduce you to Facebook. This is Alan Wainwright's timeline. Seems he didn't close it down, after all.'

Jojo watched as Kate scrolled through it. There were lots of photographs of places. Temples, sunsets, beaches. She recognized some. There were a few of people too. She'd been right about the women. In some he had his arms draped around them. The occasional one would be looking at him adoringly. The stick-thin models she'd always dreaded. It didn't hurt as much as she'd thought it might. Maybe because she'd moved on since she'd met Daniel.

'You okay?' Kate glanced at her.

'Yes, I'm fine . . . Although I'm not sure how this can help.'

'Trust me. You will be in a minute. I'm going to take you on a journey back through Mr Alan Wainwright's past. Facebook keeps posts from previous years. Look, we're already back to 2012.'

'The year we got married,' Jojo said bleakly.

'Yes.' Kate touched her arm. 'You got married in the spring, didn't you?'

'That's right. The fourteenth of April. It was one of the happiest days of my life.'

'Are you still braced?' Kate stopped scrolling and gave her a quick hug.

'I'm still braced,' she said.

Kate scrolled down to some pictures of a wedding on an exotic beach. White sands, palm trees, a turquoise-blue sea and several pictures of the bride and groom exchanging rings, kissing, lying side by side on sun-loungers.

She clicked on one of the pictures so that it was full-size on the screen. 'Take a look at the groom,' she said.

Jojo's heart stopped. It was Big Al. He was smiling – the slow, confident smile she knew so well. Just to the right of his head there was a little red date stamp: *22 Oct 2011*.

Everything in the conservatory seemed to freeze. The photo became over-bright. A Technicolor impossibility.

Jojo glanced at Kate. 'That can't be right. It must be some sort of joke or something.'

'I must admit that I thought it was something like that too,' Kate said quietly. 'But I checked. And it wasn't. These photos are of his wedding to Deanne Baker. They got married on Saturday, the twenty-second of October 2011. I've looked at their marriage certificate online.' She paused. 'I also checked to see if they ever got divorced – they haven't, Jojo. They're still married. Which means that Alan Wainwright is a bigamist.'

There was a long silence. Eventually Jojo got up and walked slowly to the kitchen. Her head was spinning and it was difficult to breathe.

She opened the fridge door, then shut it again. She sensed, rather than heard, Kate come into the room behind her.

'I probably shouldn't have told you quite like that.' Kate's voice was apologetic. 'It must be a huge shock.'

'It is.' Jojo turned to face her. 'Bloody hell, we're not even legally married, are we?'

'No,' Kate said. Her eyes were very solemn. 'You're not.' She held out her arms. 'Oh, sweetie. I'm so sorry.'

Jojo walked into her embrace. She could feel herself shaking. 'I guess I won't have to worry about giving him twenty-five thousand pounds.'

'You certainly won't,' Kate agreed. 'And I can't believe he tried to get money out of you. Did he think you were just going to meekly hand it over to him?'

'Probably. I was pretty meek for the rest of our mar— our time together,' she finished lamely. 'Let's face it, Kate, I was a total pushover.'

'But not any more.'

'Not any more, no.' She went back into the other room and picked up her mobile phone.

'What are you going to do?'

'Well, for a start, I'm going to report him to the police.'

'Go, girl,' Kate said. 'You can get seven years for bigamy in the UK. I checked.'

Jojo gave a mirthless laugh. 'Good. I wonder how I can make sure he gets the whole lot. Maybe it's worth paying another visit to our very nice solicitor.'

Kate nodded slowly. 'Maybe it is.'

'Poor Deanne,' Jojo said.

'That's typical of you.'

'Well, I doubt she knows he swanned off and married someone else six months after he married her. I don't suppose he thought to mention it.'

'No,' Kate's face was grave.

'I wonder why he did it.' Jojo abandoned her call, which had gone straight to voicemail, and walked back into the conservatory. She sat down again at the table and pushed the laptop round so it was no longer facing her. She couldn't bear to look at it any more: Big Al smiling and proud beside the pretty blonde in her slinky white dress.

She looked at Kate, who had followed her in. 'I mean, why did he even want to marry me?'

'Didn't you say you had a whirlwind romance? Maybe he got carried away.'

'He was quite drunk on the night he proposed. I do remember that. We were dancing outside on the beach about midnight. Then he proposed. He did it with the ring pull of a beer can. It sounds awful, doesn't it, but it was wonderfully romantic.' She blinked at the memory. 'It did cross my mind that he hadn't exactly planned it, but in the morning when I woke up and asked him if he'd meant it, he said of course he had.'

Kate took her hand. 'I'm sure he did mean it at the time.'

'Yeah. I guess it's immaterial now.' Jojo sighed. 'Thank you. Thank you for going to all this trouble.'

'It wasn't any trouble. It took me about an hour on the computer. It always amazes me, the things people post and say on social media. It's as though they think it's not real

– that it somehow doesn't count. Most people have no idea that the things you put on social media are pretty much there for ever. Even if you delete them, they're still there somewhere. Big Brother is watching you.'

'Sobering stuff,' Jojo said. 'Well, it is for Alan anyway. It's just lost him twenty-five grand.'

'You wouldn't have paid him, would you?' Kate looked shocked.

'No, I wouldn't. But he didn't know that, did he?'

'So what's next? Are you going to speak to him?'

'Yes. I'm going to phone him in a minute and ask him to come round.'

'Honey, do you think that's wise? Do you need back-up? I could stay. I can get Bob to come over, too, if you like. We don't need to be in the same room. We can hide upstairs or something. Just in case you need us.'

Jojo smiled at the thought of Kate and Bob hanging over the banisters or hovering in the bathroom. Bob was as tall as Alan, if not quite as wide.

'What?' Kate said.

'Nothing. No, it's all right, angel. Truly it is. I want to do this by myself. Alan may be many things, but he isn't violent. I am sure about that.'

Kate didn't look happy. 'At least tell Daniel,' she said. 'And wouldn't it be better to meet him on neutral territory? In town or something? Where's he staying, anyway?'

'I don't know, but he clearly isn't homeless,' Jojo said. 'Don't worry. I won't take any risks, I promise.'

When Kate had gone, she walked slowly back through the hall. She stopped for a moment in the doorway of the galley kitchen: her beautiful little kitchen with its copper kettles and pans and the bunches of herbs strung from the central beam. The place where she'd spent so many happy hours cooking with and without Big Al. For a second his ghost was there, a smiling, carefree version of him, bent over a pestle and mortar. Then she blinked and it was gone.

She went back into the conservatory. Beyond the windows, her patio garden sloped down to the sand and beyond that the ocean stretched out to infinity.

Big Al couldn't take any of this. He couldn't make her give up her beautiful home. Jojo's eyes blurred and she sank into the cane armchair and wept. Her tears were a mixture of relief, shock and loss, but she couldn't stop them. A while later she was aware that Sinbad had strolled into the room. He blinked green eyes at her and gave a plaintive miaow.

'It's your teatime, I know.' She stroked his head. 'You're not interested in my welfare at all, are you?'

The cat arched his body beneath her fingers and purred in a soft rumble of agreement. Jojo wiped her eyes and got up. She opened a pouch of cat food – he was on tuna at the moment – and spooned it into his bowl. He sniffed disdainfully and walked away.

'Suit yourself,' Jojo said, and went to find her phone. It was time to give Alan a call.

CHAPTER 38

He answered her call straight away with a soft 'Good afternoon.'

Jojo had thought he would. He'd be expecting her to have had second thoughts, to be worrying that he'd be angry after what she had said to him last time they'd spoken.

'I'd like to meet,' she said, without preamble. 'To discuss the way forward.' That sounded like a line from a training manual.

'Where?' His voice was clipped now.

'I don't know where you're staying.' She resisted the urge to add, *Or with whom.*

'I can come to you, if you like?'

'I'd rather not meet here.' She didn't want him in her house again. Her tears had washed him out of it. It was over and done with. She didn't want to resurrect it by letting him back in.

'The Little Chef,' she said. 'It's out by the new Tesco between Little Sanderton and Exeter.' She glanced at her watch. 'Can you make six o'clock?'

'See you there.' He disconnected.

She felt a moment's trepidation. Should she tell Daniel? They had spoken briefly, but not about the bigamy. That wasn't a subject for a five-minute phone call and he was at work. She was going to his house later for a proper catch-up. The Little Chef was on the way.

The roadside café was virtually empty. Jojo wasn't surprised. It looked in need of refurbishment. A very young waitress roused herself to come over.

'I'm meeting someone,' Jojo said.

'Big guy?' The waitress waved a hand. 'He's round the corner.'

Jojo went round and saw Alan sitting on a bench seat by the window, texting on his phone. Texting his wife, she wondered, or some newer love? He stopped when he saw her.

But he didn't get up as she reached the table. Bad manners, she thought idly. Daniel would have stood up. She knew she would always remember this: Wednesday, 22 March. *The day I discovered my husband was a bigamist.*

She sat on the plastic seat opposite him.

'You've decided it would be easier to settle out of court.' His voice was so relaxed, so unaware.

Jojo was amazed that she herself was so calm. 'Did you ever love me?' she asked.

He looked startled. She'd startled herself. She had meant to say, 'Why did you marry me?' But different words had popped out.

'Of course I did.' His eyes narrowed. 'Or I wouldn't have married you.'

'But you didn't marry me, did you?' Jojo delivered her killer line at exactly the same moment as the waitress turned up and said, 'What can I get you, guys?'

Alan glanced at her. 'Cappuccino. Large. Don't hold back on the chocolate sprinkles.' He was clearly in celebratory mode. He turned back to Jojo. 'What did you say?'

'Espresso for me, please.' Jojo smiled at the waitress, then glanced back at Alan. He was looking puzzled.

She licked her lips. 'I said, you didn't marry me. Well, you did. But you overlooked the fact that you hadn't got divorced. From the first Mrs Wainwright.'

He went very still. Then he shut his eyes. When he opened them again he didn't look at her straight away but at the table. 'I did marry you.'

'But not legally.'

'Deanne and I are divorced.' Now he met her eyes and she stared him down.

'It would have been impossible to get a divorce that quickly.' What a good job Kate had done her homework. She might have wavered in the face of such confidence. If she hadn't known for sure that he was lying.

He banged his fist on the table, rattling the cruet set and the cutlery, which were both in stainless-steel holders. Jojo watched his anger. She felt strangely removed now, as though this whole scenario were happening to someone else.

'Why did you do it?'

'Because I was drunk.' He shrugged. 'Because you wouldn't let it go, would you? You'd organized the whole thing before I'd had a chance to blink. You were desperate.'

'What?' She'd slapped him before she'd even known she was going to do it. It wasn't a very satisfying slap. Not a loud ringing belter of a slap, like the kind they faked on dramas, but a pathetic stinging attempt that hurt her hand. He had hard cheekbones.

'I'll sue you for assault.'

'No, you won't,' she said, reaching for her bag and standing up.

The waitress had just appeared with a tray. She put it down on another table, clearly unsure of what to do.

'Did you see that?' Big Al turned to her. 'She attacked me.'

The waitress didn't speak. Jojo stalked past her. 'He's paying,' she shot back over her shoulder. She could hear her heels clicking like gunshots on the tiled floor. Angry heels. And it was anger that powered her out of the door and back to her car.

'Are you sure you're OK?' Daniel couldn't do enough for her. He'd already made her drink coffee with brandy in it. Not that she'd taken too much persuading. Now they were sitting next to each other in his lounge on his incredibly comfy couch.

'I wish you'd let me know what you were doing, Jojo.

301

Anything could have happened. He could have been violent.'

'It was me who was violent,' she said ruefully. 'Years of anger, I think.'

'Do you really think he'll try to sue you? He sounds a bit unhinged.'

'He'd have to be totally insane to go anywhere near a police station.' She looked at Daniel. 'And my only regret is that I didn't hit him harder.'

'Yes,' he said. 'I'm sure.'

'Can we talk about something else?' she said to Daniel. 'I don't want to think about him anymore.'

'Of course.' He rested an arm along the back of the sofa, and stroked her hair. It was good to feel the warmth of him next to her, to feel cocooned in the safety of Daniel's house.

For a few moments there was silence, but for the ticking of the clock and the soft tap-tap of the central heating system.

Jojo let her gaze wander around the beautiful old room. The pictures that had belonged to his mother had been removed from the walls, then put back again because they had left pale oblongs behind them.

'I'll have to redecorate,' he had said yesterday, 'before I take them down permanently.'

'Baby steps,' she'd told him. 'Do you like those paintings?'

'I like the one of the lighthouse. And the landscapes are beautiful too.'

'Then why not keep them?'

He'd smiled as if he'd never considered that.

'The portrait of her that's on your bedside table,' she'd said. 'Why don't you bring that down here? You could give it pride of place on the mantelpiece.'

'Good idea.'

It was there now. For a moment, Jojo met Avril's dark eyes. They were the same shape and colour as her son's, and they held the same warmth. *A proper mother*, she thought. What must it be like to have a proper mother? One who looked like you. One who clearly loved you. Mind you, that hadn't exactly worked out for Simon, had it?

Daniel's voice interrupted Jojo's musings. 'What are you doing on Sunday?'

'Nothing,' she said, 'but if we're going out for dinner it's definitely my shout.'

'It's Mother's Day,' he said quietly. 'Everywhere will be packed out.'

'Of course.' She bit her lip. After she'd sent Carol's card she'd just tried to blank it out. She'd chosen the card in haste and it wasn't until she'd written in it that she'd noticed the words inside: *To the Best Mum in the World.* Jojo had contemplated going out and buying another, but in the end she'd decided against it. Carol would probably raise an eyebrow at such a sentiment. Jojo usually sent her staid, quiet cards with staid, boring greetings. Presumably it would have arrived by now. As usual there had been no reaction.

'It must be a hard day for you too,' Daniel said, his voice breaking into her thoughts.

'Hard? No. Why should it be?'

303

'Because I think we all want a good relationship with our mothers.' He stroked her hair again.

'Maybe.' He didn't miss much, her perceptive man. 'So what would you usually do?' she asked softly.

'Nothing special. Although I might raise a glass to her at some point in the day.' His face was thoughtful. 'How would you feel about having a few friends here for drinks and maybe a little buffet? I'd really like to meet Kate and Bob.'

'That sounds lovely.'

He touched her arm. 'I also thought I could ask Anoushka. It would give you the chance to get to know her properly.'

Clearly she hadn't hidden her expression of horror as well as she'd thought, because he added swiftly, 'I think you two would get on. If you knew each other better.'

'I'm not convinced. I still think she may have a thing for you.'

'She doesn't,' Daniel said. 'Trust me on that.' He stroked her face. 'For a start she's spoken for.'

'Anoushka's got a partner?' Jojo said surprised.

'Indeed she has.' Daniel laughed. 'And the last thing I heard was that they were trying for a baby.' He raised his eyebrows. 'She's quite a dark horse, our Anoushka.'

CHAPTER 39

Anoushka's partner turned out to be a very pretty, very blonde English girl, who held out her hand to shake Jojo's and said she was pleased to meet her. She had a dimple in her smile and she smiled a lot. She also had a glow about her that set Jojo's instincts on full alert. If she wasn't much mistaken the trying for a baby thing had worked.

'I'm very pleased to meet you too, Beth,' Jojo said, aware of Anoushka hovering behind them, like a territorial lioness, in Daniel's hall. She wondered what had been said about her. She couldn't imagine it had been complimentary, but it seemed Anoushka was on her best behaviour today.

'You make nice couple with him – yes?' she murmured, when she came into the kitchen to get a glass of wine for herself and a soft drink for Beth.

'Thank you,' Jojo said.

Anoushka nodded. 'He say you deliver babies,' she added.

'This is good profession. I have been a doula also.' Her gaze darted towards Beth and now Jojo was sure. She smiled. 'Congratulations,' she said quietly.

Anoushka smiled too and didn't comment.

'Daniel tells me you're a doctor,' Jojo said gently. 'I hope you'll be able to practise medicine again some day.'

'I hope this also.' Anoushka's eyes flashed, and Jojo thought, *She'll do it again. Because she's a strong woman.*

Kate was another, she thought, glancing across at her. She and Bob were standing by the patio doors, which led out on to the back garden. It was a nice day, so Daniel had opened them and the afternoon sun flooded the high-ceilinged room with light and turned the old polished floorboards the deep colour of conker.

Kate turned suddenly as if aware of her gaze. Then she caught Bob's hand and the two of them strolled back across the room.

They looked right together, Jojo thought. Even though they were a relatively new couple too.

'By the way, how are you getting on with *Rebecca*?' Kate asked Jojo. 'Our novel of the month, I mean. Have you finished it yet?'

'A couple of days ago,' Jojo said. 'You?'

'Last night,' Kate said. 'Great twists, weren't they? I didn't see any of them coming.'

'Me neither,' Jojo said. 'Mind you, I didn't see the twists in my own life coming either. Although, actually, I think I got off lightly, compared to the main character in *Rebecca*.'

'You'd have coped,' Kate said. 'You're stronger than she was.'

'I'm not sure I was a month ago!' Jojo sighed. 'Although I think I may be getting there.'

Jojo was getting Daniel's homemade quiches out of the fridge when her mobile buzzed from its place on the side. Worried that it might be Alan, she went to check the screen. Unknown number. She picked it up.

'Hello, Jojo. I'm just calling to say thank you for the card.'

It was her mother's voice. Jojo frowned. Carol rang so rarely that she didn't even have her latest number programmed in. 'Er, you're welcome,' she said.

'It was a very nice card. I appreciated it.'

'Great,' Jojo said, surprised. 'Are you well?'

'I am very well, thank you. And yourself?'

'Very well too,' Jojo said. Which wasn't quite as much of a lie as it would have been a few days earlier.

'I may be coming back for a fortnight in June. I have errands. Will you be available for coffee?'

'I'm sure I will,' Jojo said.

'Good. I'll phone you nearer to the time. Bye, Jojo.'

'Bye, Mum. And, um, happy Mother's Day.'

Feeling curiously touched, she glanced up to see Daniel in the doorway. He was smiling. 'You phoned her, then. Did it go well?'

'Actually, she phoned me. She liked the card I sent her. She must have been having a maternal moment. She doesn't have them very often either.'

'Baby steps,' he said, and she threw a tea towel at him.

'That's my line, get your own!' Laughing, they carried the

quiches into the drawing room. 'She's coming over in June,' Jojo told Daniel, 'so you might get to meet her. Actually, she might even approve of you – at least you've got a job!'

Daniel raised his eyebrows. 'Let's hope so,' he said. 'Because I intend to hang around. If you want me to, I mean.'

'Oh, yes,' she said, glancing up through her lashes, and she saw that shyness flash into his eyes. 'I was hoping you might.'

Much later, when they had chatted and eaten and chatted some more and still no one seemed in a hurry to leave, Jojo fetched the bottle of champagne she'd sneaked into the fridge earlier. She brought it into the lounge on a tray with six glasses and put it on the coffee table. Everyone turned as the cork popped and she poured the fizz.

'I'd like to propose a toast,' she said, handing everyone a flute and glancing at Daniel. 'In fact, I think we'd both like to propose a toast, wouldn't we?'

He smiled at her. 'You go first.'

'To strong women,' she said, raising her glass in the direction of Daniel's mother's portrait.

'And to mothers,' Daniel said. 'Past, present and future.'

'To strong women and to mothers, past, present and future!' everyone echoed, as Jojo smiled around at them all.

And they all smiled back at her, even Anoushka.

APRIL

Serena

CHAPTER 40

Serena walked through to the orangery, which had always been her favourite room of the house, although sometimes, lately, visiting it had become bittersweet. The big old extension with its arching glass roof was a room made for socializing. It came alive when it was crammed full of people, but that was a rare occurrence these days.

When she and Liam had bought this place, it was the orangery that had clinched the deal. For her, anyway. Liam had loved the fact that there was tons of outside space: the drive, the double-fronted workshop, not to mention the garden that sloped gently downwards to a back gate, beyond which was a footpath that wound its way along the Jurassic coast.

'We can hear the sea from our garden,' she'd said as they'd stood in the doorway of the orangery. 'Isn't that something?'

'I expect we can hear it from every room in the house.'

Liam had acted casually non-committal, but she had seen the excitement in his eyes.

Behind him the estate agent had smiled, sure of a sale.

Indeed, they'd bought the Old Lighthouse – a misnomer, because it had never been a lighthouse. Although its position, up there on the Devon cliffs, would have been perfect.

Serena sighed. They'd had a near-perfect life, but three years ago – when she'd been thirty and Liam thirty-five – it had suddenly ended. An aortic aneurysm. They'd found out afterwards that they ran in Liam's family. A silent, symptomless killer, deadly as carbon monoxide. After Liam's death, his three brothers and an uncle had been diagnosed with the same thing. You could do something about it if you caught it early.

But Liam had been the first.

His death had saved the lives of his brothers and uncle. Sometimes she clung on to that. On good days she was grateful he hadn't died for nothing. On bad days she raged at God. Why Liam? Her soulmate – the only man she had ever really loved.

Today was a good day. In a very short while her four best friends would be here. Her house would echo with their laughter. Their problems would put hers in perspective, as they always did.

The doorbell rang.

'It's only me, angel!' She heard Jojo's voice in the hall. The front door was on the latch, but Jojo still rang the bell out of courtesy.

Serena's heart warmed. She didn't have a 'best friend', but if she did it would probably be Jojo; Jojo, who wore her heart on her sleeve and who'd give you her last fiver without blinking.

'Hello, lovely.' Serena kissed her. 'We'll be in the orangery. Do go through.' She giggled. 'Oh, listen to me. I've been spending too much time at PTA evenings. I've gone all formal.'

'I can do formal,' Jojo said. She held out a bottle of red wine. 'I can uncork this if one thinks it would be of benefit, does one?'

'Oh, one most definitely does.' Now they were both smiling. Serena felt her melancholy mood lifting. An evening with the Reading Group was just what she needed.

In the orangery, Serena had pushed the sofas closer together so they weren't too far apart. This was their summer meeting room – in the winter they used the snug, which had a wood-burner. It wasn't exactly summer, but there was a definite touch of spring in the air and the cherry tree in the back garden looked like an oversized stick of pink candyfloss.

Kate and Anne Marie arrived together and Grace arrived last, out of breath because there had been some drama with one of her triplets. Serena darted about doing her hostess bit.

By the time they got through their first bottle of wine Serena's mood had completely changed.

In fact, she felt slightly tipsy. 'I can't remember who was choosing our book of the month,' she said into a rare gap in their conversation. 'But we should probably crack on.'

'It was me,' Jojo said. They all watched while she rummaged in her bag.

'Are we still on classics?' Anne Marie asked. She sounded worried.

'We are for this month,' Jojo said as she produced the book. 'This is a mega-classic. Even if you haven't read it, you'll know the characters. We've all heard of Mr Rochester, haven't we, angels?'

Anne Marie frowned. 'Is there a film?'

The youngest member of the Reading Group got a few indulgent looks.

'Yes, there's a film,' Serena said, at the same time as she thought, *Oh my gosh, Jane Eyre.* It was one of her all-time favourite novels. Partly because she and Jane Eyre had quite a bit in common, what with Jane being a governess and Serena a headmistress, but also because she loved Charlotte Brontë's writing. Still fresh, even today. A timeless tale of love and passion.

'Mr Rochester,' Kate sighed. 'Wasn't he the original brooding hero?'

'That's right.' Grace was nodding. 'And we all like brooding heroes, don't we, girls?' There was a ripple of laughter.

'Oh wait, isn't that the book where there's a mad wife locked up in the attic?' Anne Marie suddenly asked.

'Considering you haven't read it yet, that's very impressive,' Serena said crisply. 'Yes, you're right. But at its heart, *Jane Eyre* is a passionate love story.'

'Yes,' Jojo said, with a lovely smile on her face. 'I think nearly all the classics have a love story at their heart.' She

314

paused. 'I picked *Jane Eyre* though because she's a really nice character. She has the worst start possible and yet she never gives up.' She glanced at Serena and Serena felt the need to add something.

'She's not beautiful either. Charlotte Brontë made that clear. And Mr Rochester – well, he's not exactly your typical hero type. He's a bit rude and arrogant. Not to mention craggy-faced and ugly. Although I think he might have had a strong, square jaw.'

There was more giggling.

They all agreed that *Jane Eyre* sounded like a happier kind of book than last month's novel, which had been *Rebecca*. They moved on to other subjects. Serena was only half listening.

She was still thinking about *Jane Eyre* and the similarities between herself and the main character.

Jane Eyre had grown up well aware that she did not have the kind of looks that would grant her a smooth passage through life. In fact, Jane Eyre did not have much going for her at all. She had been orphaned and then bullied by her late uncle's family. She was the kind of heroine who got through life by relying on her inner resources, her strength painfully acquired by years of not fitting in.

Serena had a lot more in common with Jane Eyre than anyone in the room could have guessed, she thought, as she glanced around at their glowing faces.

CHAPTER 41

Serena flicked through her diary as she sipped her morning coffee. Mr Rochester versus Mr Winchester. The two names weren't *that* close. Yet it was an odd coincidence that a Mr Winchester should turn up in her life on this particular morning. Yet there he was – pencilled in for an appointment at 11 a.m.

She took off her glasses, polished them and put them back on again, and told herself that Mr Winchester, father of ten-year-old Hannah, was unlikely to be a brooding hero.

Though when he arrived, she noticed that he did have a square jaw, and there was a definite hint of cragginess in that face – this was her first impression at least. No smile, either, as she shook his hand and ushered him to a seat in front of her desk. Though he had said upfront that he didn't want to complain but to seek her advice about his daughter.

Since his call – in fact, since his several calls over the last week – Serena had spoken to Hannah's teachers and had established that Hannah was a pleasant girl, if a little quiet, who got on well with her contemporaries and was average in most of her subjects. Certainly she didn't seem to have any problems that warranted her father requesting an appointment with the head. But Serena prided herself on being accessible. So here they were.

'Coffee, Mr Winchester?' she asked, settling herself beside him.

'Yes, thanks.' His voice was at the lower end of gravelly.

While she arranged it, Mr Winchester stared out of the window and she took the opportunity to look at him more closely.

He had a rumpled look about him. His dark hair was unruly and his nose was slightly crooked. He wasn't your average Poppins parent, she thought. Definitely more Topman than Gucci, but there was a certain class about the man. It was the way he carried himself, she decided. He seemed at ease in her office. Many parents didn't.

They tended to be nervous, facing the headmistress, a hangover from their own schooldays, but Mr Winchester clearly had no such qualms.

Serena liked him. She liked the way he held her gaze when they talked, his eyes (a deep brown) were assertive but not arrogant. Not so similar to Mr Rochester in that regard then.

'Thank you for seeing me,' he said. 'I realise that this must be a very busy day for you.'

On the last day before the Easter holidays, 'busy' was something of an understatement. 'You're very welcome,' she said. 'How can I help?'

'This is a little sensitive,' he began, 'but I think Hannah is learning some bad habits.'

'In school?' She hadn't been expecting that.

'No, no.' He waved a hand. 'I mean from her mother.'

There was a small silence. She waited for him to elaborate. 'Hannah's mother and I are recently divorced.' He took a deep breath. Now he did look uncomfortable. 'It's been . . . hard.'

Serena nodded sympathetically. He had very dark eyebrows, she noticed, that matched his thick dark hair.

'Don't worry,' he said, with a sharp glance back at her face. 'I didn't come here for a counselling session. I'm just worried about the effect it's all having on our daughter.'

'Of course you are,' she said.

'Yes.' He paused. 'We have joint custody of Hannah – a few days each a week. It seemed a fair way of doing things when we arranged it.'

It might have been fair for Hannah's parents, but Serena thought it sounded terribly unsettling for Hannah.

Judging by the look on Mr Winchester's face, he didn't think it was very fair either.

'Do you think this might be having an adverse effect on your daughter?' Serena asked gently.

'I do. Yes. She's developed an issue with . . . food.'

Serena's ears pricked up. 'Do you mean an eating disorder?'

'Not exactly, no. But she's developed what she says are allergies. Food intolerances that she never used to have. Her mother has the same problem. She's sensitive to wheat, gluten, dairy, fish, sunflower seeds, grass – you name it.' He checked her face, she guessed, to see if she was listening.

He spread his hands. 'I'm not unsympathetic to food intolerances – believe me, I know they make people's lives a misery.' He paused again. 'But Hannah's are inconsistent. I wonder if you had noticed anything in school at all?'

'Girls do sometimes follow fads,' Serena began. He was shaking his head. She decided to change tack.

'I will certainly look into it for you,' she added.

A beat. 'There's something else.'

'Do go on.'

'Hannah's mother has . . . anxiety issues.'

'I see,' Serena said, even though she didn't. She smiled encouragingly.

'That's why I wanted to talk to you and not to Mrs Mc-Allister. Hannah's mother has seen her already, I believe . . .'

'Right.' It was starting to make sense. Maggie McAllister had said that Hannah's mother fell into the overprotective category. 'Neurotic doesn't really cover it,' Maggie had told her with a pained frown.

'Please continue,' Serena said to Hannah's father.

Mr Winchester shifted in his chair, leaning forward a little, his eyes on hers. 'And, well, over the last few weeks Hannah has become very anxious.'

For a moment he looked so anguished that Serena felt her heart tighten in empathy.

'I'm not a doctor,' she said slowly. 'But have you considered that she may be anxious as a result of your separation? That can have a huge effect on a child.'

'I think it's more than that. To tell you the truth, I'm worried sick. She used to be such a sociable little thing. But these days she spends hours on her own . . .'

'Have you talked to Hannah?'

'I have. She says she's fine. But she's not fine. She's losing weight. It's hard to get her to eat anything. I don't know what she's like at her mother's. It's bloody hard these days for us to have a civil conversation, to be honest. Me and her mother.'

Serena nodded. 'I think – for now – we should just continue to monitor the situation,' she said gently. 'We have a pastoral care team at Poppins, as I think you know. I'll put you in touch with them too.'

He looked at her. She could see the resignation in his eyes and she knew that he wanted her to do more. But she didn't know what else she could do.

He sighed.

'Why don't we talk again?' Serena suggested, reaching across the desk for her table diary. 'Maybe at the end of April?'

He nodded, hope flaring briefly in his eyes.

'If you're worried before then, do call me.' She gave him a business card. 'This is my direct line.'

As it happened, they were destined to meet again a lot sooner than either of them anticipated. Serena didn't usually do Waitrose on a Friday evening, but she was out of coffee beans – the one item she couldn't live without – so she dropped in after work. She was just reaching for the packet on the top shelf when she heard a commotion in the neighbouring aisle.

At first she thought it was the tail end of a toddler tantrum. She could hear a woman's angry voice and a child's urgent sobbing. And the commotion was coming her way. The little girl, who looked vaguely familiar – although that applied to most children in Little Sanderton – appeared first. Blinded by tears, she ran slap-bang into Serena, almost knocking her flying.

Instinctively, Serena put out a hand. 'Hey,' she said. 'What's the rush?'

The girl clung on tight. Beneath her coat, Serena recognised the familiar Poppins navy-and-red uniform. More slowly, she recognised that the sobbing, trembling little girl was Hannah. Still holding her, Serena looked around for Hannah's parents. She'd never met the estranged Mrs Winchester, but it wasn't difficult to spot her. Seemingly oblivious to her crying child, she was shouting at a man with a tin of baked beans in his hand.

'How many times have I told you? You stupid, brain-dead moron. If you feed her those she'll die. You don't deserve to be a father. What is WRONG with you?' The last sentence was screamed into her companion's ear at close quarters. Serena winced.

A small crowd of onlookers had gathered, and she could see a Waitrose manager heading over, a placatory smile fixed on her face.

Serena stroked Hannah's hair. 'Hush, hush,' she said. 'Everything's going to be fine.'

'I don't think so, Mrs Tate.' Hannah looked up at her with dark, tear-washed eyes that were very similar to her father's.

Serena fished around in her pocket for the mini-pack of tissues she always carried and hunkered down to the child's level.

'Wipe your eyes now. Mum and Dad are just having a little disagreement.' Blimey, that sounded like an understatement, even to her. Hannah wasn't going to be fobbed off with that.

'They're always fighting,' Hannah said, taking the tissue. 'It's because of Merissa.'

Who was *Merissa*? Serena wasn't sure she wanted to know.

'Merissa's a hussy,' Hannah went on, so softly that Serena wasn't sure she'd heard her right. 'Mum says she's a marriage-destroying hussy. What's a hussy, Mrs Tate?'

'Um . . .' Serena wasn't usually at a loss for words. Deciding discretion was the better part of valour, she said nothing.

Mr Winchester hadn't mentioned that part of the story, that was for sure. She suddenly didn't feel quite as sympathetic towards him. Mind you, nothing gave Mrs W the right to scream at her husband like she just had.

'I think Mum and Dad have stopped arguing now,' she said to Hannah, looking over. Mrs W was hugging her arms around herself, her face was mutinous. She didn't appear to have noticed that her child had gone AWOL.

Serena couldn't see Mr W's face. He was talking to the manager. He used his hands a lot in conversation. He was doing it now – waving them about in an agitated manner. The manager was nodding.

'Shall we head on back?'

Serena took Hannah's hand gently in hers.

Hannah nodded reluctantly, even as her eyes told a different story.

Serena didn't blame her. It took all of her considerable acting skills, tact and diplomacy to fix a neutral smile on her face in preparation for facing the feuding Mr and Mrs Winchester.

CHAPTER 42

To give him his due, Mr Winchester was incredibly apologetic to Serena too. Turning away from the Waitrose manager, he saw her approaching with Hannah and looked stricken.

He was white-faced, Serena observed with interest. The quiet confidence she'd seen in his eyes the first time they met had been replaced with a rather haunted look.

She was starting to feel sorry for him again, but then she remembered 'Merissa the marriage-destroying hussy' and decided that he didn't deserve too much sympathy. Clearly his ex was a little unhinged, but it was equally clear from what Hannah had said that Mr W was no angel either.

'Hannah was upset,' was all she said, as she met his gaze.

He nodded, bit his lip, and glanced at his daughter. Then, crouching down to her level, he said, 'I'm so sorry, darling. There's not going to be any more shouting.'

'Do you promise?' Hannah's voice was tremulous.

Despite her resolution never to get overly emotionally involved with a child in her care, Serena ached for her. She heard Mr Winchester's deep sigh and then his gravelly voice.

'I'll do my best to make sure there's no more shouting today.'

At least he hadn't made a promise he couldn't keep, she thought, feeling a glimmer of respect for him. At least he'd done that.

For the rest of the weekend, thoughts of Hannah and her warring parents kept flicking into Serena's head. She felt deeply unsettled, though she knew it was not all about them. The scene at the supermarket had stirred up some unpleasant memories from her own past.

Reading *Jane Eyre* again wasn't helping. Jane Eyre had grown up an orphan and had struggled through a nightmare childhood amongst cousins who bullied her, finding only the odd friend to give her solace.

Serena knew exactly how that felt. Although not because she'd grown up an orphan. Sometimes, she thought, there were worse things than losing your entire family at birth. At least then you had a *reason* to feel excluded. A reason for feeling that you would only ever be on the outside, looking in.

Serena was the middle child of three sisters. Christina, the eldest (by six years), had the brains – she was a consultant cardiologist like their father. Her younger sister, Angelina, had the beauty, not to mention the musical talent. She was an opera singer like their mother.

Serena had neither brains nor beauty. She wasn't sure whom she took after – apparently there was an aunt some-where who had a similar large nose – and the same bad eyesight (thanks a million, Auntie Laura). But she was clearly a disappointment to her entire family, and always had been.

Her school grades had been good – but that was more because she worked her butt off. Serena had known from a very young age that results were the only thing that mat-tered in her family. Unfortunately, her talents leaned more towards languages than sciences, so her father quickly lost interest. And her mother, once she realized that Serena wasn't ever going to be a pretty little songbird, also lost interest, particularly when Angelina came along.

At the tender age of seven years old, Serena gave up trying to win her parents' attention and concentrated on her studies.

Winning a place at Oxford didn't particularly impress them. Christina had already been there, so it was kind of expected. And when she went into teaching with a first-class honours degree – well, that was kind of expected too.

Unfortunately, landing the position at Poppins – which had a superb reputation – happened around the same time as Christina was given her consultancy and Angelina was cast in her first *Rigoletto*.

Even being promoted to headmistress a year ago didn't earn her parents' attention for long. But by then Serena didn't care. She had long since given up on ever impressing her family. They all lived in or around London anyway, and she had moved to Devon when she'd met Liam. It was peaceful and beautiful and enough out of the way that she had an excuse not to join in on every family occasion.

Her family didn't often get in touch. They were all heavily into social media, but Serena hated social media, so her family had to call when they wanted her for anything. But this was rare, so when she saw Christina's name flash up on her mobile on Sunday morning, she frowned.

There were no birthdays she'd missed, were there? Christina didn't usually do social calls.

'Hello, darling.' Christina's voice was light and cheery. 'How are you?'

'I'm very well, thank you. What can I do for you?'

Christina's laugh tinkled. Serena imagined her sitting at her breakfast bar in her ultra-modern kitchen. Her hair would be caught up in a chignon. Christina always wore her hair up, even at breakfast. Not a single shiny hair would be out of place.

'What makes you think I want something. Ha ha! Although, you're right, as it happens, I do. Dodie, bless her little cotton socks, has decided not to follow in the family footsteps. She wants to be a teacher.'

Serena didn't miss the slight incredulity in her voice as she pronounced the word 'teacher'. Or maybe she was being paranoid. Years of fending off mocking comments from her family had made her oversensitive.

Good for you, Dodie, she thought. Her niece had mentioned her career plans a couple of months earlier, but Serena hadn't known how serious she was. It wouldn't have been an easy choice to make in a family that thought a career outside of medicine wasn't worth getting out of bed for.

'We're kind of hoping she'll grow out of it,' Christina went on. So Serena wasn't being oversensitive then. 'But for now we're going along with it. You know what Dodie's like – if we object at this stage it'll just make her more determined to pursue it.'

Serena had always had a sneaking respect for her niece. She had never been a yes-child. Even when she was tiny, she'd been quick to disagree with her parents.

She reminded Serena of herself at that age.

'So, what I would like from you is a recommendation,' Christina said. 'Dodie needs a placement – in London, I mean. We thought maybe one of the inner-city schools, to give her a taste of the reality of being a teacher. We were hoping you could recommend a place – the rougher the better.'

Serena felt slightly aggrieved on Dodie's behalf. Not to mention irritated that Christina assumed she'd be happy to collude with her.

'I've got a list of prospective schools here,' Christina continued. 'If I just read them out to you, maybe you could tell us which ones are – er – most suitable?'

She read out the list. Serena smiled inwardly and picked the one she thought Dodie would enjoy the most.

'Wonderful,' Christina said. 'Now, I must love you and leave you. Trust you're OK, darling?' She didn't wait for an answer before disconnecting.

Serena sighed. Why did conversations with her family always leave her feeling flat?

Never mind. She had two whole weeks off school and she was spending them decorating. With luck she would get two bedrooms done – hers and the biggest guest room.

She'd also planned coffee with Jojo and possibly a touch of retail therapy with Kate. No school. No awkward parents, and only a small amount of paperwork. Bliss.

All of it went like clockwork. It had been fun catching up with Jojo and Kate. Both of them were loved-up – Kate with her builder and Jojo with the paediatrician she worked with. It was good to see.

'No sign of a Mr Rochester in your life yet then?' Jojo had asked idly, as they'd sipped lattes at the Costa in Exeter. 'You might be our Jane Eyre this month.'

'Sadly not,' Serena said, wondering why she hadn't mentioned Mr Winchester. Probably because there was nothing to mention, she thought.

Or was the truth actually that there was a tiny, deeply idealistic part of her that had hoped for that too.

Her first Monday back did not start well. When she got in there was a list of messages on her desk. All of them were marked urgent.

'Sorry, Serena.' A harassed-looking Lynn popped her head around the door. 'How was your break?'

'So-so,' Serena replied. 'Yours?'

'Manic.' She smiled. Lynn had three young children. 'And speaking of manic, one of your call-backs – Mr Winchester

– popped in first thing. He wanted to see you. Didn't you meet right before we broke up?'

'We did. Don't make another appointment,' she said. 'But if he rings again, put him through. Although preferably not until after lunch. I've got to go through the new fire regulations.'

At ten past two – just as Serena had decided she should probably get something to eat before she was too far into the afternoon – the phone on her desk rang.

'Mr Winchester!' Lynn announced. 'He's very persistent.'

'It's fine.' Serena took the call. Her brain threw up a tangle of images. Square jaws, intense dark eyes, marriage-wrecking hussies called Merissa. Ignoring them all, she kept her voice crisp.

'Good afternoon, Mr Winchester. What can I do for you?'

'Thank you for speaking to me.' There was a very brief silence. He'd clearly thought she might not. Then he continued, 'I wanted to apologize for what happened in – um – the supermarket.' There was a slightly loaded pause.

'There's no need to apologize—'

'And also to thank you. I'm very grateful to you for being there for Hannah.'

She fiddled with a paperclip on her desk. Maybe now was the time to tell him that Hannah was the loser in all this. But he knew that anyway. Contrary to what his ex-wife had said to him in Waitrose, Mr Winchester was clearly neither stupid nor unaware of the effect all this was having on Hannah.

She was just trying to think of a tactful way to phrase what she wanted to say when he beat her to it.

'Hurting my daughter is the last thing I want to do.' There was such distress in his voice that she felt that ache of empathy start again.

She sighed. 'Marriage break-ups are always difficult. It would probably be helpful if you and Mrs Winchester were on better terms.' She'd probably overstepped the mark there – it was definitely none of her business – but the incident in Waitrose *had* been extreme.

'I know. We did talk during the holidays. I think we're getting somewhere.'

'Good,' Serena said. 'And in the meantime we'll keep an eye on Hannah.'

'Thank you.' There was another pause. She had a feeling he wanted to say something else, but she didn't give him the chance.

'Goodbye, Mr Winchester,' she said. 'And thank you for phoning.'

She still had the paperclip in her hands. It was metallic with a red plastic coating and it was now bent completely out of shape. Talking to him was clearly more stressful than she thought.

CHAPTER 43

On Wednesday morning, Hannah Winchester didn't turn up for school. Serena probably wouldn't have been aware of this as quickly as she was had she not chosen that particular morning to go along to class registration and speak to Hannah's teacher.

'Have you had a phone call?' Serena asked, her senses suddenly on full alert.

'Not that I'm aware of.' Maggie McAllister frowned as she stepped out into the corridor and closed the door quietly on her class. 'She was fine yesterday. Although perhaps a wee bit quiet.' Her eyes narrowed as she looked at Serena. 'What's the story there?'

'Her father's worried about her. What's the mother like?'

'As I said before, she's a worrier,' Maggie said. 'More than most. There have been incidents.' She opened the door a crack and glanced in at her class of pupils, then shut it again.

'At the beginning of last term,' Maggie continued, 'Alison, in the art department, asked the students to bring in some materials for a class. Debbie Winchester texted Alison about it *nineteen times*. It was a little extreme.' She rolled her eyes.

'I'll say. What did Alison do?'

'Well, you know how laid-back Alison is. Although I think she did ask her not to text in the middle of the night.' Maggie grimaced. 'I had an issue with her once about school dinners. Her daughter has developed allergies, it seems. Well, as you know, we're pretty hot on that one. I think we managed to reassure her. And I've since noticed that Hannah is more sensible when it comes to what she can and can't eat.'

'I see.' Serena hesitated. 'Thank you. I'll just go and check and see if anyone's phoned in about her. I'll keep you posted.'

'Thanks.'

No one had phoned. Serena glanced at her watch. 'I'm a little concerned,' she told Lynn, 'I think I'll phone her parents.'

Mr Winchester answered her call within four rings. 'Good morning.' His voice was brusque. When she told him Hannah hadn't arrived at school he got brusquer.

'I'll phone her mother,' he said. 'Hannah's with her at the moment. Thank you for letting me know.'

Serena couldn't settle, despite the pile of paperwork on her desk needing her attention. She paced up and down her office, occasionally glancing out of the window. She could see the main gates from here – locked, as they always were at this time of day – but there was no sign of a lone child.

It was a beautiful day. Warm and sunny, yet Serena felt cold. Poor Hannah. Life couldn't be much fun for her lately. Serena knew what it was like to have rowing parents, although hers had mainly confined their arguments to the house.

Two enormous egos in the same house always leads to trouble, Christina had told her when she was older. Christina had never been bothered by their parents' rows. But Christina was thicker-skinned than both of her sisters.

Christina had enjoyed the drama, but Serena had yearned for peace. Sometimes when her parents had been fighting she had hidden in the back utility room. It was also where the catflap and food was, which meant that their old tom, Wagner, could often be found there.

Wagner was the one creature in the house who was always pleased to see her. Serena spent a lot of time crouched beside him, stroking his warm ginger fur and listening to his rumbling purrs while she waited for her parents to stop fighting.

Wagner represented love in the early part of Serena's childhood. Love with four legs and soft fur and a kind old rumble of a purr.

The phone on Serena's desk rang and she was jolted from her musings.

'Hannah was dropped off as usual at eight fifteen by her mother.' She could hear the strain in Mr Winchester's voice. 'I'm leaving work now. I'm going to come over to the school. Do I need to contact the police?'

'I think that would be prudent,' Serena said. Her instincts were telling her that there was unlikely to be a third party involved, but protocol told her to cover all bases. 'Mr Winchester?' she said. 'Please try not to worry.'

He'd already hung up. She didn't blame him. That had been a stupid thing to say. Of course he would worry. Anyone would worry.

She would start the search herself. Serena knew she shouldn't have got emotionally involved like this, but it was too late. She'd become involved the moment Hannah had run into her arms in Waitrose.

She had just put on her coat and was heading back along the corridor when she saw Mr Winchester's tall frame hurtling towards her from the opposite direction.

'Any news?' she asked him.

He shook his head. 'Debbie's dealing with the police. She definitely dropped her off. And she watched her walk through the gates – she was adamant about that.'

Serena nodded. It shouldn't have been possible for Hannah to leave the school again. Once she'd come into school there were teachers around – more than one, usually. But then again, there were dozens of pupils and if a child really wanted to slip back out again, they could probably do it.

'Does Hannah have a mobile phone?'

He nodded. 'A pay as you go. It's switched off. She only puts it on for emergencies.'

His face was white. The poor man. She touched his arm. 'Just supposing that she did decide to leave school, is there anywhere she might go? A friend? Or a relative? Maybe someone who lives nearby?'

'I can't think of anyone.'

Serena frowned. Hannah really was all on her own, wasn't she? She thought about Wagner and of safety and about the warmth of the utility room. If Hannah had run away then she would surely go somewhere that felt safe. 'Perhaps an after-school club?' she ventured.

Something sparked in his eyes. 'There is somewhere – it's a bit of a long shot. But it's worth a try.'

She looked at him.

'The stables,' he said. 'She's just started having riding lessons. She loves it down there and it isn't far from here. Definitely walking distance.' He was already turning away.

'Wait!' she called after him, and her voice must have been sharper than she'd intended because he turned back immediately. 'I'll come with you.'

This was definitely above and beyond the call of duty, but Serena didn't care. She knew the stables he was talking about. It would also explain why no one had seen her go out of the gate. She wouldn't have needed to. There was a shortcut across the school field.

They went in Mr Winchester's car. She'd expected something flash, a Mercedes or a Range Rover maybe, but he had a red Berlingo. The back seats were covered in bits of straw and it smelled faintly of horses. There was a riding hat rolling about in the passenger footwell.

'Sorry about the straw,' he said distractedly. He waved a hand. 'I keep meaning to clean it.'

'It's fine.' Inwardly, Serena smiled. Funnily enough, the car made her like him more. It made him more human. She remembered Merissa. Maybe that made him human too.

Little Sanderton Stables offered lessons, forest hacks and beach rides, according to the white painted sign outside.

They negotiated two five-bar gates, both closed, and Mr Winchester parked in a gravelled area alongside a couple of other cars. Behind them, a row of loose boxes, all of them empty and with the doors hooked open, curved around a yard, which appeared to be a hive of activity.

A teenager pushed a wheelbarrow past them. Another one carried a saddle over her arm. A third was filling up buckets with water. The air smelled of manure and horses.

Surely someone would have noticed a stray ten-year-old girl, Serena thought.

Her father seemed to be of the same mind. He glanced at her. 'I'll just check with the office. If she's here, I think they'd know.'

She followed more slowly, but before they'd got to the prefab building a woman emerged. She was very tall, quite glamorous, with skin-tight, immaculate beige jodhpurs, shiny riding boots and a perfectly made-up face.

'Eddie,' she greeted him with a smile. 'I thought I recognized the car. Were you just passing?'

So they're on first-name terms, Serena noted, wondering if this was marriage-breaking Merissa. *Don't be so judgemental,* she berated herself. *You know nothing about it.*

Mr Winchester didn't waste any time on small talk. He explained what had happened and her smile faded immediately.

'I haven't seen her. But let's have a walk around – just to be on the safe side, yah?' She threw Serena a curious look, clearly hoping to be introduced, but Mr Winchester – Eddie – was in too much of a hurry for niceties.

The place was spotless, Serena observed as they crossed the yard, Miss Glamorous Jodhpurs asking her young staff, none of whom could have been more than eighteen, if they'd seen Hannah.

All of them shook their heads.

Where would I go if I were Hannah? Serena wondered, thinking again of the utility room. Certainly nowhere there were lots of people. Because then Hannah would have to explain herself.

She cleared her throat. 'Do you have somewhere you store food – or tack, possibly?'

'We do.' Miss Glamorous Jodhpurs looked at her thoughtfully. 'Follow me.'

She showed them a feed room, which smelled of something earthy and faintly sweet. Around the walls were metal containers, all big enough to hide a child, but none concealing one, they discovered, as Eddie lifted them up one by one to check. He was looking very grim again. *He'd been so sure Hannah would be here,* Serena thought. So had she.

The tack room, which smelled strongly of leather and horses, was also empty, and there were fewer places to hide.

As they emerged, Serena glanced towards a barn a few feet away. 'What's in there?' she asked.

'Just hay. She won't be in there. We keep it bolted.'

'It's not bolted now,' Serena pointed out, feeling her heart quicken as she stepped across to the door.

Moments later they were all inside, surrounded by the musty scent of hay. After the bright sun outside it took a little while for their eyes to adjust to the gloom.

'There's not a lot in here at the moment—' Miss Glamorous Jodhpurs began, but Eddie held up a hand to stop her.

'Did you hear that?' he said.

They all strained their ears. Then it came again. A barely muffled sneeze.

'Hannah?' Eddie called.

For a few moments there was silence. But then they heard the tiniest sound. A scratching, rustling sound. As if someone were moving not very far away.

Serena hoped it wasn't rats. She wasn't a big fan of rats.

'Hannah?' Eddie called again, his voice soft. 'Are you in here, love? You're not in any trouble. I just want to know you're safe.'

Silence again – and then one of the hay bales in the stack furthest away from them moved. Slowly at first, followed by a more definite shift to the left, as if someone were shoving it from behind. A pair of shoes emerged. Little shoes that were attached to ankles encased in polka-dot socks.

'Oh, Hannah . . .' Mr Winchester's voice cracked a little as he strode across.

Serena and Miss Glamorous Jodhpurs glanced at each other, united in a moment of glorious relief. Serena swallowed a lump in her throat as Hannah climbed out of the hay and then rushed into her father's waiting arms.

CHAPTER 44

On Friday afternoon, when Serena had left school for the day and was looking forward to a quiet night – a box set and a bottle of red left over from Reading Group – Mr Winchester phoned.

He called her mobile, and she knew it was him because she'd programmed his number into her phone. She had told him to call if he was in the least bit worried about Hannah. She had decided that he wasn't the kind of parent who would abuse the privilege of having her number.

And so far he hadn't.

She hesitated for only a second before answering it. 'Is Hannah all right?' she asked.

'Yes, everything's fine. Thank you.' There was the tiniest pause.

Serena filled it. 'So what can I do for you, Mr Winchester?'

'Eddie, please,' he said. Another little pause. 'I may be

completely out of line here, but I was hoping you might come for a drink with me. Or a coffee,' he added, when she didn't answer immediately. 'I wanted to say thank you. Properly, I mean.'

Serena glanced at the glass of red she'd just poured. 'Tonight?'

'Well, er, not necessarily tonight. Although tonight would be good if you're free? Of course you're not free. You have plans. I apologize. My head's not really in the right place, I'm—'

'Tonight would be fine,' Serena interrupted. What the heck! What else was she going to do? Get quietly tipsy by herself? That wasn't exactly top of her list of fun ways to spend an evening. And she was concerned about Hannah. There was something about the little girl that reminded her strongly – painfully – of herself.

'Tonight would be fine,' she said again. 'I did have plans. But they were cancelled. So I'm free.'

Why on earth had she said that? Some urge to make him think she was massively popular and that her calm, in-control headmistress persona wasn't just a façade?

'Great,' he said. 'Have you eaten? Would you like supper too?'

'Er, no, I haven't. Yes, OK, why not? That would be lovely.'

They arranged a place to meet and she smiled as she got ready. A man who said supper – that was unusual. It was a word her parents would have used.

They went to Ocean Views and began the evening with an aperitif (sparkling water for him, still for her) on the cliff-top terrace. It was a mild evening and a montage of peach and pink and gold streaked the sky. They leaned on the rail that surrounded the terrace and watched the sea turn into a shimmer of coloured glass.

'Isn't that beautiful?' he remarked, his face in profile as he looked out at the horizon and then back at her. 'Have you always lived in Devon, Serena? May I call you Serena?'

'Yes, you may. And no, I haven't.' She smiled at him. 'Can't you tell by my accent?'

He frowned. 'Accent. Hmm, let me see. Middle-class, but not posh – I'd say Estuary.'

'Well done,' she said. 'I was born in Hyde Park. Well, not literally. But yes, that's my background. Most of my family have got really posh accents. I spent ages trying to get rid of mine. And no, I moved here three years ago for my job.' She wouldn't mention Liam. He could assume what most people did – that her career was her life. Thirty-three was young to have a headship. 'How about you?'

'I'm not local either.' His eyes warmed. 'We moved down here when I was small. I got picked on at school. Although not because my accent was posh. I'm from the other side of the river. Vauxhall!' He smiled at her surprise. 'Yeah. Proper Sahf Lahndan.' That eyebrow raise again. He had quite bushy eyebrows.

'You did a good job on the accent,' she said. 'Not a trace of Sahf Lahndan.'

'Except when I've had one too many beers, apparently. So my friends tell me!'

There was a part of her analytical brain that was already niggling away at her. She had never gone out with a parent socially before, was she attracted to him? Yes, probably, to be honest. She hadn't done dating lately either. Although she had tried it. Eighteen months or so after Liam had died, she'd given in to the relentless chant of family and friends: *Liam wouldn't expect you to stay alone forever.*

Online dating had scared her senseless. After two nights of being besieged with messages from men who 'wanted to meet her' she'd deleted her profile. She wasn't ready to sit in a restaurant with a stranger, trying to fill in the awkward pauses with inane chitchat.

There had been one or two pauses tonight, but they hadn't felt awkward at all.

She pulled her coat a little tighter around her. The evening was beginning to cool – a sea breeze whispering through the peachy air.

'I love Devon, though,' she continued. 'I've no plans to go back.'

'Me neither,' he said. 'Shall we go inside to eat? It'll be warmer.'

He was perceptive, but not pushy. She wondered why his marriage had broken down. Then she remembered Merissa. And she reminded herself that this was not a date. She was here because she had helped out with his daughter. Perhaps he wanted to ask her advice again.

At their table, she laid her serviette across her lap and went into headmistress mode. 'How is Hannah? Have you had a chance to talk to her properly yet?'

He nodded. 'A little. I didn't want to push her. She said . . .' He sighed and took a sip of his water. 'Well, Hannah said she thought it would be different now we're separated. But it isn't. She said that she doesn't feel as if it's ever going to end – the arguments.' He swallowed. 'That was hard to hear.'

'Yes,' Serena said. 'I bet.'

'I've agreed with Debbie that I will step back a bit. We're going to try and make things more stable for Hannah. We both feel it would be better if she had her base at Debbie's but came to me just for alternate weekends.' His eyes shadowed and Serena knew it wasn't what he wanted. He paused. 'Do you think that would work?'

'Will it mean there will be fewer rows?' she asked gently.

'I'm hoping so.' They paused to order. Mixed grill with fries for him, Dover sole for her. She would insist on paying her half.

'The truth is,' he said, 'Debbie doesn't trust me.' Did his face colour a little or was it a trick of the light? She couldn't tell. 'But she's going to try harder. When it's my turn to have Hannah, I mean.' He blinked.

He bit his lip. 'Debbie has been in the habit of texting Hannah when she's with me to ask where we're going. Then she turns up – like she did at the supermarket. It's happened a few times now.'

'Good grief,' Serena exclaimed. 'That must be extremely difficult for your daughter. She must feel torn in two. Sorry,' she added hastily.

'No. It's me who should apologize. I didn't ask you here to dump all this on you.' He paused. 'I asked you because I wanted to say thank you, and ...' He paused again. 'The truth is, I wanted to ask you out.'

Now she could see it was no trick of the light. His face was definitely flushed. He rubbed his nose nervously with the side of his index finger. 'I'm completely out of line now, aren't I? You said yes in, um, a professional capacity, didn't you?'

'I don't usually go out for dinner with the parents of pupils in a professional capacity,' Serena told him. Her glasses were steaming up. How embarrassing. She took them off and wiped them.

She could see him clearly again now. He looked very vulnerable. She would need to find a tactful way of broaching the subject of Merissa. She could hardly just dive in and say that Hannah had mentioned a marriage-destroying hussy. She would ask him, she decided, if Miss Glamorous Jodpurs and Merissa were one and the same person, but she wouldn't do it tonight. She would see how things went first.

'I said yes because I wanted to,' she added, and smiled. 'Shall we start again?'

'Yes. Thanks.' There was relief in his eyes. Warmth, too. 'This would be a really good time for the waitress to arrive, wouldn't it?'

'Yes,' she said, and looked over his shoulder. 'But I'm afraid there isn't one in sight. Life is rarely that neat, is it?'

'Nope,' he agreed. And for the first time, Serena felt as though they were perfectly in tune.

At the end of the evening he said, 'Would you like to do this again? Shall I call you?'

She nodded. 'Sounds nice.'

'We could maybe catch a movie?' They'd established they had very different tastes: she liked arty French films with subtitles and he liked three-hour historical epics, but surprisingly they both liked Disney films too. 'It's Hannah's fault,' he had said. 'I've seen so many with her that I've developed a taste for them. What's your excuse?'

'Candyfloss for the brain,' she'd replied. 'OK, next time there's a Disney film, we can catch it together.'

She drove home smiling. When she got in and switched her mobile on – she'd turned it off in the restaurant – she discovered she had two missed calls and three messages on her voicemail from Dodie.

She played the most recent one. 'Hi, Auntie Serena. Can you call me when you get this? I think Mum's lost the plot.'

Serena glanced at the time – it was almost eleven. Probably not too late to phone her sixteen-year-old niece. She would almost certainly be awake.

Concerned, she sat in the orangery and called her back.

Dodie answered straight away. 'Hi, Auntie S. Did you get my messages? I'm at the train station. Just waiting for a taxi.'

'A taxi?' Serena blinked rapidly. Clearly she had some catching up to do. 'Are you coming here?'

'Yes – if that's OK? Sorry to spring it on you. But I've fallen out with the old folks. And I knew you wouldn't mind.'

Well, that last bit was true, although she was shocked.

'Oh,' Serena said. 'Of course I don't. Shall I come and get you? I've only just got in.'

'No, don't worry. The taxi's just turned up. I might need a loan to pay it though. It's a bit more than what I was expecting . . . Hang on a minute! How much? That's extortion,

347

mate. It's not even midnight. I thought London rates were bad.'

Serena sighed. 'Are you in Exeter?' No wonder it was pricey. 'Look, I'll come and get you. Cancel the taxi.'

She could hear the argument going on in the background as she moved into the hall to get the coat she'd so recently abandoned. 'I'm on my way,' she told Dodie. 'Is there somewhere warm you can sit?'

Dodie laughed. 'You are funny. I'm tougher than I look.'

You and me both, Serena thought as she pulled on to the A3052 a short while later. What a strange old evening it had been. She was still processing her 'date'. It didn't mean they would end up in a long-term relationship, she told herself.

Romance had been the last thing on her mind lately. Though it rather had a habit of turning up when you weren't looking.

That was what Jojo had said the other day. They'd been chatting about Daniel and how well it was going. 'I hadn't realized how out of practice I was,' Jojo had said.

Serena could certainly relate to that.

Her thoughts turned back to Dodie. They had always got on well – kindred spirits from day one. Like Serena, Dodie was bright, oversensitive and stubborn as hell. Serena had had plenty of fallings out with her parents too, not to mention her sisters.

Still, she frowned as she pulled into the car park of Exeter St David's Station. Dodie had never turned up on her doorstep unexpectedly before.

CHAPTER 45

Dodie was sitting on a bench texting when Serena found her. 'Oh, hi.' She glanced up.

'Have you got any bags?'

'Just my backpack.' Dodie pointed over her shoulder with her thumb. 'Don't worry; I've got everything I need. I'm an expert on smart packing. Did you see the pictures of my Croatia trip on Facebook?'

'I think I did see a few,' Serena said, studying her niece's face. She looked the same as she always did. Slightly thinner, maybe, but then her mother was gazelle-like too. She was a little pale. Serena thought she may or may not have been crying recently.

'I'll tell you about it in the car,' Dodie said. 'Thanks, Auntie S. I really appreciate you coming.'

'I take it your parents know you're with me?' Serena said, as they pulled out of the station car park.

'I said I was staying with a friend.' Catching her aunt's look, she added quickly, 'If I'd told them the truth, Mum would be straight on the phone to you. I'm sure you don't want that, do you?'

Serena didn't, but it seemed disloyal to admit it. 'So what happened?' she asked, as Dodie finally stopped texting and put away her phone – or more likely lost the signal.

'Well, as you know, they want me to go into medicine.' Dodie tutted. 'And I have as much interest in medicine as I do in Japanese ceramics.'

'Hmm. So you're not keen on going into medicine, then?' she prompted.

'No. I am not!' Serena could hear the passion running through Dodie's voice now.

'Last time we spoke you wanted to teach,' Serena said. 'Is that still the case?'

'Yes. I've wanted to teach for as long as I can remember.'

Serena supressed a smile. A couple of months would have been a more accurate description. Sometimes Dodie was much more like her drama-queen mother than she would ever like to hear.

'I thought your mum was being supportive about the teaching,' Serena ventured.

'She's supportive to my face whilst plotting behind my back to sabotage it. Do you know what she did yesterday?'

'What?' Serena asked guardedly.

'She told my careers adviser to cancel a placement at a school I'd chosen. She tried to get her to change it to some dodgy school in Hackney. It's not even in our district.'

'How do you know that?' Serena felt slightly shocked. That was pushing the boundaries, even for Christina.

'Because I heard her trying to do it on the phone. She thought I was out. Well, I wasn't. Ha! So I had it out with her.'

'I take it that didn't go well?'

Their conversation was interrupted by the pings of several texts coming through to Dodie's phone. Dodie was diverted for a few moments while she answered them, tapping away at top speed. *How did teenagers cope before phones?* Serena mused. No wonder kids' concentration spans were shot to pieces these days.

She stared out at the dark road. There wasn't much traffic about now – just the odd taxi. She wondered what Eddie was doing. Their bright, flirty evening seemed hours ago.

'She didn't even apologize,' said Dodie, continuing the conversation as if they'd never been interrupted. 'She just kept repeating, "I only want what's best for you, Dodie." Well, it's about time she worked out that what's best for me is being honest. And if she can't even do that then we're through!' She harrumphed loudly.

'Right,' Serena said. She felt exhausted already and they were still ten minutes from home.

'You think I shouldn't have stormed out on her.' Dodie's voice was suddenly quieter and not so indignant.

Serena negotiated a roundabout. They were on the home stretch. 'Darling, I don't know what I think.' She kept her voice soft. 'What I do know is that it's way too late for serious discussions about anything.' She pulled into the

351

driveway. Thank heavens they were back. 'We can talk about everything in the morning. Are you sure your mother knows you're safe?'

There was a part of her that wanted to text and check, but it wasn't a very big part. The prospect of Christina ranting at her didn't appeal one bit.

'Yes, she knows. I promise.'

Serena doubted that Christina would be pleased when she found out where her daughter really was. Dodie had stayed here before – lots of times – but never without her mother's permission.

It was becoming a habit – getting involved with other people's children. What was going on? She took a mug of hot chocolate up to bed and put it on the bedside table, but she was asleep before she had time to actually drink it.

In the morning, the house was its usual quiet self and it took Serena a little while to recall the events of the previous evening.

Not that Dodie will be up, she mused, as she went downstairs. It was nearly quarter past eight – anything before nine would be early for Dodie. She was a night owl.

She wondered whether she ought to phone Christina, just to let her know that Dodie was fine.

Probably not yet. But she would try to persuade Dodie to phone her later.

She made breakfast instead. A full English consisting of fat pork sausages that spat in the pan, sizzling bacon, hash browns, scrambled eggs, tomatoes – the whole works. She doubted whether Dodie had eaten much yesterday.

It did the trick too. Dodie appeared before she'd finished cooking.

'OMG, that smells amazing. Can I move in with you permanently?'

'No,' Serena said, shooting her an amused glance. 'Not unless you're going to cook breakfast for *me* every day. Then I might consider it.'

'Like you'd want this every day,' Dodie said with a sceptical tilt of her head. 'You'd be as big as a house. And speaking of houses – wasn't there talk of you downsizing once?'

'Mm,' Serena said, putting a plate in front of her niece.

'Let me guess. Our *family*' – Dodie mimed inverted commas in the air – 'thought it would be a good idea for you to downsize for practical reasons. But you wanted to stay here because of Uncle Liam's memory.'

Ouch. Her words were so unerringly accurate that Serena felt an arrow of pain heading straight for her heart. It must have shown on her face because Dodie said instantly, 'Sorry. That was really bloody insensitive.' She reached across the table and touched Serena's arm. 'Sorry,' she said again.

'It's ok,' Serena said, blinking rapidly. She was amazed how close tears were.

'We're all tactless sometimes, darling,' Serena told her niece. 'And you don't need to apologize for saying it how it is. Actually, that's one of the things I like about you.' She put her knife and fork down. 'I probably should downsize.

It's bittersweet sometimes. This house should be full of people, but apart from having the Reading Group here once a month it's empty.'

There was a pause. Dodie put a piece of sausage in her mouth and chewed thoughtfully. 'You're not seeing anyone then? There's no one in the Reading Group you fancy?'

'It's all women,' Serena told her with a smile. 'Although there was talk of a man joining once. But I don't think he was much interested in reading. I think he had an ulterior motive.'

'I bet he did,' Dodie said, attending to a text. 'Pity it wasn't you.'

Actually it had been, but Serena didn't want to go there. 'We wouldn't rule out a man,' she said idly. 'But there's not so many men that read fiction. We're on *Jane Eyre* this month.'

'Oh, yes!' Interest sparked in Dodie's eyes. 'That was on our reading list in English. Quite a few of the girls thought Mr Rochester was hot, but I thought he was a sexist pig.'

'Things were different in those days,' Serena said.

'He lied and cheated and shagged his way around Europe, whilst keeping his wife locked up in an attic and feeding her gruel! No wonder she set his bed on fire.'

'She set his house on fire in the end,' Serena pointed out. 'So he did get his comeuppance.'

'Quite right too!' Dodie said. 'Anyway, they knew how to write books in those days. Not like today.'

'There is plenty of good literature on the shelves today,' Serena responded, aggrieved, and Dodie laughed.

'I know, Auntie S. I'm just winding you up.'

'For that you can stack the dishwasher!'

Serena escaped upstairs before Dodie could object.

'I did like the character of Jane Eyre though,' Dodie said when Serena came back down, although not to the sparkling kitchen she'd hoped for. Dodie had got as far as putting the side plates in the dishwasher, which was now full of toast crumbs. 'By the way, your phone just rang. It was someone called Eddie Winchester. He wanted to thank you for dinner. He thought I was you,' Dodie said, widening her eyes innocently.

Serena shook her head, half-amused, half-irritated. 'And you didn't contradict him, I suppose?'

Dodie lifted her hands, palms spread. 'Of course I did, just not straight away. Who is he anyway? Nice voice. Very James Arthur.'

'He's the father of a girl at school. Did he say what he wanted?'

'He said something about Beauty and the Beast being on at the Odeon.' Dodie narrowed her eyes. 'But he clammed up when he realized he wasn't speaking to you. You kept that quiet!' She giggled. 'Hey, he hasn't got a mad wife with arsonist tendencies, has he?'

'You are impossible.' Serena shook her head.

'I know.' Dodie smiled. 'Mum says that all the time. I'm going to call her in a minute. She's phoned about eight times.'

'Hey, I thought you were doing the washing up?' Serena said, as Dodie exited the kitchen hastily.

There was no answer. Serena sat back down at the kitchen table. She could deal with a whole school of pupils with one hand tied behind her back, yet her sixteen-year-old niece could run rings around her. How did that work?

CHAPTER 46

'What are the chances of me coming into school with you, Auntie S? That would be a great place to get some work experience.'

They were in the orangery with some fresh lattes, and the sun was streaming through the glass and reminding Serena that she needed to dust more often.

'I'm sure it's possible,' she said, wishing her niece would put away her phone. Every conversation they had was fragmented with texts. 'But we would have to arrange it. You can't just turn up with me on Monday.'

Dodie nodded. 'No. I thought you might say that.'

Serena yawned. She was tired. She wasn't good at late nights and, lovely as her niece was, she was also pretty full on. She also felt a little unnerved by the fact that Eddie Winchester had phoned her up so soon. And that he'd found a Disney film. She'd expected that he might call in a couple of days. Mind you, it would have been easier to process if Dodie hadn't turned up unexpectedly.

'Dodie,' she ventured. 'I'm going to ask you a question and I want you to be honest with me. If your parents weren't so against the idea, would you still want to be a teacher?'

Dodie looked at her thoughtfully. 'That's a really good question. Actually, I'm not sure.' Her eyes grew very bright. She blinked rapidly.

There was a box of tissues on the coffee table between them. Serena pushed them towards her niece. 'Oh, sweetie,' she said. 'Tell me what's wrong.'

Dodie sniffed loudly, plucked a handful of tissues from the box and blew her nose. Then she began to speak in a voice that had none of her usual bravado in it. 'I don't know what I want to do,' she said, and a tear dripped down her nose. 'The honest truth is there's too much choice and I'm really, really scared of getting it wrong.'

Serena went and sat beside her on the couch, putting a comforting arm around her niece's shoulders. 'You don't have to know now, sweetie,' she said. 'You've got ages and ages to make up your mind about what you want to do.'

'But I haven't,' Dodie murmured, and she gave a quiet sob that tore at Serena's heart. 'We've got to decide on our work experience and things. Mum says it's really important to get it right.'

'But that doesn't mean you have to get it right *first time*. That's the whole point of work experience. So you can try things out. No one's expecting you to plan out your whole career right now. Do you want to know what I did for my work experience?'

Dodie wiped her eyes and nodded.

'I went into a veterinary practice in London. I thought it was the one branch of medicine I might actually fancy.' She paused. 'I was getting a certain amount of pressure in that direction too.'

'Yeah, I can imagine,' Dodie said. 'So why didn't you want to be a vet? I thought you really liked animals?'

'Yes, I do, and that's one of the reasons I decided against it,' Serena said. 'I couldn't, for example, go into an abattoir without being completely heartbroken. And it was one of the things we would have had to do if I chose that career.'

Dodie shuddered. 'I couldn't do that either.'

'OK. Well let's think about this practically.' Serena reached for a notepad and pen that were on the coffee table. 'Do you know what else you definitely *don't* want to do?' she asked. 'Maybe we could start there?'

By midday they'd established quite a lot about what Dodie definitely didn't want to do. She didn't want to be a vet either, and she definitely didn't want to go into anything to do with agriculture or horticulture. She didn't want to work in any kind of office. She didn't want to work with small children – although being a university lecturer was still on the table. She didn't want to work in the catering industry, or in a shop (not even a posh boutique – too much standing up), and neither did she want to work for local government.

'How about a career in the media – does that appeal? You'd be a great journalist. You can be very eloquent when you want to be.'

'You're not just saying that?'

'I'm not just saying that. I'd suggest you became an author but I don't think there's a lot of money in it.'

'No.' Dodie shuddered. 'It's bad enough being named after one! She was a proper author, wasn't she? Dodie Smith. She didn't just do *The Hundred and One Dalmatians*?'

'She was a brilliant author – and a playwright,' Serena said with affection. 'Her best book was *I Capture the Castle*. You should read it some time.'

Dodie screwed up her face. 'Isn't it out of print?'

'No,' Serena said crisply. She chewed the end of her pen and looked into her niece's face. At least she'd cheered up. She'd been quite worried earlier.

'What I would really like to do,' Dodie said thoughtfully, 'is help people.'

'Maybe fundraising then?' Serena suggested.

'Nope.' Dodie frowned. 'I've got it,' she said. 'Law.' And all at once her voice was confident and decisive. 'That's what I'd like to do. I want to go into law.'

'Gosh,' Serena said.

'What? Don't you think I'd be any good at it?'

'Let me see.' Serena tipped her head on one side, considering. 'Now what attributes do I think a person might need for a career in law? Fearlessness, persistence, stubbornness, a brilliant analytical mind.' She counted them off on her fingers. 'Independence, a fondness for a good argument if the situation demands it. I'm thinking taxi drivers!' she said as Dodie widened her eyes incredulously.

'So do you think Mum and Dad would approve of me being a lawyer then?'

Both Hugo and Christina were terrible snobs. Serena had a feeling they'd enjoy boasting about their lawyer daughter.

'I think they might do, yes,' she said with a little smile. 'What shall we do for lunch?'

'Can we go out?' Dodie asked. 'Can we go to Exeter? I'm bored with looking at the sea. And my ears are starting to ring with the quiet.'

Serena smiled. 'Of course we can. So will you go into a law firm for your work experience then?' she asked.

'No, I think I might go to Bart's.'

'Bart's hospital?' Serena looked at her in amazement. 'Where your father works?'

'Yes. I like your theory that you should try out things so you can rule them out. Besides ...' She flicked Serena an amused glance. 'It'll shut Mum up, won't it?'

Much later, when they'd had lunch, been on an impromptu shopping spree and were having a breather in Costa Coffee, Dodie decided that she might as well go back to London.

'Most of my stuff's in my backpack,' she explained. 'There's a few bits still at yours, but I can pick them up next time. It'll give me an excuse to come and see you.'

'OK, if you're sure?'

'Yeah, I think I am. Tonight I can stay with the friend Mum thinks I'm staying with.' She dipped a piece of shortbread into her latte. 'Then it wouldn't be so much of a lie, would it?'

'I guess not.'

'I will tell Mum that I've seen you if you think I should though? Do you?'

'I think that if you want your mum to be honest with you, you need to be honest with her too.'

'Yeah, I guess you're right.' Dodie stirred her coffee thoughtfully. 'Anyway, tell me about your Mr Rochester – what's he like?'

'His name's Winchester,' Serena corrected, realizing suddenly that she hadn't called him back and resolving to do it as soon as Dodie had gone.

'They've got the same first name though, haven't they?' Dodie licked her spoon. 'That's a coincidence.'

And one that hadn't escaped Serena. 'Yes,' she said. 'Although I can't really imagine Jane Eyre calling her man Eddie, can you?'

'No.' Dodie sniggered. 'So does this Eddie bloke have a mad wife?'

'Nothing like that,' Serena said, thinking of Debbie Winchester and feeling a little uneasy.

'But the million-dollar question is . . .' Dodie paused for dramatic effect. 'Do you think he's hot?'

Serena stared into her coffee thoughtfully.

'We're being totally honest, remember?' Dodie added with a smirk.

Serena cleared her throat. 'I have to say hot isn't the first adjective that springs to mind either.' She thought about

Eddie Winchester's craggy face, his slightly wonky nose, those intense dark eyes. 'But he's got a certain something, yes. Definitely.'

Dodie's eyes sparkled with mischief. 'So he's ugly then?'

'No! No, he isn't ugly. I didn't say that. Stop putting words in my mouth.'

'Mind you,' Dodie went on idly, 'since *Beauty and the Beast* came out, ugly is the new hot. People are holding *Beauty and the Beast* parties all over London. The girls get really glammed up and the guys have to black out their teeth and walk with a limp and stuff.'

Serena blinked. 'Really? I'm not sure I believe you!'

'Total truth. Ugly blokes are "on trend". It's awesome.' She paused for breath. 'It's a bit of a coincidence that he's asked you to go and see it, isn't it?'

Serena smiled. 'Not really. We both like Disney. Besides,' she added a little wistfully, 'I hardly fit into the category of beauty, do I? Don't answer that,' she warned, as Dodie opened her mouth to comment.

Wisely, Dodie didn't pursue it.

Soon afterwards, Serena dropped Dodie off at the station. They stood by her car at the drop-off point and hugged.

'I've had such fun today,' Dodie said. 'Yesterday I thought I was never going to smile again. You have no idea how much you've helped.'

'I've not done much,' Serena said, suddenly feeling a little choked at the expression in her niece's eyes.

'You have though, Auntie S. You've given me a new

perspective. You've stopped me from making the biggest mistake of my life. In fact, you've changed the whole course of my future.'

'Don't over-egg it,' Serena said.

Dodie giggled. 'OK, but you know what I mean. Thank you.'

'Any time.'

'One more thing,' Dodie said. 'Promise me you'll go to *Beauty and the Beast*. Have some fun with your ugly man.'

'OK, I will. Now get going. You'll miss your train.'

As she watched her niece walk into the railway station, her backpack slung casually over her shoulder, Serena thought, *Maybe I should go to see* Beauty and the Beast *with Eddie. Fun hasn't really been a big word in my vocabulary for years. Maybe it's time I got it back in there.*

CHAPTER 47

Serena phoned Eddie Winchester at just after 9.30 on Sunday morning. She'd tried him the previous evening but had got his answerphone and she hadn't wanted to leave a message.

'Hello there.' His voice was soft and, she fancied, a little strained.

'Is now a good time? Too early?' she asked.

'I've been up a while,' he said. 'In fact, I've already been to the gym.'

'Very impressive.'

'It means I can eat more doughnuts,' he said. 'I'm partial to them.'

'I won't hold that against you.'

He sighed. 'It was easier when I didn't have a desk job. I moved around more. Anyway, I'm sure you didn't phone me to talk about doughnuts!'

She laughed. 'No. I'm returning your call from yesterday. Sorry I haven't got back to you sooner, but I had an unexpected guest. My niece. I think you spoke to her?'

'I thought she was you,' he confessed.

'She said that you'd mentioned *Beauty and the Beast*.'

'Yes, I did. But if it's not your cup of tea, I'll understand. I guess it's for children really.'

'Aren't all Disney films for children?' Serena asked him. 'Grown-up children as well as the usual variety?'

He gave a little harrumph of acknowledgement.

She let the pause run and eventually he broke it. 'So – does that mean you would like to see it with – er – me?'

'Yes,' she said. 'I would. If you're sure you wouldn't rather go with Hannah?' *Or Merissa*, she thought, but didn't say. She would ask him about her when they met.

There was another little pause, and Serena thought, *So that's what the strain's about: Hannah.*

'How are you fixed for Tuesday night?' he said.

They made the arrangements.

Serena put the phone down. She was surprised to realize how much she was looking forward to seeing him again.

On Tuesday night when he picked her up he had stubble on his chin and dark shadows beneath his eyes. Though his shirt was freshly ironed and he smelled faintly of some musky cologne, she noticed, when he came round to open the door for her.

On the way to the Odeon they swapped chitchat, but she could tell that he was stressed. When he pulled into a space in the car park she turned to look at him. 'You look worried. Is everything all right with Hannah? I hope you don't mind me asking?'

'Hannah's fine. And no, I don't mind. Not at all.'

'There's something else I've been meaning to ask you, actually. And this is probably none of my business – but . . .' She took a deep breath. 'Is there anyone else in the picture? In a romantic sense, I mean?' There. It was out there. She looked at his face. His profile was stern.

'There isn't, no,' he said eventually. 'But things are a bit complicated. I can see how you might think that.'

I bet you can't, she thought, deciding not to mention what Hannah had said just yet.

'I don't want to put a dampener on our evening,' he continued. 'Just bear with me a second.' He went to get a ticket from the parking machine, came back and locked up the car. They began to walk across the tarmac of the car park, but he didn't elaborate further. Serena was beginning to think he'd forgotten when he said quietly, 'The short version is . . . that Debbie, my ex, she's been, well, following me again.'

'You mean when you have Hannah?' She stared at him in alarm.

'Not just when I have Hannah, no.' He gave her a quick sideways glance. 'Yesterday afternoon she came to my office – she caused a bit of a scene. I work at a firm of accountants. The senior partner, although she's not that senior in years, is a woman called Merissa. Debbie accused her of having an affair with me – of breaking up our marriage. Merissa was very upset. Understandably.'

'Gosh.' Serena felt a bit numb. Thank God she hadn't blundered in and asked him if he was having an affair too.

'It doesn't help that the other senior partner is Merissa's husband,' Eddie continued. 'He wasn't very happy either. It took me – and Merissa – a couple of hours to convince him we weren't having an affair. He's older than both of us, and a bit paranoid at the best of times. Although not as paranoid as my ex,' he added ruefully. 'He kept repeating, "There's no smoke without fire." The thing is, there isn't even any smoke. Merissa and I don't even work together very often.

'Fortunately I'm really good at my job.' He turned to smile at her. '"Everything passes," as my old nan says. I enjoyed our meal on Friday. And I've been looking forward to tonight. So let's enjoy it.'

'Hear, hear!' Serena said. They had reached the door of the picture house. He opened it for her.

The foyer was full of people. She glanced around, half afraid she would see Debbie Winchester somewhere. She felt his gaze.

'I don't think my ex will make any more impromptu appearances,' he said, accurately reading her face. 'I told her in no uncertain terms that I won't stand for it. That it would have an impact on the agreement we'd made about Hannah.'

Serena nodded, slightly reassured.

He touched her arm. 'Would you like some popcorn?'

The film was classic Disney. Poignant and humorous. Pure romance. Every so often she stole a glance at his face: that slightly crooked nose, the stubble on his strong, square jaw.

Once he caught her looking at him, but he didn't say anything, just offered her his tub of popcorn – hers was already empty.

She took one, letting its caramel sweetness melt on her tongue. It was odd, going to the pictures with someone who wasn't Liam. Not that they'd ever been to the pictures that much. Maybe once or twice when they'd first met. She couldn't even remember what they'd seen.

Sometimes it seemed like a thousand years since she'd seen Liam's face, or cuddled up to him in bed. And sometimes it seemed like only the previous week. Sometimes she could remember his voice – his very faint Dorset accent – and sometimes she couldn't recall it at all.

What was it about films that stirred up your emotions? She hadn't watched a Disney film since she'd lost Liam. Although she'd certainly watched her share of box sets. She'd spurned the weepies though, in favour of dramas like *Breaking Bad*. She wondered if she'd have behaved like Walter White if it could have saved Liam. And at times she'd wondered if indeed she may actually have become a little like Walter White: cynical and hardened, maybe even a little ruthless. Only in her case, she'd focused on the teaching career she already had. She'd focused on getting the headship at Poppins; thrown everything into it.

She was so immersed in her thoughts that she didn't notice the film had ended and the credits were rolling until Eddie touched her arm. 'Hey, you,' he said. 'You look miles away.'

'Sorry.' She blinked and turned towards him. 'I wasn't. Did you enjoy that?'

'Yup. I did. Promise me you won't tell anyone. Especially not my daughter. My street cred will be blown sky-high.'

'I won't tell a soul,' she said.

As they negotiated their way out of the cinema in the flow of people, Serena heard her name called. 'Mummy, look, there's Mrs Tate. Hey, Mrs Tate!'

She turned to look and wished she hadn't. A few feet away from them she could see Emily Cotswold-Smythe, from Year Six, with her mother, known (not without good reason) by the staff of Poppins as Gossipy Gail.

The pair were heading rapidly towards them. They were both smiling widely. Gail had a determined expression on her pretty face.

'*Beauty and the Beast*, Mrs Tate?' Gail asked in her rather plummy voice. She made it sound like an accusation. 'Is it just the two of you?' She looked at Eddie.

Serena knew Gail was angling for an introduction she had no intention of giving.

'Hello, Emily,' Eddie said, a little wearily, and stood with his hands in his pockets, the picture of awkwardness.

'It's Hannah's dad,' Emily filled in helpfully for her mother. 'Is she here too?'

'Not tonight,' Eddie said.

Gail gave a little laugh. 'Very cosy.'

'Did you enjoy the film?' Serena asked pointedly. 'Masterful, wasn't it? Anyway, I really must get back. Lovely to see you.'

She was aware of Eddie behind her, but she didn't stop until they were both outside again. Then she turned and said, 'Sorry, I just thought a swift exit might be called for.'

'Masterful?' His mouth twisted in amusement.

'I know. I'm hopeless when I'm put on the spot.'

He snorted with laughter. 'Well it was a lot better than my efforts, standing there shuffling my feet. Are you up for supper?'

'I am.'

'Good. Let's get out of here.'

They went to an Italian restaurant, tiny and intimate, full of the scent of garlic and Parmesan.

'I don't know why I felt so caught out back there,' Serena said as they were shown to a table tucked against a wall at the back of the restaurant.

He nodded. 'I know. It's mad. But I do know what you mean. I've spent so long feeling guilty I've got into the habit. Guilt was my default setting when I was married. Whatever I was doing was bound to be something Debs would take issue with. It was hard work. I need to move on.'

The waitress brought them a jug of water and he poured it. *Do I feel guilty too?* Serena reflected. *Going out to dinner with another man. Liam wouldn't have minded. He would have said, 'Go, girl – you only live once. Right here, right now!'*

Eddie's voice broke into her thoughts. 'Are you OK?'

She nodded. Then she shook her head. 'I am and I'm not,' she said, and then she told him about Liam.

'We had it all mapped out,' she said. 'We'd buy a house by the sea, have children, I'd reduce my teaching hours, if necessary, but we'd share the childcare. Liam was an electrician, but he worked for himself – it all seemed so ideal. But then suddenly – bang! It was all gone.' She blinked and sniffed. 'Gosh. Sorry. I don't often talk about it.'

He was nodding slowly and there was such compassion in his eyes that it made her want to cry even more. 'I'm sorry,' she said again. 'Now *I've* put a dampener on the evening.'

'No you haven't.' His voice was rough and a bit raw. 'Never apologize for having feelings, Serena. You lost the person you thought you were going to spend your life with. It doesn't get much tougher than that.'

'No,' she said, blowing her nose and taking off her glasses. 'No, I know. Thank you.' She paused. 'As they say, it's more a case of getting used to it than getting over it when you lose someone you love.'

'I can imagine.' He sipped his drink. 'So being a headmistress wasn't in the plan then?'

'I doubt I'd have gone for it quite so soon. But focusing on work saved me from going insane.'

'I'm with you on that one,' he said and picked up his glass, 'Here's to jobs that keep us sane.'

They clinked glasses and smiled at each other.

CHAPTER 48

'Serena, darling, it's me, Christina. Do please phone me. I've got some very exciting news.'

Serena deleted the message, Christina's fourth, from her answer machine and sighed.

Apart from a brief text saying thank you when she'd got back to London, she hadn't heard from Dodie since her impromptu visit. But presumably Christina's news centred around her daughter's career change. That would be pretty exciting in Christina's world – her daughter going into law, her daughter wanting to do a placement at Bart's.

Serena couldn't avoid her sister forever. She supposed she may as well get it over with. She sat in the orangery, her mobile in her hand, but still she hesitated. *Jane Eyre* was on the table, cracked open at the spine and face down – she'd just got to the part where Jane had left Mr Rochester and had realized that she was now totally alone. She had just walked away from the love of her life and was facing a bleak future. With no money, and already cast out by the only family she had, begging was about to become her only option.

My family might not be the most supportive in the world, but at least they do love me, Serena told herself. And thanks to the life insurance policy Liam had insisted they take out, she didn't have any financial worries.

She called Christina.

'At last. I was beginning to think you were dead. Ha ha! How are you?'

Serena was about to answer, when Christina hurried on. 'You'll never guess what!'

Serena kept quiet – she didn't want to break any confidences.

'Angelina's won a competition. Not just any old competition either, but an amazing competition. Hugo and I couldn't believe it when we heard. Neither could Mum and Dad. We've all been so excited.'

A competition? She hadn't been expecting that! Serena felt a little stab of hurt. Why was she always the last to know about anything that went on in her family? It was as though she was an afterthought: *Has anyone told Serena? No? Oh golly, you know how sniffy she gets if we don't tell her things.*

'It's a trip to Disney World – the proper one in Florida!' Christina continued. 'An all-expenses-paid family holiday. Get this – it's over Christmas too.'

'It sounds amazing,' Serena said softly, watching the dust motes swirl in a beam of sunlight slanting towards the orangery floor. Disney World – it was a place she and Liam had planned to go, one day. Hope fluttered around in her chest. Going with her family would be lovely too, though.

'We're all so excited! When I say family, the trip is actually for six. So we thought, Angelina and Josh – he's her latest chap, have you met him? Another singer, of course. Mum and Dad and Hugo and I. Dodie doesn't fancy it. I know we said you could come up to us this year for Christmas, but, well, these are extenuating circumstances – an unmissable opportunity. You *do* understand?'

'Of course.' Was that a little break in her voice? She was determined not to let Christina know how hurt she was. 'Yes,' she went on. Her voice was stronger now. Not a glimmer of the crushing disappointment she felt – or the anguish that Christina didn't think she would mind being left out. She managed to force it all back down into her heart. Put the lid on it. Press it down tight.

'You could come with us?' Christina babbled on. 'I mean, I'm sure they could tack on an extra person. You know, on the flight – you'd be on a different seat on the plane, not near any of us possibly. But that wouldn't worry you, would it? Ha ha. There's plenty of room in the apartment. I think the sofa in the lounge converts to a bed. You wouldn't be in the way there.'

Serena felt a little numb now. Maybe it was the shock. *In the way?* Was that really how her family saw her?

'The other thing that might not work for you is the timing,' Christina rattled on, oblivious. 'The flight out is before you break up for the hols. Could you manage that?'

'I'll have to let you know.' Serena hung up. After a few seconds the phone rang again. But she didn't answer it. Then again. This time there was the little ping of a voicemail message immediately following it.

'Sorry!' Christina's bright voice continued. 'Must have lost the signal. The other thing I wanted to say was thanks so much for talking some sense into Dodie. You're a star. Speak soon.'

Serena felt a solitary tear roll down her cheek. She had never felt so bereft. Or so alone.

Work, as always, was her salvation. Over the next few days she threw herself into it, going in early and leaving late, clearing up dozens of outstanding little jobs. One of them was to go and see Hannah's teacher to enquire how things were going. She hadn't heard from Eddie Winchester since their night at the pictures, which had been more than a week ago now.

She knew she could have called him. But she didn't want to bother him. OK, the truth was deeper than that. She couldn't face another rejection. She didn't want to hear his surprise when he heard her voice. 'Serena, what can I do for you?' he would say.

And she wouldn't know how to answer him. After all, they weren't dating. All they'd really done was to go out for a couple of meals together, exchange a few confidences. She barely knew the man.

He probably didn't need to schmooze his daughter's head-mistress any more, now that he had got what he wanted from her in respect of Hannah.

All of these uneasy suspicions were confirmed when she saw Maggie McAllister and enquired about Hannah's welfare.

'She's a lot happier than she was,' Maggie said. 'Her parents have obviously reached some kind of agreement.'

'Good. That's great news,' Serena said.

'You look tired, though,' Maggie went on, a thread of concern in her voice.

'I'm fine,' Serena said. When had she got so good at lying?

'Right,' Maggie said, clearly not convinced. 'Well, don't overdo it. No sense in making yourself ill.'

'I'm never ill.' Serena gave her a reassuring smile. She was heading back to her office when she bumped into Hannah. 'Good morning,' she said, stopping in the corridor. 'How are you?'

Maggie was right. Hannah was not the same little girl she'd seen at the stables that day when she'd climbed out of the hay bales, so vulnerable in her little polka-dot socks. She was rosy-cheeked and bright-eyed. What on earth had caused such a transformation?

It wasn't long before she found out.

'Good morning, Mrs Tate.' Hannah beamed at her. 'I'm very well, thank you.' There was a little pause. Serena waited.

Hannah looked at the floor, then back up at her. 'Mummy and Daddy are getting back together,' she whispered. 'Daddy's going to come back and live with us again.'

'Gosh,' Serena said, feeling a thump of shock in her chest.

Hannah glowed with happiness. 'We're going to be one big happy family, Mummy says.'

'That's lovely to hear,' Serena said, although actually she was amazed. How peculiar. He'd seemed to be hell-bent on moving on from his ex, not getting back with her. But who knew what went on in other people's relationships? No wonder he hadn't been in touch.

She wanted to ask when he was moving back in, but she was aware that this would have crossed a boundary. Instead, she cleared her throat.

Hannah shuffled her feet. 'Mummy thought it might be last weekend,' she went on, 'but then something came up so Daddy couldn't come. I think it might be this weekend though. What do you think, Mrs Tate?'

'I don't know, dear,' Serena said. 'But I'm sure your mum's right. What does Dad say?'

Hannah's eyes clouded. 'He didn't tell me anything, but it might be a surprise.'

Serena gave Hannah her best reassuring smile. She would phone Eddie Winchester, she thought. She would phone him tonight. She could congratulate him – that wouldn't be out of place, would it? Not in the circumstances.

He didn't answer his phone, so Serena left him a message – very neutral, very harmless. The last thing she wanted to do, if he and Debbie were truly getting back together, was to cause any trouble. 'Just a quick courtesy call,' she said, 'to discuss Hannah. Maybe you'd like to call my office and make an appointment for a follow-up meeting?'

She put the phone down and turned her thoughts

resolutely to the following day. Or more specifically, the following evening.

Tomorrow was the eleventh of May and the Reading Group were meeting. They usually met on the first Thursday of the month, but Jojo and Daniel had been on holiday last week so they'd postponed it.

Gosh, that had come around quickly. Well, at least she could tell them that the spell they'd had of reality echoing fiction had been broken. Her life, this past month, had been nothing at all like Jane Eyre's.

OK, so she may have met a Mr Rochester aka Winchester. Funny how they had the same Christian names too. And she may have established that her entire family saw her as an outsider and didn't actually like her very much at all. *Oh, don't be so melodramatic. It's only Christina who does that.* And Christina had always had the hide of a rhinoceros. For a moment she allowed herself a very pleasing image of a rhinoceros with Christina's face lolloping across a savannah, its great clumsy feet punching up dust. Christina had big feet. She'd hated it when she was younger. It was the only big thing about her.

Serena blinked a few times. For goodness' sake, why on earth was she thinking about rhinoceroses?

Perhaps she was sickening for something. She did actually feel very hot all of a sudden. She would take herself off to bed, she decided, with a hot toddy. Yes, that would be lovely.

In the morning when she woke up – after a night of strange dreams involving rhinos and Mr Winchester – she felt awful.

She felt as though several hangovers had all descended at once. Bleary-eyed, she turned over in bed and saw that it was just after 7 a.m. Already half an hour after her usual getting-up time. She must have slept through the alarm.

One thing was certain though. She couldn't go into work like this. She phoned Lynn, the school secretary, and took her first sick day since she'd started at Poppins.

CHAPTER 49

A little later on, Serena wobbled out of bed and got herself some painkillers. It wasn't flu, as she'd originally thought. It was a migraine. She'd had a spate of migraines in her teenage years. They'd been so debilitating that she'd seen a neurologist, had an MRI, even had an EEG, but all had been clear.

The neurologist had referred her to a child psychologist.

'Stress,' the psychologist had finally declared.

'She hasn't got any stress,' her mother had objected. 'She's a child.'

'She's fifteen,' the psychologist had countered. 'She comes from a high-achieving family.'

Serena could have hugged the psychologist. Finally, it seemed, someone understood.

Even though it wasn't flu, she decided it might be prudent to cancel the Reading Group too. She was not going to be at her best, that was for sure. She rang Jojo and asked her to tell everyone else.

'Of course I will, angel,' Jojo said. 'So how's everything going? Are you up to talking?'

Serena had thought she wasn't, but judging by the amount of time she spent on the phone to Jojo, she clearly was.

When she put the phone down she felt drained. She hadn't realized how hurt she still felt about Disney World. It was that age-old feeling that she wasn't good enough. That she didn't fit in.

The migraine had gone, but in its place was a fuzzy, fragile feeling. Serena fetched her duvet from upstairs and curled up on one of the chesterfields in the orangery. It was somehow better to be downstairs in this room, where she had so many happy memories, than to be upstairs in bed alone.

At lunchtime she made herself a sandwich, but she couldn't face eating it. She took some more painkillers and fell asleep. When she woke up there were long shadows in the room and she realized that she'd been out for hours. It was almost seven.

She made herself a cup of tea and splashed water on her face from the kitchen sink. She was just trying to decide whether it was worth making anything else to eat when the doorbell rang.

For a few seconds she contemplated not answering it – she must look a sight. But the caller was insistent, and rang again. Could it be school? She'd switched her mobile off earlier. Barefoot, she padded along the hallway to answer it.

'Hello, angel,' Jojo said, as Serena gaped at her in surprise. 'I just thought I'd pop by and see how you were.' She held up a carrier bag. 'I've brought some things you might need.'

Serena smiled despite herself. 'Not wine, is it?'

Jojo wagged a finger. 'Not wine. Naughty girl. Well, there might be a bottle in there actually.' She rolled her eyes. 'How did that happen? I'm sure I meant to pick up sparkling water. I've got cupcakes too. They're low-fat, vegan ones. Are they bad for migraines?' She didn't wait for an answer. 'I also picked up one of those uber-posh ready meals. In case you haven't eaten.'

Serena was touched beyond words.

'I can just drop this off and leave you in peace. I don't want to make you feel worse.' Jojo paused meaningfully. 'But I am free for the evening if you're up to some company?'

'I am,' Serena said, blinking rapidly. 'Oh, Jojo, thank you.'

'What are friends for?' Jojo wafted past her in a cloud of Prada. 'I'll take this through to the kitchen. You go and put your feet up.'

Serena sat obediently on the chesterfield in the orangery, pulling her feet up underneath her like a child.

A few moments later, Jojo came in with a tray. 'You probably shouldn't mix alcohol with strong painkillers,' she said. 'When did you have your last lot?'

Serena showed her. 'Before lunch. I'll go easy on the wine.'

'Never let it be said that I am not a responsible member of the medical profession,' Jojo said, pouring her half a glass. 'Have a cupcake with it. We don't want you drinking on an empty stomach, do we?' She winked.

Serena was just taking a bite when the doorbell jangled again. 'Gosh,' she said, frowning. 'I'm not expecting anyone. You did tell the Reading Group, didn't you?'

'I did.' Was it a trick of the light or had Jojo gone a little pink? She was jumping to her feet. 'Don't worry, I'll go and get rid of them,' she said.

Serena could hear voices in the hall. She finished her cupcake. Wow, it was good. Homemade. Jojo was a superb cook. Serena could have eaten at least three. Luckily Jojo seemed to have brought half a dozen. She was just reaching for another one when her friend reappeared.

She wasn't alone. 'Hello, honey-bunny,' Anne Marie gave her a brilliant smile. 'I know Reading Group's cancelled tonight, but I was a bit worried when Jojo said you weren't well so I thought I'd drop round some nibbles.' She had a plate in her hand, covered in cling film. 'They're little sausagey things. I didn't cook them, don't worry.' She giggled. 'They're M&S. Very yummy. Shall I put them in the fridge? I won't stop.'

'Put them on the table,' Serena said, looking at Anne Marie's face and feeling like a breath of fresh air had just wafted into the room. 'And you are very welcome to stop – I'm feeling a lot better.'

'Really? That's excellent news.' Anne Marie perched on the arm of a chair.

Serena wasn't sure whether it was the company of her friends or the food that was helping, but she did feel better.

Much, much better. She felt as though someone had wrapped a warm blanket around her. She was in the middle of telling them about the holiday at Disney World – when Kate appeared at the door.

'Serena, I hope you don't mind, but the door was on the latch, so I just thought I'd pop in. I didn't like to think of you sitting here feeling ill on your own.' She smiled at the group. 'I brought you some fruit. I wasn't sure if you should have chocolate when you've got a migraine. In case it's a trigger, you know? But I did pop in a little bar of fruit and nut for when you're better. Shall I go and put the latch down – on my way out, I mean?'

'Yes, put the latch down,' Serena said, 'but don't go. It's lovely to see you.'

A few minutes later, Kate reappeared with Grace. 'Look who I found lurking outside,' she said. 'Serena, are you sure that you don't mind us all descending on you like this?'

'I'm feeling a lot better actually,' she said. 'In fact, I feel like a total fraud. Especially after I told you all not to come.'

'That went well,' Jojo said happily.

'I've brought you some feverfew,' Grace said. 'Oh, and some peppermint and lavender essential oils. That's supposed to be good too.' She handed over a little package.

Serena took it. As she thanked her she could hear the huskiness of her own voice. 'You lot are amazing,' she said. 'When I got up this morning I was having ... well, I was having a major attack of the blues. As well as a migraine,' she added softly.

Jojo and Anne Marie shifted up to make room on the sofa for Grace and Kate, who were shrugging off their coats.

'Well, it's hardly surprising in view of what you were just telling us about Disney World,' Jojo said, her voice hot with indignation. She repeated the story for the benefit of the new arrivals.

Everyone made appropriate sounds of shock and dismay.

'Actually, I've got some news,' Anne Marie announced suddenly into the thrum of voices. 'I wasn't going to tell you tonight because tonight isn't about me – it's about making you feel better, Serena. But I think this might help.' She studied her fingernails, which were silver with little sparkly bits.

Everyone looked at her expectantly.

Anne Marie is glowing, Serena thought, wondering fleetingly if she were pregnant. She'd looked happy from the moment she'd walked in.

'No, I'm not pregnant,' Anne Marie said. 'If that's what you're thinking. I know what you lot are like! But Thomas has asked me to marry him. And I've said yes.' Clearly unable to contain herself a second longer, she gave a little squeal of excitement. She rummaged in her bag. 'Hang about, I'll get the ring. I took it off.' She flashed Serena a shy smile and Serena thought, *Bless her, she must have been bubbling over with wanting to tell us, but she kept it to herself.*

'Gorgeous girl, why didn't you tell us straight away?' Serena exclaimed, as Anne Marie slid a very sparkly diamond cluster on to her finger. 'That is absolutely brilliant news. You have made my day.'

'And mine.'

'Hear, hear!'

'Is there any wine left? We need to have a toast,' Jojo said.

Anne Marie preened and glowed some more beneath their congratulations.

'When's the big day?' Serena asked. 'Or haven't you decided yet?'

'We haven't firmed up the details yet. But we don't want to wait.' Anne Marie paused. 'One thing we have decided on is that we want to get married in the sun. Florida has been mooted actually ... Florida being the sunshine state. And we'd like you guys all to be there. The hotel will be our treat. You'll need to get your own flights, but there's some quite good deals around ...' She held Serena's gaze. 'I reckon you could all sit together at the back of the plane – in the naughty corner!'

There were roars of approval. Serena's heart thumped in her chest. *Oh my friends, my amazing friends*, she thought. *Whatever would I do without you?*

CHAPTER 50

It was the morning after the night before, and contrary to what she'd thought might happen, Serena had slept like a baby and had woken feeling refreshed and alert.

Nevertheless, Serena decided that Poppins could manage without her for another day. It was Friday anyway. It seemed senseless to go in. Why take the risk of sparking off another migraine?

She phoned and made her apologies, then she did a little bit of paperwork so she wasn't being completely idle. Then she got on with a few chores. The Old Lighthouse was a big house to clean, despite the fact that she didn't use half the rooms. Maybe she should downsize. Maybe Dodie had been right and it was time to move on a bit from her past. Maybe she should even start dating again. Going out with Eddie Winchester had reminded her that dating could be fun.

Once the thought of him was in her head, it was hard to get it out again. He hadn't returned her call. She wondered what he was doing. Getting ready to move back into the family house maybe? Perhaps he was already back. Perhaps they had all eaten a family breakfast this morning before going off in different directions to start their days.

This left her feeling wistful and a little sad. *Oh, get over yourself, Serena. Life isn't a fairy tale.* Life isn't even an old classic like *Jane Eyre*. None of the Reading Group had mentioned April's novel last night. They had talked about real life instead. Anne Marie's amazing news had been the high point of the evening, but after that they had talked about nitty-gritty stuff, like the fact that Grace's washing machine was on its last legs and how you couldn't get things repaired these days – you had to sign up for insurance plans that cost £16.99 a month by direct debit.

Broken washing machines. That was the reality of life, wasn't it? One day she would tell the Reading Group about the crazy fanciful notion she'd had that this month it was her turn. That she was the one whose life would echo the novel the group were reading. That she would get the chance to be a romantic heroine. A Jane Eyre. But of course she wasn't anything of the sort. She was Serena Tate. Widow. Bossy headmistress. Family outcast.

Serena gave herself a little shake and went and cleaned the bathroom. Bleach and bloody broken washing machines. Yep, that was the reality of life. And most of the time she was perfectly fine with it.

I should have gone to work, Serena thought then. Solitude left her mind free to ramble along strange tracks.

She looked in the mirror as she scrubbed. Her face was pale and her eyes were puffy. She couldn't pull off crying like your tragic romantic heroine either. She didn't look wan and fragile when she'd been weeping – she looked washed out. No wonder Eddie Winchester had gone back to his wife. Debbie was a beautiful English rose. OK, a beautiful English rose with a strong streak of paranoia – but he clearly no longer held that against her.

When her mobile rang and she saw Eddie Winchester's name flash up on the display, she thought for a moment that she had conjured him up.

'Good morning,' she said, wondering if he knew she wasn't at work.

'Good morning, Serena.' His voice was cool. 'I hope I'm not disturbing you? I just heard you were ill and I wondered if there was anything you needed. I know how horrible it can be being ill on your own.'

'How thoughtful,' she said. 'Thank you. But I'm fully stocked up with everything I need. I've got some good friends.'

'Good.' There was a pause. 'Right, well I'll leave you to it then.' Another pause. Why was it suddenly so awkward? Was it the unspoken elephant in the room? Serena decided to drag it out into the spotlight. She took a deep breath. 'Hannah told me,' she began, 'about you and her mother reconciling. I just wanted to say that I wish you luck.'

There was a longer pause.

'When did Hannah tell you this?' His voice was quiet. 'Was it recently?'

'Yes. Er, Wednesday.' She heard his sigh and there was another little pause before he spoke.

'It's not true,' he said. 'But that does explain your message on my answerphone the other day. I thought I'd done something to upset you. But now I see.'

Serena was confused. 'I thought that was why I hadn't heard from you,' she began. 'Because of the – er – reconciliation.'

'I've just been busy,' he said. 'End of year accounts for lots of our clients. You've been on my mind.'

'I have? Oh ...' She could feel her face flaming. She wanted to ask *why* she had been on his mind. But it wasn't the time for it.

'Yes, but I'm worried now. About what you've just told me. Sorry, Serena. I think I'm going to have to try and sort this. I'll call you back.'

Her mobile rang again five minutes later and she had answered it almost before she'd registered that it wasn't Eddie but Christina.

'Hello,' she said cautiously. If she'd been totally compos mentis she would have just hung up again, but it seemed rude to do that now.

'Serena, it's about Dodie,' her sister said, and her voice sounded so odd and strange that Serena felt ice hit the pit of her stomach.

'What's happened?'

'She's in hospital. She's got ... she's got ... meningitis.'

'Which type?' Serena said, even though she already

suspected it was bacterial, the most dangerous kind. She'd heard the horror stories. A child waking up in the morning with a headache, dead by the evening.

Christina confirmed it softly. 'She has septicaemia too. She's in ICU. They're doing everything they can. I thought you should know.'

'I'll come,' Serena said. 'Are you at the hospital? Can you text me the postcode?'

'I will. Thank you.' Christina's next words were a whisper. 'You need your family around you at a time like this.'

Serena arrived at St Mary's just before 7 p.m. Christina was in the visitors' room. She was sitting with her chin in her hands, staring into space. *Please let her still be alive.* Serena sent up a fervent and passionate prayer. *Dodie has her whole life ahead of her. Please, God, who I'm not sure I even believe in. Please don't let it be too late.*

And then Christina looked up. Serena walked slowly across the room and sat in the plastic seat beside her. She took her sister's warm, limp fingers in hers. 'What news, darling?'

'She's still here. But she's very, very ill. They've said that if she gets through the next few hours, she's got a chance. It's a case of fighting the infections and praying there are no complications.'

Serena squeezed her fingers and nodded. There were a dozen things to say, but they were all clichés. Even the most obvious one – 'She'll be OK' – didn't seem appropriate, because neither of them knew if that were true.

'They're not keen on having more than one person at a

time in ICU. I've been sitting with her while Hugo pops home. But I couldn't bear it anymore.'

Serena found a mini pack of tissues in her bag and handed it over. 'Do you mind if I go in?'

Christina shrugged.

Five minutes later, Serena was standing, complete with gown and mask, in the dimly lit warmth of the little room where Dodie lay, pale as wax. A nurse was doing something to a machine on the right of the bed. He nodded at Serena as she approached from the left.

'Is it OK to hold her hand?' she asked. 'Will she be able to hear me?'

'Of course. And yes – possibly.'

'Hello, darling. It's your Auntie S come to visit.' It was hard to keep her voice normal as she looked down at her niece's face. Her long eyelashes were dark against her pale cheeks, her hair fanned out on the pillow, her hand with the IV line in resting lightly across her stomach. She looked terribly small in that bed, surrounded by machinery. No wonder Christina couldn't bear to be in here.

Serena picked up her hand very gently. The skin looked sore where the needle went in. She bit her lip. 'You'll be out of here soon, sweetie,' she said. 'You're going to be a roughty-toughty lawyer, remember? You haven't got time to lie around in here.'

She spoke nonsense for a while. Dodie didn't move, not that Serena had expected her to. The doctors had explained that she was heavily sedated to give the medicines that were fighting the infections in her body time to do their work.

The machines hummed away in the dry air. Eventually the nurse finished what he was doing. He smiled at her from the doorway. The controlled smile of a professional who sees death every day.

CHAPTER 51

The night drew on. Her parents came; Mum, pale and a bit puffy-eyed – Mum didn't do crying well either – and Dad with lines around his eyes that she'd never seen before. Was it possible to grow old overnight? Angelina came alone, smelling of expensive scent and with a sprinkling of rain on the woollen shoulders of her coat. She clung on to Serena's arm like a little girl.

'She's not going to die, is she, Serena?' Her eyes, so blue and so wide, were the eyes of a child who had never in her life faced anything bad. Serena kissed her forehead.

'Shall we go and get tea for everyone?' she said.

Death has rarely touched my family, Serena thought as she and Angelina strolled along a white corridor to the vending machine. Even their grandparents were still alive and kicking. Both sets. One lot in Surrey and one lot in Padstow, Cornwall, where they'd retired by the sea.

When Liam died they had all come – but not until his funeral, once they'd had the time to adjust and to compose themselves and to say the right things to her. They hadn't come to any hospital for a deathbed wait. Liam had never made it to hospital. He'd been at a railway station when the aneurysm had ruptured. He'd been dead before he'd hit the platform. He hadn't suffered, the paramedics said. She had always been grateful for that.

Serena found the right change for the vending machine and they carried the drinks back in shifts. They all took it in turns to go in and out of ICU, and they all took it in turns to comfort Christina – and Hugo, when he came back, bleary-eyed, to the visitors' room.

Christina kept saying to no one in particular, 'She's going to be a lawyer, did you know that? She's decided to be a lawyer.'

And Hugo kept saying, 'If she gets through the night . . . if she just gets through the night, she's got a chance.'

Dodie got through the night.

Some time just before dawn Christina spoke. 'There's no sense in everyone staying here. We should take it in turns to get some sleep. We only need one of us to be here in case there's any change.'

Hugo nodded. 'That's right. I'll stay a bit.'

Their father said, 'I'll take Mum home. Come on, my love. You're dead on your feet.'

Serena looked at her sisters. 'Is it OK if I stay with someone? I didn't think to book a Premier Inn.'

'Stay with us,' Christina said. 'Of course you can stay with us.'

It felt odd going up to Christina's guest room at six in the morning, which it was by the time they got back. She didn't think she'd be able to sleep; the adrenalin that had kept her going all night was still swirling around her veins. But she did. It was like falling into the black hole of oblivion. When she woke up, sunshine was streaming through the cracks between the curtains. She drew them back to reveal a beautiful day. The clearest of blue skies and a bright yellow sun worthy of a child's painting. The tree at the foot of her sister's garden was covered in pink blossoms. The buds of new life were springing up everywhere; even the grass was fresh and new. It was not a day to end your life on. She cleaned her teeth in the en suite bathroom and glanced at her mobile. It was nearly eleven o'clock.

She was scared to go downstairs.

When she did she found Hugo in an armchair in the lounge and Christina curled up on the sofa opposite, snoring softly. Pongo, their Dalmatian, was lying on the rug by her side.

Hugo stirred when he saw her and untangled himself from the throw that covered him. He got up. He was fully clothed.

'We did go to bed,' he said, 'But we couldn't sleep, so we came down again. Would you like coffee?' He had his polite host's voice on, even though he looked as if he were on total autopilot.

'I can do it.' She followed him into the kitchen. 'Any news?'

'No change as of an hour ago.' He yawned. 'But that's good news. She's a fighter.' There was a glimmer of pride in his voice.

He put coffee beans into the grinder. Ground them. Stopped talking out of necessity. Then, when the machine had finished its shrieking, he shook his head. He wasn't looking at her, but far away into the distance. And then, quite suddenly, he said in a voice hoarse with pain, 'We can't lose her. We can't . . .' He slumped down at the breakfast bar, rested his head in his hands and began to sob.

Serena went across to him. She wanted to hug him, but she felt as if she didn't know him well enough. How ridiculous not to know your brother-in-law of seventeen years well enough to hug. Instead she rubbed his shoulder with the flat of her hand. Round and round, as you would if you were winding a baby.

A few moments later he stopped as suddenly as he'd begun. He wiped his hand across the back of his face. 'I'll make you that coffee,' he said.

At midday, Serena drove them all back to the hospital. At just after one, Hugo and Christina saw Dodie's consultant for an update.

Serena waited for them in the visitors' room. They were gone a long time, which she hoped meant it was good news. She wondered if it was better or worse, the fact that they were both in the medical profession. It made things easier to understand, she supposed, but it also meant that they were both totally aware of every little thing that could go wrong. Apparently with this type of infection there could be all sorts of complications, from deafness to brain damage. She shuddered.

It was three quarters of an hour before they came back. They both looked a bit shell-shocked. Serena got up, not sure whether to smile or not.

'She's going to make it,' Christina said. 'She's still very poorly, but she's going to be fine.'

'There may be some complications.' Hugo's voice was wary.

'Yes, but she's alive.' Christina rounded on him. 'And she knew who we were too. We've just been to see her.'

'I just don't want us to be complacent,' Hugo said stubbornly.

'That does sound like very good news though,' Serena said.

'It is.' Christina hugged her. 'It's bloody amazing news. Ignore him. He's just being his usual pessimistic self. Do you want to go and see her? It's so brilliant to see her awake.'

'She needs to sleep,' Hugo said.

'I don't want to tire her out,' Serena acknowledged, glancing at Hugo. 'Why don't we all go for lunch, my treat, and then if you think it's OK I'll pop in and see her before I go back to Little Sanderton.'

So that's what they did: had a burger in the hospital canteen in an atmosphere that was strained despite Serena's best efforts at tact and diplomacy. They were both tired out, she thought, no wonder they were sniping at each other. The last forty-eight hours had been hell for them.

Just before she left she went back into ICU. Dodie was asleep, so she didn't stay. She blew her a silent kiss from the doorway and then she dropped Hugo and Christina at home and began the long drive back to Devon.

'Thank you, God,' Serena said, as she finally left the motorway. 'Thank you so much. I'm not going to start going to church, but is it OK to thank you from my car?'

This felt slightly ungrateful, so when she was about five miles from home, Serena pulled into a lay-by, alongside a footpath sign, just off the road. It was a place she was familiar with, a place Liam had shown her long ago, and although she hadn't been here for a few years she was pretty sure that not much would have changed.

She opened the hatchback, got out the pair of walking boots she always kept there, and pulled on an old raincoat, fastening it tightly around her. She climbed over the stile, breathing in the sharp scents of the country with pleasure. The path led uphill for a few hundred yards and then it curved to the right and came to a fork. The left-hand side continued upwards and the right-hand fork led towards a woodland copse. Near the woodland copse there was another footpath sign, half-hidden in the undergrowth, and another stile, crisscrossed with brambles, which clearly didn't get much use.

Serena climbed over it carefully, picked her way along the overgrown path beyond and then paused to catch her breath and to gaze. Her timing couldn't have been more perfect. The bluebells were at their best. They stretched in all directions, a vibrant carpet of them spread out beneath the trees. Bluebells as far as the eye could see

They glowed in the dusk. Their unearthly colour was otherworldly, magical. Serena swallowed a huge ache in her throat. The first time Liam had brought her here, she'd been blown away. From the main footpath there was no clue that such magic existed. Many a hiker passed by, oblivious.

She continued carefully along the path, which wound its way through the woods and finally came out in a clearing. A huge old tree trunk lay on its side. It had been there for years. They'd had a picnic here once, just Liam and her. They'd brought a backpack of cheese and bread and a bottle of wine. She had a photo somewhere of them sitting amongst the blue.

She climbed on to the tree trunk, which was covered in lichen and mould and smelled of damp and decay, and sat with her knees hugged up to her chest, remembering.

'I love you so much,' he had said, touching her face, so tenderly, so gently. 'I think I'm going to remember this moment forever.'

'Me too,' she'd said, leaning her head against the solid strength of his shoulder and closing her eyes, letting the sun touch her skin. A few moments later he had tapped her arm with quiet urgency and when she'd opened her eyes he'd put a finger to his lips and pointed.

On the other side of the copse she'd seen movement. Then a stag had emerged from the trees. For a few seconds it had stood, totally still, with its head raised, scenting the breeze. Then it had turned, ghost-like, and disappeared back into the trees.

Now, Serena smiled at the memory. She could smile at many of her memories now. It no longer felt as if she were betraying him. She no longer felt guilty for feeling happy.

And it was here that she said thank you again to God for sparing Dodie's life. It seemed a much more fitting place to say thank you than in her car, a throwaway line on a motorway. There was no stag today. But she fancied that she could sense Liam's spirit moving close by amongst the trees.

CHAPTER 52

It was odd being back at school on Monday. She felt as if aeons had passed since she'd been in her office, not just a few days. She'd had a couple of missed calls from Eddie, one on Friday and one on Saturday, but he hadn't left a message and she hadn't phoned him back yet. She didn't feel up to it.

Eddie Winchester felt like part of another world. A world that wasn't as important as the one where her niece was in ICU. Although actually Dodie was doing really well. Christina had phoned just before lunch.

'All the indications are that there is no permanent damage.' Her sister had sounded slightly awed. 'I can't get my head around it, Serena. She's been so bloody lucky.'

'How are you? Is everything OK at school?' Before Serena could reply, she had hurried on. 'By the way, did Angelina tell you she's split up with the singer – she's heartbroken.

But clearly the man wasn't good enough for her. So that means there's a spare place. For Disney World, I mean, at Christmas. Oh, do say you'll come.'

'I might actually be going to Disney World before then, as it happens,' Serena said. 'I've got the opportunity to go in the summer.'

There was a pause as Christina took this in. Serena wished she could see her face. 'With a man? I didn't know you were seeing someone. You kept that quiet, you dark horse. Who is he?'

'I'm not going with a man. I've been invited to a friend's wedding.'

'What friend? Surely you'd rather go with your own family than a friend . . .' She tailed off. 'Oh, well, obviously not.'

Serena took the diplomatic way out and didn't answer that question. 'I'm a bit late for a meeting actually,' she said. 'I'll phone you later, shall I? I'm so pleased Dodie's OK.'

Dodie would be fine. All was right with her world again. It was amazing how the prospect of losing someone you loved, followed by the relief of realizing they were OK, could shake every atom of self-pity from your body.

She was about to go and grab a sandwich when she heard voices outside her door. One of them was Lynn's. 'You can't just go in. I'm afraid you'll have to make an appointment.'

Serena hesitated as she heard another woman's voice, raised in anger. She recognized it. Where from? She had about five seconds to work it out before her door flew open.

Ah yes. Debbie Winchester. A red-faced, extremely angry Debbie Winchester.

'Good morning, ladies,' Serena said peaceably.

'I'm so sorry—' Lynn began.

'It's fine,' Serena said. 'Take a seat, Mrs Winchester.'

'I don't want to sit down,' Debbie Winchester said. 'What I want is an explanation.' She stormed across the room, her face suffused with rage. Serena felt rather glad that her huge old desk was between them.

'An explanation about what?' Serena asked.

'You've been trying to steal my husband!'

Serena took an involuntary step back as the other woman nipped around the desk. Lynn was close behind her. But neither Lynn nor Serena was quite quick enough. Before either of them could take any further evasive action, Debbie Winchester thrust something in her face and Serena felt an intense burning sensation. Suddenly it was impossible to see. Then she was choking. Her skin was on fire. For a few awful seconds she thought she was going to die.

'Police, Lynn,' she gasped, putting up her hands to protect herself from further attack. And then she was on her knees, gasping and spluttering, trying to find her glasses, which seemed to have come off at some point, and only dimly aware of the torrent of abuse from above.

After that, time seemed to take on a surreal kind of roller-coaster motion. She wasn't sure whether the police or the paramedics arrived first. But as time looped in and out between fast and slow she was aware that her office was full of people. A PC taking statements, paramedics telling her it would be OK. Everything was going to be fine. Just pepper gas. Very nasty to experience, but there wouldn't be any long-term effects.

The short-term ones were bad enough, though. She was shaking, her whole body outraged at the attack. At some point, the paramedics had helped her to remove her blouse, because it was the only way to be sure of removing all traces of the irritant, and she was now wearing a T-shirt that someone had found in lost property. She was also wrapped in a very soft throw that Lynn kept in her office.

It was a long time before she could see properly. Her throat and chest still felt raw, possibly from all the coughing. And she felt intensely vulnerable.

'What will happen to Debbie Winchester?' she asked Lynn. 'The police said they would charge her. Do I have any say in it? Is that the best thing to do? What about Hannah?'

'I think you should let them get on with it,' Lynn said with a little shudder. 'The woman is at best deranged and at worst completely psychotic. No wonder her husband was worried. Have you had any dealings with her before?'

'No, not really,' Serena said. 'I saw her in Waitrose once, having a meltdown. I didn't realize quite how dangerous she was though.'

'I dread to think what could have happened if you'd suffered from asthma or anything like that,' Lynn said. 'That stuff could have killed you.'

Serena blinked a few times. She was still trying not to rub her eyes. 'I *have* been out with Eddie Winchester, Lynn,' she said quietly. 'In a platonic sense, I mean. We went to the pictures. She must have found out.'

Lynn gave her a direct look. 'There's no reason you shouldn't go out with him if you want to – platonic or not. They've been divorced at least six months by all accounts.' She paused. 'Of course! You weren't here on Friday, were you? She was up here then, arguing with him in the play-ground.'

'Poor Hannah.'

'Yes, that's what I thought. I was tempted to get the police, Mrs W was causing so much disruption.' She sighed, her eyes dark. 'I'd already told pastoral care. There's a note on your desk about it somewhere.'

'I was still working my way through the pile.' Serena smiled wryly.

'Well, I shouldn't think that little outburst will have done her much good,' Lynn said. 'Mrs W, I mean. They'll probably award him full custody after that.'

'Oh, that life were that simple,' Serena said. 'Although I sincerely hope you're right.'

'She needs to be locked up,' Lynn said. 'And after today, I very much hope that's what happens.'

It was a few days before Serena found out what had hap-pened to the unfortunate Mrs Winchester. It was Friday evening and she hadn't been in long from school when there was a ring on her doorbell.

She checked through the security spyhole she'd had fitted the previous day. It was unlikely that anyone was going to turn up on her doorstep and assault her, but the incident at school had unnerved her so much that she'd decided she might as well protect herself.

Eddie Winchester was standing on the doorstep. He had something in his hands. A bouquet of flowers, Serena saw, as she opened the door.

'I'm sure I'm the last person you want to see,' he said, 'but I had to come and make sure you were all right.'

'I'm fine,' she said. She pulled the door a little wider. 'Please. Come in. Are they for me?'

'Yup.' He followed her through to the kitchen and she was aware of his presence behind her.

Chemistry, she thought, as she stood at the sink in her kitchen, snipping the cellophane wrappings from the flowers. It was such a long time since she'd felt the electricity of chemistry that she'd forgotten what it was like.

He'd really gone to town with the flowers. They filled the Belfast sink, the fragrance of their blooms strong in her nostrils.

She turned to catch him watching her. 'Would you like a coffee?' she asked. 'Or something stronger?'

'A coffee would be good,' he said, and she was reminded of the first time they'd met.

'I also came to apologize,' he said. 'For what Debbie did.' He paused.

'You're not responsible for her actions,' she said.

He nodded an acknowledgment. 'Thank you.'

'Is she OK?'

'She's gone into St Augustus Hospital – it's a psychiatric unit.' He paused. 'She went voluntarily. I haven't seen her, but I did speak to her mother – now there's a nice woman – and it sounds as though Debbie is actually very remorseful about what happened.'

'I see.'

'It doesn't mean she won't be punished for it.' His dark eyes held hers.

'I have no desire whatsoever to see her punished,' Serena said. 'But I hope she gets the help she needs. How's Hannah?'

'Hannah's OK. Thankfully her gran and I have quite a good system going. Hannah knows her mum's not very well but that she will be better in time. It's surprising how much they understand at that age.'

'Yes.'

They sat in the orangery and drank tea. And then more tea. Eddie didn't seem to want to go. And Serena didn't want him to go. She told him about the previous weekend's events. 'That's why I didn't answer your calls,' she said. 'I was at the hospital. I wasn't avoiding you. In case you were wondering.' A beat. 'Of course you weren't wondering.'

'I was, as it happens.' He looked at her. 'I know we haven't had a very good start. In fact we've had a bloody terrible start, and please stop me if I'm talking out of turn.'

She was about to speak, but he put his hands out, palm forward. 'Just let me get this out or I'll lose my nerve.'

Serena suppressed a smile.

'I like you. I've liked you from the moment I met you. I don't suppose it's going to be totally straightforward, what with Hannah being a pupil at your school, although she will be leaving soon anyway. And with, well, my ex. But I was wondering whether we could maybe start again – you and me. Maybe another dinner … or something. What do you think?'

He had flushed a deep red. He looked more awkward than Serena had ever seen a man look. Dodie's words flashed into her head. *Go out with your ugly man, Auntie S.*

Serena smiled at him and, feeling like a proper nineteenth-century romantic heroine, she said, 'Who needs straight-forward, eh? I like the idea of another dinner …' She left it a beat. 'Or something – very much. Yes, Mr Winchester. Let's do it.'

SUMMER

Grace & Mikey

CHAPTER 53

I don't want to get married. Anne Marie knew this was not a good thought to have when you were on your way to your wedding.

Well, strictly speaking, they weren't on their way. The actual ceremony was on Saturday, and today was Monday, just about. She glanced at the display on her mobile – it was five minutes to midnight. But they were kind of past the point of no return.

It wouldn't have been quite so bad if it was just her and Thomas, but it wasn't. There were ten of them in the wedding party, including Michael Collins who was their best man, her father and several of her closest female friends. They were all currently squashed into a jumbo jet hurtling at 550 miles an hour towards Orlando International Airport.

From there they'd be travelling on to one of the best hotels outside Disney World, where they were all booked to stay until her dream wedding, which was scheduled to take place at the Cinderella Castle at 3 p.m. on Saturday.

Her father would kill her if it didn't happen. This whole expedition was costing him a fortune. Not that the money would be the major issue. Dad would be far more disappointed that she'd changed her mind about marrying Thomas, who was a family friend and his osteopath.

Anne Marie felt sick with fear. Why hadn't she stopped it before?

She glanced at Thomas, who was asleep in the seat beside her. His face in repose was very handsome. He was kind. He was solvent. He made butterflies flutter in her tummy. No, he didn't. Not anymore. Although he certainly had back in January. She'd been totally in love with him then and that was only six months ago. What had gone wrong?

Thomas stirred in his sleep. His lips twitched in what could have been a smile. Anne Marie closed her eyes. *What have I done? And, a million times more importantly, what on earth am I going to do about it?*

She wasn't the only one who couldn't sleep. Michael Collins, known to his friends as Mikey, was also awake. He was in the aisle seat in the row in front of Anne Marie, sitting next to a man who had a black hangman's hood pulled down over his head. Just after they had taken off, the man had smiled pleasantly at Mikey and said, 'Ah good, it looks as though you're settling down for the night too. For a horrible moment I thought you were going to watch a film.'

Mikey, who had been intending to do exactly that, had shaken his head. 'Er, no, mate.'

The man had nodded approvingly and then, like a magician, he'd produced an array of little packages, which he'd laid out on the pull-down table in front of him. Mikey had watched in amazement as he'd unleashed a foam pillow that sprang into shape as soon as it was free of its wrappings, a red airline blanket, a blindfold, earplugs and noise-reducing earmuffs. He'd tipped back his seat to maximum recline, put in the earplugs, donned the earmuffs and blindfold and finally pulled the hangman's hood over his head.

Ten minutes later he'd been snoring, making it impossible for Mikey to get any rest. He'd always been a light sleeper. Although for a brief while, when he'd been going out with Annabel, he'd slept soundly. *That had been contentment*, he thought, with a little sting of sadness. The kind of contentment that had been unimaginable since she'd left him.

He wished he hadn't thought of Annabel. Mostly, these days, she was banished from his head. But something about being up here in this tin can, roaring through the great empty hole of the night sky, had conjured her up. Actually, it wasn't all that surprising: the last time he'd been on a plane he'd been with Annabel.

His heart contracted with pain. He guessed he wasn't over her yet then.

'This is your captain speaking. We will be serving breakfast shortly.'

The voice on the tannoy crept into Anne Marie's dreams

and she awoke with a jolt of surprise. Maybe it was all a nightmare – she wasn't really on a plane, and now she was awake the awful doubts about her wedding would be gone . . .

She definitely was on a plane. The buzz of early morning chatter was all around her. Her mouth felt dry and the faint body odours of the other passengers hung in the air.

Just before she'd fallen asleep, she'd tried to console herself with the fact that what she was feeling may just be a touch of pre-wedding nerves. Loads of people had them. Not for the first time lately she wished Mum were still alive, or that she was closer to her sister. Would asking them be easier than talking to one of her friends? Maybe she would wake up and look at Thomas and feel an almighty rush of love for him and be certain that she did want to get married after all.

That hadn't happened either, although she was certain about one thing. She needed the loo.

'Do you mind if I get out?' she asked him. He was in the aisle seat.

'Course not, lovely.' He yawned and stretched. 'I'd come with you and clean my teeth but I expect there's a bit of a queue.'

There was. Anne Marie stood in it, clutching her washbag. She glanced out of the nearest window. The sky was the bluest of azure blues out there. It was a perfect day. She should feel jittery with excitement.

Someone tapped her on the shoulder and she glanced round. It was Grace, and she was smiling. 'Hello, gorgeous, did you get any sleep?'

'A bit. You?'

'I slept like a log,' Grace said. 'I'm lucky. I've always been able to sleep on planes. Besides,' she added happily, 'when you have triplets, you learn to sleep when you can. But hey, you've got all that to look forward to, haven't you?'

She must have caught Anne Marie's look of horror, because she added hastily, 'Babies, I mean, not triplets . . .' She tailed off. 'Not that there's any rush, I mean, you're only young . . .'

Anne Marie didn't feel young. She felt at least twice as old as her twenty-two years. 'Phew!' she said, trying for a flippant tone but aware that this probably hadn't come off – judging by the expression on Grace's face.

Luckily at that moment the door of the in-flight toilet opened and she escaped inside.

She should feel gloriously happy, but there was a cold ball of fear in her stomach.

This was definitely more than pre-wedding nerves.

417

CHAPTER 54

On the website, the hotel had been described as opulent and spectacular. But these words didn't really do it justice, Anne Marie thought, when their minibus pulled up outside the impressive marble entrance.

The Aurora was set on the shores of a lake, which was bordered by a forest of pines. The rooms at the front overlooked the glassy dark water. There was also an outdoor pool, which lay before them like a turquoise diamond. At one end was a bar, but most of it was open to the sky.

The hotel wasn't just in a beautiful setting – the interior was pretty impressive too. It had three restaurants, four bars and a huge lounge area, which featured some original works of art by Damien Hirst on the walls. Or so claimed the information packs for guests in each of the rooms.

It was such a hot day that once they'd unpacked and orientated themselves, the members of the wedding party had either gone for naps to recover from the flight or had congregated in the pool bar, which was all marble floors, fountains and foliage. Grace was standing beside Anne Marie, looking out at the pool. A bronze statue of Venus rose from the furthest point of the diamond.

'I don't think I've ever been to a place as beautiful as this,' Grace said, touching a sumptuous red velvet cushion.

Her voice was wistful. Anne Marie looked at her. 'I know,' she said softly. 'I don't think I have either.' This wasn't quite true. Dad had taken her to some pretty amazing places. But Anne Marie wasn't as oblivious as she'd once been to the fact that she was lucky to have led a very privileged life. And that most of her friends hadn't. Especially Grace.

The previous year, Grace's son Harry had been diagnosed with cancer, and the family had fallen behind on their rent for a time while they focused on his care. The extra expenses also meant that money was still tight for Grace and her family.

How lucky Anne Marie was to be able to host her closest friends at this luxury hotel for her wedding. Ah yes, her wedding. For a brief while, beneath the excitement of rocking up at this fairy-tale hotel, she'd forgotten that she didn't want to marry Thomas.

'So have you ever been to Disney World before?' Grace was saying slightly impatiently. As though she'd already asked the question, maybe more than once.

'Sorry, I was miles away. But no, actually, I haven't. I've always liked the idea of the Disney bit, but I'm not a massive fan of theme parks . . .'

Distractedly she scanned the room for Manda.

Her chief bridesmaid and best friend had only got married in January herself – she'd had a bit of a wobble too, although it hadn't been quite as last-minute as this. Anne Marie was desperate to ask her if she'd stopped feeling that way. And if she regretted getting married – even though she was pretty sure she knew the answer to that one. Manda and Jack seemed happy.

Manda was nowhere in sight, but she could see Mikey and Jojo and Thomas over at the bar buying drinks. That was a good idea. She was pretty dehydrated herself.

Grace was feeling dehydrated too, not to mention on edge. It was too hot and she was tired out. There had been a million things to organize before she'd come away in order to make this trip possible. Ben wasn't used to having sole responsibility for the boys. If she hadn't been so fond of Anne Marie she wouldn't have come.

She glanced back at her friend. Anne Marie didn't look like a girl who was heading towards the happiest day of her life. She was about to say something when Jojo arrived with a large glass of white wine in her hand.

'Have you got jetlag too, angels?' She smiled at them both, clearly oblivious to any tension. She held up her glass. 'Blimey, this is good. Mind you, it ought to be – at twenty-four dollars a glass.' She took a sip. 'Your best man sent me over,' she added, with a glance at Anne Marie. 'He's getting a round in. He wants to know what you both want to drink.'

'Twenty-four dollars a glass!' Grace felt faint. 'Tap water will be fine.'

'Have a proper drink,' Anne Marie said, looking at her anxiously. 'Don't worry about the cost. Mikey won't be expecting you to buy him one back.'

'I'd just prefer . . .' Grace said.

It was too late. Jojo was already shouting across to Mikey. 'Three more of these, please. Where's everyone else? Where are Manda and Jack?'

'I don't know,' Anne Marie said.

'They've probably sneaked off to their room for a lie down,' Jojo said with a chuckle. Her laughter was wickedly infectious.

Grace smiled back. The throb of a headache was starting at her temples. She hadn't realized they were coming to such a plush place. She wasn't sure how she was going to survive here for a week. She couldn't afford to drink anything, let alone eat.

She hadn't told the girls, but money was still tight. She and Ben were struggling. His business wasn't doing as well as it had even a year ago, and taking care of Harry had been surprisingly expensive, even through the NHS.

'Penny for them, angel.' Jojo's voice broke into her thoughts and Grace was jolted back into the room. Jojo's eyes were kind, but Grace knew she couldn't share what was on her mind. This was Anne Marie's moment.

Mikey arrived with a tray of glasses. 'Help yourselves, ladies. Isn't this place awesome? I could live here. Absolutely no doubt about it.'

'You'd need to win the lottery first,' Jojo said.

'Yes.' Grace felt guilty as she sipped her glass of wine. 'Thanks for this, Mikey.'

'No worries, babe.'

She tried not to bristle. *Babe*? She must be at least five years older than him. She wondered idly how he earned his money. He was wearing expensive clothes but his shirt wasn't properly ironed and his jacket looked rumpled and creased. He hadn't changed clothes since they'd arrived, but then neither had Thomas and he didn't look like a tramp.

Then again, Mikey wasn't like his cousin at all. Thomas always looked smart. There was something very *together* about Thomas, whereas Mikey was unruly. Even his thick dark hair was unruly. And while Thomas was quite serious, Mikey had a cheeky sparkle in his eyes, which Grace was sure got him a long way with women. So why did he grate so much on her?

Stop being so judgemental, she told herself. *You're tired, not to mention envious.* When he'd leaned forward to put the tray on one of the low tables, his jacket had swung open, weighed down by his wallet, which she had seen was stuffed full of notes. How amazing it must be not to have to count every penny.

'Jojo tells me you're in a reading group,' Mikey said politely to Grace. 'So what does that involve?'

'Reading!'

He looked slightly hurt and she gave herself a mental kick. *Play nicely, Grace. You can't go around disliking people just because they have more money than you – you'd have to dislike 90 per cent of the population.*

'We pick one book a month and we all read it.' She managed a smile. 'Then the next time we meet, we discuss the book . . .' She waved a hand. 'You know . . .'

He nodded as if he did. *Actually we don't discuss the books much*, thought Grace. *Most of the time we're too busy sharing stuff about our lives, which is much more interesting.*

'What are you reading this month?' Mikey asked.

'*The Great Gatsby*,' she told him. 'It's about unrequited love. I thought it would make a change from all the happy-ever-after romances we've been reading lately. Also, I thought it might help us to buck the trend.'

'Buck what trend?' Thomas asked. He was standing beside Anne Marie, and Grace wondered whether she should have been more discreet. The reality-echoing-fiction trend was something they'd discussed quite a bit in their monthly meetings, but she wasn't sure they should be discussing it in public. It was a bit weird. To say the least.

Anne Marie was smiling though, so maybe it was OK. She looked at her fiancé. 'You know, how when we were reading *Emma*,' she began, 'there were some – um – striking similarities between the plot of the book and my life? With the matchmaking and stuff.'

'I remember,' Thomas said, narrowing his eyes.

Anne Marie blushed. 'Well, that kind of thing happened every month,' she said. 'When we read *Lady Chatterley's Lover*, Kate ended up falling in love with her gamekeeper. Well, kitchen-installer, actually, but you get the picture.'

'And when we read *Jane Eyre*, Serena ended up going out with a Mr Winchester, who had a mad ex,' Jojo chipped in.

'And when we read *Rebecca*, Jojo ended up living at Manderley,' Anne Marie finished.

'No, that didn't happen,' Jojo objected. 'But there were a few strange coincidences, it has to be said.'

'So this month,' Grace said, 'I decided to pick a book that was about a man.'

'So what exactly is *The Great Gatsby* about?' Mikey asked. He was looking at her expectantly.

Grace shrugged. 'I haven't actually started it yet.'

Serena came to her rescue. 'It's set in Long Island. Which, before anyone gets excited, is a long way from here. The Great Gatsby is in love with a married woman. He was in love with her before she was married, but felt that he wasn't good enough.' She looked at them over her glasses. 'So he sets out to earn a fortune to prove himself worthy. Unfortunately, by the time he's done this, she's gone and married someone else.'

'Typical,' Jojo said, outraged.

Serena nodded. 'Most of the book is about him trying to win her back. With tragic consequences.'

'So it doesn't have a happy ending then?' Anne Marie looked at her aghast.

'I'm afraid not,' Serena said.

'But as you said earlier,' Jojo said to Grace, 'it's just a book. And we're not men.' She shot Anne Marie a playful glance. 'None of your wedding guests used to have a secret crush on you, did they?'

'Not as far as I know,' Anne Marie said quickly.

'Can men join your Reading Group?' Mikey asked. 'It sounds like my kind of thing.'

Thomas shot him a disbelieving look. 'I didn't have you down as a reader, Mikey.'

'I'm always reading.' Mikey sounded indignant. 'Really ladies, I am. I'd love to join your Reading Group. I'll download *The Great Gatsby* on my phone.'

'I suppose we could make you an honorary member while we're in the USA,' Anne Marie said. 'When we get back to England, Serena can decide whether or not you can have a permanent membership, as we meet at her house.'

Mikey turned the beam of his smile on to Serena and her gaze grew thoughtful.

'We may need a secret ballot,' she said, 'when we get back. But Anne Marie's right. You can become an honorary member while we're here. If you're sure you want to?' She paused. 'Bearing in mind what Anne Marie just told you. About the trend. The main character in *The Great Gatsby* ended up dead in a pool.'

'That's not going to happen to me.' Mikey glanced at the pool, which shimmered blue, just a few metres away from where they all stood. He gave an exaggerated shudder and then grinned. 'I promise I won't go near any pools.'

'That's settled then,' Anne Marie told him. 'Welcome to the Reading Group.'

CHAPTER 55

Grace's headache was getting worse.

When Thomas said he would get them another drink, she excused herself. It might only be afternoon in Florida but it was coming up to the boys' bedtime in the UK and she was missing them desperately.

'I'm going to pop up and call home,' she told Anne Marie. 'Do you mind?'

'Of course I don't, honey-bunny.'

At least she looked happier now. Although that might have been the wine.

Grace escaped to her room with relief.

She rummaged in her luggage for her phone and saw there was a text from Ben. They'd agreed to keep texts to a minimum, because of the cost, though she'd upgraded her package so she could still phone home. Speaking to the triplets and Ben every day was a necessity, not a luxury.

Call me before you go to bed, the text said. Grace frowned, then speed-dialled his number.

'Hi, darling.' Ben sounded as though he were in the next room. 'How's it going?'

Some of her tension ebbed away at the sound of his voice. 'It's going great,' she said. 'This hotel is amazing. I wish you could see it.'

'Take photos,' he said. 'Have you got free Wi-Fi? You could put them on Facebook. I can show the boys.' The words *It'll be cheaper* hung in the air.

'Sure,' she said, suddenly aware that his voice sounded over-bright. 'How are the boys? Everything OK?'

'They're great. I think they're missing you.'

'I've only been gone a day,' she said, smiling. 'But I'm missing them too. And you,' she added softly. 'Are you OK, Ben?'

There was the tiniest of pauses and this time she knew she wasn't imagining it. There was something he wasn't telling her. 'Ben,' she said. 'Has something happened? Please tell me.'

'We had a letter from . . .' The signal fluctuated a bit.

'Can you hear me?' he repeated. 'Town and Village Rentals. We had a letter from our landlord. It's actually dated from a few weeks ago . . . we must have missed it. Anyway, he's written to inform us that they're putting up the rent, and if we don't pay a significant portion of it upfront, it may result in eviction.'

'He can't!' Grace felt a sinking coldness in her chest.

'He can, sweetheart. Apparently the fact that we haven't been very regular in our payments counts against us . . .'

427

'Oh,' she said quietly. 'How much?'

He told her. 'I know it's a lot,' he added quickly. 'We'll figure something out, but ... don't go overspending, will you?'

'I won't,' she said tightly.

There was a pause. 'Sorry, Grace. I know you won't. What I meant was that I don't want you to be putting too much on the credit card if you can avoid it, we may need to make that payment quite soon. I do want you to enjoy yourself though.'

Grace had an urge to burst into hysterical laughter. She wouldn't tell him about the price of the drinks. He'd be appalled. 'OK. Can I speak to the boys?'

He put them on, one by one. As usual, Harry was the most talkative, wanting to know if she had seen Mickey Mouse.

'No, darling,' she told him. Hearing them all made her feel more homesick, not less. When she finally disconnected, she sank down into the fresh linen scent of her bed and burst into tears. There was a part of her that wished she hadn't come.

It would be impossible not to spend money here. At the very least she would have to buy a round of drinks and they would be going out to eat too. Maybe she could skip a couple of meals? She could say she wasn't hungry, though she couldn't really play the diet card. Lately she'd actually lost a bit through worry. She hadn't been this skinny since she was twenty.

For the first time since she'd known her, Grace envied Anne Marie. How amazing it must be to bounce along through life knowing that all your bills would be picked up. That you never needed to do a job you disliked, just to make ends meet. That you never needed to work at all if you didn't want to – you could just play at running a cleaning company.

For goodness' sake, she had to get a grip. These women were her closest friends. Anne Marie was a lovely, generous girl. It was hardly her fault that she'd been born into such privilege. There were downsides to having lots of money too. Not that Grace could think of any at that particular moment.

Standing at the window, looking out over the glitter of the lake, she wiped the tears from her face and straightened her shoulders. This wasn't about her. This was about Anne Marie. It was her week – her wedding. Grace went into the bathroom and repaired her make-up.

Given the choice, she would have curled up in bed and gone to sleep. But she wasn't going to do that. She was going to get herself togged up, go back downstairs and make sure Anne Marie had the time of her life.

CHAPTER 56

Mikey was already downstairs. He'd been chatting to Jojo about her work as a midwife and, much less interestingly, about her new boyfriend.

'I reckon I'd have made a good midwife,' Mikey said recklessly. 'I love women, me!'

'You love chatting them up,' Thomas said, appearing by his side and slapping him on the shoulder.

'It's not too late,' she said, a challenge sparking in her eyes. 'We need more male midwives. You could train up.'

Mikey nodded uncertainly. 'I love babies,' he said. He wasn't so sure about the birth bit, although he'd definitely have been by Annabel's side, rubbing her back and not minding when she dug her blood-red nails into his palm and cursed him to hell and back.

He took a deep breath and tried to push the painful image from his mind. It would never happen. *Don't go there, Mikey.*

Jojo was laughing. He liked older women. Annabel had been thirty-six, five years older than him, but she hadn't been as brash as Jojo, with her bright scarves and her jangling bangles and her awesome cleavage. It was extremely hard not to stare at Jojo's breasts, but Mikey prided himself on being a gentleman, so he'd just sneaked the odd look.

If he was honest, he was slightly scared of Jojo. She was so confident. Not to mention tall. In her heels she must be at least six foot, which was two inches taller than him.

Now if you'd asked him about Grace – beautiful, willowy Grace – well, she was a different story. Where was she anyway?

Suddenly, as if he had conjured her up with the power of his thoughts, he saw her heading across the room. She smiled as his gaze met hers. That was one of the things he'd clocked earlier: that lovely smile, which rarely left her face, despite the fact she was obviously tired.

Annabel had been able to melt him with her smile. His love for Annabel had welled up from some deep place within, rendering him powerless to think clearly or to have any perspective at all when he was in her company.

Stop thinking about Annabel.

He turned his attention to Grace, who had just arrived beside Jojo.

She'd redone her make-up. Was that for his benefit? He hoped so. 'Can I get you a drink, lovely?' he asked. 'White wine, wasn't it?'

She put up a hand, palm outwards. 'I'd prefer water. Besides, it's my turn. May I get you a glass?'

'Certainly not,' he said, liking her more and more. Most women didn't offer to buy him drinks either. Not once they saw the size of his wallet. They were quite happy to let him subsidize them indefinitely.

Annabel had even let him pay for the taxi she'd called on the day that she left him.

Grace was asking Jojo if she'd like another glass of wine.

'Not for me, I think we're going to eat soon. Anne Marie's booked a table in the bar.'

He would engineer things so he could sit next to Grace, Mikey decided.

As the others drifted in, he stuck close to her side. And half an hour later, mission accomplished – he was sitting on her right at the round table they'd been shown to.

He'd ordered a couple of bottles of wine for the table. That way, he figured he could top up her glass without her feeling beholden to him, because he was sure now that's why she'd refused his offer of a drink.

Mikey and Grace request the pleasure of your company at their engagement party . . .

As their main courses arrived, along with the bread and the side salads that they hadn't ordered – Mikey had forgotten that the Americans didn't like anyone to go hungry – he began to enjoy himself.

Grace seemed to be enjoying herself too. Right now, she was laughing and joking with Anne Marie, sitting on her left, as if she hadn't a care in the world.

Mikey waited for a gap in Grace's conversation and then

he dived in. 'So what do you do back in England then, beautiful?'

She turned towards him, those gorgeous dark eyes thoughtful. 'I'm a full-time mother,' she said, 'so I spend most of my time looking after my triplets and my husband Ben.'

Whoa – Mikey felt the bubble of his fantasy burst. Everything in the room seemed a little duller. He should have known she was married. All the beautiful women were married.

'Sorry,' he said. 'I wasn't . . .' Wasn't what? Hitting on her? Of course he was, which was probably why she'd just mentioned her husband.

'It's fine,' she said. 'It's nice to chat.'

'Yes, it is.' He fiddled with his napkin, struggling to rebuild the conversation on safer lines. 'Triplets, eh? Do they run in your family?'

'No.' Her eyes shadowed. 'We had trouble conceiving, so we had fertility treatment . . .'

'Ah,' he said. Clearly that was a sensitive subject too. He was digging himself into a hole. He bit his lip. 'Um – how old are they?'

'Six. Do you like kids?'

'I love them. I've always wanted a big family. I think it's because I was an only child. I really missed not having any siblings.'

Grace smiled at him. 'We wanted a big family too. Although we didn't actually plan to have them all in one go.'

Mikey began to relax again. Maybe Thomas had been right. Maybe this was exactly what he needed. Some downtime in the sun, away from his work, surrounded by pleasant company. And Anne Marie's friends were pleasant. It didn't always have to be about romance.

That was his trouble. He was a born romantic. He looked at the world through rose-tinted glasses. He couldn't be the only guy who felt like that, but it was an attitude that had got him into lots of trouble. He sighed.

'So is there anyone special in your life?' Grace asked. 'Are you married?'

He shook his head. 'I got close once.' He didn't usually tell people that. Was it the heat? Even though it was evening, it was still hotter than the hottest of English summer days.

'What happened?' she said, 'If it's not too difficult to talk about?'

Mikey hesitated. Her eyes were kind. Suddenly he did want to talk about it.

'Her name was Annabel,' he said, aware that the rest of the table were too deep in conversation to overhear what he was saying. 'I took her to the Seychelles for a week and on the last night I proposed.'

Grace nodded, and after a moment he went on. 'We hadn't been seeing each other that long – about six months. But for me it was serious. I was besotted with her.'

'But she didn't feel the same?'

He shook his head.

Grace lowered her eyes. 'That must have been awful.'

'Yeah.' It was his cue to make some flippant remark. But neither of them spoke.

He was grateful to her for that. Grateful that she hadn't minimalized what he'd told her.

As dessert arrived, and the rosy glow of wine and the holiday feeling settled over the table, they got on to life dreams. Hers had been to go to art school, she told him. 'I'd probably have done it too,' she said. 'If I hadn't met Ben. What about you, Mikey?'

'I don't know. I was never much good at anything at school. I wasn't academic.'

'He's an ace diver,' interrupted Thomas, leaning over with a glint in his eyes.

Grace looked intrigued. 'What kind of diver?'

'I dive off boards,' Mikey said. 'Or fall off them sometimes.'

'Don't do yourself down,' Thomas said. 'He did it at county level at school. He's got medals.'

'Really?' Grace had admiration in her eyes. So why did he feel so embarrassed?

'You'll have to show us,' Grace said.

'I can't,' Mikey said. 'I'm not allowed near the pool. Remember?'

'He can also win medals for talking,' Thomas added. 'He's one of the best salesmen I've ever known.'

'Is that what you are?' Grace asked. 'A salesman? What do you sell?'

'Houses,' Thomas said. 'He's made a fortune at it.'

'I've just been lucky,' Mikey said, glancing at his cousin

and noticing that his eyes were slightly unfocused. He didn't usually drink very much. That probably explained his verbal diarrhoea.

'He's being modest,' Thomas said. 'He owns a rental company too. It was a little tinpot company when he bought it two years ago and he's completely turned it around. It's a thriving business now.'

'Oh yes, which one?' Grace asked.

'Town and Village Rentals,' Mikey told her. He didn't enjoy talking about work, but it seemed there was no getting out of it. 'I haven't done much. Thomas is exaggerating.' He broke off. Grace's expression had changed.

There'd been a flicker of something in her eyes. Shock? No, that didn't make sense. It was gone almost before he'd registered it, but now her face had settled into a kind of frozen grimace.

He touched her arm. 'You OK?'

She nodded, then snatched up a serviette and wiped her mouth. And then she was pushing back her chair, the metal legs scraping on the polished marble.

'I'm so sorry. I'm afraid I'm not feeling very well. I think I'd better . . .' And then she was gone.

Mikey looked at Thomas. 'Was it something I said?'

'I don't think so.' Thomas frowned. 'Maybe she ate something that didn't agree with her.'

From the other side of the table, Jojo exchanged glances with Anne Marie. 'I'll go after her,' she said, 'just to check she's all right.'

CHAPTER 57

Grace could feel her heart pounding as she got in the lift, clutching her bag tight to her chest. It had been such a shock, hearing him say that name. *Town and Village Rentals.* Her conversation with Ben had still been swirling at the back of her mind.

All she could hear was the strain in Ben's voice when he'd said, *'Don't go overspending, will you?'*

And there was Mikey, boasting about what a good salesman he was. Splashing his cash about without a care in the world.

No, he hadn't been doing that. He'd actually seemed quite embarrassed when his cousin had bigged him up. She had put aside her negative first impressions of him. In fact, the more they had talked this evening, the more she had felt that she'd been wrong. She'd actually begun to like the guy.

But now she didn't know what to think. In her room, she dumped her bag on the bed and then poured herself a glass of water. She felt slightly sick.

There was a knock on the door. Tentative. Surely he wouldn't have followed her? She went across and looked through the spyhole. It was Jojo.

With a sigh of relief, she undid the catch.

'I won't come in if you'd rather I didn't?' Jojo said softly. 'But nothing's wrong, is it? You haven't had some bad news from home? Is Harry OK?'

'Harry's fine,' Grace said. 'Fighting fit at the moment, thank heavens. No, it's nothing like that. It's just, well . . .' Oh, what the heck. Jojo would be discreet. And actually she did need to tell someone. She opened the door wide.

Five minutes later they had raided the minibar – she would regret that when she got the bill, but needs must – and they were sitting on the huge bed.

'So let me get this straight,' said Jojo. 'Anne Marie's best man is also the Scrooge who threatened to kick you out of your house if you don't pay up,' Jojo said.

'Um, yes.'

Jojo frowned. 'What are you going to do?'

'I'm not sure. But I'm not going to say anything to him.' Grace sighed. 'Anne Marie can't find out. This needs to stay a secret.'

'My lips are sealed,' Jojo said thoughtfully.

There was another knock on the door. Jojo got up and went to have a look. 'It's Kate,' she said. 'Shall I let her in?'

438

Five minutes later, they had put Kate in the picture. 'Not a word to Anne Marie, though,' Jojo said.

'Of course not.' Kate smiled at them both and fidgeted on her corner of the bed. 'Actually, I've got a secret too. I wasn't going to say anything, but I'm too excited.'

Jojo looked at her with a knowing smile. 'You're pregnant aren't you?'

'How on earth did you know that?' Grace and Kate said in unison.

'Years of experience,' Jojo said smugly. 'Congratulations, darling. How many weeks?'

'Eleven.' Kate was smiling so much she was aglow. Grace felt some of her tension slip away beneath the lightness of Kate's news.

'Bob the builder's a fast worker,' Jojo said, clasping her hands behind her head and leaning back against the oak headboard.

They all giggled. 'We probably should have been more careful,' Kate said, not sounding as if she meant it in the slightest, 'But me and Anton . . . Well, we'd been trying and it hadn't happened, and there was a part of me that was beginning to think that maybe it couldn't happen. So Bob and I, well, we didn't bother with – you know . . .'

'Shocking behaviour,' Jojo said. 'I'm guessing he's pleased too, is he? Bob, I mean, not Anton.'

'He's over the moon,' Kate said softly. 'He adores kids. Of course, he already has a daughter, with his ex-wife.' Her eyes were soft. 'But they're not in the country. Daisy lives in Italy with her mum.' She held her arms out to them. 'You two are the first to know. I didn't want to steal Anne Marie's thunder.'

'So you want us to keep mum?' Grace asked. 'If you'll excuse the pun?'

'Well, maybe just until after the wedding,' Kate said. They both looked at Jojo. Her cheeks had gone a little pink, Grace noticed. Was she hiding something too? Her intuition was suddenly on full alert.

'Jojo . . .' She touched her friend's arm. 'Is there something on your mind too? You're not pregnant, are you?'

'No,' Jojo said. 'Although I wouldn't mind if I was actually, but no, I'm not.'

'But there is something?' Grace pressed.

'Yes, there is.' Jojo paused. 'Wow! It's impossible to keep secrets round here, isn't it?'

'Yep,' Kate said. 'Well, it is from your friends!'

They both waited expectantly. Grace couldn't believe how much better she was feeling.

Jojo looked at Kate. 'I only found out the day before yesterday . . .'

'Found out what?' Grace prompted. 'Come on. Spill.'

'I've tracked down my biological mother,' Jojo said softly. 'I couldn't have done it without Daniel. Emotionally, I mean. I've thought about it lots of times over the years but I've always been too scared.' She had tears in her eyes.

Grace, who was sitting on her left, grabbed one of her hands and Kate grabbed the other. 'You've done the right thing, you would have always wondered if you hadn't.'

440

Jojo blinked and sniffed and rubbed her face. 'Have either of you got any tissues? Sorry, I didn't mean to do this.'

'It's totally normal,' Grace said, getting up and going into the bathroom to fetch her a loo roll. 'Have you met her yet?'

'No,' Jojo said, tearing off a strip. 'I've had an email.'

Alarm bells were beginning to ring in Grace's head. There was so much hope in Jojo's eyes, so much expectation. She didn't want to think about the fact that Jojo might still be disappointed.

'It was quite brief,' Jojo said, hesitant now. 'It said yes, she's my mother, and that she would be in touch. That's good, though, isn't it?' She leaned forward. She was like a child at Christmas, Grace thought. A child who had been given a present, but had it taken away again before she was allowed to open it.

'It sounds very promising,' Kate said.

'I know she may still come back and say that actually she doesn't want anything to do with me because she has a new family and all that,' Jojo acknowledged.

'Do you know anything about her?' Kate asked.

'I know she lives in Cornwall. In a little place called Padstow.'

'Padstow's beautiful,' Kate said, her eyes alight with enthusiasm. 'I've been there for a holiday.'

'Yes, we have too,' Grace said, and she thought, *God, I'm so lucky. I have my mum and my dad and my boys and Ben. I have a family and I have brilliant friends. All Jojo wants is to meet her mum.*

441

'I'm sure she'll be proud to have a daughter as lovely as you,' she said softly.

'Hear, hear,' Kate said.

'Stop it, you'll make me cry again.' Jojo tore off more loo roll. 'I've asked her for a photo, but she hasn't sent one yet. That doesn't mean anything though, does it?'

'No,' Grace said.

'You do get why I haven't told Anne Marie yet?' Jojo sounded anxious.

'Yes, of course we do.' Grace sat back on the bed beside her friends. 'I don't think we can tell her any of this stuff,' she added with a little frown. 'I definitely can't say anything about Mikey.'

'I hadn't really planned on saying anything until I'm twelve weeks anyway,' Kate added. 'Also, Anton and I aren't divorced yet. It could affect things – even though it was Anton who broke up our marriage, not me.' She sighed.

'I don't really want my news to be public knowledge either,' Jojo said with feeling. 'It's all a bit too new and raw.'

'So we keep it all between the three of us for now then,' Kate said. 'That shouldn't be too difficult.'

'No, it shouldn't,' Grace agreed. 'I'll just avoid Mikey.'

'I'll just avoid alcohol,' Kate said. 'Should be an interesting week!'

'And I think I'll just avoid getting drunk and talking too much,' Jojo said, making a zipping motion across her lips. 'How hard can it be?'

CHAPTER 58

Oh, famous last words, Grace thought the next morning. She'd just pressed the lift button on her floor and a few seconds later the doors had slid open to reveal Mikey.

He smiled and gestured for her to join him. 'Grace, how are you? Are you feeling better?'

Panicking, she stepped back. 'I'll catch you up. I've forgotten my phone.'

Before he could say anything else, she swung round and walked back towards her room. Her heart was thumping.

She waited a few moments more and then took the stairs.

When she walked into the breakfast room, she could see some of the wedding party, including Anne Marie and Thomas, sitting at a table for six by the window. There was no sign of Jojo or Kate.

There was a breakfast table set up for four alongside the bigger table, she realized as she got closer. But it was empty and there was only one place left on the bigger one. Right next to Mikey.

Maybe she should make a tactical retreat. But it was too late. Mikey had spotted her.

He patted the seat beside him. 'Please – come and join me.'

He sounded so kind that Grace felt guilty as she dropped her gaze. Why on earth was she feeling guilty? He might do a good line in patter, but he was not a kind man.

Ruthless and pragmatic were better words for the kind of man he was. She had felt for him when he'd told her about Annabel, but she realized now that her sympathy had been misplaced. Annabel had clearly known him better than she did.

'Are you OK now?' he asked, his eyes solicitous.

'Yes, thank you.' She kept her voice coolly polite. 'I had a migraine, that's all. I get them sometimes.' She turned slightly away from him and towards Anne Marie, who was sitting opposite and who also looked concerned.

'Are you OK, honey-bunny?'

'I'm good. A bit washed-out.'

A waitress arrived and Grace felt obliged to order something light from the breakfast menu, to underline the fact that she was feeling washed-out. She went for, 'Poached eggs, no toast, thank you,' instead of the full works that she'd intended to have, because this breakfast was going to have to see her through until teatime.

Mikey offered to fetch her a peppermint tea from the breakfast bar. 'Mum used to swear by it for migraines,' he said. 'Coffee used to trigger hers. Is coffee a trigger for you?'

'No,' Grace said. She was desperate for a coffee.

Kate arrived with Jojo. They called out cheery hellos and then sat at the other table. Oh, why hadn't she left it a few more minutes? She could hardly change places now. But perhaps it was just as well. Kate had only been seated for five minutes when she suddenly put her hand over her mouth, leapt up and fled from the room.

She was in the direct line of sight of Grace and Mikey, and he turned to her and said, 'Blimey. Are you sure it was a migraine you had? Maybe there's some bug going around.' He called across to Jojo. 'Hey, are you feeling all right, babe?'

'Yep, I'm good.' Jojo's voice was cool. Were they all going to ostracize Mikey? Grace felt a pang of guilt, which she dismissed swiftly. He deserved it.

There was no chance of Kate's sudden disappearance going unnoticed now that Mikey had alerted everyone.

Anne Marie was looking worried. 'Oh dear,' she said. 'I do hope there's not something going around that everyone's going down with.'

'I'm sure there isn't,' Jojo said.

'Mine was definitely a migraine,' Grace agreed, just as the waitress turned up with her coffee.

'Ma'am, if you are in any way prone to migraines, I recommend you avoid coffee.' She hovered with the cafetière, but didn't put it down.

'She's right you know,' Thomas said. 'Should you be

445

risking coffee?' He smiled at the waitress. 'Leave the cafetière up this end though, please. We could do with a top-up.'

Grace had an urge to scream. A minuscule breakfast she could deal with, but no coffee was unthinkable. 'Oh, what a tangled web we weave,' she whispered to Jojo as they got up together and went to the breakfast bar for juice. 'Is Kate all right?'

'Just a bit of morning sickness,' Jojo said. 'Have you forgiven Mikey already?'

'No, I haven't. It was just bad timing. Do you know what the plan is for today?'

'We're all going to Disney World.' Anne Marie had arrived behind them. She was smiling brightly. 'What was bad timing?'

Grace blinked. 'Er, sorry?'

'I thought I heard you say bad timing? Oh, never mind.' Her voice was high. 'You are both enjoying yourselves, aren't you?'

'Absolutely,' Jojo said.

'Yes,' Grace agreed, wondering how she was going to wangle a coffee without anyone noticing.

Anne Marie frowned. 'Manda and Jack have had a row,' she confided. 'I don't think they're having a very good time.' Her gaze flicked back towards the table, where her bridesmaid and her husband were both immersed in their mobile phones. You could almost see the ice crystals forming between them.

'I expect they'll sort it out,' Jojo said, touching her arm.

'Do you think it's a good idea that I booked tickets for the Magic Kingdom? Daddy said I should have asked you first.'

'I'm up for it,' Jojo said.

'Me too,' Grace said staunchly. She had never seen Anne Marie looking so tense. She was usually so bright and bubbly. But then she forgot sometimes how young she was. Getting married was a big step for anyone, and a dream wedding at Disney World might seem like a fantastic idea, but Grace suspected it also ramped up the pressure big time. She remembered fleetingly what it had been like when she and Ben had got married. Several times during the build-up, she'd wished they could sneak off and get married quietly – just the two of them with a couple of strangers they'd dragged off the street to be witnesses.

'Are *you* enjoying yourself?' she asked softly, 'Because that's the most important thing.'

'Of course I am.' Anne Marie's voice was hollow. 'I'm going to ask everyone who wants to come to Magic Kingdom to meet in the downstairs reception at ten o'clock.'

Back at the table, Grace ate her breakfast in silence. Mikey got up to get a drink and on his way back he stopped to chat to Jojo.

Grace could hear snatches of their conversation.

'So have you been to a theme park before, Jojo?'

'Nope.'

'Are you looking forward to it?'

'Yep.'

'What do you think of the weather?'

'Great.'

447

Grace glanced across at them. Jojo was looking at her phone. Her face was very flushed. Then she too leaped up and fled from the table.

Mikey caught Grace's gaze and rolled his eyes. 'This is getting to be a habit. Woman running out on me halfway through a conversation.'

She nodded, wondering if Jojo had got some more news.

'A guy could develop a complex,' Mikey went on, sitting back down beside her.

She smiled at him. She was going to have to change her game plan. Avoiding him was clearly going to be difficult.

But to her immense relief, Mikey wasn't one of the group that gathered in reception. In fact, with the exception of Kate, who'd cried off for obvious reasons, it was just Anne Marie, Serena, herself and Jojo – the girls from the Reading Group.

'Manda and Jack are doing stuff, and Dad and Thomas are playing golf,' Anne Marie said, looking around at them all. 'Are you sure you really want to go? I don't mind if it's not your thing.'

'Of course we want to go,' Jojo told her. 'It'll be the highlight of the holiday.'

'Apart from your actual wedding, of course,' Serena intervened quickly.

'Yeah, of course, apart from that,' Jojo agreed. 'And the hen night. We are having a hen night, aren't we? I love hen nights.' She was certainly fired up about something, Grace thought, trying to catch her eye and failing. She was so fidgety; her bangles were constantly jingling.

'Yes. Manda's organizing it.' Anne Marie looked very summery. She was wearing a gorgeous sundress, sunhat and sensible flat shoes, and a pair of scarlet-framed retro sunglasses hung around her neck on a chain. Grace suddenly had sunglasses envy. She had a pair of very old Ray-Bans she'd found on eBay years ago.

Stop it, Grace. Money isn't everything, her sensible voice cut in. The Ray-Bans were very nice. They were probably almost retro too.

Everyone else was in shorts and T-shirts. Even Jojo had her legs out.

They stood outside on the terrace, waiting for the transport to arrive, and Grace breathed in the smell of summer; coconut tanning oil and the scent of the roses in a nearby bed drifted on a soft breeze. It reminded her of long-ago days when, as a teenager, she would go off on trips to the beach with her friends.

She missed her boys and Ben, but on the other hand it was certainly easier not having them all here. It felt freeing, not having any responsibilities. As though she could let her hair down for once, be a child again instead of a responsible adult. She felt a prickle of excitement in her stomach. Today was going to be fun.

The minibus taking them to the park pulled up into the waiting area and they began to climb in. Grace was last. She was just settling into her seat near the front when she spotted Mikey strolling out of the hotel entrance and into the sunshine.

He was wearing an oversized Mickey Mouse T-shirt, shorts, sandals and a huge Stetson. 'Not trying to sneak off without me, I hope,' he called out to the minibus driver. Then he climbed in and sat beside Grace.

Her heart sunk. Why did he have to sit next to her? She swallowed her annoyance.

'Hiya.' He seemed oblivious to her coolness. 'I've always wanted to go to Disney.'

'I'm surprised you haven't been then,' she said crisply, and resisted the urge to add, 'After all, money obviously isn't a problem.'

'Would you believe I've never had anyone I wanted to bring?' Some of the cockiness had left his voice and she glanced at him. His smile was uncertain. Not quite as insensitive as he appeared, then.

Nevertheless, she didn't want to get involved in conversation with him. She didn't want to hear any more about his disastrous proposal. After all, wasn't there a saying about reaping what you sowed?

Mikey was perplexed. He'd clearly done something to upset Grace, but he had no idea what it was.

Maybe it was because he was the only guy. Maybe they had wanted a girly day out, just the four of them, and he'd come blundering along in his size tens and spoiled it. He hadn't missed the look on Grace's face when he'd turned up. And yet last night she hadn't been like that. He'd thought they were getting along well.

He must have misread the signals. But hey, he had form,

didn't he, when it came to misreading signals? He'd got Annabel completely wrong too. He had thought she loved him. He had thought she wanted to marry him. How dumb could you get?

He hadn't told Grace the whole story. He was glad of that now; glad he hadn't made a bigger fool of himself than he evidently had. As the minibus pulled away, he laid his head back against the headrest and closed his eyes and he was back there.

Back on that beach in the Seychelles: the white sand, the pink sunset, the whole shebang. That perfect moment when he'd got down on his knees and pulled the jewellery box out of his pocket, fumbling a bit in his nervousness because, hell, this was the most important – and the most scary – thing he'd ever done in his life.

She had looked a bit surprised; he had clocked that. 'What are you doing down there, silly?' she had said, flashing him one of those sparkling, beautiful smiles.

But he'd carried on regardless. He'd been past the point of no return – and anyway, he'd wanted to carry on. He'd dug into his savings for the ring. Proper diamonds – no costume replicas this time.

'Will you marry me, Annabel? I . . . I love you so much.'

Her face as she'd looked down at him kneeling on the sand had been a picture. He'd seen all different expressions flit across it, quick as shadows on the sea: shock, pleasure, irritation, embarrassment. *Embarrassment?* Then she'd just giggled again and said, 'I love you too, silly. Come on, get up. People are staring.'

She was right. They were. A little crowd of onlookers was watching them from the railings.

'Yeah, but will you?' His voice had gone a little hoarse. He knew with hindsight that he must have sounded desperate. Who was he trying to kid? He *had* been desperate by that stage, hadn't he? Because he'd been starting to cotton on to the fact that the wonderfully romantic dream in his head may not have the wonderfully idyllic ending that he'd planned.

'I can't decide something like that overnight,' Annabel had said, folding her arms and looking a little irritated. 'Just get up, Mikey.'

So he'd stumbled to his feet, his face burning with humiliation. Annabel had turned her back and walked away from him. A girl in the crowd of onlookers had giggled. He had brushed sand from his knees and stumbled after Annabel.

Back at their hotel, they had sat in a stiff silence, which had morphed into a tight, cold space in the bed between them.

Rather like the tight, cold space between him and Grace now, Mikey thought. If it was possible to have cold spaces in hot minibuses.

Yeah, it was, he thought, as they pulled into the car park of the Magic Kingdom, Grace staring firmly out of the window. It definitely was.

CHAPTER 59

Jojo didn't seem as friendly as she had the previous night either. This had to be paranoia, surely? He racked his brains to think of something he could have said to upset either of them. There was nothing.

He put it out of his mind. Serena clearly didn't have a problem. As they joined the queue for a log flume, Serena smiled at him brightly.

'So what do you think?' She gestured around them. Mickey Mouse and Minnie Mouse were strolling by, hand in hand. When Mikey glanced across, Minnie waved at him. He waved back. Somewhere in the distance he could hear a brass band booming over the shrieks of children, and the air was full of the scents of food and perfume mingling with the sweet fragrance of flowers from a nearby bed.

'It's amazing, isn't it?' he said, answering Serena with a question.

'Yes.' She had a sparkle in her eyes that he hadn't expected. Serena had struck him as the most serious of all the women; he hadn't been surprised to learn she was a headmistress. He found her slightly intimidating, just as he had found school intimidating, but she didn't seem at all scary now. They had just eaten ice creams and she still had a blob of hers on her top lip.

He told her.

'Oh my gosh, I must be regressing to childhood,' she said. 'Thank you.' She wiped it away with a paper tissue, produced swiftly from her bag. 'I've always wanted to come here. It's a place where fairy tales happen, isn't it?'

'Is it?' He knew he sounded cynical but she was unfazed.

'Yes, I think it is. Well it will be for Anne Marie and Thomas on Saturday. Are you looking forward to being best man? Have you done your speech?'

'Er, yeah. To both,' he said.

She smiled. 'And have you had a chance to start *The Great Gatsby*?'

'Um, no to that one. I did download it though.' He tapped his pocket. 'I've got it on my phone. If we end up standing in too many queues at least I'll have something to read.'

'Good.' She looked at him over her glasses. She was back to being a headmistress again, enquiring whether he had done his homework.

Mikey nodded at her and she turned to answer something that Anne Marie had said.

He felt alone again. Out of place amidst the couples and the crowds of kids, the sunburned Brits, the women with strollers, the fake smiles of the actors and the glitter. A group of young women were approaching. He could hear their excited chatter and as they got closer he could see their perfect bodies and their stunning faces. They were as beautiful and as out of his reach as the stars.

He was beginning to feel like a spare uncle at a wedding. You have to invite him because he's part of the family, even though he's a bit weird and no one really knows what to say to him. And certainly no one wants to sit next to him, although the nice ones will take it in turns to chuck him a line of chat now and then. Duty done.

Bollocks. Thomas had asked him to be his best man, hadn't he? He wasn't a spare uncle at this wedding. He was important. He had a job to do. Thomas wouldn't have asked him if he didn't rate him.

Yeah, he would. Thomas knew about Annabel. Thomas had always been there for him. He was that sort of bloke. Decent. Kind.

Thomas was the brother he had never had.

Annabel had told him it was over the day after they'd got back from the Seychelles.

'I'm just not feeling it any more,' she'd said. 'Not enough to, well, you know.'

'To get married,' he'd finished. 'I'm sorry. I shouldn't have put you on the spot.'

She had smiled her loveliest smile. 'It was very sweet of you, and please don't think I wasn't hugely flattered.'

He felt as though she'd kicked him. Hugely flattered! Wasn't that something you might feel if a casual acquaintance gave you a compliment? He'd thought they'd been so much more to each other than that.

He had helped her carry the few possessions she had at his house out to the waiting taxi.

'We will stay friends, won't we?' Her eyes had glittered blue.

'Sure,' he'd said, knowing that would be impossibly painful.

She'd waved at him like a child out of the back window of the taxi, as if she'd just been going out for the day and not walking out of his life for ever.

Mikey dragged his thoughts back to the present as the queue inched forward. He decided to give the log flume a miss. They didn't have to go around the park joined at the hip, did they? With a muttered apology to Serena, he separated himself off from the group and headed back in the direction of the cafe they'd passed a little way back.

Grace waited until Anne Marie and Serena were a little way ahead and then she tapped Jojo's arm. 'So, um, I couldn't help noticing your sudden departure from breakfast,' she said. 'Was it good news?'

Jojo smiled. 'Is it that obvious? I'm almost bursting with trying to keep it to myself.' Her eyes were sparkling with excitement. 'I got another email with some more information. You'll never believe it, but she's a nurse.' She darted an anxious glance at Anne Marie, who was now chatting to Serena, and then looked back at Grace. 'So we're both in the same profession – *that* can't be a coincidence, can it?'

Grace agreed that it couldn't. 'What kind of nurse?'

'Psychiatric, so she's dealing with patients' heads not their bodies, but it's still amazing, isn't it. I'm blown away.'

'I can see that.' Grace felt warmed. Her friend's happiness was infectious.

'So did she send a photo?'

'Not yet. She said she isn't very good with computers. I'm not either. Hey, maybe that's genetic too.'

'Maybe,' Grace said indulgently.

'That she thinks about me often and that she hopes I'm doing all right and that, best of all . . .' Jojo's voice went a little husky. 'She wants to meet me.'

'That's fantastic,' Grace said. Clearly they'd been talking louder than they'd thought because Serena and Anne Marie were both now looking at them curiously.

Jojo went as red as the frames on Anne Marie's sunglasses. 'It's no good,' she said, 'I can't keep this to myself a second longer. I've got some amazing news, girls.'

Mikey was standing in a queue at the cafe, but thankfully it wasn't as long as any of the lines for the attractions. As he waited to be served, he felt his phone buzz in his pocket. It was probably a text from work. He rarely got texts from anyone else.

The waitress got him his coffee. There was nowhere to sit, inside or out, so he took it outside and stood by a bin. Snow White walked by with her entourage of dwarves, and blew him a kiss.

So he could pull a cartoon character – *whoop-de-do*.

He pulled out his phone to check the text. Annabel's name flashed up on the screen. For a long, hot second he thought he was seeing things. He hadn't seen Annabel for two and a half years. Why on earth would she be contacting him now?

Serena's words rung in his ears: *It's a place where fairy tales happen.* Maybe Annabel had changed her mind. Maybe she had been thinking about him all this time. Maybe she had realized that she was in love with him after all. Maybe she had known that for a long time, but she'd only just plucked up the courage to contact him. The last thing he had heard, via a mate on Facebook, was that Annabel was going out with a billionaire playboy. Well, maybe not a billionaire, but a well-heeled lawyer with a boat. Annabel would like that – she loved boats. She loved all the good things in life.

Wasn't that why he'd built up the business? Thrown himself into it in a workaholic frenzy. It had been an attempt to forget her, but it had also been an attempt to build up his finances. Maybe if he were rich enough he could win her back. Maybe, maybe, maybe . . .

Maybe he should just read the text.

With his heart banging and his fingers slippery with sweat, Mikey opened it. It was brief. *Hey, Mikey. Hope you're good. Can you call me, please? Annabel.*

Holy crap! What the hell could she possibly want? Could he phone her now? No – it was too noisy. The last thing he wanted, if she was going to ask him if they could try again, was to be saying 'pardon' every couple of minutes.

Besides, he didn't want to appear too keen, did he? He didn't want her to think he was just kicking his heels waiting around for her to phone. He wanted her to know he had a life. Hey, maybe she already did. Maybe she knew he was doing pretty well these days. Maybe that's why she had texted.

His heart dipped a bit. He had focused everything on amassing money in order to impress her, but he didn't want her to want him for his money. That was a paradox if ever there was one.

He would find somewhere quieter to phone her. Somewhere none of the others would accidentally happen upon him. He needed to find a bench out of the way of kids and music and photo-snapping tourists. There were lots of quiet spots. He began to walk.

Every so often he got his phone out and thought, *Is this a good place? Should I do it now?* He was sweating profusely. He shouldn't have worn the flaming Stetson. That wasn't helping. What if Annabel's text was urgent? What if she was phoning because she needed him? He couldn't bear it if anything was wrong.

He was in a part of the park he didn't recognize. He glanced up. He was standing by a great metal archway with two giant retro-futuristic light bulbs either side of the lettering. *Tomorrowland*, said the sign. Now wasn't that a thing. He was standing in the gateway of the future in more ways than one. It had to be a good omen.

He took a deep breath and dialled her number. With every ring his heart thumped a little louder. At this rate he wouldn't be able to hear what she said.

Should he cut the call? A kid carrying a hot dog bumped into him. Mikey sprang away from him like a scalded cat. Shit! The ringing had stopped. Had he cut her off? No. She had answered the phone.

'Hello?'

'Hey, Annabel, it's me. Mikey.' He'd been trying for cool. But knew he hadn't achieved it when she said, 'Who?'

'Mikey – your old flame.' Oh God, this was getting worse. It was cringeworthy.

'Mikey.' Finally there was recognition in her voice. 'How are you? Long time no hear. How's things?'

Had she forgotten she'd asked him to call?

'Things are great, thanks. Business is going great guns. Business is booming, as they say. Ho ho.' His face flamed. He could feel a river of sweat pouring down the back of his neck. 'Actually, I'm in the States.' Should he say he was at Disney World? That may not be cool enough for Annabel. 'Do you remember Thomas, my cousin? Well, I'm here for his wedding. I'm the best man. We're staying in this amazing hotel.' He couldn't keep the edge of pride from his voice.

It didn't seem so impossible that she'd got in touch because she wanted him back. He was doing OK. He was single; he was solvent. Come on – he was a *best man*.

'That's really cool, Mikey darling.'

The warmth was spreading up through his chest. Half pride, half love. *Darling*. He'd never thought he'd hear her say that word again.

'But anyway ...' Her voice cut through the warmth. 'Talking of weddings, that's why I got in touch. I'm getting married. I wanted to tell you. Because we were close once – and I wanted to know . . .' Her voice disappeared and then came back in and she was saying something about music.

He was still stuck on the sentence before. Had he heard her right? She was still speaking. 'So I was wondering if you could remind me, please? I hope you don't mind.'

'Remind you of what?'

'Of the name of that jazz band your mate hired for his thirtieth. You must remember – they were so brilliant. Dominic is a real fan of jazz and so I was thinking that I could hire them.' She giggled in that breathy little-girl way she had and Mikey felt his heart begin to break.

She was getting married. She had phoned him to find out about a band. She didn't want him back. On the contrary, she had moved on so completely and utterly that it hadn't even occurred to her that he might be jolted by her news.

He swallowed hard.

'Mikey? I don't think the signal's very good. Would you mind phoning me back when you're in a better area?'

'Sure.' He disconnected and leaned heavily against the railings. Above his head, the word *Tomorrowland* glittered brightly in the midday sun.

CHAPTER 60

Mikey's first instinct was to walk. No, it was to hide. To get lost in the anonymous crowds. He hadn't realized just quite how big a torch he'd been carrying for his erstwhile love. A torch that had been fanned into a mighty inferno by her text. Why had he let himself hope? What the hell was wrong with him? He thrust his hands deeper into his pockets and kicked violently at an empty Diet Coke can that was lying on the ground. It spun across the cinder path.

Almost immediately, a Mad Hatter character materialized at his side. 'Don't get mad, get tidy,' the Mad Hatter said. A female voice – a breathy, female, little-girl voice. Annabel's voice. He swung around and found himself staring into the smiling dark eyes of the Mad Hatter. His mind was playing tricks on him. Of course it wasn't Annabel.

'Is everything OK, sir?' She was slightly less sure of herself now. Caught in the glare of his anger.

He closed his eyes. 'I'm fine. Thank you. I'm fine.'

She bent to pick up the Coke can. 'Have a lovely day, sir.'

His anger was threaded through with shame. It was a familiar enough emotion, one that had stalked him on and off for most of his life.

Oddly, it often cropped up when he was around Thomas. He never had got his head around that. Thomas had been like a brother to him, his elder by just four months, but the gap had always seemed much more. Thomas had been wise and sensible for as long as he remembered. He'd probably been born wise and sensible.

While Thomas was doing well at school, getting good grades, being chosen as a prefect, excelling at sport – Mikey had been failing exams and getting into trouble, not to mention getting bullied.

He'd spent the first half of his school days trying to be invisible, in the hope that would keep him off the bullies' radar. That had kind of worked, but it hadn't worked nearly as well as the tactic he'd deployed for the second half of his school days: pulling dangerous stunts.

It had begun with dares – I dare you to cross over the train line, I dare you to jump off the bridge – and Mikey had realized two things: one, that if he impressed the bullies they didn't pick on him as much, and two, that he wasn't actually scared of very much at all. He wasn't scared of heights or deep water or the dark in the slightest. Or, to be more accurate, he was far less scared of any of these things than he was of people.

It was why he'd got into diving. He'd joined a club at the local pool when he was barely ten. He'd become expert very quickly because he was prepared to take more risks than anyone else. He would jump higher, do the extra somersault, do the stuff that everyone else thought was impossible. He became known as Mad Mikey, and became a bit of a cult hero. Unfortunately, this had been at the cost of his school-work, which he figured didn't really matter, as he'd never been academic.

Besides, street cred protected him from the bullies far better than qualifications.

While Thomas had left school with a clutch of A-stars, Mikey had left with a handful of nothing. Thomas had gone on to be a very fine osteopath and Mikey had had a string of sales jobs, which ranged from renting jukeboxes to pubs to selling fruit and veg at the market. Selling was easy. He didn't know what he wanted to do, apart from the fact that he didn't want to work for anyone else.

Then, just as he'd turned twenty-two, he'd found his niche in life. Property. And he hadn't done badly in the big scheme of things. He was currently the owner of seven flats. He'd bought the first property with a small legacy from his grand-mother, who had died when he was twenty-one. Ignoring the advice from everyone he knew, including Thomas, he'd got a really good deal on a knackered, run-down old house in a not very good part of Exeter, and spent the next year refurbishing it and converting it into two flats. Luck had been on his side and the timing was right. He'd bought in a dip and he'd made a nice profit when he sold again.

Confident for the first time in his life that he had made a good decision, Mikey had trusted his instincts and done it again. He lived in one of his properties and he rented the rest out. He wasn't rich. There were mortgages on some of them, but he wasn't doing badly. And there was the agency. That was doing well too. It was doing even better since he'd recently got rid of the manager, Dick Barton. Dick by name and dick by nature, Mikey had realized when he'd caught him with his fingers in some pretty unsavoury pies. He had a new bloke in the driving seat now. Things were on the up.

Yeah, on a financial level he could hold his head up high, Mikey thought. On a personal level though, Mikey was supremely unconfident. When it came to women, he was still at ground zero.

He lifted a hand to his sweaty forehead. It was too hot; the whole park was a suntrap. He decided to ditch the bloody silly hat. Bugger the sunstroke.

Anne Marie and the girls were having lunch. Anne Marie knew that she was not doing a very good job of pretending everything was fine. She wasn't going to be able to hold them off much longer. Today, both Grace and Serena had asked her on separate occasions if she was OK.

Each time she had smiled her brightest smile and said, yes, of course. She was a bit tired maybe, a bit overwhelmed – but yes, thank you, she was fine.

She didn't even know why she was lying. It wasn't because she thought they would judge her. They weren't like that.

She sipped her berry smoothie and looked up. On the other side of the table, Jojo met her eyes.

'So then,' Jojo said, 'are you going to tell us what the format of your hen night is, or is it a surprise?'

'No, it's not a surprise,' Anne Marie said. 'We're meeting for cocktails first, then we're going on a boat on the lake.' Anne Marie had imagined her hen night – way back when she and Manda had first discussed it – as being one of the best bits of the whole wedding. She and her very best friends, drifting along the lake in the evening sun, chattering about men and marriage with wisdom and maturity, laughing together, a little wryly, about being part of a couple and what that meant; her on the brink of a new life and the sun beginning to set above the pines, the lake a glorious sheen of pink glass. There would be laughter and warmth and the boat would cruise gently towards the most perfect of pink sunsets. The sun literally setting on her old life – what a brilliant metaphor – before it rose again the following day on her new one. The day when she would leave behind her single life – which, let's face it, hadn't been all that much fun anyway – and become a married woman. Mrs Thomas Hanson. Although they had discussed the whole name thing, and Thomas was open to doing something different. They could do the double-barrelled thing. Anne Marie Hanson-Hambledon. Or even Anne Marie Hambledon-Hanson. That had a slightly better ring to it.

She was brought back to the present by Jojo's anxious voice. 'Angel, why are you crying?'

Anne Marie swiped at her eyes. *Oh crap.* She hadn't meant to cry. The tears had slipped out without her consent, the sneaky buggers. But suddenly they wouldn't stop.

They were all looking at her now. Serena produced a mini-pack of tissues from her bag and pushed them across the table. She was always so organized. Grace's eyes were sympathetic. Jojo's were kind. Their loveliness wasn't helping. Anne Marie couldn't hold it in any more.

'I'm so sorry,' she began.

Jojo squeezed her hand. 'Is it all getting a bit much?'

Anne Marie shook her head, gulped and swallowed more tears. 'I don't want to get married,' she said. 'I don't want to marry Thomas.' It was such a relief to say it. She looked at her friends. 'I'm really, really sorry.'

'Darling girl, you don't need to apologize to us.' Serena's voice was gentle.

'But I've brought you all here under false pretences,' Anne Marie said.

'Don't be silly,' Jojo said. 'I'm sure you were planning to marry him when you asked us, weren't you?'

'Yes, of course I was.' She didn't know whether it was making her feel better or worse, the fact that they were all being so understanding and nice. But then what had she expected them to be? Manda, who had a tendency to be a drama queen, may have been a bit more shocked, she guessed, and a bit more judgemental. Perhaps that's why she hadn't told her, even though she was her best friend.

'When did you realize?' Jojo asked.

467

Anne Marie looked at her. Everything in the restaurant was very bright, quite surreal. 'I'm not sure. Maybe a month? It's been more like a very slow dawning.' She paused and bit her lip. It was so hard to explain. 'I've known Thomas for ever,' she said slowly. 'And well, I guess, when I realized he was interested in me I was really flattered because he's so nice and lovely.' She wiped her eyes again. 'And he's much older, as you know. And I kind of got caught up in it all.'

They were all nodding. 'It was quite a whirlwind romance,' Grace said.

'Have you talked to him?' Jojo asked.

Anne Marie shook her head. 'I don't know what to say. I should have said something before. It's not fair not to, but I just don't know what to do. I don't want to break his heart.'

There was silence around the table. Their faces were grave. She wished she had a time machine so that she could fast-forward into the future. Fast-forward to a time when they were all back at home. When this was a distant memory: *Oh, you know, that time that I nearly got married.* Or perhaps it would be better to go backwards, back to the moment when he'd asked her to marry him, and instead of saying yes she would say . . . What? What would she say?

'Putting the marriage thing aside for a minute,' Grace began, 'what would you do if you could start over? Would you still date him, do you think?'

Anne Marie thought about it. She thought about his quiet humour, the way he made her laugh, his kindness. He'd come to the homeless shelter once, where she worked as a volunteer, and he'd helped out with the washing up. It hadn't been beneath him, like she knew it would be for some men – like Manda's Jack for instance. Or even her father.

Fresh anguish spiked through her at the thought of her father. He would be almost as heartbroken as Thomas if the wedding didn't happen. It would ruin his friendship with Thomas. At the very least, it would alter things irrevocably between them. She closed her eyes. 'Yes, I would definitely have gone out with him,' she told Grace. 'I like him very, very much.'

'Like or love?' Jojo asked softly. 'It's so hard to tell sometimes, isn't it?'

Anne Marie nodded. 'I really don't know,' she whispered.

CHAPTER 61

Anne Marie wasn't the only one who was wishing there was such a thing as a time machine. Mikey could have done with one too. He had just reached the entrance of the 'Transit Authority People Mover', which sounded pretty promising, but which turned out to be just a boring old environmentally friendly transport system. He got on it anyway. What the hell! He wasn't exactly making the most of his complimentary ticket. He might as well go on something.

As his carriage glided along the rail, he thought about time machines. He would have used his to fast-forward himself into the future, to a time when this wedding was over. To a time when his role as best man was a distant memory. Right now, he didn't think he could face even going back to the hotel, let alone watch his cousin and Anne Marie all loved-up and happy, heading off into their future as newlyweds with their whole lives ahead of them, while he sat on the sidelines, visualizing Annabel doing the same thing with the billionaire tosser playboy and aching with loneliness.

It would have been better if he was having fun. Which he had been last night. He frowned. He and Grace had been getting on great once they'd established the boundaries.

I, friend of bride, happily married with triplets. You, cousin of groom, sensible best man.

No flirting. Well, OK, maybe a little bit of harmless flirting. But only because they were in a large party of other people and it was a time out of time. And yes, they'd connected. He was sure they had. Yet this morning she had acted as if she disliked him intensely. How – and more importantly, when – had that happened?

He hadn't bought her migraine story at all. She'd reacted to something he'd said. Something she hadn't liked. He racked his brain to think what they'd been talking about just before she left.

Maybe he should have a quiet word with Thomas and see if he could shed any light. Maybe Thomas would slap him on the back and say, 'No, mate, nothing to do with you – she'd had some bad news.' That was possible, wasn't it?

It didn't have to be about him.

It would be better, though, simply to talk to Grace. Much better to ask her outright what he'd done to upset her. If it wasn't anything to do with him, then he could forget about it; and if it was, then he could put it right. Either way, it would make the next few days more enjoyable.

He probably wouldn't see her again till that night. This

place was far too vast to find them again. What were the chances of bumping into them? Practically nil. He could speak to her later. That way, he'd have ages to work out what he was going to say.

But he hadn't taken Sod's law in to account. He had just stepped off the transport system when he saw them. Or, to be more precise, he saw Anne Marie.

'Hey, Mikey,' she called, spotting him immediately. 'We were just talking about you.'

'All good, I hope?' How easy it was to slip into his usual banter. Fix on his happy mask. Did Anne Marie even like him?

She smiled. 'Of course all good.'

There was no edge to her voice. Maybe he really was just being ultra-sensitive, worrying about nothing. Talking to Annabel hadn't helped. It had hauled all his old paranoia, his feelings of not being good enough, back up to the surface.

'I was telling the others that you'd go on Space Mountain with them. It's four to a carriage. And I wouldn't go on it if you paid me a million pounds.'

'And why's that, babe?'

'It's too dark!' She gave an exaggerated shudder. 'And I don't like heights.'

'A theme park is a pretty strange place to come if you're scared of heights?' he said gently.

'Yes, I know.' Her voice was a little rueful. 'I guess I thought I was braver than I am.'

'I'm surprised you didn't drag Thomas along to hold your hand,' he said, and her face dropped a little.

'He's playing golf with Dad.'

'Ah,' he said, thinking that if he were Thomas he wouldn't have left her to go off alone for the day.

Not that she was alone, of course. She was with her girl-friends. Even so, if he'd been Thomas he'd have stuck with her. There was something very vulnerable about Anne Marie. She seemed so young. He could see why Thomas had fallen for her. She brought out a guy's protective instincts.

'So what are you going to do while we're on the ride?'

'I'll look after everyone's bags.'

It wasn't four to a carriage, but three, he discovered when they got to the head of the queue, and you were seated one behind the other. Somehow he ended up behind Grace.

He would never have a better opportunity than now, he thought, as the ride began to move. Just himself and Grace in the dark. He wouldn't even have to look at her face. So he leaned forward and touched her shoulder and just blurted it out. 'I've done something to upset you, Grace. What is it?' He was blunter than he'd intended to be and at first she didn't answer. He wondered if she'd heard. It was noisy in here.

'Grace,' he said urgently. 'Please tell me.'

'OK,' she said. 'I'll tell you later. But not in front of Anne Marie.'

'Cool,' he said, and his stomach crunched with nerves. Now he knew that he *had* upset her, he didn't know whether he felt better or worse.

The ride began to speed up, their carriage shooting for-ward into pitch-black darkness. From somewhere ahead came the sound of maniacal laughter. Mikey settled back in his seat. At least he had stopped thinking about Annabel. There was always a bright side.

Their opportunity to talk came quicker than he'd expected. As they met up with Anne Marie and walked away from the ride, they naturally fell into two groups. Anne Marie, Jojo and Serena were chatting about the ride a little way ahead on the walkway, and he and Grace dropped back.

'So,' he began. 'Was it something I said? Or something I did?'

Grace frowned, and shot him a quick sideways glance. 'It was something you did,' she said quietly. 'We have to keep this conversation between ourselves. I don't want to create a shitty atmosphere for Anne Marie.'

'Agreed,' he said, curious now. What the hell was she talking about? There was music everywhere in this place, but they'd just got to a quieter spot. As they passed the entrance to a picnic area, Grace turned to look at him, 'You're my landlord,' she said. Her cheeks were bright pink.

'I'm your *landlord*?' He began to smile. 'And that's a problem because ... ?'

'It's a problem because you think it's perfectly OK to raise the rent and threaten to kick me and my family out of our home if we don't pay up immediately.' A beat. 'Out of your home,' she amended. Her eyes were very bright.

He still didn't have the faintest idea what she was talking about.

'You've lost me,' he said, shaking his head. 'That's not how my company operates. What's your address?'

She told him and he thought hard. Cogs were beginning to click into place. She was living in one of his properties, that was for sure. It was one of his nicest ones, not even in Exeter, but Little Sanderton. But he certainly hadn't known she was one of his tenants.

'We got behind with the rent,' she said tightly. She looked so mortified that he was beginning to wish he hadn't started this. 'And because of this, we were threatened with eviction.'

'Not by me,' he said.

'But presumably by one of your staff,' she shot back.

'Yes,' he said, thinking of Dick Barton. Last March he had evicted some tenants on a technicality, because he'd taken a backhander from someone who wanted the property. In any case, Dick's contract had recently been terminated – his last day had been the day before this holiday.

Mikey hadn't known that Dick had pulled the same stunt again. But that was exactly what this sounded like. Not, Mikey thought, that explaining all this to Grace was likely to cut any ice. She looked pretty pissed off. He looked at the others before turning back to her.

She quietly added, 'Look, we aren't the type of people who normally miss payments. But one of the boys was ill earlier this year and we took our eye off the ball.'

He cleared his throat. 'I'm so sorry, Grace, that you received this kind of treatment from my company. I really am.'

Grace looked disbelieving.

'I didn't know about it,' he added. 'If I had, it wouldn't have happened. You must be worried sick.'

Grace shrugged. He felt compelled to say something else. 'What would you like me to do about it?'

There was a pause, then she shook her head. 'That letter ... we've been treated as though we – our circumstances – don't matter.'

He nodded. Yes, that sounded exactly like Dick Barton, the little troll. A nasty, callous little troll.

'One of our boys has cancer,' Grace went on quietly. 'He's in remission, thank goodness.' She paused. 'I'm not trying to get the sympathy vote. I'm just explaining why we weren't always on time with our payments, and why we don't have the money to pay the rent increase all in one go.'

Mikey felt cold, despite the heat of the sun. Bloody hell. No wonder she'd been shocked when she found out who he was.

They were passing a balloon-seller; the helium balloons, pink and purple and blue, bumped together against a backdrop of blue sky as they strained for freedom.

'Grace,' he said. 'I'm so sorry. I think I know the staff member responsible for that letter. He was fired last week. But I will look into this when I get back, and make sure nothing like it ever happens again.'

'OK.' There was doubt in her eyes. He got the impression that she wanted to say something else, but she didn't.

'Can we start again?' he said.

After a moment's hesitation, she nodded. 'Of course, Mr Collins.'

'Mikey,' he said. 'Please.'

'Mikey.' She wasn't smiling, but she didn't look pissed off any more either. He had a sudden urge to ask her if she had any sisters who were single and might fancy a date with a property management entrepreneur, but he managed to resist it.

CHAPTER 62

Anne Marie had made a decision. Somewhere amidst the unreality of Disney World, she had realized that she had to talk to Thomas. And she had to do it tonight.

They had separate rooms at the hotel. Or at least they did for the first part of their stay. She knew it was a bit mad and also pretty extravagant, but it was in keeping with tradition. Once they were married, they would move into the bridal suite for their last night. But until then, they weren't just in different rooms – they were on different floors. She was on the ninth floor, along with Manda and Jack and all the girls from the Reading Group. Thomas, Mikey and her father all had rooms on the tenth floor.

When they got back from the Magic Kingdom, she went straight up to Thomas's room and knocked on the door. There was no answer. There was no answer from her father's room either. She guessed they must still be out somewhere.

The sick feeling of dread in her stomach receded a bit. So she had another stay of execution then. For at least a few more hours.

When Mikey got back to his room, the first thing he did was to phone the office and get Charlene, his PA, to look up Grace's tenancy agreement.

'They fell behind on their payments last year,' she told him. 'Happens all the time, they probably overspent on Christmas.'

He didn't comment.

'They've been paying OK ever since,' Charlene went on. 'Hang about, what's this?' There was a pause, and then she said, 'We've just advised them of a rent increase with payment upfront. Do you need details?'

'Yes,' he said, and was surprised when she read out the amount. 'That's quite a bit of money.'

'Well, would you like to adjust it? Apart from that one blip they are good tenants, from what I can see.'

Mikey chewed the end of his pen idly. What the hell! It was peanuts to him, but it was a lot to Grace and her family.

'Put it back to what it was,' he said. 'Oh, and write them a letter, would you? Apologize about the previous letter, and tell them not to worry about paying upfront. That was one of Dick's stunts,' he added. 'There are extenuating circumstances, but I've only just found out about them.'

'No problem,' Charlene said. 'Anything else?'

'Yes. One more thing. Give them a one-month rent holiday, as a gesture of goodwill. Word it so they know it's a one-off. But make it clear they don't owe us for September – or whenever the next month is due.'

'My, we are feeling generous.' Charlene giggled. 'Must be that Florida sun. I take it you're having a good time?'

'Yeah, I am, thanks,' Mikey said, and they said their good-byes.

He felt better for doing that. There was a lightness in him that hadn't been there an hour ago. *Never let it be said that Michael M. Collins doesn't put things right*, he said to himself.

He pondered on whether he should phone Annabel back and give her the name of the jazz band she wanted. He didn't want to talk to her again – he knew that, so in the end he texted it to her. Then, with a little stab of regret, he deleted all trace of her from his phone.

He had a shower, washing the dust and the sweat from his body. Then, not wanting to stay in his room with thoughts of Annabel he went downstairs.

Serena was on a sunlounger by the pool, reading. He was just wondering whether he should sit somewhere else so as not to disturb her when she beckoned him over.

'*The Great Gatsby*,' she said, showing him the cover. 'I don't suppose you've had a chance to read much of it yet?'

'No,' he said. 'I guess I should get cracking. Having gate-crashed my way into your Reading Group.'

'It's quite good. Not our usual kind of book at all.' She laid it down on a low table beside her. 'The story is told by a narrator.' She smiled at him. 'But he's not the hero.'

'Yes, we talked about it before. The hero is in love with a married woman, isn't he?'

Serena nodded. 'Always a risky business.'

'And not something I've ever done,' Mikey said crisply, thinking of Annabel. She'd be married soon, but he wouldn't be chasing after her. He was done. Trying to win her back would be senseless. Although he knew that there was a part of him that had been trying to do exactly that ever since they split up.

He swallowed. 'In the film, the Great Gatsby was quite heroic, wasn't he? Is it the same in the book?'

'Yes, it is.'

'What did he do? I forget.'

'There was a car accident and someone got killed. Gatsby took the blame – even though he wasn't driving. He did it to protect the woman he loved.' Serena took off her glasses, polished them and put them back on her nose. 'So have you ever done anything crazy for love, Mikey?'

'No, I don't think so.'

'Neither have I.' There was a pause, and she glanced across at the statue of Venus, which was a few feet away from them. 'Mind you, the Great Gatsby's woman wasn't worth it in the end.'

He nodded. Annabel hadn't been worth it. All this time he had carried a torch for her, she had been getting closer to the billionaire.

She hadn't given him a thought.

'I don't think I've ever done anything heroic in my life,' he told Serena.

'Maybe you will,' she said.

'Maybe.' There was a pause. 'Can I get you a drink?' he asked.

'I'm fine at the moment, thank you.'

'So this thing,' he went on. 'This trend that you were talking about – what's your take on that? Was reality echoing fiction?'

'I'm not sure,' she said. 'At first it did seem pretty spooky. There were definite elements in our lives that seemed to be following what had happened in the books. But then I also think that if you start focusing on something then it gets bigger. Say, for example, you decide you're going to buy a black Chevrolet – then you suddenly start seeing black Chevrolets everywhere. Have you ever had that experience?'

'I dunno,' he said. 'I've never bought a black Chevrolet.'

Serena gave him her headmistress look. 'You know what I mean. But to get back to your question, I think maybe it was us. I think that because we were reading a particular book we just got caught up in it. We saw elements in our own lives that were a bit similar and our imagination did the rest. We're quite an imaginative bunch! But that's just my take on it,' she added. 'Ask Anne Marie or Kate and you might get a different story.'

'Where is everyone else?' he said.

'I've no idea. Maybe they're all getting a little time out. It's quite hard work, isn't it, being with people 24/7?'

He took that as his cue to leave. Or at least to make a tactical retreat. He moved to a seat a little further from the edge of the pool. God, it looked inviting. It would be good to go for a swim. Maybe he'd go later when no one was around.

*

Grace felt slightly shaky after her chat with Mikey, but at least it had cleared the air between them. Now she wouldn't have to avoid him for the rest of the week.

She went and knocked on Kate's door to see if she was OK.

'I'm good, thanks,' said Kate as she let her in. 'A bit tired, even though I've had a very chilled-out day. How was the Magic Kingdom?'

'Actually, it was quite fun,' Grace said. 'Pretty crowded. The boys would love it – one day, when they're a bit older. And we're a bit richer.' She smiled. 'It's a place for children really.'

Kate patted her stomach. 'Do you hear that, bump? We'll go when you're a bit older. Give me time to save up too!' She yawned. 'Gosh, I'm sorry. Morning sickness takes it out of you, doesn't it? But I'm really looking forward to the wedding, aren't you?'

Grace hesitated. But only for a moment, because there didn't seem any point in keeping it a secret. 'Actually, it looks like there might not be one,' she said, and told her what Anne Marie had said in the cafe.

'Oh, the poor love. She must be terribly upset.' For a while they talked about marriage and whirlwind romances and what it was like to get married really young, which Kate had done too.

'What do you suppose will happen if she does call it off?' Kate said. 'Do you think we'd have to change our flights and head back a bit earlier? I mean, it would be awful for them, wouldn't it? Staying here all week and then not getting married on Saturday. Like rubbing salt in the wound.'

'Yes,' Grace said. 'Poor Anne Marie.' She sighed. 'I was feeling jealous of her earlier. And now I feel like a right cow.'

'Because she seems to have so much. It isn't the be all and end all, though, money, is it?' Kate's eyes held a wisdom that was far beyond her years.

Grace nodded. She told Kate about her conversation with Mikey.

'Well, well,' Kate said. 'You just never can tell, can you. Maybe he's not such a bad guy then, hey?'

'No, I think he's OK. I'm so glad I didn't say anything to Anne Marie,' said Grace. 'What do you think we should do? About Anne Marie, I mean?'

'I don't think there's much we can do, apart from wait and see what she does. And whatever that is, we'll support her.'

Grace nodded. 'We're just going to have to give her as much love as we possibly can, aren't we? Bless her. I think she might well be talking to Thomas now.'

Anne Marie was waiting for him in the foyer. Where was he anyway? She'd tried phoning him earlier and her call had gone straight to voicemail.

She couldn't get hold of her father either. She had glanced out at the pool earlier and seen Mikey and Serena chatting. They were sitting near the statue of Venus. Venus, the goddess of love. How ironic that seemed now.

Then suddenly Anne Marie looked up and there they were, Thomas and her father, strolling in through the main doors, looking suntanned and happy. Her father had just said something to Thomas that had clearly made him smile. He was nodding. Anne Marie wondered if they were talking about her.

She hoped they weren't. She hoped her father hadn't been saying, 'Just a couple more days and you'll be my son-in-law.'

Standing in the foyer of this most beautiful hotel, watching these two men she cared deeply about and knowing she was going to break both their hearts, was a raw moment. She didn't think she had ever felt so bereft.

She hugged her arms around herself. She had lost weight lately. Most of the time she had been too churned up to eat. A few months ago, losing weight would have been cause for celebration. But it wasn't now. Maybe she had grown up then, just a bit.

It was Thomas who saw her first. He must have felt the heat of her gaze because he looked up and he gave her a little wave. Carefree and casual. Would she ever see him that carefree and casual again?

'Hello, sweetheart.' The two of them reached her together. Thomas kissed her on the cheek. Her father smiled.

'Did you have a good game of golf?'

'Stonking,' her father said.

'He thrashed me,' Thomas said. 'You could have warned me. I didn't know he could play so well.'

'He spends a lot of time on golf courses,' she said. 'It's where he strikes most of his deals, isn't it, Daddy?'

'Absolutely, Princess.' He nodded indulgently. 'Did you enjoy the Magic Kingdom? I've just had word from your sister. She's arriving Friday lunchtime. They had to change their flight. Problem with one of the kids.' He shook his head. 'Don't you two go rushing into having kids, will you?' He winked at Anne Marie. 'They're more trouble than they're worth.'

'We won't rush into anything,' Thomas said, taking her hand. 'Will we, darling?'

She shook her head. She was too choked up to speak.

CHAPTER 63

'You look worried,' Thomas said when they were clear of her father. 'What's going on in there? Do you want to talk?'

'Yes, please.'

'My room or yours?' he asked.

She shrugged. 'Either.'

'Is it urgent? Would you mind if I had a shower first?' He screwed up his face. 'It's hard work, golf.'

'Of course I don't mind. It's not urgent.'

'Great.' He smiled at her. 'Give me, say, half an hour? And then come to mine and we can catch up. Is that OK?'

'That's absolutely fine.' Neither of them said anything else. The lift glided upwards, and she got out on level nine. He didn't attempt to kiss her. She wondered if there was some part of him that already knew what she was going to say.

Anne Marie had a shower too. Then she applied her make-up carefully. She wasn't really sure why she was bothering. Earlier on she had cried off every bit of mascara. Tears, she had thought idly, were the best mascara-remover in the world. If you could bottle tears and sell them as mascara-remover you would make a fortune.

It was slightly over half an hour later when she got to Thomas's room. She knocked on the door, her heart pounding in her chest. After tonight, it would all be over. He was never going to speak to her again when he found out she didn't want to marry him. She wondered if they would be able to claim any of the money back on the wedding insurance. Probably not. She was pretty sure the company didn't make refunds if the bride changed her mind.

She was so caught up in agonizing that it didn't register straight away that he hadn't answered the door. She knocked again. There was still no answer. With a little sigh she got out her phone and saw she had a text from him: *Sorry, sweetie, I'm just helping someone out. It was urgent. Can we talk later? T x*

She read it again with a frown. Helping someone out? What on earth did he mean? And how could it possibly be more urgent than this?

Not that he knew it was urgent, of course. With an even bigger sigh, she began to retrace her steps. It was almost seven. They wouldn't have time to talk now before dinner. It would have to be afterwards. Which meant it would be really late. And also there would be an atmosphere over dinner.

Half the Reading Group knew how she felt. She paused as she passed Manda and Jack's door. She should have told Manda too. She was her best friend. But it was difficult because she was always with Jack. She lifted her hand to knock then withdrew it, torn with indecision.

She knew she was just making excuses. She could tell Manda she wanted a quiet word and Manda would be there. Of course she would. On the other hand, she should have told Thomas first. Not everyone else. She wouldn't tell Manda now, she was going to find out soon enough. She decided to go on downstairs to the bar. Being alone with her endlessly circling thoughts was the last thing she wanted.

Rather ironically, Manda was the first person she saw. She was perched on a bar stool, and as far as Anne Marie could see, she was alone.

'Girlfriend,' Manda called, waving at her frantically from across the bar. 'There you are. I was beginning to think you weren't coming.'

'I didn't know I was supposed to be coming.' Anne Marie said as she reached her. 'We didn't arrange to meet, did we?'

Manda hopped off her bar stool and they air kissed. Manda smelled of Loulou and it reminded Anne Marie painfully of home. Of normality.

'Thomas said he'd tell you.' Manda paused. 'He forgot to pass on the message, didn't he?'

'I think he must have done,' Anne Marie said. 'What was the message?'

'Well . . .' Manda signalled to the barman. 'It's a bit of a long story. I'll get you a drink. I had a cocktail earlier. I'm road-testing them for tomorrow. They're amazing. They're an amazing price too,' she went on. 'But hey, it's not every day your bezzie mate gets married, is it, so I thought I'd splash out. We haven't had a proper chat since we got here. How are you feeling?'

'I'll get them,' Anne Marie said. A cocktail suddenly sounded like a very fine idea. Come to think of it, getting drunk suddenly sounded like a very fine idea. Why hadn't she thought of it before? 'What are you having?'

'Sex on the Beach.' Manda gave her a sly smile. 'What else.'

'Two Sex on the Beach please,' Anne Marie told the barman, who didn't smile, but just raised an eyebrow and said, 'Coming up, ma'am.'

She couldn't decide if he was making a joke or not. Probably not. The Americans weren't as subtle as the English.

While they waited for him to mix them, Manda said, 'Jack has put his back out and your darling fiancé offered to see if he could sort it out. That's what they're doing now.'

'Right,' said Anne Marie. 'How did he put his back out?'

Manda giggled. 'Well, I could tell you, but I'm not sure I should. Put it this way – we have been quite active since we got here. We are still newlyweds, after all.' She clapped her hand over her mouth and giggled again. Her eyes were a little glazed.

'How many cocktails have you had?' Anne Marie asked.

'Just the one. They are quite strong, though.'

Anne Marie didn't know whether to believe her or not. But one thing she was sure about was that she couldn't go confiding in Manda when she was in this state. No, she definitely had to speak to Thomas first.

Their drinks arrived. Anne Marie took a sip. Manda was right – they were strong. By the time they were joined by everyone else in the wedding party, which couldn't have been much more than twenty minutes later, Anne Marie was on her way to being drunk.

Jack and Thomas came in together. 'This man is a genius,' Jack announced, patting Thomas on the back. 'I could barely walk earlier and now look at me.' He gave a little hop and a skip.

'Don't get carried away,' Thomas warned. 'You'll be sore for a day or two.'

'Let me buy you a drink,' Jack said, smiling across at Manda and Anne Marie. 'What are you ladies drinking?'

Thomas came across to stand beside her. 'Sorry, darling. About postponing our chat.' His eyes were contrite. 'But I didn't want to leave poor Jack in agony.'

'Of course not.' She smiled at him. 'He seems OK now.'

Thomas leaned forward and stroked a strand of hair back off her face. The gesture was so tender, so loving, that she wanted to weep. What was he going to do when she told him? She was sure now that he didn't know. There was nothing in his eyes. No trace of worry. She must have imagined what she had seen earlier.

But the whole world had gone into a rosy, soft-focus haze. In fact. the whole evening passed in a kind of rosy, soft-focus haze. Anne Marie remembered chatting and laughing with

Manda and Jack and her father and Mikey. They all seemed on really good form.

Every so often she got a searching look from one of the Reading Group. But hey, maybe she was imagining that. They all seemed happy enough too. From what she could hear, they were discussing *The Great Gatsby*. She must start reading it. Especially if it had Leonardo DiCaprio in it. Hang on a minute, he was in the film, not the book. Actors weren't in books. She was getting muddled. It was these flaming cocktails.

Had she had three or four? She thought it was three, but there had been wine on the table too. Was it her fault if people kept topping up her glass?

At the end of the evening, Thomas went with her in the lift to help her to bed. 'I'm fine,' she kept telling him, but actually she was glad of his help. It did seem a little bit harder to walk than it usually was.

He insisted on coming into her room too and making her coffee.

'Don't think you're sneaking into my bed.' She wagged a finger at him. 'Naughty, naughty. I know your game.'

'I'm not trying to sneak into your bed. I'm going back to mine, don't worry. But I just want to make sure that you're safe.' He kissed her forehead. His eyes were very tender. 'I'll always want to make sure that you're safe, Anne Marie.'

'Aw, thanks.' His niceness was penetrating through the fog in her brain. There was a niggling thought too, somewhere else. A thought she couldn't quite put her finger on. Why had he said 'always' in that odd tone of voice? Ah, of course – he would always be there. He would be by her side, for ever, as her husband.

Ah yes, husband. Was he going to be her husband? Had she told him that he wasn't? No, she definitely hadn't. Or he wouldn't look so happy.

She'd planned to tell him tonight, hadn't she? But she couldn't tell him now. She couldn't think clearly enough.

He stayed while she drank her coffee, and then he made her another one.

'You're not feeling sick, are you?' His voice was grave. 'If you are, I'll stay here and keep an eye on you.'

'I'm not feeling sick,' she assured him. She was almost feeling sober, which was a shame.

'OK, well, I'll say goodnight then,' Thomas said. He pecked her on the cheek. A very chaste kiss, Anne Marie thought, from a man who was going to be her husband.

She wanted to call him back and say, 'Oh, Thomas, what is going on with us? Did I imagine the passion that we used to have?'

But she didn't. She couldn't. They would have to talk when she was properly sober. Tomorrow, which was the day of her hen night. The hen night that wasn't going to happen, Anne Marie thought, as she closed the door of her room behind him.

CHAPTER 64

Anne Marie felt as if she had only just gone off to sleep when she was woken by the wail of a siren. For a couple of moments she stayed where she was in bed. It must be the fire alarm. Was it a drill? Would someone switch it off in a minute? No one did. She threw back the covers, slipped on her sundress, which was on the chair by the side of the bed, and put on her shoes without socks.

The movement made her feel slightly giddy and her mouth felt ash-dry. Oh crap, was she still drunk? Or did she have a hangover already? Perhaps she was caught between the two. There was something very spooky about the sound of that alarm. She could hear doors banging outside her room. Clearly all the other guests were taking it seriously.

You weren't supposed to stop to collect any of your possessions, but bugger that. She tugged her phone from its charger on the bedside table and her bag from the back of the chair and opened her bedroom door.

Smoke was seeping along the corridor outside her room. Her heart jolted in shock. For the first time, she felt fear. The emergency lighting had come on, but that just added to the spookiness. There were more doors banging further down the corridor. Jojo and Serena were in the rooms directly opposite hers. Anne Marie pounded on their doors. 'Fire! We've got to get out,' she shouted, surprised when her voice came out all high and shrill. Serena's door opened but there was no answer from Jojo. Could she already be out?

'Shit,' Serena said, glancing past Anne Marie. She was wearing a pink robe but no shoes. She must have only just woken. 'Where's Jojo?' she said, her voice low and urgent but still totally calm, as it always was.

Anne Marie couldn't imagine Serena ever getting ruffled.

'I don't know.' Anne Marie hammered on her door again. The smoke didn't seem to be any worse, but it smelled stronger now, even in that few seconds.

The fire door further down the corridor was closed. Did that happen automatically?

'We have to go, Anne Marie.' Serena tugged at her arm.

Anne Marie nodded. Fear was properly alive in her now, flooding her with adrenalin, which was chasing away the hangover. But oddly, she also felt strangely calm. Jojo couldn't be in her room. She would have answered. But what if she were a heavy sleeper? As she followed Serena up the corridor, she kept looking back over her shoulder.

What if Jojo were still in there? She had to have one more try. Breaking away from Serena's grasp, she raced back in the direction she'd come. This time she pounded on the door with both fists and screamed at the top of her voice. 'Jojo! Get out! We've got to get out!'

The door opened. Jojo was blinking at her like a startled goat. She was wearing a voluminous nightshirt and a head-set, which clearly she'd only just tugged away from her ears. No wonder she hadn't heard.

'My shoes,' she gasped.

'No time!' Anne Marie shouted. 'It's not a drill.'

They hurtled down the corridor and met a white-faced Serena, who was waiting at the emergency door at the corner of the building. 'We need to go down the fire escape,' she shouted. 'It's going to be a bit hairy. We're bloody high. I just had a look. There's a lot of people already out there. On the lower floors.'

'Go for it,' Jojo said. 'We just need to take it steady. One at a time. You OK, Anne Marie?'

Anne Marie gulped and closed her eyes. 'I'm terrified of heights,' she whispered. 'I couldn't even manage Space Mountain.'

Jojo grabbed her hand. 'It's nothing like as scary as Space Mountain,' she said. 'It's a proper staircase and there are lights on it. It's not dark. It's going to be absolutely fine.' Anne Marie swallowed as Jojo's fingers tightened around hers. She could feel the draft of the cooler night air beyond the open door of the fire escape.

She sneaked a glance over her shoulder. The smoke was thicker still. 'Oh my God, what about everyone else? Should we go back?'

'Listen to me, angel.' Jojo's voice was very firm. 'We have to worry about getting ourselves out. We may very well be the last ones on this floor. Do you understand?'

Anne Marie nodded and clutched her bag to her chest. Just ahead of them, the dark shape of Serena hovered in the doorway.

'Serena's going to go first,' Jojo continued, 'and I'm going to be right behind you. And we're going to take it really, really steady.' She drew out the words, her voice calming and confident.

'You OK with that, Serena?'

Serena nodded. She didn't look convinced, but she stepped out onto the grid-like stairs and Anne Marie followed.

The night air touched her face and she felt her head spin slightly as she saw the lights of the ground far, far below them. The fire escape was very dark; there were lights further down, but the ones higher up hadn't come on. Anne Marie shivered and her foot slipped on the grid, which was damp with condensation. She gave a small moan and sat down, frozen with fear.

'I don't think I can do this.'

'Yes, you can.' Jojo sat beside her and grabbed hold of her hand. 'We can't stay here. Look at me, angel.'

Anne Marie did as she was told. 'Right then,' Jojo said. 'This is what I want you to do. I want you to breathe. To the count of five, take one breath in, hold for five, and breathe out for five. Five seconds in, five seconds hold and five seconds out. That's it. And again.' Her eyes were soft. 'Feeling better?'

Anne Marie nodded.

'Now then, hang your bag around your neck. Then with your left hand, you grab the rail, and with your right hand you hold on to me. All we have to do is one step at a time. That's it.'

Her voice was rhythmic. Soothing. Almost hypnotic. *One day, when I have babies, I want her to be my midwife*, Anne Marie thought. Bloody hell, that was random. Where had that thought come from? She wasn't going to have any babies. She wasn't even going to get married. Misery flooded through her. Where were Thomas and Dad? What if they were trapped? Good God, they were on the floor above. She looked up. No one was on the fire escape above them. Couldn't they get out?

From the landing below, Serena cleared her throat. 'You two OK?' She smiled encouragingly.

'Five in ... five hold ... five out. Do it with me,' Jojo instructed. 'One, two, three, four, five.'

Anne Marie did as she was told. It was definitely working. Everything had begun to feel slightly surreal. As if none of this was really happening. As if the siren that they could still hear from the building, now mingling with the sirens of the fire engines far below, were a part of some other life that didn't belong to her.

And in this way they went slowly down the fire escape. When they were about three floors from the ground, Serena said, 'God, I hope everyone got out. Do you think the fire started on our floor or the one below? Which floor were the others on, Anne Marie?'

'Daddy and Thomas and Mikey were above us,' she whispered. 'Everyone else was on ours, but nearer to the other end.' The same thoughts were still swirling in her head too, insidious as smoke. It was unthinkable that any of the people she loved might be trapped. When she risked a look up, she could see plumes of smoke curling up into the night sky but no flames. It was very possible that the fire had started on the other side of the hotel – the side that overlooked the gardens, not the lake – and none of the wedding party were on the other side of the hotel. She had to hold on to that thought.

Then finally they were on the ground and the officials were taking over, shepherding them into the car park, which was obviously the place to gather. There were dozens of people milling about in various states of undress. One man had a towel wrapped around his head like a turban. Had he just washed his hair at 2 a.m.?

Two ambulances with their backs open, spilling out light, were parked over to one side, and she counted five fire engines – and three more driving into the car park behind them. She began to shiver, the enormity of it all suddenly hitting her.

'Can I have your names, please, and room numbers?' a man with a clipboard was asking.

As he ticked them off his list and looked like he was about to move away, Anne Marie grabbed his arm. 'Can you tell me if you've got a Stephen Hambledon and a Thomas Hanson on your list?' she asked, in a voice that didn't sound anything like hers.

He scanned the list and gave a brief shake of his head. 'Not yet, ma'am. But there are people coming out all the time.'

Jojo stepped forward. 'We also need to know about—'

He put up a hand to stop her. 'I haven't checked everyone off, ma'am. Please let me do that first. Can I ask you to join the group over there on the left, please?'

Jojo nodded. The three of them began to walk towards the group. Then suddenly, high above their heads, there was an explosion, followed swiftly by another. They all looked up and now they could see that the top floor of the hotel, on the side of the building that was closest to the lake, was ablaze.

A few of those rooms had balconies, and in the flickering light people were clearly visible, standing close to the railings in a bid to get away from the smoke.

'Oh my God,' Serena murmured, as the low boom of a third explosion rent the air. A silence fell across the car park as dozens of pale, upturned faces focused on the drama that was being played out above them.

CHAPTER 65

Mikey had also woken up to the sound of the fire alarm, but he had known immediately that it wasn't a drill because he smelled smoke. With adrenalin coursing through him, he tugged on his jeans, getting his feet tangled up in his haste and hopping around like a demented dummy before finally freeing himself.

Grabbing a T-shirt but not stopping to put it on, he hauled open the door of his room and saw that the corridor outside was thick with smoke. To his right, a couple of shadowy figures were moving away. The emergency lighting was on, but he couldn't see who they were. 'Thomas?' he yelled.

'No,' a disembodied voice called back. 'Sorry!'

Mikey pounded on the door opposite. Somewhere close by must be well ablaze. All that smoke had to be coming from somewhere, but he couldn't work out the direction. It seemed to be just as dense whichever way he looked. Shit, he didn't even know which way the fire escape was – why hadn't he checked?

Had those blokes been going the right way? Or had they been guessing too? The door in front of him opened and Thomas stumbled out. 'Christ,' he said. 'Mikey, is that you?'

'Yeah, it's me. Which room is Stephen in?'

Thomas pointed to their left, the opposite direction to the one the blokes had been heading in. Then he broke into a fit of coughing.

'We have to make sure he's out,' Mikey said. 'Hold on a minute.' He darted back into his room and soaked a towel in the bathroom sink. It was mad, but he'd seen it done in the movies. A wet towel over your mouth. Wasn't that supposed to give you more time?

Emerging seconds later, he handed one to Thomas, and even though every instinct he had was urging him to do the opposite, they began to edge along the corridor towards Stephen's room.

On the ground, Anne Marie, Jojo and Serena had just found Manda and Jack.

'Oh my God!' Manda sobbed as she saw them approaching. 'Thank heavens you're OK.'

'Have you seen anyone else?' Anne Marie asked urgently.

'Grace and Kate are safe,' Jack told them, his eyes serious. 'Kate's in an ambulance, they're checking her over.'

'She's pregnant,' Manda said, wiping streaks of grime from her face. 'She just told us.' She pointed back over her shoulder. 'Grace is sitting over there on the grass.'

'Gosh,' Anne Marie said, trying to take this in.

'We haven't seen your dad or Thomas or Mikey,' Jack added. 'Which side of the hotel were they on?'

'This side,' Anne Marie said, looking up. 'The same as us.'

The firefighters had several hoses trained on the front of the building and the air was full of smoke and ash. Over to their left, another fire engine was lifting a square platform on the end of a crane into the air. They could hear the hydraulic whirr.

'They'll get them out,' Serena said in her confident head-mistress voice. 'Don't worry. They know what they're doing.'

Mikey pounded on the door. 'Stephen!' he shouted, before bursting into another fit of coughing. 'Are you in there?'

Thomas pounded on the door too. One thing was certain, Mikey thought – they couldn't hang around here. They should be moving. They should be getting out. Every instinct was screaming it. *Get out, get out, get out!*

The door opened.

Stephen was fully dressed. Before he could speak, there was a sudden and powerful explosion. It came from some-where behind Mikey. It was difficult to work out the direction, but it had the effect of propelling Thomas and Mikey through the open doorway. The air in Stephen's room was still rela-tively clear.

'Didn't you hear the alarm?' Thomas said.

'Not until just now. Earplugs,' Stephen said. He looked past them to the smoke-filled hall, a panicked expression on his face. 'What's going on? What was that noise?'

'Which way's the fire escape?' Mikey said, abandoning the towel and pulling on his T-shirt. 'We really should be heading there.'

'It's to the left,' Stephen said. 'We're about as far away as we can get from it.'

'I think we should still try.'

Thomas was shaking his head. 'If it's blocked we'll be cut off.' He pulled the door closed, cutting off the smoke that had been streaming into the room, and walked towards the floor-length windows. 'What about the balcony?'

Mikey followed him. It was easier to think in here. He had to admit that the thought of going back out into the blinding, choking smoke was the last thing he wanted to do. The towels hadn't helped. The towels had been useless.

He pulled open the doors. The balcony was big, wide enough for a table, four chairs and several pot plants. Wide enough for a bloody party. They overlooked the lake. What a pity they weren't a bit closer. A hundred metres closer and they could have jumped. No, it was an optical illusion. They weren't even that close.

Directly below, he could see the shiny blue diamond of the pool. If they'd been a couple of floors lower that would be doable. From up here, the force of hitting the water would probably break your neck.

He, Stephen and Thomas weren't the only ones who had gone out on to balconies. There was a couple one floor below them, over to their right. They were leaning out over the railings, shouting and waving sheets. From the room to the right of this couple, smoke was pouring out of the windows.

Below that, the hotel looked fine. The fire must have started on the floor below them – the floor that the women were on.

He shuddered and hoped no one else had worked that out. Behind him, Stephen said, 'Hobson's choice. We take a punt with the smoke and try for the fire escape. Or we wait here and hope someone rescues us.'

'Or that they manage to put the fire out,' Thomas said, his voice wry.

'They're doing their best,' Mikey said. He couldn't believe how calm they were all being. They could be within an hour of death. Half an hour even. *Don't go there, Mikey.* An over-active imagination was no help at all in a situation like this. The *what ifs* were already niggling away in his head. The main one being what if the emergency services didn't have a crane long enough to get up here. They were a bloody long way up.

Anne Marie, Grace, Serena, Kate, Jojo, Manda and Jack were all huddled together at the edge of the car park by the lake.

They had established that none of the men except Jack was outside. Grace and Manda had searched, going from group to group, asking the fire wardens, checking. No one had seen them.

Grace glanced at Anne Marie. She was very white. Grace felt a surge of compassion. What a nightmare this must be for her. What a nightmare this whole week had been for Anne Marie. And now she was facing the prospect of losing not only her fiancé and cousin but her beloved dad too.

Grace couldn't even begin to imagine what that must be like.

She put an arm around Anne Marie's slender shoulders. 'It's going to be OK, sweetie,' she said, even though she knew that was a mad thing to say because she couldn't possibly know. But she had to say something. They couldn't all just sit here with no hope.

'They're getting the fire under control,' she added softly.

Anne Marie burst into tears.

'It's all my fault,' she sobbed. 'I'm being punished.'

'Don't be silly . . .'

'I am.' Anne Marie wiped her nose and gulped a bit. 'It's because I don't want to marry Thomas and now I'm going to lose him. God's taking him away to punish me.'

'No. That's not what's happening.' Jojo, who was standing close by, took a step towards them.

She and Grace exchanged glances.

'You're in shock, that's all,' Manda said, looking at her sympathetically. 'And the other thing is pre-wedding nerves. I had them too. Remember? Of course you want to marry Thomas. You love Thomas.'

'I know. I love him a lot.' Anne Marie's eyes were as bright as stars as she stared around at them all. 'I don't know what to do. I'm so scared for Dad and for Thomas.' She began to shiver in her thin dress.

'Anne Marie, darling, you do not have to get married if you don't want to.' Serena was the voice of authority and they all looked at her.

'Precisely,' Jojo said. 'It can all be cancelled.'

No one mentioned the obvious. Thomas and Stephen and Mikey were still missing. And after the fire, it seemed highly unlikely that the wedding would go ahead anyway, whatever happened.

On the balcony, Mikey thought, *I wonder what it would have been like with Annabel. If she'd accepted my proposal and married me, I may very well have been making her a widow tonight. But then maybe if we had got married, our lives would have taken a whole different turn. Maybe I wouldn't even be here – being Thomas's best man.*

Good grief, how selfish he was being. Poor Thomas was supposed to be getting married on Saturday.

As if Thomas had picked up on his thoughts, he looked across at him. 'I love her,' he said. 'These have been the happiest eight months of my life.'

Stephen, who was standing beside him, blinked a few times, and his Adam's apple bobbed. 'She couldn't have chosen a better man,' he said, his voice low. 'I'm proud to have you as a son-in-law.' He clapped Thomas on the shoulder.

Mikey bit his lip. In the room beyond them, through the glass doors of the balcony, which were closed, he could see the door of Stephen's hotel room. There was an orange glow beneath it.

CHAPTER 66

Thomas moved towards the balcony and leaned over the metal railings that bordered it. 'Hey!' he shouted at the top of his voice. 'Hey! We're here! Up here!' He turned back towards them, gesturing wildly. 'You two, get over here. We've got to make sure they see us.'

When they reached him, Mikey saw that the fire crew had the aerial platform level with the balcony below them. It looked like it was on its maximum extension. Jesus, it was never going to reach them.

The adrenalin was coursing through him. Until he'd seen that glow, he'd been confident that they'd have time, that the balcony had been a good idea – a place of safety that would be their sanctuary, rather than a trap that would become their coffin.

Don't think like that, man.

Thomas and Stephen were scared too; he could see it in their faces. They were both hollering over the edge of the balcony. 'Up here, guys! We're up here!'

Smoke temporarily obscured the platform. Thomas cursed. 'Do you think they saw us?'

Who knew? It was impossible to see the ground for a moment. Then the smoke thinned enough for them to see the platform.

In that instant, one of the firefighters turned his face up towards them and gave them the thumbs-up. They'd got the couple on to it now. They were huddled together, plainly terrified. There was room for more people on that platform. But how the hell were they going to get to it?

Something smashed in the room behind them. The standard lamp, Mikey thought, or the glass door of the minibar, exploding in the heat. The fire was in the room now, raging across it with terrifying speed. His skin prickled as the temperature rose.

An unfamiliar emotion was threading through the adrenalin that powered through him. Fear.

The platform was edging up towards them. Mikey hoped to God they were the last people on this floor. What if they weren't? How did the firefighters decide whom to rescue?

When it was about four metres short of the bottom of the balcony, the platform stopped.

They had a ladder, he saw. Holy crap, they were going to stretch it between the platform and the balcony. That was dicey. But he guessed they didn't have much choice. He and Thomas reached out to grab the hooked top of it as it came up through the smoke. Between them, they got it into place on the railings as flames licked at the inside of the balcony doors. Stephen was backing away. Mikey glanced at him. His face was ghost-white.

The ladder clanked as the firefighter ascended and then suddenly he was there with them on the balcony. He was quite bulky, Mikey thought, reassured. Bulky and commanding. 'OK, guys, one at a time. Let's get moving.' He had a voice that was gruff to match the bulk.

'Who's first?'

Stephen gave Thomas a shove. 'You go, son.'

Thomas looked like he was about to argue, but the firefighter was already putting a harness over his shoulders and clipping on carabiners, deft and swift. For a second they were both straddling the balcony. The firefighter went first, guiding Thomas's feet onto the ladder, and they disappeared.

Stephen looked at Mikey. His face was grey. 'I don't think I can do that,' he said.

'Yes, you can,' Mikey told him. 'Nothing to it.'

Stephen shook his head. Sweat was pouring off his face. His eyes were dark with terror. There was another bang as the fire smashed out the glass doors behind them, spraying them both with glass.

It was a while before the firefighter was back, his face black with grime. 'Quickly,' he said. 'Who's next?'

Mikey shoved Stephen forward. 'You want to see your daughter get married, don't you? Think of her. Think of Anne Marie.' He could feel the fire's heat on his back.

'Go,' he said. 'Go. If the worst comes to the worst, I'll jump. I can make the pool from here. I can do it. GO!'

The firefighter was shaking his head as he helped get Stephen over the edge. 'I'll be quick,' he said. 'Don't move.'

Mikey nodded. Fuck, it was hot. Through the gaps in the smoke below, he watched the two men inching towards the platform. They seemed to be going in slow motion. There wasn't going to be time. There was fire all around. If he left it another ten seconds he was going to be burned alive.

Brian and Angela Collins invite you to the funeral of their only son, Michael.

Bollocks to that.

He straddled the balcony. OK, so he wasn't sure about the pool – his assertion that he could reach it had been designed to galvanize Stephen into action.

Should he go for the platform? If he went for the platform, he might land on someone. If he went for the pool, he'd be clear of the platform. Even if he didn't reach it, he wouldn't take anyone out with him. What was it Serena had said earlier about heroics? Suddenly, his mind was immensely calm.

The choking smoke was in his face. Suffocating him – like a wall of dust in his lungs. There was no more time. He had to make a decision. He jumped.

CHAPTER 67

It is possible to survive falls from heights of a hundred feet into water. Much depends on how you land. And on how deep the water is. Therefore, if he hit the pool, and if the pool was deep enough, he had every chance of surviving.

It was amazing what thoughts flashed into his head in the moment before he jumped. Images too – adrenalin sharp. He saw a hangman's hood over the head of the man on the plane, and the loop of rope dangling from the fire-fighter's belt. Would he have time to feel pain? This was about the last thought he had before impact.

On the ground below, there was a great deal of chaos and shouting and disorder as people searched for their loved ones, going from group to group, ever more frantic as the fire and the firefighters battled it out. By 3 a.m., the fire appeared to be winning.

They were still standing in a tight-knit group. The keep-your-chin-up chatter had receded into a worried silence as time passed and Thomas, Mikey and Stephen didn't materialize.

'They're still getting people from the top floor,' Serena began, but the rest of her sentence was cut off by a muttered cry from the direction of the pool. 'Oh my God, it's a jumper. It's a jumper . . .' The words echoed back through the crowd.

'Don't go over there,' Serena said, catching hold of Anne Marie's arm.

Anne Marie shrugged her off. 'I have to.'

She was shivering violently, despite the fact that she'd been given a blanket to wrap around her shoulders and it wasn't cold anyway. Her legs felt like sponges, not solid enough to support her, and her bare feet felt clammy in her shoes, but those words, *It's a jumper*, forced her on.

She arrived at the poolside in time to see that they were bringing something – someone – out of the water. The body of a man, wearing jeans and a T-shirt. She couldn't see any more than that. She couldn't see his face. They had him on a stretcher – did that mean he was alive? It must mean he was alive – or they wouldn't need the stretcher.

Her thoughts jumbled and churned, shot through with fragmented images. Thomas, his eyes tender, leaning forward to stroke a strand of hair back from her face. Thomas beside her during their holiday in Ecuador, listening to something the guide was saying about extinction. Thomas laughing. *Oh, Thomas, please don't leave me.* 'Please don't leave me.'

She was sobbing as she reached the ambulance where they'd just taken the man on the stretcher. Someone was closing the doors from inside, but she was hammering on them.

'Anne Marie, love, Anne Marie, wait.' Serena's voice was at the edge of her mind, the edge of her consciousness. Quite distant and surreal.

Anne Marie let Serena lead her away as the ambulance drove off into the night. They stood in a patch of darkness a little way from the pool. She had no idea how long they stood. Time seemed to have lost all meaning.

And then there was another voice. 'Anne Marie, oh my darling, my love.' And it was Thomas's voice. Her darling Thomas. How was that even possible? Thomas was in the ambulance. But he wasn't in the ambulance. He was behind her. He was standing up. He was tall and alive and talking. She rushed into his arms, not sure until she was actually touching him that he was real. They clung to each other tightly and she buried her face in his shoulder. Breathing in the scent of him, the stink of smoke and of life and of love.

It was only when they drew apart that she saw her father, just behind him. His face blackened by smoke, his eyes very serious.

'Hello, Princess.' His voice was cracked and hoarse. A paramedic was already hurrying towards them.

'Oh, Daddy. Are you OK? Everyone else is OK. Oh God, I've been so worried.' In a moment she had left Thomas's arms to go into her father's.

'Sir, I'll need to check you over. Can you just step this way, sir? Please.'

Neither of them took any notice of the paramedic.

Her father kissed the top of her head like he had when she was a child. For a while, she couldn't speak. Her eyes and her throat stung with shock and relief. She was dizzy with the aftermath.

And then everyone else was there, and they were all talking at once. There was backslapping and there were hugs and questions and more questions. Finally, Anne Marie untangled herself from her father enough to take a step back.

'Where's Mikey?' she asked. 'Have you seen him?'

Her father nodded. Then closed his eyes and shook his head. Just the tiniest of shakes.

There was another explosion from somewhere at the top of the building, and cries of, 'Get back, get back!' from the officials. 'Everyone needs to move back, please. The building is becoming unstable.'

'He saved our lives,' Thomas said. 'He wouldn't come off the balcony. He made us go first. My stupid, crazy, brave bloody cousin.'

She could see tears on his face, tracking through the grime.

'Someone jumped,' Anne Marie said softly. 'I thought it was you.' She glanced around. The ambulance behind them had just started to move.

Her father pressed his knuckles to his eyes.

'Wait a minute,' Serena said. 'We don't know that he's

dead. The person who jumped – whoever it was – he landed in the pool.'

'It's not deep enough, surely.' Thomas's voice was incredulous.

'He said it was though, didn't he?' Her father was looking at Thomas. 'It was the last thing he said to me. He said he could make it if he jumped into the pool. Could he make it, Thomas?'

Thomas shrugged. 'I don't know. I don't think he could have known either.'

'One thing I am sure about,' Serena said quietly. 'Is that they don't take dead people to hospital in ambulances with flashing lights.'

CHAPTER 68

It was two days later. The evening of Saturday 27 August, the day they should have got married. Instead, Anne Marie and Thomas were arriving at Celebration Hospital, Orlando. Everyone else was back at the hotel they'd been moved to. They were visiting Mikey in shifts.

Not that he had been aware of this until today, because he'd been heavily sedated. He had a fractured pelvis, two broken legs, a cracked collarbone and numerous cuts and grazes. He was extremely lucky to be alive, his doctor had said.

If he'd landed two feet to the left, he would have missed the pool completely. Two feet to the right, he'd have hit the statue of Venus. As it was, they hoped there would be no permanent damage. Although it was going to take a while for his injuries to heal.

Today he was compos mentis enough to know what day it was, apparently. His parents had flown in from England and they would be here in a couple of hours.

Neither Anne Marie nor Thomas said much on the long walk to the ward. There had been quite a bit of talking going on for the last couple of days. A lot of soul-searching too.

They'd had to cancel the wedding, although their wedding-planner had pointed out that if they still wanted to go ahead, she would pull out all the stops to ensure that they could.

The venue – the Cinderella Castle – was, of course, unaffected. Their wedding clothes could be replaced. They could spend their wedding night at another hotel. But rescheduling the whole thing was also absolutely fine. They would have a full refund regardless of what they did, and compensation too. Her father, it turned out, had taken out a belts-and-braces insurance policy.

But they didn't want to get married without Mikey.

'I've been worried that you may have been having second thoughts, actually,' Thomas had said softly when he and Anne Marie were alone on the day after the fire. His grey eyes had held hers. 'Was I worrying unnecessarily?'

'No,' she had said, shaking her head, because the time for keeping things to herself was long past. 'I *was* having second thoughts.'

'I see,' Thomas said with a barely perceptible sigh. 'It's OK, you know.' He paused. 'I've often thought that I was punching above my weight with you. I . . .'

'No,' she said hotly. 'You weren't. You've never been doing

that. It's not that I don't love you. I do. I only realized how much when I thought I had lost you.' She caught hold of his hand. 'There was a moment when I thought that it was you who had jumped off the balcony. I thought it was you they were putting into that ambulance and I was terrified. The thought of not having you in my life was unimaginable.'

He looked at her. 'I can still be in your life, Anne Marie. You don't have to marry me. I can go back to honorary big brother status, if you like.'

'I don't want you to do that.' She paused. 'I think . . . that we should just give it some time. I think that I got caught up in the romance of being engaged and getting married. But actually, it was all too quick. I think – if you don't mind, Thomas – that we should wait a while.'

There, she had said it. It was all out in the open and he didn't look shocked and hurt like she had thought he would. He was nodding. Smiling.

'That's fine by me,' he said. 'We can wait as long as you like. A year? Five years, if you like? In fact, I think it's a good idea.'

'You do?'

'Yes, I think it was all too quick too.'

'Really?'

'Yes.' She saw the sincerity in his eyes. 'You were driving it, Anne Marie. Not me. I thought it was what you wanted.'

He was right. She had been driving it. She had suggested the early date on impulse and then everything had snow-balled towards it. An unstoppable avalanche of preparations, getting bigger and brighter the faster it moved.

'I'd be quite happy,' he added softly, 'if we had a very quiet wedding somewhere – just you and me and your dad. And Mikey. I think that Mikey should be there. He saved our lives, you know. Your father was terrified of leaving that balcony. I don't think he'd have done it without Mikey.'

'He was incredibly brave,' Anne Marie agreed. 'Dad said it too. A total hero.'

She was thinking that now as she pushed open the door of Mikey's room and they went in. Mikey was lying back on the pillow with his eyes closed, but when he heard their footsteps on the tiled floor, his eyes flickered open.

'Hey, you,' Anne Marie said.

'Hey.' He frowned at her. 'Shouldn't you be getting married or something?' He sounded husky and drowsy, a combination of tiredness and smoke, she guessed.

'Can't do that without our best man, can we?' She moved to his left side and took his hand. 'Are you in lots of pain?'

'Nothing I can't handle.' He squeezed her fingers and gave a terrible groaning sound.

'Mikey, what is it?'

He winked. 'Just kidding. I've had worse. Haven't I, Thomas? Tell her about the time I jumped off the fountain in Exeter when we were drunk.'

'He broke both his ankles,' Thomas said, rolling his eyes. 'Didn't you have a pin put in one of them or something? Mind you, that was on to concrete. I'm surprised you didn't break them again this time.'

'I don't think I did them much good,' Mikey said. 'I think

I may have bent the pin, but hey-ho. I don't think there's a shortage of pins in the NHS.'

He slumped back into the pillow. His face had gone pale and Anne Marie guessed this was a lot of effort for him. Much more than he was letting on.

'Were there any fatalities?' he asked.

'No,' Thomas said. 'I don't think so. Everyone except you was either rescued or got out in a more traditional way. That was nuts. What you did.'

'Yeah, I know. It seemed like a good idea at the time.'

Their eyes held for a moment.

'Thank you,' Thomas said gruffly.

Anne Marie swallowed. 'You're a hero,' she said. 'Totally and utterly.'

'You're very lucky you're not dead,' Thomas said.

There was a little pause. 'I'm really sorry about your wedding. You must be gutted.'

'We're OK with it,' Thomas told him.

'Yeah, we're happy to wait,' Anne Marie confirmed. 'We've decided there's no rush. By the way, Grace says thanks. She said you'd know what for.'

'Tell her she's welcome,' Mikey said.

'I will. And Serena says to tell you that you're now a fully-fledged member of the Reading Group. We had a vote. It was unanimous.' She swallowed a lump in her throat.

Mikey smiled, but he didn't say anything. He closed his eyes and there was another long pause. Anne Marie was beginning to think he'd fallen asleep. She glanced at Thomas and mouthed, 'Should we go?'

They had just reached the door when Mikey said, 'Hey, guys . . .'

They both turned.

'Can you give Serena a message back for me?'

'Sure,' Anne Marie said, moving a step closer to his bed again.

'Say, "I told you I wasn't going to die in that pool."'

She looked at him, perplexed.

'The Great Gatsby ends up dead. Face down in a pool. *Comprende*?'

'Does he?' Anne Marie said with a little shiver.

Mikey was overtaken by a fit of coughing. 'Yeah,' he said when it had stopped. 'But I reckon that, thanks to me . . .' he gave her a cheeky wink, 'the Reading Group may have finally bucked the trend!'